SINGLE INDEMNITY

BRIANNE GILLEN

This is a work of fiction. Names, characters, places, and incidents either are the product of the author's imagination or are used fictitiously. Any resemblance to actual persons, living or dead, events, or locales is entirely coincidental.

Single Indemnity: Phoenix Pictures, Book 2

Copyright © 2022 by Brianne Gillen

All rights reserved. No part of this book may be reproduced in any form or by any electronic or mechanical means, including information storage and retrieval systems, without written permission from the author, except for the use of brief quotations in a book review.

Edited by: Michele Chiappetta of Writing By Michele, LLC

Cover Design by: www.DaybedBooks.com

Print ISBN: 978-1-7372403-2-7

E-book ISBN: 978-1-7372403-3-4

Published by Brianne Gillen

www.briannegillen.com

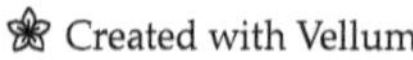 Created with Vellum

To my fellow Splooshies
—Amanda, Daria, Genevieve, & Jillian—
for your support on this writing journey, & for your friendship.

Prologue

Parkmoor Studios Costume Department
Hollywood, California
1936

"So, Miss Reynolds, not married yet?"

Natalie "Nate" Reynolds heard the record needle scratch in her brain.

She shouldn't have been discombobulated by the question. Her job interview with Parkmoor Studios' head costume designer, Glenn Chambers, was going swimmingly. She had this job in the bag.

Unlike the one she'd lost out on at RKO Studios only a week earlier. Where they apparently didn't want a "career girl" in name only, who'd quit and leave them in the lurch the minute she found a husband. As if Nate would ever. Hitching herself to a man—like her former beau—who'd expect her to settle down as her sister had was the dead last thing on her to-do list.

Adding insult to her heart's recent injury, one of her fellow graduates from the Mount Hollywood Art School—who *had* landed the RKO job—had oh-so-benevolently informed her of what he'd overheard about the reason they'd passed over Nate. Her eyes rolled of their own accord every time she thought about his little heads-up.

But she wasn't bitter. Of course not.

All that aside, *this* job was different. It had to be. Chambers appreciated her talents, and after less than an hour in his company, Nate sensed she would not only enjoy working with him, but also learn a great deal in the process.

And yet…

This is nothing but small talk. You've already gotten a better feeling from this interview. He wants to hire you. Your marital status does not matter in the slightest.

Nate's smile spread across her face.

Own it. Be confident. It doesn't matter.

She prepared to answer, ready to be honest. Forthright. Unmarried, and the very best person for the job regardless of whether or not she had a man in her life. She wanted this career-launching position so much, she could taste it.

Nate opened her mouth on the expectation that the word "no" would roll off her tongue.

For the rest of her life, she would never be entirely certain why, then, the following tumbled out instead.

"As a matter of fact, I am married."

The record scratch turned into a full-on crash as the player tumbled over, spilling its contents on the floor of her brain in a mess of broken black vinyl.

Where the fuck did that come from?

Surprise registered on Chambers's face as he looked down at her left hand. "Oh, I'm sorry for assuming. When I didn't see a ring, I thought…"

You can still get out of this. Turn back, cover your way into a misunderstanding.

Nate waved the hand in question. "Right, well, we've only

been married a few months and my husband hasn't been able to afford a ring yet, so…"

"Of course. And who needs a ring when you've got him, right?" Chambers winked.

An unfamiliar laugh escaped her throat. "Exactly!"

What is happening?

She had never grasped what people meant when they described out-of-body experiences. Until now. Now she knew. It was horrifying.

Chambers leaned forward slightly. "And he doesn't mind you working? That's wonderful."

Nate swallowed against the acid collecting in her mouth. "Yes. I mean, no. He doesn't mind… One of the things he loves most about me is my passion for my work. Plus he travels a lot; I think he likes the thought of me keeping myself occupied when he can't be here. And we're not in any hurry for children or anything…"

Oh. My. God. Stop talking.

But she was clearly incapable.

"That must be especially difficult on you both, being so newly married." Nate felt her head nodding as Chambers continued. "What line of work is he in, that keeps him on the road?"

Crap.

Travel. A job involving travel. Salesman? No, people hated traveling salesmen. True, Hollywood wasn't exactly some tiny, insular town, but still…

Nate's eyes fell on a newspaper, discarded in the wastebasket. A face looked out at her from the sports page, that new Italian kid the Yankees had just signed who was poised to take the game by storm.

"Baseball," she blurted. "He's a…baseball…scout." Chambers's eyes lit up, indicating she'd chosen well. As if her mouth was giving her brain even a smidgeon of choice in any of this. "He's out scouring the country for the next big hitter," she added cheerfully.

"Wow. That's exciting. You must be so proud."

"*So* proud."

Chambers frowned. "And I can see why he wouldn't be able to take you with him on the road. I doubt baseball's any place for a lady."

"No. No, it's not."

Nate felt sure her organs must be folding in on themselves, given how hard she cringed internally. She wanted nothing more than to lean forward and hit her head on her potential boss's desk. Maybe then she'd return to her senses. Instead, she kept the smile plastered on her face.

Please let this interview be over soon.

"Well, I for one am grateful it isn't. If it was, you might not be sitting here." Even though they were alone in the office, he leaned in with a lowered voice. "I do have to get final approval from the studio heads, but that's just a formality. I'm fairly confident in assuring you that once it comes through, the job will be yours if you want it."

Oh, thank god.

"I do. Thank you so much, Mr. Chambers."

He stood and extended his hand to her. "You'll make a wonderful addition to the department, Miss...pardon me...*Mrs.* Reynolds."

As she shook his hand, her mouth decided it still had more fight left. "Oh, Reynolds isn't my married name. It's my own. Wa...a...alter..."—*sure, why the hell not?*—"Walter agreed that it would be better for me to keep my own name professionally. So I wouldn't ever be riding on his coattails...when he starts making a name for himself in baseball...you know, because of the occasional crossover between studio execs and ball club owners."

Jesus Christ, you have the job. STOP TALKING.

Chambers considered for a moment before smiling at her. "Your Walter seems like quite a smart, forward-thinking man. You're a lucky woman."

"I really am, aren't I?"

Nate picked up her portfolio, eager to make her escape as

quickly as humanly possible, before she put her foot in it any further.

Walking her to the door, Chambers added, "You can expect a call from us in a day or two, and then we'll have you back in to make it official."

"Thank you. I'm looking forward to joining the team." She held her head high as she exited the office.

Nate had just landed her dream job.

With an extra helping of fictional husband.

Chapter One

Phoenix Pictures
Twelve Years Later

*N*ate Reynolds stood back and tapped her marking pencil against her lips, heedless of the dark red lipstick stains she left on it, as she assessed the two photos tacked to her office wall. The actor in the costume test stills looked every bit the pirate, but Nate couldn't shake the feeling something was missing. As head of the costume department at Phoenix Pictures, and lead designer on this particular film, it fell to her to fix it. If only she could figure out what, precisely, needed fixing.

Anyone looking at the stills would find these pirate costumes perfectly acceptable. Good, even. But "acceptable" and "good" weren't what had propelled Nate this far, or shaped her reputation. Her perfectionism when it came to her work always paid off.

She simply had to nail that elusive extra detail.

Reflecting her constantly busy schedule, her office lay cluttered with sketches, fabric samples, and the endless supply of snacks she stashed everywhere—pretzels when she needed salt,

M&M candies for sweet days…and a little booze for extreme emergencies. But Nate purposely kept one wall free from the chaos—simple cream paint, no adornments—allowing her to block out distractions, concentrate on the images, let them speak to her. Sometimes the message rang loud and clear. Other times, like this, it wasn't even audible.

As her eyes drifted over the photos, Nate's attention caught on the actor's cheeky grin and she laughed to herself. Leave it to Nick Bradley to lighten the mood. He was one of the good ones, for a lot of reasons. Chief among those, in Nate's estimation, was his ability to make his wife, Lois Ashford, happy. Lois was not only a talented actress and the head of Phoenix Pictures; she also happened to be Nate's dearest friend in the world. And the amount of joy Nick brought her scored him never-ending points in her book.

Nick was also empirically, almost obnoxiously, handsome. Nate could dress him in a burlap sack and he'd look good, a fact that often eased her job considerably. Unfortunately, those good looks didn't do anything to help her solve her current, tricky problem.

Nate groaned in frustration. With shooting set to begin in a week, the pressure was on to figure this out fast.

At a knock on her open door, she turned. Rose Lockwood, her secretary, hovered in the doorway.

"Am I interrupting?" Rose asked.

Nate shook her head, grateful for the chance to clear her thoughts for a moment. "Not at all. What's going on?"

"Marie called to say they just finished the extras' fittings for the party scene. Only a couple of minor alterations, and they'll be all set for tomorrow."

"That's perfect. Thanks."

"You were concentrating pretty hard there." Rose gestured to the photos. "Everything okay?"

"Not yet, but I'm *so* close."

Nate waved Rose over. The secretary glanced at Pirate Nick and smiled.

"Very roguish."

"But something's still missing. I can't put my finger on it."

Rose appraised Nate, the corners of her mouth twitching up. "That's driving you nuts, isn't it?"

Nate laughed at her astute observation. "You have no idea." She squinted at the wall. "What do you think?"

"Oh, I couldn't say…"

"Of course you could. You've got a great eye. If you ever wanted to move away from that desk out front, you have plenty of potential elsewhere in my department, you know." Nate gestured. "Please…"

Rose's eyes lit up at the compliment. "Thanks. I'll keep that in mind." She focused her attention on the costume stills, absently twirling a strand of hair around her finger—she'd been various shades of blonde the entire time Nate had known her, but had settled on a rich honey shade of late, and it suited her. "Huh."

Nate pounced, eager to hear the young woman's ideas. "Got something?"

"Maybe…I mean…" She stepped closer and nodded decisively. "Can I be blunt?"

"Are you kidding? Blunt and I get along famously. Let me have it."

Rose faced Nate and squared her shoulders. "His pants aren't tight enough."

Nate's eyebrow shot up of its own volition, and she snapped her gaze to the photos.

That's the ticket.

"I'm curious. What made you draw that conclusion?" she asked Rose, intrigued.

Rose's eyes widened slightly, registering both surprise and pride, as if she wasn't used to being asked her opinion. That was a damn shame. Nate gave her secretary an encouraging smile.

"It's all about the visual cues we give, right?" Rose responded.

"When you were talking about the script the other day, you said it's a satire. Mostly about how inept Mr. Bradley's character is as a pirate. None of his foils can understand why he's got all the power and women fall at his feet. But it all hinges on how much you can get away with when you look the part."

Nate smiled at her insight. "That's exactly it. And for the first few scenes, the audience isn't in on his incompetency. Just when they're starting to fall under his spell, they're hit with precisely what a jackass he is."

"And the more visually stunning he is from the get-go," Rose agreed, "the more jarring it'll be. Hence…"

"The pants need to be tighter." The two women grinned at each other. "Rose, you've got great instincts."

"Thanks." She looked back at Nick's photos. "Do you think Ms. Ashford will mind?"

"That we're effectively turning her husband into a bigger piece of meat? Nah, she knows that about him already." Nate winked. "And knowing Nick, he'll agree wholeheartedly too."

Rose laughed. "Well, I should get back to my desk. Anything else you need?"

"No, thanks." Nate gestured to the wall. "You're a lifesaver."

"You would've gotten there yourself. I just came along with fresh eyes."

"Well, thank you and your fresh eyes just the same."

Rose turned to go, but as she passed Nate's big, ash-gray desk, she paused. She reached out a finger to the object that snagged her notice, stopping just shy of touching it.

"I still think it's awfully nifty that your husband got Joe DiMaggio to sign this for you." She raised her head, uncharacteristically reticent. "Sorry, you're probably sick of hearing me say that."

Nate tried to ignore the clump of lead that settled in the pit of her stomach. Forcing a smile, she responded, "Not at all. It is a pretty nifty thing."

"Yeah." Rose sighed. "Well, see you later." She headed off with a wave.

Nate wandered over to the desk and picked up the weathered-looking baseball, emblazoned with the signature of America's favorite Yankee.

Or so everyone thought.

She usually kept the ball and its little stand on the back shelf under her sizable window, framing a picturesque vista of the studio. But things had been so hectic of late that the sketches over-flowing from her drafting table had overtaken the shelf as well. After knocking it over several times, Nate relocated the baseball to a corner of her desk, but she really needed to move it back. It attracted more attention in its current spot, and the last thing she needed was anyone examining it too closely.

And drawing the correct conclusion that she was the one who'd signed it, not DiMaggio.

Not that she wasn't proud of her accomplishment. It *was* a pretty good forgery, if she did say so herself. After picking up a brand-new, blindingly white baseball at Sears, she'd spent the better part of an afternoon beating it up and applying multiple coats of shoe polish and fake dirt from her costume kit. Once it looked sufficiently filthy, she'd taken a marker and added the signature she'd studied for days. The result appeared rather convincing. Especially from a few feet away.

Anyone passing through her office would easily believe her husband, the eternally-traveling baseball scout Walter Guffman, had detoured at some point to ask one of the greatest baseball players of their time to sign a little souvenir for the wife back home.

And that's exactly the way Nate wanted it.

Her charade might have launched with career-driven inten-tions, but over the years Walter had become unexpectedly handy when it came to relationships. Or rather, her lack thereof. This business was hardly a breeding ground for quality matches. In her experience, the men interested in more than a casual fling typi-cally fell into two categories—those who'd expect her to abandon her hard-won career for them, or those who'd feel threatened by her success while pretending otherwise.

She'd much rather be with no one at all than one of those. Luckily, Walter provided her a neatly wrapped excuse to keep to the casual fling category herself, when she felt the need.

Yes, the situation left her a little lonely sometimes, especially now that her best friend had a new partner-in-crime who stood out against the sea of creeps... But her fiction was still worth it. Truly.

Nate tossed the ball from hand to hand a couple of times before returning it to its stand. She shook her head.

Enough of that. I have work to do.

She returned to Nick's photos and took them back to the drawing board. Literally. She marked up the changes she wanted made to the pants, jotted down a few additional notes for her head seamstress, and dropped everything in a big envelope in her outgoing mailbox.

She'd have to remember to run the changes by Nick as well. She'd been truthful when she told Rose he wouldn't mind, but also needed to ensure he could still move in them. He might be a master pratfaller, but a man could only do so much when hamstrung by his own pants.

Nate had just settled down to start some preliminary sketches for another film, this one a modern melodrama, when Rose popped her head around the office doorway once again, appearing slightly moony this time.

"Sorry to bug you, Nate, but you've got a phone call. It's that new comedy writer, Colin Canfield." She practically sighed the name.

Ah, that explained the mooniness. Nate had yet to meet the man, but Lois had mentioned he was British, pointing to his accent as the likely culprit for Rose's current state.

Not that she could blame Rose. Nate knew for a fact that if Cary Grant waltzed into her office and spoke to her in his lovely posh voice, she'd be absolute putty in his hands.

"Did he say if it's urgent?" Nate asked.

"Um, no. He didn't say. Did you want me to take a message?" Rose looked comically torn—aghast at Nate for not wanting to talk to the writer, but elated she'd get to spend more time on the line with him.

Nate glanced longingly at her sketches, hesitant to break her creative momentum. But this small interruption had already broken it anyway. She *was* curious about what Canfield wanted. Writers didn't often emerge from their cave to have any direct dealings with her. And Nick and Lois were always gushing about this one in particular.

Sighing, she turned back to Rose as she stood. "Go ahead and put him through, Rose. Thanks."

She reached her desk chair as the phone buzzed. "Hello?"

"Nate? Hello. This is Colin. Colin Canfield. New writer here at Phoenix."

Oh my.

The deep, rich register of his voice reverberated all the way through her, and she sank into the comfortable cushioning of her chair. Despite his slightly awkward and hesitant delivery, his clipped British diction mixed with a warm baritone, resulting in a combination that...well, it was downright potent.

A girl could get used to that voice.

Nate rolled her eyes at herself, fully aware of the ridiculousness of that thought. She was a professional, not some silly bobby-soxer swooning over a nice voice. A nice...*sexy* voice.

That was currently silent. Waiting her for reply.

Crap.

"Mr. Canfield. Hello. It's nice to finally meet you...at least vocally." She let out a lame chuckle. She normally prided herself on her witty retorts. What was wrong with her?

"Oh, believe me, the pleasure is all mine. And please, do call me Colin." He paused. "I hope you won't think me too forward... You don't mind I called you 'Nate,' do you? It's just everyone seems to refer to you that way..."

Colin's bumbling uncertainty was downright endearing, and thankfully stood in direct contrast to the timbre of his voice, putting Nate at ease a bit. Her lips relaxed into a smile.

"Of course not. 'Nate' is just fine."

"Brilliant." The relief in his dreamy voice came through loud and clear.

Professional. Keep it professional. There is nothing dreamy about his voice. Nothing.

"So, Colin. What can I do to you?" *Shit.* "*For* you. What can I do *for* you?"

She slumped forward and dropped her head into her free hand. Thank god Rose had closed the office door when she left to put the call through.

Her gratitude deepened when he answered as if he hadn't noticed her blunder.

"Well, I'm beginning work on a new script for Nick to produce, and I wondered if I might run a few ideas by you before I take it to him."

"Me?"

"Yes. You see, a fair amount of the costumes are going to stem from the comedy bits. Or, rather...the other way around, I suppose. The comedy bits will come from the costumes." She could practically see him shaking his head on the other end of the phone. "Either way, the costumes are going to be quite crucial. But I want to make sure what's in my head is even possible. Which is where you come in."

"Wow. Okay. I'm not typically brought in this early, but sure."

"Oh, dear. Am I making an unusual request? I just thought... well, I figured it would be easier this way. No sense in coming up with an idea that everyone falls in love with, only to discover later that it's impossible, or creates a mess of work for you and your team. Better to stave off your inevitable headache before anything gets too far outside my own head, you know?" He heaved a sigh. "Sorry, I'm rambling, aren't I? Have I completely overstepped?"

Nate grinned, forgetting he couldn't see her. "Absolutely not.

As a matter of fact, it's damn refreshing. More often than not, that's exactly how the process unfolds. Your forethought is very much appreciated."

"I'm so glad. And believe me, if you can somehow make the images in my head come to life, I'll be the one who's appreciative." Colin drew in a sharp breath. "But I don't mean to pressure you." He groaned softly. "Be honest, how badly am I cocking this up?"

Nate laughed, at both his honesty and his casual profanity. "Oh, you're doing just fine." *So very fine.* Her throat needed a quick clearing before she continued. "Like I said, the fact that you're involving me now puts you ahead of the game."

"I can't tell if you're trying to make me feel better, or if you've had some terrifically stressful jobs. For your sake, I hope it's the former."

"Thanks, but I'm afraid it's the latter. I love my job tremendously, but you wouldn't believe some of the whoppers I've had to deal with over the years."

Colin chuckled. "I can imagine. We writers really do need to get out of our own heads more often, don't we?"

"Usually, the directors are just as bad. And don't even get me started on…"

"The actors," they finished simultaneously, their mingled laughter hovering cozily between them.

"It'd be nice if I had the power to snap my fingers or wave a magic wand and deliver on a moment's notice like they seem to think I can."

"Might not make your life easier, but I'd say it's a testament to your talents that people think you can. It's certainly why I've been eager to work with you. From everything Nick and Lois have told me, you possess a considerable amount of magic."

An odd heat started at the crown of Nate's head and spread quickly and thoroughly down her entire body. What on earth… was she actually blushing? *Jesus, when was the last time a man made me blush? Oh, this is not good.*

Before she could respond, Colin interjected a quick, "Hold a moment!" She heard him tell someone in the background about pages that needed to go out, before he returned to their call.

"Sorry about that. I should be going anyway. I've probably taken up entirely too much of your valuable time," he said, sounding sheepish. "And yet here I am, about to ask for more. Might I pop in soon and share my thoughts? I have a bit of time this afternoon, as a matter of fact…"

"This afternoon?" If this phone call was any indication, Nate was going to need more time than that to prepare herself. Her eyes landed on her drafting table, and she mentally lunged for the lifeline it offered. Sketching. Right, she had been in the middle of sketching.

"I'm a little loaded up today. But I should be able to squeeze you in tomorrow morning?"

"Excellent! I'll come to your office. See you tomorrow. Thanks awfully, Nate."

"You bet."

I wonder what you look like, Colin Canfield?

As she replaced the phone receiver on its cradle, the cord brushed the stand on the corner of the desk, knocking its inhabitant to the floor, where it proceeded to roll toward her chair. Nate stopped it with her foot and bent to pick up the…

Baseball.

Damn it.

Chapter Two

Colin Canfield picked up the battered leather portfolio case containing his notes, grinning as he prepared to leave his office. As a matter of fact, he hadn't stopped grinning since his phone call with Nate Reynolds the prior afternoon. He understood why Lois and Nick spoke so highly of her. She was delightful. And she hadn't seemed to bat an eye at all his rambles. Downright miraculous, that.

He had no problem putting words on a page, weaving together the right combinations and scenarios, culling them down to find precisely the right expressions. But when the words came directly out of his own mouth? That's when his filter faltered.

And boy, had it faltered with Nate.

Colin had no idea why talking to her had flummoxed him as much as it did. It should have been simple. Just business. He'd started at Phoenix Pictures only a couple of months ago, and everything was going smoothly. Everyone at the studio was simply lovely and welcoming.

Nate sounded a lot more than lovely.

Colin exhaled. Okay, so maybe he did know why he'd been a bumbling mess. Only one brief telephone call, and one thing was abundantly clear already.

Nate Reynolds was a wise-cracking dame.

He had quite the soft spot for wise-cracking dames. Every heroine he'd ever had a crush on fell into that category. They were his very favorite to write. He made a point of incorporating at least one sassy lady into everything he churned out, even when they weren't entirely necessary to the story. A tribute to all the ways they enhanced his life.

Until you let them disappear from it.

Colin's shoulders sagged as the familiar dull ache bloomed in his chest. His appreciation for those interesting, fun, wise-cracking dames wasn't limited to the romantic. His sister—half-sister if he was being technical—had brought tremendous fun into his life. Their familial situation might not have allowed them all that much time together growing up, but it didn't stop him from missing her now. From wondering if he had any right to enjoy his new job when he'd primarily relocated here in order to continue his search for her.

But that would have to be a problem for another day. He did have a job to do, and in order to achieve that, he had to get it together and act like an intelligent human being around Nate. He adjusted his tie and straightened the hem of his jacket.

I wonder if she was as affected by our call as I was?

Doubtful. What reason would she have? She was cool, collected, professional. Wise-cracking. They were two colleagues, about to work together on the first of many projects.

He pushed his glasses up the bridge of his nose and glanced at the clock.

Right. Get it together, remember? He'd have to continue the process on the way to her office, if he wanted to arrive on time. Like a professional.

Colin would absolutely *not* develop a crush on Nate Reynolds. At all. End of story.

THE MINUTE COLIN left the confines of the writers' building, he squinted in the bright sunlight, chiding himself for not having invested in proper sunglasses yet.

He was still adjusting to life in California. An Englishman through and through, the near-constant sunshine astounded him, especially in October. Back home, fall would be well and truly underway, readying to give way to winter. But here, hardly a cloud marred the sky. Just last week it had been nearly as hot as summer.

The mild breeze fought for dominance with the sun warming his skin, making for a delightful combination. Colin smiled to himself.

As different as it was, it delighted him no end to be here. Everything felt shiny and new. Fresh. The war had cast quite the pall over everything, and he had started to worry he might never emerge from it. London would always be home, but despite the rebuilding efforts, the rubble still remaining on many of the streets kept the memory of those dark days in the forefront of his mind, stirring a painful pang in his chest every time he ventured out of doors.

His move to New York to join the Broadway scene a couple of years ago had proved a good step in the right direction. And that had in turn led him here, to what truly felt like the beginning of a grand adventure. He would find his sister, and gain the fresh start he needed.

His creativity roared back to life more each day, his writing muscles continuing to flex and gather strength. Focusing almost entirely on comedic scripts liberated him tremendously, as did working with so many people who trusted his voice. Lois Ashford had brought such vitality to his words on the stage as an actress, but having her as a boss was equally thrilling. Her husband Nick pulled double duty as an actor and producer, and he frequently paired with Colin. Lois pretty much gave the two of them free rein to experiment and try new things with their comedy films. He'd never laughed as much at work in his life.

Guilt flared again over the one drawback to his exciting new career. Thus far, it kept him busier than he'd expected. Leaving him less time to devote to his search. But if his writing was soaring to new heights, surely his sister couldn't be far behind. He had to believe that.

An emerald-green awning cheerfully announced his arrival at the studio's costume building. The awning itself featured only simple white lettering, while a silhouette of an elegantly gowned woman painted on the glass door below it invited him inside.

Colin pulled open the door and headed down the hallway toward Nate's office.

Here we go. You can do this. No bumbling.

The toe of his shoe caught on the doorframe leading into her reception area, and he barely managed to catch himself from sprawling his long limbs across the floor in a heap.

A woman sitting at the desk in front of him—Rose, presumably—gasped and raised startled eyes to him as he awkwardly straightened up. He pushed his glasses back up before they slid further down his nose.

"Everything okay out there, Rose?" Nate's voice called from her office.

Superb. She had to hear that, didn't she?

A flush crept up Colin's neck. It would reach his cheeks in seconds, he knew it.

Rose, undeterred, called back to Nate, "Everything is fine. Mr. Canfield is here."

"Oh! I'll be right out."

Rose leaned her chin in her hand and grinned up at him. "She'll be right out."

Colin attempted a smile of his own as he tried to calm his breathing. "Thank you."

Nate materialized in her office doorway, and he no longer needed to worry about controlling his breathing. The breath left him altogether.

She was inordinately striking. Her glossy brown hair was

pulled up in a style he was sure had a name he couldn't recall, which drew particular attention to the lighter, almost blonde streak in front. She wore a bold rust-colored blouse tucked into dark brown wide-legged trousers, with what appeared to be a wildly patterned men's necktie around her waist as a belt. She resembled an autumn leaf, come to life in the form of some kind of…sophisticated wood sprite.

Sophisticated wood sprite? Bloody hell.

Colin hoped she didn't notice how hard he swallowed.

Her dark red lips curved into a smile as she assessed him with the warmest brown eyes he'd ever seen.

"Colin, hello. Is everything all right?" Her eyes trailed over his clothes—*of course that would be what she takes in*—which he now realized remained slightly askew from his run-in with that blasted doorframe.

He attempted to smooth his tweed sport coat and straighten his tie. "Yes. Thank you. Sorry you had to hear that." He gestured toward the doorway. "Just had a little trip. Hoist by my own clumsiness, I'm afraid."

Nate chuckled. "Don't worry, it happens to the best of us. That entryway is a bit of a menace."

Colin doubted that was the case, but appreciated her attempt to make him feel better nonetheless.

They grinned at each other. He so thoroughly enjoyed her smile that he almost missed how perilously close they veered toward awkward pause territory.

Luckily, Nate seemed to come to the same conclusion. She straightened her shoulders and cleared her throat, saying, "Shall we?"

"Yes, of course."

He started to follow her into the room when Rose interjected, "Would you like me to hold all your calls?" Colin turned his head, surprised to find her staring at him, when it was Nate she addressed. Strange.

"I'd appreciate that. Thank you, Rose."

Nate closed the door behind them. Colin made toward her desk, but she gestured him toward the surprisingly spacious couch and glass coffee table to their right.

"Let's sit over here. More room to spread out."

"Right, sure."

He set his portfolio on the table and hovered while she grabbed a notepad and pencil from her desk. Once she took a seat in the armchair, Colin settled on the couch. Nate cocked her head, looking vaguely surprised. Didn't most men do that? His mother had taught him from an early age that a gentleman never sat down before a lady did. Perhaps it wasn't much of an American custom?

Nate cleared her throat and flipped to an empty page in her pad. "Thanks for coming in."

"Oh no, thank *you* for agreeing to meet with me. I know how busy you are. But hopefully this will give you a head start, rather than make more work for you."

"It's certainly a step in the right direction." She smiled warmly. "Let's hear what you've got. You said it's a comedy you're planning, right?"

"Yes." He took out his notes. "Nick wants to put together some comedic projects that are a little different, unexpected. He especially wants to explore the television angle."

"Smart idea. It's still so new you can take more risks, get away with a lot more."

"Right. So I've been toying with shorter stories. Little vignettes, if you will. They center around a common theme, but mostly stand on their own. But because they're shorter…"

The corner of Nate's mouth hitched up. "They need to pack a bigger punch, the sooner the better."

"That's exactly it!" Colin grinned. He had been a bit nervous about his ideas. That Nate understood his intentions right out of the gate felt tremendously satisfying.

"At least for this first few I've been writing," he continued, "the comedy relies pretty heavily on visuals."

"And what better way to tell an immediate visual story than with the right costume?" Nate smirked, projecting well-earned pride in her skill.

Dear god, working with her is going to be a romp.

"From all I've gathered, you are exactly the person to deliver on that."

Oh no. Was that too much?

A hint of color painted its way across her cheeks, her smile almost shy. "Thank you."

Okay, maybe not too much then. Good.

Their eyes met and locked, the sudden intensity between them making him momentarily dizzy. The warmth in her eyes turned practically molten, and it was all he could do to remain upright. He'd never felt so thoroughly knocked on his arse in all his life.

It was sublime.

And colossally stupid.

You are at work. *Stop being ridiculous.*

At the same moment, Nate blinked, and when she opened her eyes to him again, the fire had been doused.

"So. You want to know if your ideas are possible."

Somehow Colin jolted his brain back to life and regained focus. "Possible. Yes. My ideas." Okay, perhaps he hadn't achieved it as completely as he thought. "Right. I have some pictures in my head, but I have no idea if they'll translate to reality. It's entirely possible I'm overthinking."

Nate smiled reassuringly. "I know how that goes. I was completely in my own head over Nick's costume for the pirate movie; I thought I'd never figure it out, until Rose weighed in with fresh eyes." She paused. "You wrote that one, didn't you?"

"I did. Can't wait to see what he does with it. And what you've come up with for him. What was the missing piece, then?"

Nate hesitated for a fraction of a second, before a defiant glint sparked to life. "Tighter pants."

Colin's eyes widened. "Tighter *pants*? I don't recall writing any scenes where he's..." Clarity dawned as he remembered what country he was currently in. "Oh. You mean trousers."

She raised a pair of bemused eyebrows at him. "Of course. What did you think I meant?"

"Well, in England..." He stopped himself. A discussion of underwear would surely plunge them into the realm of dicey—the last thing either of them needed. He waved his hand. "You know what? Doesn't matter."

"If you say so."

Now that he understood—and steadfastly ignored the potential for embarrassment—Colin had the chance to process what Nate said about the costume.

"So you're tightening his trousers to make him more attractive, yes?" At her nod, he continued. "Which in turn heightens the contrast when he begins to bollocks everything up. That's bloody brilliant." Colin laughed. "And it's going to prompt Nick to ham it up even more, isn't it?"

Joining in his laughter, Nate agreed. "Oh, you know it." She narrowed her lovely eyes. "Did you say 'bollocks everything up' a minute ago?"

"I did. Is that a problem?"

"Not at all. It's just new to me. I'll have to remember it."

"Going to add it to your arsenal, are you?"

"Would you like me to credit you?"

Colin shook his head. "I'll let you have this one free of charge."

"Thanks awfully."

They grinned easily at each other for a moment, before Nate brought them back to the reason for their meeting.

"Okay, Trouser Man, let's hear those plans."

Colin launched into his ideas with the distinct sense that Nate could make just about *any* magic happen.

Chapter Three

"Okay, hear me out." Nate took a dramatic pause, savoring the anticipatory gleam in Colin's eye. "I'm thinking… lobster claws."

The two of them had been in her office for nearly an hour, talking through Colin's writing. His creative streak was a perfect match for hers. They'd done nothing but spark off each other since he sat down.

His clear appreciation for her talent, combined with that absurdly, distractingly sexy voice? She definitely needed to watch herself with this one.

At least in person, she didn't have to focus solely on his voice like she had over the phone. She let her other senses take the reins from her ears, so that her brain could apply itself to the task at hand. Her *job*.

She watched as he bit his full lower lip, and his shoulders— *goodness, they are broad under all that tweed, aren't they?*—started to quiver. He met her eyes, and promptly exploded with warm laughter.

"Lobster claws," he wheezed. "That's…oh, that's brilliant. I love it!" He finished with a snort and a downright adorable crinkle of his nose.

No. Not adorable, damn it. Do not *think of him as adorable.*

"You sure you don't mind? I mean, the bear is a funny finish, but it's..."

"No, this will absolutely serve the story better. Are you sure *you* don't mind? It would be more work."

"Eh," Nate shrugged. "Lobster claws aren't that hard."

"Oh? Good to know."

"I am a font of useless knowledge."

They both grinned.

"All right, then. I'm adding in the lobster." He bent over his notes, scribbling furiously, a stray curl of his dark blond hair escaping its pomaded moorings to brush his forehead.

As much as that curl intrigued her, Nate remained stuck on the way the word "lobster" had emerged in his British accent. She couldn't contain the giggle that escaped her.

Oh dear god, I'm giggling. *I don't giggle. What the hell?*

Colin raised his head and quirked an eyebrow at her laughter.

Nate waved her hand in dismissal as her brain raced to cover her tracks. "Just thinking about...him trying to hold her with claws."

"It is going to be a bloody fantastic visual, isn't it? I'm awfully excited to write this now."

Whew, diversion achieved.

"Me too. This is a really funny piece, Colin."

Nate was no longer deflecting. She meant it. They'd talked about several of Colin's scenarios this morning, but this was by far her favorite, centering around a young hoofer who dreamt of being the next Fred Astaire. The only job he could land did involve dancing—as a real-life model for cartoon artists, much to his dismay. Despite being partnered with a beautiful human woman, he would have to don some sort of dancing animal costume in every bit. Colin had originally planned to end with the dancer in an awkward bear suit.

Enter Nate and her lobster claws.

"How'd you come up with the idea for this one?"

A wash of pink crept across Colin's cheeks. "Just came to me, I guess."

"Really?" She couldn't keep the skepticism from her voice. "But it's so technical. Which leads to all the animal stuff being so absurd, of course. Everything you included about how much he knows about dance… That's why it's as funny as it is."

His blush deepened. There was absolutely a story there.

I'll get it out of him eventually.

Something of her determination must have shown in her eyes, because a hint of trepidation crossed his. But only a hint. "Oh, come on. I can't reveal all my secrets, now can I?" That seductive voice held the flirtatious spark of a dare. As if he welcomed her getting under his skin.

I wouldn't mind getting under all of him.

Nate blinked. She *needed* to stop having thoughts like that.

She had never been so grateful to hear a knock at her door. Shaking off the moment, she noticed Colin echoing her posture. At least she wasn't alone in this heat—although it probably would be much better if she was. Easier to turn it off if it was one-sided.

"Yes?" she called out to the blessed interrupter.

Rose cracked the door and peered around it. "I'm sorry to disturb you, Ms. Reynolds, but Ms. Ashford is here for your meeting."

"Wait, already?" *Just how long have we been at this?*

The subject of her inappropriate musings glanced at his watch. "Oh, my."

Nate looked back to Rose. "Tell Lois I'll be right out. Thanks, Rose."

Colin gathered up his notes, neatly stacking them before tucking the pages back in his portfolio. "I completely lost track of the time. I hope I haven't taken up too much of your day."

"Not at all. It was a very productive session." She hesitated as they both stood. "And a fun one."

Colin flashed her a bright smile. "It was, wasn't it? I'm very much looking forward to working with you, Nate."

"Me too." She reached out to shake the hand he extended.

Given everything that had transpired over the course of their meeting, and the phone call yesterday, it really shouldn't have surprised her. And yet... The warmth that spread up her arm and through her entire body overwhelmed her.

She had known him all of one day, and already she was in deep.

How is that possible?

Even more startling was the intensity coming at her from behind the spectacles perched on Colin's nose. They prevented her from seeing too much of his eyes from his position on the couch, but now that they stood face-to-face, those glasses hardly concealed anything. She had thought Colin's eyes might be light brown, but they were actually hazel. And no simple hazel, either—they contained a decidedly fascinating arrangement of varying shades of amber and gold, even a little green.

She desperately wanted to whip his glasses off and experience those eyes in all their glory.

At the same time, Nate knew what a mistake that would be. Those lenses were the only thing separating her from tumbling headlong into his potent stare, and if she was reading him right— if his response was anything like what she herself felt—she'd slip right into quicksand. She might never want a return ticket from that hazel fathomage.

Slipping her hand from his before it was too late, Nate made a beeline for the door. She hoped Colin followed her, but she couldn't chance a look. Despite the almost identical lighting in her reception area, Nate blinked rapidly upon opening the door, as if she'd just emerged from a dark theater on a bright afternoon.

Seeing her cool, collected best friend chatting with Rose jolted her back to reality. When had she become so dramatic? Colin was just a man.

Lois greeted her with a smile. "Hi, Nate. And Colin. Hello."

Oh, good, the just-a-man in question had followed her out

after all. Regrettably, he was not as far behind her as she anticipated.

"Lois. Lovely to see you." The words, in his glorious baritone, spoken at such a disturbingly close range, turned the entire contents of her body into hot liquid that rapidly flooded to her core.

This is it. I'm dying. That voice is going to fucking kill me.

Thank god he was talking to Lois. Nate had a vague idea that she possessed a voice of her own somewhere, but damned if she had any recollection of how to use it.

"Colin, great to see you too," Lois responded. "I didn't know you two were meeting this morning. I hope I didn't interrupt."

Her tone was all innocence and friendly business, but Nate observed something wicked stirring in her friend's bright green eyes. So much for keeping this hidden. As soon as they were alone, Lois would be merciless.

Colin answered her, blissfully unaware. "Oh, don't worry. We were just wrapping up." He held up his portfolio. "I'm working on some ideas involving a bevy of interesting costumes, so I wanted to talk through them with Nate before I took them too far."

"Oh, that's very considerate." Lois smiled. Like the damn Cheshire Cat.

"Yes, it was," Nate piped up. "We had quite a productive meeting." Good. Her voice hadn't deserted her after all.

"Oh, it was tremendously productive," Colin added. "Nate had some simply wonderful ideas."

"Our Nate is the best," Lois replied, not masking her pride.

"Thank you. But really, that's enough." As much confidence as she had in her abilities, they didn't need to dwell on them now. She turned a pointed glare on Lois.

"Well, I should be going." As Colin stepped around her, his arm brushed hers, and there went that zing again. "Thanks again for all this, Nate. I'll be in touch."

"Um, yeah. Sure. Sounds good."

"Ladies." He held up a hand in a shy wave as he backed toward the exit.

"Goodbye, Mr. Canfield," Rose breathed.

Colin gave her a startled glance before nodding and taking his leave. Nate stifled a laugh.

He really has no idea of the power in that voice, does he?

Lois cleared her throat pointedly and leveled Nate with a carefully bland expression that was anything but.

Nate's smile died on her lips, and she narrowed her eyes in a clear "shut up" despite knowing for a fact that Lois would not.

"Shall we?" Lois asked, enjoying herself far too much.

"Come on in." Nate waved her into the office.

"Oh, I almost forgot!" Rose's arm shot out, handing Nate a slip of paper. "Mrs. Haynes called. Something about a mix-up over your marital status? Looks like you left your hubby off some paperwork."

Heat flooded Nate. "Right. Thanks."

As soon as the door shut behind them, Lois turned to Nate with a smirk. "Forgetting Walter's existence again? I can't imagine why." Before Nate could respond, Lois held up a hand. "It's okay, we don't need to go into it."

Nate's gratitude was short-lived.

"So. You and Colin are...productive."

Nate crossed her arms over her chest. "Yes, we are. We're collaborating on a comedy script that will very likely bring success to *your* studio. You can thank me later."

"Mm-hmm. You sure you're not getting ready to rain scandal down on my studio?"

"For your information, our knowledge of each other consists of exactly one phone call"—*damn, that voice*—"and the meeting you just witnessed. So you can kindly get your mind out of the gutter."

Lois held her hands up in mock surrender. "My, we're defensive, aren't we? And do I need to remind you how firmly entrenched in the gutter *your* mind was when Nick and I started spending time together?"

Okay, she did have a point.

"Fine, I suppose I earned that." Nate crossed to retrieve her notebook from the couch. "But you're wrong. There is absolutely nothing going on between me and Colin."

"Really? Because your face out there said otherwise."

Oh, no.

Nate turned back to Lois warily. "Did it really?"

"Oh, geez, don't panic. I'm sure I was the only one who noticed."

"Good." Nate chewed on her lower lip. "So…um…how did my face look?"

To her relief, Lois laughed. "Mostly just mildly guilty."

Good. Guilty wasn't so bad. Easily shrugged off.

Lois continued, "That is, until Colin started speaking…"

Damn.

"Oh, really?" Nate tried for nonchalance, but knew Lois could see right through her. "And just how did I look at that point?"

Lois grinned. "Like you were having impure thoughts."

Nate sputtered. "I was not!" At the skeptical quirk of Lois's eyebrow, she relented. "Okay, fine, I was. Have you heard that voice? It's…it's like…I don't know…like velvet sin."

Lois stared at Nate for a moment before a bark of laughter erupted from her.

"I'm sorry. It's just…" A snort escaped as she tried to contain her mirth at Nate's mortifying voice-crush. "*Velvet sin*? Are you serious?"

"Hey, he's the writer. I speak the language of clothing, remember?"

"Fair enough." Lois sobered ever so slightly. "Would it help if I told you the way he looked when he came up behind you?"

As much as she wanted to know, Nate sincerely doubted it would help one bit. Just the opposite.

She donned her best impression of haughty and imperious as

she made her way to the desk. "I haven't the slightest need to know. You can keep it to yourself, thank you very much."

"Wow. All right then." Lois paused. "May I interest you in the reason I scheduled this meeting, or do you not need that information either?"

Facing her friend, Nate kept her voice casual while seizing on the subject change. "As a matter of fact, that would be useful information. Go ahead."

She gestured to the chair across the desk as she settled into her own. Lois smiled and took the offered seat.

"At the risk of sounding terribly banal," Lois began with an affected tone contradicted immediately by a wink, "I really just wanted to invite you over for an early dinner on Sunday. Nick bought a barbecue and wants to show off his apparently masterful grilling prowess."

"Are you kidding me? You booked time on my busy schedule —and yours—for a *social* invitation?"

"Please. It was the only way I'd be sure to catch you. Plus, I needed to get out of the office and stretch my legs."

Nate smiled. "And let everyone on the lot see you out and about, instead of perched in your tower, surveying the kingdom from above?"

Lois chuckled. "Exactly. I hope it worked."

"I'm sure it did." In a delayed reaction, Nate's mind finally took note of Lois's invitation. "Wait a minute. Did you say *Nick* got a *barbecue*?"

"I did."

"But it's October."

"It is. But it's October *in Los Angeles*, according to him. Apparently, that stretch of warm weather we had last week inspired him." Lois lifted an elegant shoulder.

"Is he really any good at it?"

"I guess we'll find out on Sunday."

"Yikes." Nate studied her. Underneath the sardonic resignation lurked a barely banked spark of pure joy. "You find it thoroughly adorable, don't you?"

Lois rolled her eyes as her cheeks flushed. "I really do." They laughed together. "So you'll come?"

"I will. And I will even pretend to like it if it tastes like shit."

"You are a true friend, Nate Reynolds."

"I know."

Their conversation might have offered a welcome distraction, but talk of Nick and Lois's domestic bliss brought Nate's attention back to her own lack thereof...and of the Brit with the magic voice.

She blew out an exhale. "Okay, fine. Go ahead and tell me."

"Tell you what?"

"Oh, don't play coy. You know what."

Lois smirked. "I knew you couldn't let it go."

Nate made a circular motion with her hand. "So...?"

Lois leaned forward conspiratorially. "You ever imagine what would happen if Clark Kent forgot to take his glasses off before unleashing his heat vision? Like he could probably burn a hole right through them?"

Nate forgot how to breathe. Had Colin actually been looking at her like that?

He was looking at you like that when you fled the office, you dingbat.

She swallowed as heat crept up her neck. "Are you saying Colin...?"

"He did. Precisely like that." Lois sat back in her chair with a smug grin, continuing in an offhanded tone, "That is, if Clark Kent was blonde, of course. And British. With a voice like *velvet sin...*"

Nate threw an eraser at Lois. "Oh, shut up."

Lois cackled as she caught it, before sobering. "Can I ask you a question?"

"If I say no, you'll ask anyway, won't you?"

"Yes, I will." She took a breath. "What would be wrong with

letting yourself explore a little? He's a good guy, from everything I can tell."

What, indeed?

"I don't shit where I eat." Nate pushed up out of her chair. "And you just said it yourself—do you really want two of your studio's most valuable employees generating all kinds of potential drama?"

"Most valuable employees, huh?"

"You know we are."

"I do know. I'm glad you do, too. But you've always been discreet, Nate."

She had the odd sensation that Lois was fishing for something. Nate turned to the window in avoidance, and her gaze fell on the baseball on the shelf.

"What's stopping…" As Lois trailed off, she knew her friend's had as well. "Right."

"Right." Nate faced Lois again, leaning on the shelf and crossing her arms.

"You know, I don't blame you for that paperwork thing. I honestly forget sometimes too. That you're married."

"Yeah."

A shard of icy guilt lodged in Nate's chest. The truth about Walter remained the one—and only—secret she'd ever kept from Lois.

And as secrets went, it was one hell of a doozy.

She hated keeping it. She'd wanted to tell Lois a million times over the years, but just…hadn't ever known how. The one time she had shared her lie with someone hadn't exactly ended well. Her sister Mallory's complete lack of understanding had caused such a shift in their relationship that they'd pretty much stopped speaking by the time Nate met Lois.

A dull ache still bloomed in her chest at the thought of Mallory, and she could only imagine how much more acute the pain from a Lois-shaped absence would be. The thought of driving her best friend away… It was too much.

So she held her tongue. Again.

Lois inhaled. "I know you don't talk about it much, and whatever your reasons for not leaving Walter altogether, haven't you had…over the years…from time to time…"

Nate quirked an eyebrow. "Dalliances? Flings?" At Lois's nod, she affirmed, "I have."

"I thought as much. Then let me ask again. What's stopping you now?"

"Are you kidding me?" She made a broad gesture with her hands. "Shitting…eating… It would have an end date. Making things complicated. Working together after…complicated. And I don't want to do that to you. Or anyone else around here."

"Or yourself."

Nate's head snapped up at that. "Or myself. It would be a mistake. For a lot of reasons. And you know it." She paused. "And what is with you anyway? You're a nauseating walking advertisement for wedded bliss, and you're encouraging me to do this?"

Not that it was actually infidelity, but Lois didn't know that.

"I just want you to be happy."

God, I really need to tell her.

Lois continued, "But I get your point. And I won't push."

"Then why do I get the feeling you have more to say?"

She opened her mouth to protest, but stopped when she saw Nate's face. "Look, I really am not going to push. Only…"

"What?"

"The way you two looked around each other. And your lack of composure"—she held up a staying hand—"that no one else could see, don't worry. Anyway, it was the most heat I've ever seen you generate with someone, especially considering how briefly you've known each other."

Nate had a sneaking suspicion where Lois was headed, and she hated how right Lois probably was. But something about Colin already felt bigger than just a dalliance, and she was in no rush to examine why. As a result, her reply slipped out more sharply than she intended.

"Is there a point in there somewhere?"

"As a matter of fact, there is. All that heat's going to need somewhere to go eventually. You might want to get it out of your system before it consumes you."

Lois rose and came around the desk. Placing an affectionate hand on Nate's arm, she added, "You know I love you, and I only want what you want."

Nate met her eyes. "And you think I want to fling Colin Canfield?"

"He's tall, but I don't think he weighs very much. I'm sure he'd fling easily."

Nate couldn't help her snort of laughter. "Don't you have a studio to run?"

"All right, all right, I'm going." She gave Nate's arm a squeeze and turned to go. "See you Sunday?"

"See you Sunday."

Lois winked before closing the door behind her. As Nate stared at the door, all the thoughts she'd rather avoid swirled in her head. She eventually had to come clean with Lois. And she needed to get the idea of Colin's fling-ability out of her head.

So she did the only thing she could, the thing she did best. She made her way to her drafting table and threw herself into sketching the best damn dancing lobster costume Hollywood would ever see.

Chapter Four

Colin's fingers flew furiously over the keys of his typewriter, barely keeping up with the words building up in his head. Reaching the end of the page, he whipped it out and added it to the stack on his left. His mouth tightened into a hard line as he fed the new paper into the machine. He wasn't quite sure why he executed the flourish with every page change, but he'd become vaguely aware of the habit ages ago, and at that point it was far too ingrained for him to change it. Now it happened every time he got in a writing frenzy.

His office-mate was needed on set this afternoon, so Colin had the radio on a little louder than usual, as both treat and distraction. As he continued on with his fresh page, he registered the lively drumming of Gene Krupa coming at him from the speaker, and reveled in its perfection. Krupa always paired well with his typewriter's rhythm.

Especially appropriate, given that he currently worked on his dancer comedy, as his feet began to absently tap out a combination under his desk along with the music. A holdover of his past, from what felt like a lifetime ago. Maybe two lifetimes.

Channeling that past might have given him inspiration for this particular idea, but it wasn't the only reason this scene was coming to him so frantically. He'd been riding a fantastic creative streak for several days now, and could pinpoint exactly when it started.

Or rather, exactly *who* started it.

The second Colin had taken Nate's hand at the end of their meeting, a jolt of pure electricity singed his entire body. He was, quite frankly, a little astonished that he hadn't needed to be carried out of the office in a dustpan, having been reduced to a smoldering pile of ashes.

He could only—desperately—hope his glasses had masked the conflagration he tried, and likely failed, to keep out of his eyes.

Unfortunately, that heat had congealed the minute he stepped out of Nate's office lobby. He'd only taken a step or two when he heard Rose call out a message to Nate...referencing her *husband*.

Nate was married.

A fact Colin wished he'd known before spending the entirety of their meeting flirting with her. True, she had been flirting as well, or so he'd thought. Perhaps he'd read far too much into it.

But that was neither here nor there. All potential for a delightful romantic entanglement was over. Now that he knew of her husband, there was no other way it could go with Nate but complete and abject disaster.

Even if she continued their flirtation, he'd be an utter cad to return the parry. Especially since they worked together. At a studio in need of proving itself, a studio where he very much liked working. He didn't want to have to leave it in disgrace after a punch in the nose from Nate's husband. Or Nate herself.

It was simply impossible.

So Colin took all that pent-up spark and disappointment, and threw himself into his writing. He'd been afraid it would impede him, but instead it worked like a charm. Of course, it helped that his meeting with Nate had been productive in substantial creative ways as well, giving him a deep well to tap into.

Despite his ill-timed attraction to her, they worked well together. She'd appreciated his ideas and added to them, and he had inspired her right back. The lobster claw plan was utterly brilliant, and he couldn't wait to pitch it to Nick.

Colin reached the conclusion of his current scene. Feeling triumphant, he punched the final period with gusto and whipped the last page out of the typewriter with one last flourish.

"Well, that looks like a satisfying conclusion."

Startled, Colin looked up to find Nick Bradley himself leaning against the office doorway, hands in his pockets, grinning. *Speak of the devil.*

Except he wasn't the devil. Quite the opposite. Stupidly handsome, to a degree that would be intimidating on anyone else, Nick also exuded a friendly and approachable nature, and uncommon humility. Not to mention razor-sharp comedic instincts. He and Colin had become fast friends these last few months.

"Sorry, didn't mean to startle you," Nick added.

Colin smiled as he placed the last paper on the pile and tapped the stack on his desk to straighten them. "Don't worry, you didn't." He reconsidered. "All right, actually, you did. But no need to worry yourself. Truth be told, just about anything would have startled me right now."

Nick pushed off the doorframe. "It certainly looked that way." He took a step before stopping himself. "You don't mind if I come in, do you?"

Colin gestured him in. "Of course not. Your timing was quite serendipitous. Just finished this scene." He patted the pages reverently. "I do hope you weren't standing there long, were you?"

"Not at all," Nick answered as he strolled into the room. "Just long enough to know what a terrible idea it would be to interrupt you while you were entrenched so deep. But when you executed that beautifully dramatic ending, I figured it was safe."

"Sorry, that was a bit much, wasn't it?"

"Don't apologize." Nick perched on the edge of the other desk. "It makes me even more intrigued to read it now. That the new one you've been keeping under your hat?"

"It is. I need to give it a quick once-over, but then it's all yours."

Nick held his hands up. "Of course, take your time. Whenever it's ready."

Nick's enthusiasm at seeing the script both bolstered and terrified Colin. He hoped he hadn't built up too much anticipation, though he felt pretty confident about this one.

"Hold on a moment." Colin tried to inject suspicion into his tone. "Is that why you're here, to check up on me?"

Nick flushed. "No! Of course not… Okay, maybe a little. But not to pressure you, I promise. I'm just excited to see it," he ended with a sheepish grin.

Colin went easy on him. "Your vote of confidence is most appreciated. I think."

Nick laughed. "I have no doubt it will be well-earned. And really, I only stopped in because your office was on the way back to mine from wardrobe, so I thought I'd say hello."

"Oh, were you at wardrobe?"

Was that casual? I hope it was casual.

Not that he needed to be casual about Nate. Not at all. Not anymore.

"Yeah, for my final fitting before next week. Wait till you see the great pirate getup they've got me in."

"I've heard. I'm looking forward to seeing it realized."

"Uh-oh. How did you hear about it already?"

Bollocks.

"Oh, Nate told me about it when I met with her the other day." At Nick's raised eyebrow, he explained. "I wanted to run a few ideas by her for this script before I committed it to paper."

"Huh. That's a good idea." A devilish glint entered his eyes. "So the new one involves costumes already… Intriguing indeed."

Colin chuckled. "Relax, you'll have it soon. I promise."

Nick pushed up from the desk and gave him a salute. "I will let you get back to it, then." He was nearly to the door when he whipped back around. "Oh, I almost forgot. What are you doing Sunday?"

"Sunday? Not much of anything, really."

"Perfect. Then you can come over to our place for dinner." Nick puffed out his chest. "I'm barbecuing."

Despite his best efforts, Colin was fairly certain his confusion showed on his face. "Barbecuing? As in, on a grill?"

"Of course. Is there another kind?"

"No, I suppose not. But it's October."

Nick made an exaggerated shrug. "In sunny Hollywood. Seasons don't really matter here. And so I am going to be doing wondrous and smoky things with meat." He pointed a finger at Colin. "You'll come?"

California was indeed a strange place, but he smiled anyway, catching Nick's infectious mood. "I will be there."

Nick clapped his hands together once. "Excellent." He pulled a scrap of paper off the desk and bent to scribble on it, before handing it over. "Here's our address. Come by around five."

"Thanks. I'll see you then."

"See ya!" Nick left the office with a wave.

It wasn't until he was gone that it occurred to Colin who else might be at this barbecue.

Nate.

He leaned his head back with a groan. He was supposed to be focusing on the professional here. He pulled himself upright and squared his shoulders. Professional. Of course he could keep this professional. Sunday would simply be a social gathering with a group of work colleagues who got along well. And were all friends. *Just* friends.

With any luck, he might even meet Nate's husband at this dinner. Yes, an excellent thing to hope for. The husband. That would certainly curb this silly crush once and for all.

"DON'T WORRY, I stashed an enormous cheesecake in the fridge. We can easily make a meal of it if we have to." Max Mitchell, Nick's best friend and bakery-owner extraordinaire, winked at Nate as he handed her a beer and joined her at the patio table.

She laughed. "I was hoping you'd say that."

"Hey!" Nick whirled around from the barbecue, brandishing his spatula like a weapon. "Cheesecake is not a meal. Certainly not tonight." He aimed the spatula accusingly at Max. "And you of all people should know that."

Max held up his hands in surrender, but didn't bother to keep the mischief from his eyes. "Okay, fine, but helping our dads years ago isn't exactly the same as doing it all yourself. Can you really blame me for being a little leery?"

"Yes. Yes, I can. You know I'm a pretty good cook." Nick scowled.

Of course, that scowl's impact was greatly diminished as soon as one looked below his neck. For hanging on it, covering his torso, was a bright green apron, embroidered with a gleeful-looking witch stirring a cauldron. The fact that the witch bore a striking resemblance to Lois was no coincidence—Nate had done the embroidery herself and gifted the apron to her years ago as a joke.

Lois wandered over and planted a kiss on Nick's cheek. "Don't listen to them, darling. I can't wait to taste your masterpiece."

"You're a terrible liar, but thanks nonetheless, love." He gave her a return peck before turning back to his task.

Lois chuckled as she took her own seat. "You know, Max, if you're so worried, you could get up there and pitch in. Or at least supervise."

"Not necessary!" Nick called over his shoulder.

"I hate to admit it, but he's right. My magic is restricted to my oven. I would be no help at all here. You see, *I* can actually own *my* shortcomings."

"Oh, shut up," Nick muttered. "We'll just see who's coming back for seconds and thirds later."

They all laughed. Nate genuinely loved spending time with this bunch. While she and Max did have a tendency to pile on Nick, he took it in the good-natured spirit it was intended, and gave as good as he got.

"So, Frannie couldn't make it tonight?" Max asked casually.

Frannie Haynes, who often joined their circle, was an accounting whiz at the studio. When Nate and Lois had first met her, she worked as a manicurist—a gig she'd taken after losing her finance job to the boys returning home from war, in order to support her daughter Lucy. When Lois took over at Phoenix, she offered Frannie the chance to return to her original passion, and it worked out beautifully for everyone.

"No, she called to say Lucy wasn't feeling well," Lois answered. "She didn't want to leave her."

"Oh, that's too bad." Max took a sip of his beer, still nonchalant.

Or so he thought. Nate inspected him closely. Yep, definitely too nonchalant. Lois regarded him with similar scrutiny, then met her eye, matching slow grins spreading across their faces. Luckily for him, Max didn't notice their silent exchange.

"Too bad?" Nate chided. "I've never been in the presence of the two of you for more than five minutes without it getting…let's just say fractious. At best. I think Tom and Jerry get along better."

With a tiny smirk, Lois added, "Yes, I'd think you'd be relieved Frannie wasn't coming."

Max's eyes darted between the two of them. "I simply meant it was too bad her daughter's sick. She's a lovely little girl. And no one wants to see a child suffer."

To his credit, he covered himself quickly. But Nate and Lois would most assuredly be investigating this further.

Their unwitting victim was saved by the sound of the doorbell echoing through the open patio door.

Max jumped up in an instant, comically eager to escape. And suspiciously hopeful despite his efforts at pretending otherwise. "You guys stay comfortable. I'll see who it is."

Nate snorted as soon as he disappeared. "Okay, we have *got* to find out what's going on there."

"Oh, you know it."

"Is it possible Lucy made a miraculous recovery, and things are about to get fun?"

"Don't think I didn't catch the implication behind that," Nick interjected. "And not to burst your bubble, but it's probably Colin."

Nate was certain she actually heard her stomach hit the ground beneath her.

And then all other sound ceased to exist as a certain distinct British baritone floated toward her from inside the house. Even muffled and distant, that voice incinerated her insides.

Imagine it right next to your ear.

Repressing a shudder, she crossed her arms and leveled a glare at Lois across the table.

"Don't look at me like that," Lois hissed. "I didn't know he was coming, I swear." She turned to Nick and raised her voice sweetly. "Hon, you didn't mention Colin would be here too."

"Oh, didn't I? Sorry, I thought I did. Yeah, I was in his office the other day and figured it would be nice to include him. He's still pretty new here." Nick glanced over his shoulder and asked quietly, "You don't mind, do you?"

"Of course not. The more the merrier."

Lois kept her eyes on Nate and mouthed an apology.

Nate barely had time to register that this wasn't some grand scheme on Lois's part before the velvet that put her in a fog grew louder, and Max ushered Colin outside. She was powerless to stop the flush creeping up her neck and face.

Of course, his eyes had to find her first.

He gave her a lopsided smile, but his Adam's apple worked furiously for a moment before he quickly turned to survey the rest of the patio, oddly detached. Before she could read too much into it, though, their focus was pulled elsewhere.

"Colin! So glad you could make it!" Nick spread his arms wide, spatula still in hand, apron on full display.

Nate noticed a tiny quirk at the corner of Colin's mouth, but he masterfully contained his mirth.

"I'm delighted to be here. Thanks again for the invitation." He paused briefly before deadpanning, "That's a most dapper apron you've got on there."

Nate cackled, which got Colin's attention. He flashed her a quick—and devilish—smile, as if unable to help himself.

Aw, shit.

What business did he have pairing glasses and argyle—yes, he wore an argyle sweater to a barbecue—with rakish wit and that obscene voice? It simply wasn't fair to do that to a woman.

Nick looked down at himself and grinned. "Thanks. It's my favorite." He winked at Lois.

Lois shook her head as she stood. "Of course it is. It's mine," she stage-whispered conspiratorially. "Colin, welcome. It's great to see you."

"You too, Lois. Your home is just lovely." He gestured toward the house, which seemed to remind him of the bottle he held in his hand.

Huh. His hands are nice, aren't they? Wonder why I didn't notice that the other day…

This just grew worse and worse, didn't it?

"I brought this," Colin continued, oblivious to her infernally expanding catalogue of his virtues. "I wasn't sure what went well with…whatever we're having. But I hope everyone enjoys something red?"

"Of course. It's perfect," Lois replied as she took the wine from him. "I see you've met Max. And obviously you know Nate."

Thanks a lot, friend. Draw his attention back to me.

Feeling the need to speak up before he uttered one more word and left her completely at sea, she jumped in. "Colin. Nice to see you again."

Her words ran together. *Jumped in a little too hard, I guess.*

"You as well." Colin's eyes darted away from hers. He cleared his throat so roughly Nate worried he'd damaged the nap of that velvet sin, before he turned his attention elsewhere. "And Max, it's a pleasure."

As he and Max made small talk, Colin's gaze kept flickering back in her direction, though he hardly seemed happy about it. Had something happened since their meeting the other day? His easy manner had vanished, which worried her. Of course, she wouldn't have taken note of it at all if she was capable of looking anywhere but at him. Her damn eyeballs clearly didn't want to even try.

She diverted her mind to the task of discovering an answer to a much less distressing question—precisely how it was possible for him to simultaneously look so square and so delectable—until Lois's voice snapped her attention back to earth.

"Would anyone like some wine?" Lois asked. "This looks fantastic, Colin."

At everyone's assent, Lois headed for the door. "Nate, can you help me with the glasses?"

"Huh? Oh, absolutely."

Nate shook her head as she followed Lois inside. She should be grateful for the interruption. There was no reason to be analyzing Colin's delectability, especially in front of a crowd. Who all knew why she wasn't supposed to go after him.

But really, who knew argyle could be so damn appealing?

"Wow. Coming back anytime soon?" Lois asked as they reached the kitchen and she fished a corkscrew out of a drawer.

"I've been here the whole time."

Lois snorted. "Sure, you have. Grab the glasses, will you?"

Nate followed Lois's instructions. "You really had no idea he'd be here?"

"I promise you, I was as surprised as you were. Well...maybe not *quite* as surprised." Lois chuckled at the metaphorical ice Nate hurled her way. "Really, though, I wouldn't have ambushed you."

Nate sighed. "I know you wouldn't." She chewed on her lip. "What do you think he's doing here?"

Lois arched an eyebrow as she poured the wine. "By accepting an invitation to socialize with some work colleagues in a town where he's relatively new? I can't imagine. Must be one hell of a sinister plan he's cooking up."

"Your sarcasm is a real pain in the ass sometimes, you know that?"

"Says the queen of sarcasm herself. Not so enjoyable when you're the target, hmm?"

Nate stuck her tongue out, like the child she was, and Lois laughed.

"I guess I was just looking forward to today, that's all. I didn't want to think about…" She trailed off, not wanting to admit the rest, even to herself.

"How right I was that you want to fling the hell out of Colin?"

Nate rolled her eyes. "Fine. Yes. Happy now?"

"I suppose so." Lois paused, an odd, knowing expression on her face. Nate didn't like the look of it. "It's too bad Walter's not here to save you from yourself."

Nate's stomach dropped again, a riot of thoughts crowding her head. And her heart. The usual guilt over deceiving Lois. And the most confusing pull. On the one hand, everything would be so much easier if Walter was here—if he existed, of course. She had grown rather used to using him as a shield over the years.

But if she had never invented him, her current mess wouldn't be a mess at all. She'd be free to act on the attraction building between her and Colin. See where it went…and risk all that came with it.

At this point, she didn't know which option scared her more— holding onto her lie, or letting go of it.

Lois waited for an answer, though, so her turmoil would have to wait. "It is always too bad he's not here, isn't it?"

Only half the truth, but half was better than none.

Before Lois responded, Nate plowed on. "You know, *you* could help me out here. Say something to get my mind out of the gutter so I don't make a bigger fool of myself out there."

Lois filled the last glass, finally sympathetic. "He's wearing argyle to a barbecue? You must have thoughts about that."

"I know! Who does that?" Nate's mind filled with the vision of him in his sweater, and her mouth softened. "It works on him, though, doesn't it?"

Lois smirked infuriatingly.

"Hey, wait a minute. Are you really one to criticize, when your husband's out there wearing *your* apron?"

"Touché." Lois's face went dreamy. "It does work on him, too, though."

"You're hopeless."

"I am. And proud of it." She picked up three of the glasses in a careful balancing act, leaving the remaining two to Nate. "Come on, let's go hopelessly ogle the meat." She threw a wicked smile over her shoulder. "And whatever Nick's grilling."

Chapter Five

"If you put away any more of that steak, you'll be all out of room for cheesecake," Nick intoned smugly. "I believe an apology is in order?"

Max glared at him as he lifted another forkful to his lips. "Fine. If you insist. I may have underestimated your barbecuing skills."

"Well, this is one rare instance where I am not proud," Nate piped up. "That was delicious, Nick."

"See, that wasn't so hard, was it?" Nick smiled.

Max rolled his eyes as the whole table laughed. Colin sat back and took it all in, grateful to Nick for including him tonight, despite his regrets over not being able to flirt with Nate anymore. The wine and the humor flowed freely. Since arriving in Los Angeles, he'd been primarily focused on work and the hunt for his sister, and tonight he felt a sense of kinship and belonging for the first time in ages.

And once they'd begun eating, he had managed to keep his longing stares at Nate to a minimum. A worthy achievement, if he did say so himself.

Though he wondered why Nate's husband hadn't come with her, he knew better than to ask. None of his business, after all.

As the group settled into a satisfied lull, not yet ready for that cheesecake everyone raved about, their talk gravitated toward the subject that inevitably came up whenever a handful of men their age sat in a room together. The war.

Nick and Max had a long-shared history, which likely extended to their service, as well.

Curiosity getting the better of him, Colin asked, "So did the two of you serve together?"

Nick nodded as Max answered, "Sort of. We were in the same regiment, but I wasn't allowed near any action. Stuck on mess duty." He tapped his left ear. "The lingering effects of an…incident…when I was a kid."

"It's a pretty funny story," Nick chimed in.

"Which we do not need to rehash tonight. I've already been humbled enough by that meat apology I had to make."

"Fair enough," Nick chuckled. "What about you, Colin? Were you in the service?"

"Of a kind." At everyone's questioning looks, he elaborated. "An old injury kept me from most of the action as well. But I did serve in intelligence. Wrote radio plays for the BBC, to be precise. I know it doesn't seem like much, but…"

He glanced at Nate in time to see understanding—and intrigue—dawn across her face.

"You planted secret messages in them, didn't you?"

Colin answered her smile with one of his own. "I did."

"You may not think it sounds like much, but it is," Nick said earnestly. "I mean it. Our unit was on the receiving end of a lot of those kinds of broadcasts, and believe me, they were one of our greatest lifelines. Thanks."

"You are most welcome." Feeling the need to lighten the mood again, Colin added, "You have no idea how rewarding it can be to hide troop movement and coordinates in loo jokes. Flatulence makes a lovely substitute for explosions."

The table erupted in laughter.

As they moved on to Max's cheesecake—which was, in fact, unreasonably delicious—a sobering realization took hold of Colin.

All this time they'd been chatting, not one person had yet to mention Nate's husband, even through all their talk of the war.

Is it possible I overheard wrong? Bollocks, have I been standoffish all night over nothing?

Hope flared back to life in his chest. But he needed to make certain.

"Nate," he blurted, "did I hear correctly that you're married?"

Nate had been in the process of picking up her fork, and it clattered to the table with a resounding echo. Out of the corner of his eye, he saw Lois nearly choke on her wine.

Way to be tactful, you arse.

Colin's face flooded with heat. He caught a glimpse of Nate's own lovely—and now thoroughly flushed—face. The bite of cheesecake he'd just swallowed morphed into a congealed ball of pure embarrassment.

"My apologies," he managed to offer. "I heard someone mention a husband to you the other day, and wondered if he might be here, and then he wasn't. And then I started wondering if I'd gotten it wrong and you weren't married after all, and so…" His ramble ran out of steam. "I thought I'd ask. In a rather abrupt way. Sorry. I am quite the fool, aren't I?"

After an interminable silence, Nate replied haltingly. "No. He's not here. My husband, I mean. Because I…do…have one. But not with me. He would be, except…well."

Her cheeks took on a distressing shade of red.

Shite on toast. I've thoroughly embarrassed her. Why couldn't I keep my mouth shut?

"He travels. A lot." The crimson faded as Nate got the most astounding blank look on her face. If he didn't know better, he'd say it almost seemed as if she couldn't remember her own husband's name. "Walter! Walter's a baseball scout."

Colin felt terrible. He couldn't believe he'd flustered her to this point. He wanted to slink under the table.

But he couldn't. He'd generated this chaos, and he needed to fix it. Compliment her husband.

But Walter. Ugh, "Wanker" more like.

No, he most certainly should not harbor thoughts like that.

"Baseball. That sounds exciting. What team does he work with?"

Not that Colin knew a damn thing about American baseball, but he would feign interest if it killed him.

"Team? Oh, he works with a lot of teams. Right now, he's scouting for…the Tigers. Detroit." She finished with a weak smile, and his heart imploded in his chest.

"Huh." Lois watched the depths of her wineglass. "I thought you said he was with the Phillies lately." She leveled a strange, unreadable look at Nate.

"Did I?" Nate rather resembled a deer caught in headlamps. "No, it's the Tigers now. Definitely the Tigers."

Colin couldn't make heads or tails of the whole scene, but one thing was certain. He had royally cocked up this lovely evening—and any chance of even a platonic relationship with Nate.

Thankfully, Max came to his rescue. And Nate's.

"You know, I could use some coffee along with this cheese-cake. Who's with me?"

Nate shot to her feet. "I sure am. Why don't I help you with it?"

She escaped inside without waiting for Max's answer.

"Be right back." With a sheepish shrug, Max followed her into the house.

Colin leaned his elbow on the table, his chin slumping forward into his hand. "Bet you're glad you invited me now."

Nick chuckled softly. "Don't worry about it, mate. It wasn't that bad."

Colin's eyebrows shot up incredulously.

Nick grimaced. "Okay, maybe it was."

Lois contemplated Colin for a moment before seeming to reach a decision.

"Nate doesn't talk about Walter too often. He's not around much…ever. It's a bit of a sensitive subject." She leaned over to pat him on the shoulder. "But you couldn't have known that. Don't beat yourself up."

"If you say so."

"I do."

"And everyone knows, Lois is always right." Nick smiled mischievously at her, and she gave his hair an affectionate ruffle.

Colin watched the two of them, so at ease with each other, so much in love. A surprising pang of jealousy sprang to life in his chest. Not over them in particular, but their intimacy. Did Nate share that kind of intimacy with her husband?

He doubted it, not if this disaster of an evening was any indication. That brought a wave of sadness to chase his green-eyed monster. Nate deserved that blissful intimacy, not some oblivious bloke who couldn't be bothered to be around for his utterly charming wife.

But there he went again, making assumptions. He knew absolutely nothing about Nate's husband or her marriage, and he had no right to pass judgment.

He did know two things, however. One, he needed to apologize, to make up for embarrassing her so utterly.

And two, if he had been lucky enough to marry Nate Reynolds, he sure as hell wouldn't let anything put that lonely, panicked look on her face.

THE REST of the evening passed without incident. When Max and Nate returned with the coffee, Nate had erased all traces of the previous awkward encounter, and was back to her usual gregarious self. Conversation between the five of them resumed its casual, lighthearted manner from earlier in the evening, before Colin's colossal misstep.

Despite the renewed ease, the group called it a night relatively early, owing to the anticipation of almost everyone's busy workday ahead. Max had a bakery to open at an ungodly hour, and Nick, Nate, and Colin were all expected on set relatively early for the pirate film's first day of shooting.

Lois and Nick waved to their guests from the doorway as the three of them departed through the front yard.

Max hesitated a moment before speaking. "Well, I'm off. Have a good night."

"Night, Max." Nate waved.

"It was great to meet you, Colin."

"Likewise."

Max shot him a small but reassuring grin before loping across the street to his truck.

Colin attempted a smile. "May I walk you to your automobile?"

"An offer that formal is hard to resist. But my car is just there." Nate gestured to the curb right in front of the house.

"Well, I can at least see you directly to the door."

He caught a hint of her smile in the faint light from the half-moon and the surrounding houses. "Sure."

As they rounded the back of the car, Colin took a steadying breath. "Nate, I…"

She turned to face him, but remained quiet.

"I would like to apologize. For earlier. And…other things."

Nate held up her hand. "There's no need."

"But there is. The last thing I wanted to do was embarrass you. I never should have said anything."

"Colin, really, it's okay."

He swallowed hard. "And please, let me assure you, when we met the other day, I had no idea."

Confusion flitted across her features. "The other day?"

"Our meeting, in your office. I…I feel I might have been… rather inappropriate. I assumed that you were…"

"Single?" She huffed, a bitter sound. "Right."

"I assure you, it will not happen again. I'm so very sorry."

"You couldn't have known." He heard her sigh, so heavily he

felt the weight of it on his own shoulders. "It's not something I talk about much. I...I wish I could explain my reasons, but..."

He couldn't help himself. He reached out and rested his hand on her upper arm, suddenly desperate to offer her gentle reassurance.

"You don't owe me any explanation." Her muscles relaxed under his hand. "If you ever do need to talk, though, my ears are always open."

Oh, god, that sounded positively lame, didn't it?

To his great relief, Nate smiled.

"Thanks. That...means a lot, actually."

Their eyes locked and the air solidified around them. Again.

The urge to lean in and kiss her overwhelmed him. With his hand still on her arm, he felt tension coming back to it, only an entirely different tension this time, a sense of anticipation in it. Hard to be certain in the semi-darkness, he felt rather than saw her gravitate toward him. Only a fraction of an inch, but it was enough.

He was close, so close. But if he bridged that distance...

You can't take it back.

No, he couldn't. As much as he wanted to, as they both seemed to want to. She was married. There was clearly a story there, and the apparent unhappiness of said story lodged like a dagger in his heart. Her husband might be a wanker who didn't deserve her, but that didn't negate his existence, which made this a path they couldn't venture down.

So Colin summoned all the strength he had—which granted, wasn't much, but at least enough—and let go of her arm.

He saw a flicker of disappointment in her eyes before she blinked. He hated having put it there, but it was for the best.

"This might be a bit presumptuous, but I do hope you know, Nate, that you can consider me a...friend."

Nate's features softened into a smile. "I already do. And...likewise."

Colin's face relaxed as well. "Good. Friends. Well. Good night, Nate."

"Good night, Colin."

He held the door as she slid into her car, and watched as she drove away, before heading to his own.

He was honest enough with himself to admit that he yearned to be much more than Nate's friend, impossible as that was. But he also knew that, despite their short acquaintance, he wanted her in his life in some capacity rather than none at all. He treasured her friendship already. And so he welcomed whatever small bit of her he could have.

Friends. They could do this.

He hoped.

ate set her kit bag at her feet and took in the massive pirate ship docked in front of her. Well, the facade of half a pirate ship, anyway. It might not be remotely capable of staying afloat, but with the right applications of movie magic, audiences would never be the wiser.

She loved this business.

Various crew members bustled past her, getting the last of the equipment set up for the first shots of the day. One of Nate's assistants hovered around the group of extras in the corner, checking their costumes.

Nate glanced around the sound stage, on the lookout for the head pirate in order to give his costume a final once-over. Based on their last fitting, Nick's costume had come together nicely. All that remained was to make sure everything looked right under the lights.

If only she could quiet her still simmering nerves about that damned barbecue.

It had been quite the sensory overload. She had miraculously kept from dissolving into a puddle every time Colin opened his mouth, even managed some intelligent conversation. Until Colin brought up her marital status, which opened the floodgates of hell. Or, it being hell, maybe more like the fire door had been firmly shut with her still inside?

However she chose to describe it, it had been a shit-load of... well, shit. One she could not afford to step in again. She'd been so busy flirting with him, it hadn't even occurred to her he might not realize she was married. Of course, he'd been so oddly resigned earlier that evening. And then the whole ordeal threw her for such a loop that she'd stumbled over the details of her story in a way she hadn't since she perfected it years ago. Her reputation and her career depended on her performing it successfully.

Not only had she actually forgotten... *Crap snacks, not again... Walter! Walter, damn it.* She really needed to remember her stinking husband's name.

But no, the worst of it couldn't have ended there. She had to go and slip up about the damn teams. *Really, who came up with those names anyway?* And Lois, of all people, caught her. As careful as Nate had always been, her friend wasn't stupid. Vague queasiness settled in her stomach. Lurking just beyond her reach was an elusive feeling. Lois had acted casual, but through her haze Nate sensed something lurking underneath. She didn't want to— *couldn't*—linger on the possibility that Lois had figured out her charade. There would be no coming back from *that* disaster.

She turned her attention to what had happened later, out at the car. Which did other things to her stomach—and destinations further south. Colin had been so sweetly apologetic, determined to preserve their friendship. So damn honorable.

She wished she didn't find that honor so appealing.

They were friends. That's all. He believed she had a husband. It didn't matter how different he was from most of the people she'd met in this business. If he found out the truth, saw her for the giant, lying fraud she was, it would change everything—the friendship, the sweetness, the spark would all vanish.

Oh, but that spark.

Even now, it threatened to overtake her. The warm weight of his hand on her arm. The fire in his eyes, shining behind his glasses, even in the dark of the evening. She'd wanted nothing more than to cement her lips to his.

But then he'd pulled back, leaving her to face reality once again. The avalanche of reasons why that was for the best turned her into a veritable snow beast.

If only Walter didn't exist.

He doesn't, *you dope.*

Was it physically possible to kick herself in her own ass? Alas, it would look awfully strange if she tried it in front of a sound stage full of people.

True, she lived in a mess entirely of her own making, but how was she supposed to have known, twelve years ago, that a deep-voiced, confoundingly sexy British square would show up and upend her carefully crafted lie. It hadn't started out all that carefully crafted, but she had buffed it to a high sheen over the years. She didn't need it falling apart now.

Or maybe I do.

Impossible. Yes, it would conveniently eliminate the barrier to her kissing the pants off of Colin and finding out just what was under those glasses…and pants. But then she'd be leaving her heart wide open, and that way lay madness. She was resigned to her secret singlehood, her protection against inevitable disappointment. Both personal and professional.

She was better off this way. Friends. That's what they'd said last night, and that was how they would stay.

A loud rumble brought her back to the present, as one of the crew rolled a huge light past her. Nate sighed and focused on the pirate ship again. She had a job to do, a job she loved. Time to concentrate on that.

"Costumes all ready for today?" A lower, much more pleasant rumble reached her ears this time.

Well, there goes that concentration.

She turned to see Colin ambling toward her, a vision in tweed. Even his tie was a nubby, knitted concoction of three shades of brown.

Irritation flared. Tweed was *not* supposed to be so adorable, damn it.

Colin approached her, expectant and slightly apprehensive, and her annoyance melted. She managed a smile, and impressed herself by actually remembering his question.

"I think so. I haven't laid eyes on our illustrious pirate yet, but I'm not anticipating any major problems." She paused to implore the costuming gods and goddesses. "Knock on wood."

He grinned. "I have no doubt you are so well prepared that no wood will need to be roughhoused today."

Crap. He can make even superstition sound filthy.

Heat singed the tips of Nate's ears. Colin's smile faltered as he seemed to catch what he'd said, and his cheeks went redder than Superman's undies.

She quickly turned to gaze up at the pirate ship, giving them both a moment to frantically attempt recovery.

"This ship is…really something."

Colin let out a strangled "Yes." Clearing his throat, he continued, "Henri and his team have really outdone themselves."

"It's a marvel, isn't it?" She latched onto the lifeline, before her traitorous dirty mind—and apparently his as well—forced her to walk the plank. "She looks almost seaworthy."

Appearing to have collected himself—*the lucky bastard*—he replied, "Oh, absolutely. I might even call her yar. So long as you stay on the starboard side."

She gave him a startled look. "Wow, you know your boats."

Colin straightened his shoulders in an attempt at bravado. "Of course I…don't." He slid her a sidelong glance and one side of his mouth hitched up. "Honestly, I've heard the terms starboard and bow used in a sentence. But I couldn't tell you the arse end of a ship from its…anchor?"

Nate laughed. "Hey, it's still more than I know."

"I suppose we should be proud we can at least identify it as a boat."

"There you go. Silver lining found."

They grinned at each other, before a cat-calling whistle from one of the lighting grips pulled their attention to the edge of the set, where Nick appeared in all his pirate glory.

"Oh, well done, Nate," Colin chuckled.

It was Nate's turn to straighten with bravado, hers in no way feigned. Pride flared at what she and her team had accomplished. Nick flipped the grip a lighthearted rude gesture before he caught sight of her and Colin. As he started toward them, Nate took in her handiwork.

His leather pants had been tailored just the right amount —tight enough to make the ladies swoon, but not so tight that they'd piss off the censors. Said pants and his matching doublet had been weathered to perfection, and the billowy shirt underneath yawned open enough to reveal a hint of hair on his chest. The sheer number of buckles on his boots had been a royal pain in the ass to craft, but the effort paid off. A head scarf and clip-on earring completed the look, as did the mustache Jackie in makeup had affixed to his upper lip.

And then Nick opened his mouth.

"Ahoy, mateys!"

Colin mock-scowled. "Do not say that once the cameras start rolling. I will not have people thinking I wrote dialogue that corny."

He held up his hand. "You have my word." He turned for Nate's approval. "How do I look, madam?"

She shook her head, unable to keep from smiling. "Every bit the buccaneer. Here."

Nate reached up to adjust the amount of shirt collar peeking out from his doublet. He needed to look carefully, artfully disheveled. There existed a fine line between roguish and just plain messy, after all. Finding that line, she stepped back for an assessment.

"That'll do."

"Excellent." Nick's nostrils flared slightly. "By the way, what am I smelling? I think it's my pants and vest. They're somehow... floral? And yet, waxy?"

Nate chuckled. "It's my aging goop. Those pants have supposedly sailed around the world with you and done all sorts of dastardly deeds. Couldn't have them looking too new, could I?"

Lois sauntered up with a smile. "What's all this about my husband's dastardly pants?"

"Don't worry, these dastardly pants are all for you, honey," Nick drawled, winking lasciviously.

Nate rolled her eyes. "Hey, I had a donut on the way over here. I'd like to keep it down, if you don't mind."

Colin leaned in to stage whisper, "Are they always like this?"

"Afraid so."

Boldly ignoring them, Nick went full pirate and reached for Lois.

"I swear to god, Nick Bradley, if I have to reapply that mustache because you can't keep your hands off your wife, you won't live to see your first take!" Jackie's voice carried across the set, from where she touched up one of his co-stars' hair.

Nate, Colin, and Lois laughed as Nick slowly lowered his arms.

"Duly noted, Jackie!" he called. "Honestly, how does she do that? I swear, she actually has eyes in the back of her head."

"Or she's just worked with you enough," Lois teased.

"Very funny." He glanced over his shoulder at Jackie. "Think she'll actually kill me if I chance it anyway?"

"Of course Jackie would never outright kill you," Nate responded. "Though I can absolutely see her making your balls into earrings," she concluded with a beatific smile.

Nick blanched.

"Let's not risk it, love," Lois chuckled. "Save the boys. There'll be plenty of time for me to ravish you later."

The director called Nick over, saving him from himself, and Lois leaned in toward Nate. "Tell me, friend, does he get to keep those pants when this is all over?"

"Gee, I don't know. I'd have to run it by the head of the studio, and I hear she can be a real tyrant." Nate flashed her a wicked grin.

"Don't let her hear you say that, or you could be out on your ass," Lois shot back.

"Eh, I'm not worried." She gestured to Nick. "I think she'll keep me around for that alone."

"I hate to say it, but you've got a point there." She smiled warmly. "It is some of your finest work."

"I know."

They shared a laugh, until one of the film's producers caught Lois's eye. She headed over to greet him, leaving the writer and the costume designer alone on the sidelines.

"They're quite smitten with each other, aren't they?" Colin observed, with an almost wistful sigh.

"Yeah, they are. I tease, but I'm really happy she found him."

Colin turned to her. "She's very lucky to have you as a friend."

Nate blushed. "Thanks. I'm pretty lucky too."

Can't go five seconds alone with him, can I?

Nate forced her attention across the room. While she feigned fascination over a serving wench's sleeve, a choked snort emanated from Colin. Expecting a smart quip about billowing linen, it surprised her to see his attention on Nick and the director, walking over to the ship's gangplank.

Well, the director walked. Nick was… Really, strutting like a peacock was the only way to put it.

"What on earth is he doing?" Colin asked, horrific fascination all over his face. "Is he getting into character already?"

Nate harbored a suspicion, and one glance to her left confirmed it. "I'm pretty sure he's performing entirely for his favorite audience of one at the moment." She nodded in Lois's direction.

Colin followed her nod and laughed. "He's shameless, isn't he?"

"Unfortunately, yes."

To her credit, Lois attempted—in vain—to keep her focus on the producer. But Nick was a master of his craft. And he knew his wife. As he continued to listen to the director's notes, he hefted a leg up onto the gangplank, leaning his elbow on his knee. An action which brought his leather-clad ass into full, prominent display for Lois.

"Dear god, now he's—" Colin stopped himself. "No, I shouldn't say."

Nate lifted her eyebrows, thoroughly intrigued. "Oh, you can't tease me like that. If you think you shouldn't, that's exactly why you *need* to say it, in my book."

He let out a huff of amusement and leaned in conspiratorially. "Ever see the way wild animals…present their arses when they're trying to attract a mate?"

A loud cackle exploded out of Nate. Heads whipped in her direction, and she suppressed it with an undignified snort.

"Oh god, that's…" Another snort. "…exactly what he looks like."

"Right? It's uncanny." Colin took in her difficulty and his grin widened.

In an attempt to remain professional on set, Nate got her laughter under control. For a minute, at least. She started to chuckle again and shook her head. She could feel Colin's mirth vibrating off him, but didn't dare look at him, lest she lose it again.

She sensed him angle his head down toward her.

"Now what we have here," he began in a low tone, perfectly mimicking a documentary voice-over, "is the male 'actorius sapien' in his natural habitat."

She stifled yet another snicker.

"See how he struts about the space, preening in his leather coverings, overly confident despite the apparent silliness of his presentation."

Nate bit down hard on her lower lip as her chest wheezed. She elbowed Colin in a futile attempt to make him stop, even though she couldn't wait to see how far he'd take this.

"But what may seem silly to an untrained eye proves in actuality to be the very behavior to snare a mate." Barely perceptible, Colin inclined his head toward Lois, and Nate grabbed his arm. Undaunted, he continued, "Observe the female of the species: the faint blush, the…almost alarming degree of possessiveness in her gaze."

Nate dug her nails into Colin's tweed sleeve as a somewhat high-pitched whine of amusement escaped her lips. Her eyes watered with the effort.

He started to lose a bit of control himself, but not before getting in one last zinger. "It would not entirely come as a shock should the female steal the director's megaphone, knock her mate over the head, and drag him from the set…"

That was it. He had killed her. Her laughter completely uncontainable, she sagged against his shoulder. It shook with his own laughter, as a deep, delectable rumble emanated from his chest. More heads turned their way, and she couldn't summon the desire to care. She hadn't laughed so hard in a long time.

Or felt a laugh echo all the way to down to her lady bits.

They had yet to calm down over Nick's presented ass when Lois finally drew her attention away from said derriere, raising a quizzical brow in their direction.

The show-off himself turned his gaze on the two of them as well. Nick brandished the script pages in his hand and called out with an annoying smirk, "Hey, Colin. Mind if I tear you away to ask a question about these lines?"

Colin cleared his throat and straightened up with a slight blush. "Of course."

Nate wiped at the corners of her eyes and attempted to regain her composure. She was on her way to doing a successful job of it, when Colin turned back after taking only one step away.

"Please do excuse me, my fellow intrepid zoologist." He inclined his head in a tiny bow before walking over to Nick.

Leaving her with the sense that she was the one who'd been clubbed over the head with a megaphone, rather than animal-kingdom Nick.

"You all right there, my friend?"

She startled at Lois's voice beside her. Her focus had been so entirely on Colin walking away, she hadn't noticed Lois's approach.

Nate cleared her throat of any remnants of laughter. "Just fine, thanks."

Lois's infuriatingly talented eyebrow hitched again. "Care to share the joke?"

"No, I don't think I do." Ignoring Lois's surprised look, she turned her attention across the room. "I should probably go check on Ava's dress. Be right back."

Colin caught her eye and flashed her a grin as she made her way over to Nick's co-star. Nate smirked. She rather enjoyed having an inside joke with Colin.

That was what *friends* did, after all.

Chapter Seven

Colin carefully juggled the grocery bags in his arms as he kicked his apartment door closed behind him. He had just made it to the small table in his kitchen when the telephone rang. Startled, he set the paper bags down with more force than he'd planned, and one promptly toppled over, sending a waterfall of fruits and vegetables cascading to the floor.

Of course it was the bag with every possible round object he'd bought.

"Bollocks on a crumpet!" he exclaimed as he executed a little jig to reach the phone without landing on his arse amid the lethal, still rolling produce.

"Hello?"

"Greetings, darling," his mother trilled. "Is everything all right? You sound rather winded, dear."

He smiled at her concern. "Hi, Mum. Just doing battle with some groceries, no cause for alarm."

"Oh." Marjorie Canfield had always known how to pack a world of emotion into a single syllable.

"Do I detect a hint of disappointment there?"

"Of course not, darling. But if you're going to forget our regu-larly scheduled phone call, it would be rather lovely if the reason was at least a young lady there stealing your breath. Groceries are just so—"

"Mum!" Colin's face burned. "First of all, I did not forget our call."

Not entirely, anyway. He'd known to expect it today, but could have sworn he had a little more time to prepare. He must have lost track of the hour while at the store.

It had nothing whatsoever to do with his stopping to look at the lobster case because it reminded him of Nate and her brilliant costuming ideas.

Ahem.

Right, his mother. Upon his move to the States, they established a standing appointment to check in once a month. They'd always shared a good relationship, but it had become especially important to both of them to stay connected after the war. It certainly was no easy task, what with the time difference and the expense of overseas calls. Colin made good money at the studio, and he'd offered on multiple occasions to pay for at least some of the calls, but his mother insisted on picking it all up herself. To his utterly endeared frustration, she maintained that it was "the least a mother can do for her son."

She drew his attention back to the subject at hand. "You know, I wouldn't blame you in the slightest if you had. You do lead such an exciting life out there in California now."

"I'm a screenwriter, Mum. It's not nearly as glamorous as you think. I'm still spending most of my time in a small room with my typewriter."

"Is there no one special to coax you away from that room now and again?" she asked slyly. "I'm sure your typewriter wouldn't mind sharing you."

Colin rolled his eyes as he stooped to pick up an apple that had landed near his foot. "No, I'm sure it wouldn't. But it won't have to. There's...no one special right now." He prayed she hadn't caught the slight hitch he'd been unable to curb over his lie.

"Are you sure about that?"

Damn it. Just once, would it kill her to miss something?

"I'm sure, Mum."

He injected as much finality as possible into the denial. Even if he wanted to admit just how special Nate was becoming to him—and how famously she and his mother would get on—it was all for naught anyway. As long as Wanker remained in the picture, they hadn't a chance.

No matter how her laughter warmed him to the core, even days later. He smiled every time he thought of how much fun it had been to egg her on, break her restraint until she'd collapsed against him with laughter.

Imagine her other restraints breaking against you.

Colin brought his forehead to the wall next to the phone with a small thud. He could not be having thoughts like that while talking to his *mother*, for fuck's sake.

"Don't take this the wrong way, dear, but are you sure you're getting out there enough?"

Thankful for the long phone cord, he moved to start putting the perishables in the refrigerator. Maybe the cold air would tame his stubborn thoughts that refused to leave his nether regions.

"That starved for grandchildren, are you?" He knew it was madness to bring it up, but anything that might get his mind off sex was worth the risk.

Marjorie scoffed. "Give me a little more credit than that, won't you? While a tiny tot or two would delight me no end if that's what you want, I am only thinking of your happiness." She paused. "You're not still dwelling on what happened with Fiona, are you?"

His eyebrows shot up at that one. "Fiona? Are you kidding? Of course not. That's ancient history."

And it was. He honestly hadn't given more than a passing thought to the split with his former flame in years. It had hurt tremendously at the time, but they'd patched things up and moved on to become friends long ago, before the war even. He'd lived multiple lifetimes since, and had no regrets now.

"I hope so," his mum continued. "There's an utterly perfect girl out there for you, and I'd hate for you to pass her by because of any lingering hesitations over that twat."

Colin barked a laugh. "Mum! You know Fiona and I are friends now."

He admonished her in an effort to be a gentleman, though her language was anything but surprising. Some of the very best—and most vulgar—cuss words in his arsenal, he had learned directly from his mother.

"Maybe so. But *you* know I can hold a grudge better than anyone. Especially when someone comes for my boy." Her tone softened. "You're a truly exceptional young man, and you deserve a truly exceptional love in your life."

Colin's shoulders softened and his chest filled with warmth. "Thanks, Mum." He heard what sounded distinctly like a sniffle on the other end of the line. "Are you crying?"

"No! I most certainly am not." She drew in a sharp breath. "Well, since you refuse to give me anything interesting about your love life, you might as well entertain me with something else. What are you working on now?"

Colin continued putting away his groceries as he regaled her with details about fake pirate ships, projects he had coming up, and the new friends he'd begun making. As difficult as it was, he carefully left Nate completely out of the discussion. He knew his mother too well. She'd pick up on his conflicted feelings in a flash, and he simply wasn't ready to have that conversation with her yet.

Not that a part of him didn't long to tell her. He smiled to himself, thinking again about how much she would absolutely adore Nate.

Ever the proper son, he turned their talk back to his mum, asking about her adventures. The woman had a bustling social life, and what seemed like a million friends—along with a handful of lovers over the years, which he steadfastly refused to think about for any length of time. Despite having divorced his late father when Colin was a little boy, Marjorie Canfield had never been lonely.

Thoughts of his father brought his mind around to the subject he never enjoyed facing. He pushed his glasses up the bridge of his nose as he debated whether to ask the ever-present question in his mind.

"I haven't heard anything more about Frances or her mum, dear."

Colin jerked off the wall where he'd been leaning.

"I swear to god, Mother. Are you actually able to read minds?"

Marjorie chuckled softly. "Only yours. Or rather, it's your silences I'm best at reading. They contain multitudes."

Colin shook his head. "So you've always told me."

"Are you ever going to stop beating yourself up about this? It's not as if you haven't tried."

"I haven't tried hard enough. If I had, I'd have found her by now. She's my sister, goddamn it. How can I have just lost track of her?" He raked an angry hand through his hair.

"There was a war, darling."

"Still. I should know where she is now. It's the reason I took this job in the first place; I'm not spending nearly enough time looking."

Not a day went by when he didn't regret it. He had been in intelligence during the war, for heaven's sake. He should have the connections to be able to track her down. But he'd failed repeatedly.

And he missed her.

They hadn't grown up together, not in any traditional sense. They shared a father, who despite loving both of them tremendously, simply had never been cut out for "staid" family life. After his restlessness got in the way of his marriage to Colin's mother, he'd gone on to give it another try with someone else. The man hadn't succeeded there, either. But to his credit, he had tried to shower his two children with as much love and attention as he could manage, albeit from a bit of a distance, before his untimely death during the London Blitz.

Luckily, their mothers had at least been amicable. Though he wouldn't exactly call them friends, Colin suspected they had bonded over their exasperation when it came to their mutual ex-husband. But the best thing they agreed on was their conviction that the half-siblings should have some semblance of a relationship. The two mothers had made sure they saw each other at least a few times a year —quite the effort considering how far they lived from each other.

Colin would be eternally grateful for their dedication. He adored his boisterous sister.

Even though adulthood, and then war, had taken them far from each other.

His sister had ventured across the pond for university, and the last he knew of her she'd married an American just before he enlisted. That had been right after the Pearl Harbor attack.

It killed Colin that he didn't even know her married name.

Which, in turn, made it that much more difficult to find her now.

Marjorie had heard through the grapevine that his sister and her own mother had ventured west at some point, but unfortunately the details ended there. He'd been so hopeful, leaving Broadway behind for Hollywood, but he'd been too successful at his job—and nowhere near successful in finding her.

His mother's solicitous voice sliced through his thoughts. "Colin. Listen to me. You have not failed her. You haven't."

"How do you know?" He knew he sounded petulant, but his guilt tended to get the better of him.

"Because her mother raised her as well as I raised you. You're both resilient. And stubborn as hell—you get that from your father. It may be taking longer than you want it to, but you *will* find each other."

"I hope so."

"Trust yourself. I do. And in the meantime, get out there and live your life. It would hardly do for your sister to find a broken shell of her brother."

Colin let out a sound that was half-groan, half-chuckle. "You can't fool me—you're still just angling for those grandchildren, aren't you?"

"Oh, you are impossible."

"Yes, *I'm* the impossible one. I suppose I learned from the best, didn't I?" Colin smiled at her huff of mock outrage.

He had no idea how she did it, but a few words from her—and the conviction behind them—had him feeling better. He still didn't possess anything remotely like a solution to the guilt that overwhelmed him sometimes over his sister's absence. But his mum believed in him, and that would have to sustain him for now.

After they hung up, Colin finished tidying up the kitchen and made his way to the bedroom to pick out his work clothes for the morning. He opened his closet door, contemplating his plethora of tweed. As happened whenever he looked at any item of clothing lately, his thoughts turned to Nate.

He smiled to himself as he pulled out a sport coat, wondering what she would think of it. Maybe he should pair it with a sweater vest. He cocked his head to one side, uncertain. Did she like sweater vests? Should it even matter?

Should or shouldn't, you know it does.

He couldn't help it. He wanted to impress her. Somehow, despite everything, he thought perhaps he did. He hadn't seen her since that first day on the pirate set—*dear god, even her snort-laughs are like music*—but they'd spoken on the telephone three times since. And she'd initiated every call.

Interesting, that.

She'd posed various questions about the costumes for the dancer skits, but none terribly urgent. It was almost as if… But no, he was being silly. What could possibly be so remarkable about his voice that she needed to hear it that often? It was nothing more than wishful thinking on his part. That would lead to nowhere.

Because they were *only* friends.

He refocused on the jacket still in his hand, then spotted his favorite three-piece suit in its place in the closet, and his chest lightened.

Yes, tomorrow felt like a three-piece suit kind of day.

A dead end might lurk ahead, on a road he shouldn't be traveling in the first place, but damn it, he'd at least look his best while marching to his doom.

Chapter Eight

Nate concentrated on the sound of her heels clicking on the pavement as she made her way across the lot. The brown alligator pumps were one of her favorite pairs, in part because of that tone. Her footsteps resonated assurance, certainty. Confidence.

Too bad her mind hadn't caught up yet.

She knew she was being ridiculous, but she waffled back and forth over the precise reason why. She had so many to choose from. One minute she chided herself for her nerves, when she was simply doing her job. The next she reminded herself that absolutely no reason existed for her to do this part of her workload so early in the process, and in person no less. She was making excuses, like she'd done an embarrassing amount of times the week before. It put her at risk of looking unprofessional, incompetent even. Which would never do.

Yet her feet pushed her forward, closer and closer to the writers' building.

She marveled at how many times she'd failed to resist calling him. Spending time with him on set that day had flipped some kind of a switch. That voice, so irresistible when forming words, held another power entirely when used for low, rumbling laughter. It pushed her over the edge, and now she could hardly go two stinking days without hearing it. In any capacity.

It simply wasn't fair.

She usually took weekends off from even thinking about work, but this last one she threw herself into sketching, in the hope that it would distract her. A pretty useless endeavor when all her pencil could manage to focus on were the things they'd talked about over the phone, amendments to her ideas for the dancer comedy. The entire time she'd worked, his voice played on an endless loop in her mind. And elsewhere.

Nate had walked into her office that morning resolved to devote the entire day to accessorizing costumes for an upcoming melodrama. Then proceeded to curse her own efficiency when she completed the task by lunchtime. Lunch with a chatty Frannie and Lois in the commissary had helped. But the minute she returned to her office, with an entire afternoon stretching in front of her, she became a detached passenger in her own body, watching as her hands grabbed her sketchbook and her feet carried her toward Colin's office.

She reached the squat building, staring up at it for a moment. Even through the door, she heard the frantic clicking of multiple typewriters. It simultaneously satisfied and unnerved her.

Nate could picture Colin, hunched over his typewriter, concentrating. She'd talked plenty with him about his work, but she had yet to observe him in action, and her eagerness fizzed inside her.

I'll bet he's adorable.

But then the doubt crept in. As adorable as he might be, he was at work. She knew how much it pissed her off to be interrupted when in her bubble, how hard it could be to rev up her creative streak again. It wasn't a particularly nice thing to do to him, showing up unannounced. He'd probably resent it. She could count on one finger the experience of her own workflow being impeded without it being a problem.

The time when it was his voice on the other end of the line that did the impeding.

Well, shit.

Nate scrunched up her mouth and glanced around her. She couldn't exactly linger in a bustling, active studio. Someone was bound to come along any minute now, and if they found her in this indecisive state it would look fishy. She'd come this far; she might as well go in and take her chances. With any luck, he'd be fine with seeing her. And even if he wasn't, she'd at least get to see him, to hear him. So there was that.

She pulled open the door and walked in, immediately assaulted by an odiferous wall of coffee. She shook her head and smiled. Writers. The scent nearly made her eyes water, which provided the unexpected bonus of actually clearing her mind—and her nerves—a bit.

Making her way down the hall, she found Colin's name sharing a placard with his colleague's outside a surprisingly quiet office. Maybe he'd stepped out. Nate fought a wave of disappointment as she noticed the door was ajar. Planning to knock before peeking in, she raised her arm. But her fist never made it to the door. Her entire body arrested, because through the half-open door—

Oh, fuck me.

She could see him in profile, staring at the wall in front of him.

But this was no version of Colin she had ever seen before.

He half-leaned on the edge of his desk, one ankle crossed over the other. His arms folded lightly over his midsection and a pencil lodged horizontally between his teeth. He'd loosened his tie and discarded his jacket, leaving him in a vest and his shirtsleeves. Which were rolled up above his elbows. In an effort clearly designed to kill her, he lifted the arm closest to her to absently rub at the back of his neck, putting his forearm in all its glory on full display. The hair in residence there appeared light enough that it might go unnoticed from a distance, but the perfect bit of light coming in the window brought it into a cloud of beautifully stark relief.

As much as his arm mesmerized her, the slight movement of his hand pulled her attention upward.

And then she was really toast.

His glasses had migrated from their usual perch on his nose to a new seat on the crown of his head, atop hair that looked like it had…exploded. She'd long held a theory that his typically pomaded hair would exhibit a life of its own if freed from its restraints, and here was the proof. He appeared to have run his hands through it multiple times, which had unleashed quite a beast of delectable curls. Even soft, his hair remained a very dark blonde, almost but not quite brown, though it was decidedly lighter without the gel.

Oh, the fun her fingers could have in that mane.

Nate was dimly aware that she should start breathing again soon if she wanted to remain upright, but the involuntary action eluded her at the moment. Buttoned-up, tweedy Colin was attractive, in a mild, unassuming way. But this messy, unreserved Colin deep in concentration was… Well, it did similar things to her insides as his voice did.

Oh, shit. He can't start talking. If he starts talking when he looks like this, there is no way I will survive it. I have to leave now, *before it's too late.*

Her traitorous feet refused to move. She would imminently expire, rooted to this spot.

A hazy memory surfaced from her teenaged years. Her family had taken a trip to Europe, which included a stop in Florence to see the statue of *David*. To this day, it remained one of the most stunning things she'd ever beheld. But disheveled Colin was somehow…magically…*better.*

He was, quite frankly, magnificent.

Nate didn't have time to process this new revelation or close her gawking mouth, because Colin's gaze flicked ever so slightly to his left, bringing her into his periphery.

Fuck.

His head snapped around and he bolted off his desk, startled.

He turned to face her, but not before she caught a glimpse of one astoundingly fine ass.

What in god's name has he been hiding under all that tweed?

"Nate! Hello!" Concern followed surprise onto Colin's face. "Oh no, did we have a meeting?"

"No!" Nate squeaked. Great, she was *squeaking* now? *The hell?* "I thought I'd pop over. Unannounced. Sorry. I hope I'm not interrupting. I can go."

It was Colin's turn to exclaim, "No!" Unfortunately he didn't squeak it, so they remained on very unequal footing.

"Please stay. I could use a break actually." He stepped closer and gestured her in. "Welcome to my cave."

Nate laughed as she stepped into the room. Bringing her nearer to his eyes. Which were, for the first time since she'd met him, not hidden behind the lenses of his spectacles.

Fuuuuuuuck.

They were, indeed, a fiery hazel. Even more than she'd realized. Dark around the edges, his irises brightened as they converged on his pupils, culminating in a perfect approximation of a ring of flames. Flames that licked all the way to *her* core and threatened to incinerate her.

She was ready to fling herself over the edge and let the devil have his way with her.

The only thing that pulled her back from the brink were those criminal eyes themselves. They widened briefly as Colin seemed to recall something, prompting him to cast his eyes down at himself. He glanced back up sheepishly.

"Forgive my appearance. When I'm working out a particularly sticky problem, I tend to…well…let myself go a bit. I swear I was far more dapper this morning." He ended with a lopsided grin, color painting his cheeks.

Aw, he's embarrassed. Because he is human, *remember?*

Regaining a hint of her equilibrium, Nate managed a smile. She hoped she came across as reassuring and not feral.

"Don't apologize. I know what it's like to be in that mode."

"Yes, I imagine you would."

They stood there, Nate fully aware she was staring, yet unable to stop herself.

Say something. Anything.

"And your appearance is anything but unforgivable. You should let yourself go more often."

Okay, maybe not anything.

As her whole face flooded with warmth, she tried to cover with an attempt at laughter that of course came out sounding unhinged even to her own ears. She'd never met someone who so thoroughly eroded her brain cells.

Colin's face still held its own tinge of pink, but his shoulders squared and his chest puffed enough to make her wonder if maybe it wasn't embarrassment she'd inspired in him after all. "Thank you." His voice dropped, barely above a whisper. "I would like my appearance to impress you."

The soft, earnest words, combined with the corresponding, barely banked fire in his eyes robbed Nate of any remaining shreds of…well, anything.

He regarded her for a moment. Something was at play behind the smolder, but she couldn't tell what he was thinking. Hell, she couldn't tell what *she* was thinking. What were thoughts, even?

Colin raised his arm, and for one breath-stealing second, she thought he might reach for her. But his hand absently drifted up the bridge of his nose in an utterly endearing move born entirely of habit rather than necessity, since his glasses sat on top of his curls.

His head jerked when he realized he adjusted nothing but air, and he let out a huff of bashful amusement. He whisked the glasses off their perch, in a gesture of half reluctance and half fierce determination, and replaced them on his nose. His armor back in place, the spell of those flaming eyes broken.

Nate took a full breath for the first time since entering his office.

"You don't always need them, huh?" she asked.

"No. I mean, most of the time I do. But they're more for close things anyway." With his head, he gestured to the wall behind him. "For some reason, it helps to take them off when I'm trying to look at the big picture."

"Is that what you were doing? Looking at the big picture?"

"It is," he replied, stepping back over to the wall. He seemed to share her relief at having something else to focus on again.

As he moved, Colin attempted to smooth his hair back, and Nate wanted nothing more than to stop him. Thankfully, she found the sense to keep her mouth shut. As his hands came back down to his sides, she smiled. As if rewarding her for her restraint, his hair steadfastly refused to be tamed, and sprang back up the instant he let go. She inwardly applauded its unfettered, rebellious spirit.

He continued speaking, oblivious to the silent dialogue between her and his hair follicles. "I've been having a dreadful time getting a handle on the flow of this script, so I thought perhaps a little rearranging might be in order."

His sweeping gesture finally pulled her full attention to the wall, where a cork board hung, covered with small square drawings.

"I thought storyboards didn't enter the picture until directors got their hands on something."

"They don't usually." Colin crossed his arms over his chest. "But they're a rather brilliant tool when I need to see if what I'm doing is going to work."

"So the big picture is really just a bunch of little ones," she quipped.

He let out a soft chuckle. "Precisely."

Nate took in the little squares, her attention captured. She squinted as she registered more detail. And then let out a little snort. "Are those…stick figures?"

"Well, we can't all be world-class artists, can we?" he countered, all mock affront.

"No, I suppose not." She flashed a grin over her shoulder as she leaned in for a closer look. "They are pretty cute."

"Thank you. I worked tremendously hard on them. Whole minutes were spent on the effort."

"I can see that."

"Hey." He narrowed his eyes and nudged her arm playfully.

Willfully ignoring the jolt of pleasure now zinging through her arm, Nate continued to peer at the simple drawings, whose lack of artistry really did add to their charm.

"Is this a new script you're working on? It's not the dancer one, right?"

"Yes, this is a new one. Well, sort of." He stepped closer to the wall—and her—but kept his eyes on the storyboards. "I've been batting this one around in my head for a while, but now that I'm finally committing it to paper, I want it to come out perfect. I just need to make a little more sense of the plot."

"Hence the little stick guys."

Colin chuckled.

Nate turned to look up at him. He certainly was tall, almost a solid head above her own height. "Is there something special about this one? That you want it to be perfect and all?"

He hesitated momentarily, throwing a glance over her shoulder toward the door. "Well, I suppose I can tell you. Chances are, you know about it already, or will soon anyway."

He had her truly curious now.

Gesturing to the board, he continued, "I'm hoping Lois will choose this one for her first directing effort."

Nate's gaze snapped back to the wall, excitement brewing for Lois. "So she's finally gonna do it. I knew she was waiting to try until she got the studio off to a good start under her reign. But I didn't know she was that close yet."

Colin hummed. "I don't know how soon it will actually be. But she floated the idea, in case there was anything I wanted her to start considering. And I do want her to consider this. If I could only…"

"Get it right."

"Exactly." Lost in concentration again, he chewed on his lower lip as he brought his hand up to rub his chin. "It can't be anything but. Lois is going to have so much riding on this, and there will no doubt be some who won't make it easy for her. I need to give her the strongest possible foundation to build upon."

Warmth bloomed in Nate's chest at the passion behind Colin's words. Passion that had nothing whatsoever to do with his own ego, and everything to do with helping her best friend's dream come to fruition.

This man. This lovely, wonderful man.

She gently grasped his arm. So touched by what he'd said, she almost didn't register the surprising firmness of the muscles underneath her hand. Almost.

"I'm sure you'll write it perfectly."

Colin looked down at her touch, and turned his body to face her. The molten flame blazed up in his eyes again, breaching the barrier of his glasses.

"You really think so?" His voice dipped deeper than she'd ever heard it. Which was saying something.

Swallowing required a herculean effort, but she managed the task. "I do. And your motivation is going to mean a lot to Lois."

"I hope so."

"I know it will. It means a lot to me, on her behalf."

"Does it? That's good."

Under her hand—*huh, I forgot to move my hand from his arm, didn't I?*—his muscles flexed, as if he struggled to hold himself still. But he didn't completely succeed. His face now hovered inches from hers. Or maybe she was the one who'd decreased the distance between them. She couldn't be sure of much at the moment. Except that she wanted desperately to throw herself into the fire and erase the distance altogether.

His Adam's apple bobbed convulsively—captivatingly—on a hard swallow, the action disposing of the last of her restraint. She shouldn't do it, she really shouldn't. *But why exactly am I even supposed to care, again?*

Nate tipped up her head and brought her lips to his.

Colin froze, and for a split second she panicked, afraid she'd made a terrible mistake. But then his body roared back to life, the fire she'd seen behind his glasses suddenly all-consuming. His hands found her waist as his lips slid against hers, their pressure gentle but not at all tentative. As if he'd been planning precisely this move for some time.

She'd had quite a few late-night planning sessions of her own recently, and so it took no effort at all to slide her arms up and around his neck. When her tongue found the seam of his lips, he opened them eagerly to let her in. As soon as they tasted each other, a soft moan slipped out of her. His answering groan—more like a *growl*, really—reverberated in corners of her body she'd never before been aware of.

One of his hands slid around and up her back, while the fingers of the other gripped her waist fiercely. All the while, his tongue acted as an intrepid explorer, claiming every inch of her mouth. She reveled in an expedition of her own, on a quest to discover the way to make him groan again.

A tiny bite on his lower lip worked wonders. A slow slide of her tongue against his was like lighting a match. When her fingers finally found purchase in his hair, it nearly felled them both.

Good lord, this man can kiss.

Air was highly overrated. Who needed it anyway? She'd blissfully stay here, burning, for an eternity.

Said eternity might have passed, or perhaps mere minutes. But the loud zip of a misbehaving typewriter ribbon down the hall permeated the smoke they'd generated around themselves. They broke apart with the sudden remembrance that they stood in his office. With the door partly ajar.

Nate looked up, preparing to assess Colin's reaction, discover if he was as singed as she felt. But she couldn't see his eyes at all. Because his glasses had completely fogged over.

A giggle escaped her.

He took note of his impaired vision at the same moment, and ripped off his glasses, wiping them haphazardly on his sleeve. He made quick, if not thorough, work of it and returned them to his face, but not before Nate got a glimpse of the fire still simmering.

He finally raised dazed eyes to hers, with a sharp, shuddering breath. Nate had barely taken a breath of her own before he pivoted away, raking furious hands through his hair.

"Oh, I cannot believe I just did that."

Evidently not a happy or satisfied disbelief, and she tried not to let that sting. "It wasn't just you. There was a whole lotta 'we' involved there."

His shoulders slumped. "And there shouldn't have been."

Her anger flared. "You didn't seem to mind when your tongue was down my throat," she hissed.

Colin whirled around and stormed over to her, more agitated than she'd ever seen him. "No, I didn't mind. But your *husband* might."

Oh. Right. Damn.

Nate's eyes drifted closed as her head lolled forward.

"This never should have happened," he continued.

Could she tell him? *Should* she? Part of her wanted to. So much. That kiss had been…everything. It had also clearly incinerated her brain, because she couldn't think fast enough. She needed more time.

Her sister's appalled face suddenly flashed through her mind, a vivid technicolor reminder of the last time she'd told someone the truth. The slow-burning disaster that followed.

The nature of their relationship was obviously different, and Colin had just inhaled her like she was life itself. But now that reality had crowded back in on them…who knew what he'd do? He already had regrets.

"Nate…" He trailed off helplessly. He made as if to touch her, but stopped himself. She felt the loss keenly.

She forced herself to talk, completely unaware of what would come out, but needing to do something. "Colin, what just happened was…" *Stupid words, still failing me.*

"It was." His expression was nothing short of anguished. "My god, it was. But you're married, Nate. We can't pretend you're not."

"We could." She tried for a flirty smile, but his distraught expression stopped her cold. "Colin, you don't understand—"

"No, I don't. And I don't need to. It doesn't matter."

"Of course it does."

"It doesn't." The quiet ferocity in his tone cooled what little warmth remained from their kiss. "Look, it's true that I don't know the details of your marriage, or how that wa— that *man* could be stupid enough to be away from you all the time." His mouth twisted into a grimace. "But I'm not someone who does this."

"Colin…"

"I'm sorry, Nate. I know what it's like when a person you've planned to spend your life with finds their bliss elsewhere. I could never do that to someone else. No one deserves that." He paused, muttering almost under his breath, "Regardless of how much I want to punch him."

Nate's heart ached for him. So he'd been hurt in the past. By someone very close to him. She wanted to tear the woman's eyes out. But she couldn't, because she had no right to. Just like he believed he had no right to slug anyone on her behalf.

All because of her stupid, stupid lie.

He watched her, waiting for a response. There was such finality in his words. And no way could she fault him for sticking to his principles. It only made him more achingly wonderful.

No, the blame lay entirely with her.

Only…she simply wasn't ready to tell him the truth. Not yet. They'd known each other an awfully short time. Too short to risk throwing away everything she'd worked for, especially if he didn't react well. Not if there was even a small chance he'd throw it back at her, use it against her somehow. He truly didn't seem like the type who would, but she shouldn't chance it.

She inhaled a fortifying breath and met his eye. "No, you're right. I'm sorry. I shouldn't have kissed you like that. It was… You know what, just forget it ever happened."

"Nate."

She held up her hand. "No, I mean it. I…um…I'm gonna go now."

Colin took a halting step closer. "You don't have to. Not now. Not like this."

The air in the room threatened to suffocate her, and she backed toward the door. "Yeah, I do. And you have to get back to work. Your little stick guys deserve your full attention."

She raised her eyes for one last look at his beautiful, disheveled self, a distant part of her taking pride in her contributions to the chaos. Then she fled the office.

When she reached the outer door to the building, she wrenched it open and gulped the fresh air. It didn't help. She glanced around, beyond grateful not to spot anyone who might need to talk to her. She couldn't guarantee her voice's cooperation.

Though fairly certain he wouldn't follow her, she set off quickly anyway, not wanting to take any chances. An unspoken rule of studio life existed that if someone bustled past, they could be holding up an entire stage full of people should their progress be halted. Taking full advantage of this, Nate kept up a steady clip all the way back to her office. She had never been so happy to find Rose's desk empty.

The second her door closed behind her, she sagged against it and expelled a slow, wheezing exhale. Her whole body vibrated, as if someone had injected Alka-Seltzer directly into her veins. She almost wished they had, as her churning stomach could use some at the moment. She pressed her lips together, which promptly made everything worse.

She still tasted Colin's kiss on them.

It was just a kiss. You can recover from this. It was just a kiss.
Such a damn good kiss.

Maybe this wasn't so bad. Maybe the kiss was so phenomenal because they'd needed to get it out of their systems, like Lois had suggested. And now that they had, they could move on. No harm, no foul. There. A perfectly reasonable explanation.

That would absolutely come back to bite her in the ass in a few minutes when she recognized it for the lie it was, but hey, she'd take whatever relief she could get for now.

Feeling ever so slightly more in control, she let her eyes absently wander around the room. They landed on her drafting table with a thud. Or maybe that was her heart.

Her sketches. She'd left them in Colin's office, untouched and forgotten on his desk.

She thunked her head back against the door with a groan. As if the action had knocked something loose, an odd moisture escaped her eyes and slid down her cheek. She brought her hand up to investigate, staring down in confusion when her fingers came away wet.

What the... Am I...crying?

Great, she was actually shedding tears over this. She took a breath, ready to berate herself. And promptly deflated.

She'd just experienced the best kiss of her life, with a man who respected her ambitions while doing all kinds of wonderful things to her insides, after which he'd expressed his regrets...not because he didn't want her, but because he had principles...which wouldn't be a problem in the first place had she not lied her way into a corner over a decade ago.

If ever there was a time to cry, this was fucking it.

She slid to the floor, buried her face in her hands, and allowed the tears to come.

Chapter Nine

Upon returning to his office after back-to-back meetings with a couple of directors, Colin stared down at his lonely desk. Not that it lay empty. It was littered with all the various stages of a script—bound finished products, partial scenes, handwritten notes, drawings of his "little stick guys" as Nate had called them. But his eyes refused to stop gravitating toward the corner, where a leopard-print portfolio case sat, vivacious as its owner.

He needed to get it back to her, despite the inertia gripping him.

It hadn't even been twenty-four hours since their kiss, but his entire body ached.

That kiss had settled itself into every fiber of his being.

Theoretically, he knew he'd done the right thing in ending it. Theoretically. One glasses-fogging, face-melting, soul-scorching kiss didn't change the existence of Nate's husband.

No matter how bloody much he wanted it to.

He held nothing but regret over the way they'd parted. She'd covered it well, but he still glimpsed the hurt in her eyes. She'd taken the leap, kissed him, and he rejected her. He had tried to convey how much it killed him to push her away, but it wasn't enough. She hadn't even left the room before he'd been tempted to rush over and pull her back into his arms. His arms hadn't felt anything shy of thoroughly empty ever since.

He'd spotted her abandoned case on his desk almost as soon as she'd departed. And then spent the better part of the day arguing with himself over whether to bring it to her. It should have presented the perfect excuse to see her, to check that she was all right, but he doubted she'd want to see him. Instinct told him he couldn't let her go without trying to repair the damage, though he hadn't the foggiest idea how.

Gutless wonder that he was, despite his yearning, he'd finally settled on writing her a note, slipping it inside, and hoping he could deliver it to Rose and dash out the door before Nate saw him.

Their friendship was unlikely to survive this, but at the very least he owed her an apology. No matter how cowardly the method of its delivery.

On top of it all, the longing for her reached excruciating levels. Every time his phone rang, he picked it up with breathless anticipation, willing it to be her. It wasn't. Every time he left his office, he prayed he'd return to a message from her left among the mess on his desk. It never appeared.

He sighed and moved around to sit in his chair. Despite the nagging knowledge that he ought to type up his meeting notes while they were fresh in his mind, he found it difficult to do anything but stare. After fixating on the phone so long he was surprised he didn't bore a hole right through the dial, he looked over to his office-mate Tom, furiously typing at his own desk. The man's focus so acute he'd barely managed a wave when Colin had come in.

Colin was envious. He needed to remember what focus felt like, before he lost the ability to do it altogether.

Perhaps a brisk walk around the lot would help.

Yes, that would be just the trick to clear his mind, reinvigorate him. He might even run into Nate.

Shite. This is supposed to take your mind off her, remember?

No. What he truly needed was to bring that damn portfolio case back to her office. His apology note was doing neither of them any good, sitting on his desk.

He rose to his feet and grabbed the case.

"Be back in a few. I'm going for a quick walk."

Tom grunted in response.

Colin chuckled wistfully as he made his way down the hall and out of the building. He missed his concentration so very much.

He breathed in a lungful of fresh air. Another lovely day. It reminded him of the one, only a few weeks ago, when he'd set out on his way to meet Nate for the first time. His mood light, hopeful. Excited.

Colin nodded an absent greeting to a couple of actors, two of Nick's pirate crew. Luckily, they didn't linger to chat.

The previous evening, he'd agonized over the note. Still analyzing it in his head, he resisted the urge to stop and edit it again, even now. Words twisted and swirled in his mind. Had he said the right thing? Sounded like a fool? Would he only make her angrier? More hurt?

I feel terribly about the way we ended our meeting yesterday.

Too formal? Too impersonal? He hated reducing what passed between them to something so mundane and businesslike, but they were at work, after all. He didn't dare reference what had actually happened, in case someone else came across the letter at some point. But would the omission offend her?

I fear I did not explain myself well enough, that I may have been hurtful in the process.

His lip curled in a sneer. At himself. Could he come across as more of an arrogant weenie? Was it even possible to be both arrogant and a weenie simultaneously? It must be, for he had most assuredly achieved it.

Should you be amenable, I would welcome the chance to apologize. But I understand if you would rather not.

He was a writer, goddammit, and that was the best he could come up with? Pathetic. Serve him right if she ignored him.

But oh, how he wished she wouldn't.

His desperation to see her mounted. To do precisely what he offered to do, apologize. He hadn't a clue what he would actually say to her face, and he dreaded having to disappoint her again. Because he would. He hadn't changed his conviction that to engage in an affair wouldn't be right.

And not entirely because he knew what it was to be the odd man out in that situation. As awful as the experience had been at the time, he was also becoming aware that to be with Nate, and then lose her, would feel far worse.

He was already falling hard for her. That kiss had provided a final shove over the cliff. He wasn't confident he had it in him to let himself get closer, only to have it end. Because even aside from the moral objections, affairs always ended. God only knew why she endured marriage to that jackass, but the fact remained she did. Which meant she wasn't likely to change her situation anytime soon.

They'd both get hurt eventually, so better to curb it now. If only he knew how to do that without obliterating their friendship in the process.

And he at least wanted to try, the more he let his thoughts simmer. Just a day without her presence in his life filled him with a tremendous, gaping emptiness.

Bloody fucking hell.

"Colin!"

Startled, he looked up to see Max heading toward him, carrying a pair of pink bakery boxes held together with a network of twine.

"Max, hello. Good to see you."

"Likewise," Max replied as they shook hands.

"What brings you here?"

Max gestured to the boxes. "Dropping off some fuel Lois ordered for a meeting she's got tomorrow."

"I'm surprised she hasn't installed you in the commissary yet."

"Oh, believe me, she's tried. As flattered as I am, I'm not ready to franchise just yet."

Colin smiled. "Well, I'm sure if you ever change your mind, everyone on the lot will go crazy. You do deliver the goods."

"Thanks." Max studied him. "Don't take this the wrong way, but you look like you could use some of the goods yourself right about now."

"Oh, well…" Colin started to wave it off, but sighed instead. "It's been a bit of a week."

"Sorry to hear that. Anything I might be able to help with?"

"Thanks, but I doubt it."

"Fair enough. Oh, hey, here's something that might cheer you up anyway. I'm thinking of having a little get-together at the bakery next week. You should join us. When I get the particulars sorted out, I'll tell Nick to pass them on."

That "us" no doubt included Nate. Equal parts hope and dread filled Colin.

"I'm not sure that would be such a good idea."

"Are you kidding? We all survived Nick's barbecuing. That makes you part of the team now."

"Thanks," he offered weakly. Despite how much that warmed him, it didn't outweigh everything with Nate.

"Ah. I think I get it." Max's eyes narrowed. "Let me guess—your 'bit of a week' has something to do with Nate?"

Colin nodded glumly. "You could say that. Wait. How did you know that?"

"You two seemed pretty tight at Nick's that night. That is, until you asked about…"

Colin emitted a grunt. And he was not a man who grunted. "Don't remind me." It might have been Max's sympathetic, trustworthy expression, or simply the fact that he didn't have anyone else to talk to. Or perhaps the intoxicatingly sweet smell wafting up to him out of those pink boxes muddied his common sense. Whatever the reason, he suddenly found himself unable to refrain from unloading an embarrassing flood of his pent-up feelings onto this man he'd only met on one other occasion.

"I really didn't know she was married at first. I stopped flirting as soon as I found out. At least, I hope I did. I certainly tried to. We were friends. Only friends. And I was perfectly fine with that. Mostly. Then one bloody kiss, and all of that effort... zoom, right in the rubbish bin. And I go and make it worse by turning her away, because of my stupid consideration for her stupid husband, my desire to not turn us into a pair of adulterers. Having a moral compass is so bloody highly overrated. And yes, I am aware of what a pretentious arse that makes me sound like." He finally took a breath and noticed Max's wide-eyed face. "Oh, dear god. My apologies. Damn it, you didn't need to hear all that."

Max chuckled. "Don't be sorry. You clearly needed to get it off your chest. So...you kissed her, huh?"

"I did. Or rather, she kissed me." He rolled his eyes at his own words. "Oh, fantastic, now I'm being an utter cad by talking about it."

Max held up a hand. "Don't worry. I am a gentleman when it comes to these things. It goes no further."

"Thank you."

Max sucked in a breath. "It does make me wonder, though... In the interest of gentlemanly advice, of course...may I say something else?

Colin inclined his head in assent.

"Look, I don't know a whole lot about Nate's marriage. I've never asked her, because quite frankly, it's none of my business. But it's not hard to tell it doesn't exactly make her happy. There's a lot more going on there than she lets on. I've also heard Nate herself mention...involvements...she's had with guys other than Walter. It might be something that's just not a big deal. To either of them."

"I suppose. Though *I'd* still not be comfortable with that."

"And I'm not saying you should. Or shouldn't. Either way,

again, not my business. But…Nate's a doll. She was a really great friend to Nick last year. And to Lois, of course, for far longer than that." Max shrugged. "She might need a friend of her own, someone to help her see that she deserves better than what she's got now."

Colin opened his mouth to protest, but Max didn't let him interrupt.

"I'm not saying you jump right to the adultery part," he conceded. "Only…keep being there for her, I guess. As her friend. Show her an alternative."

Colin huffed. "And hope to god she chooses me?"

Max chuckled. "Hey, I haven't known you long, but you seem like a good guy. The sparks were flying fast and furious between you two. I think you've got a shot." He held up a finger. "When she gets rid of the other guy, of course."

"Of course." He adjusted his glasses and shot Max a sheepish glance. "Thank you, Max. Now, if only I can get her to talk to me again after the way we left things."

Max clapped a hand on his shoulder. "I saw the way she looked at you. I think you can manage."

"I hope so."

Max lifted his parcel and slid one of the strings aside enough to reach under one corner of the top box's lid. Extracting a uniquely twisted pastry of some sort, he handed it to Colin. "Here. You could definitely use one of these. It's chocolate and hazelnut. Nick swears they can regrow a limb."

Colin eyed it speculatively. "Is that right? Won't you be short-changing Lois, though?"

"Eh, it'll be fine. If she notices, I'll just tell her Nick swiped one."

"All right then," Colin laughed. He took a bite and… "Oh," he groaned. "That *is* good."

Max saluted him. "Glad I could help after all."

"Thank you, Max. You really have."

They parted ways, and Colin turned once more toward Nate's

office, with a new sense of conviction. He plucked his rubbish note from her case, crumpling it and tossing it in a nearby bin. He needed to talk to Nate, face to face. Let her talk to him.

Max was likely right. If her marriage was so lousy, she needed friends at her side. And if she could get past his rejection of her kiss, Colin could shove aside his longing and be the friend she needed.

Chapter Ten

*N*ate's day had proved blissfully busy thus far. Between a string of fittings all morning and consulting with her cutters and drapers after lunch, time had flown by, allowing her almost no chance to think about anything but work.

As much as it had surprised her, her crying session had provided quite a helpful release. True, she'd gone to bed—and then woken—with a monstrous headache, but copious amounts of coffee kept the throbbing manageable.

She still needed to formulate a plan to retrieve her sketches from Colin's office, but since the project was in no way urgent, she could put it off for another day. Not that it was something to be overly proud of, but emotional avoidance counted among one of her many talents, and she was putting it to good use today.

As Nate returned to her office, umpteenth cup of coffee in hand, she slowed her pace. Despite the day starting to wind down, she had a bit of work left to do before she went home. The only problem was the solitary nature of what remained on her docket. Without the buffer of other people, that sweet avoidance might not come so easily.

She left the door open and tossed her notebook on her desk. Ordinarily she liked some privacy when she sketched, but at this point she'd welcome a freight truck driving through her office if it kept her mind off yesterday.

And the fact that she hadn't heard anything from Colin.

She really shouldn't be surprised. They'd left things…not at all good. She had no clue what she'd even say to him if he did call or drop by, and suspected he felt similarly. But that did little to stop her from wanting him to reach out anyway.

The mess she'd made of everything notwithstanding, she held more than a sneaking suspicion that his voice—*that magical voice*—would make her feel better.

A memory of that low rumble against her lips sent a sudden shiver through her whole body.

Why, oh why, did it have to be such an astronomically great kiss?

Nate drew in a sharp inhale. *No.* She was supposed to avoid any and all thoughts of that variety.

She grabbed the wardrobe list she'd plotted out for the costume drama requiring her attention and brought it to her drafting table along with her coffee and a handful of M&Ms. Settling into her tall chair, she forced herself to focus on the task at hand. French Revolution, good. Nothing like enormous skirts and guillotines to throw herself into. Blood-splattered opulence was exactly what she needed right now.

Letting her pencils fly, she successfully managed to turn off her head for a while. She held up a pair of similar pages to the late afternoon sunlight, comparing two variations on the same ball gown. A ringing phone out in the lobby pulled her attention to the doorway.

She held her breath in futile hope as she strained to hear Rose answer it.

"I'm pretty sure she's available, Mrs. Haynes." *Damn.* "Let me check."

The intercom on Nate's desk buzzed, and she dragged herself over to it.

"Hi, Nate," Rose chirped. "I've got Mrs. Haynes on the line for you?"

"Go ahead and put her through, thanks."

"Afternoon, Nate," Frannie Haynes's cheerful Scottish lilt greeted her.

Nate forced a bit of cheer into her own voice—her mood wasn't her friend's fault, after all. "Hi, Frannie. What's up?"

"Sorry to bug you, pal, but I wanted to check in again about that paperwork?"

Crap. In all the chaos over Colin, she'd completely forgotten to deal with—or rather, *not* deal with—Frannie's concerns over those documents.

"You know," Frannie continued, "if it were anyone else, I'd say *how in the bloody hell do you forget you're married*?" A shiver coursed through Nate. "But it's you. And I think I know what happened here."

Nate gulped. "You do?"

"Mm-hmm. It's no wonder at all you forgot. That gobshite you're married to doesn't do right by you, leaving you alone all the time."

Nate's breath left her in a relieved whoosh.

"If you'd like," Frannie continued, "the next time the arse is back in town, I can come over and sock him for you. Jaw, nuts... whatever body part you prefer."

Warmth chased a burst of laughter up Nate's chest. She didn't deserve it under the circumstances, but her friend's willingness to rise to her defense gratified her, nonetheless. "Thanks, Frannie, but I think I'm all right for now."

"Okay. But if you change your mind, just say the word."

"I will. And I'll...um...take care of that discrepancy on the paperwork." *Or not...*

"Good. You really shouldn't let it go too long," Frannie warned warmly. "It'll bite you in the arse if you do."

Won't it just?

Movement at her open door caught her notice, and she nearly dropped the telephone.

Colin hovered in the doorway. He gestured to the phone

apologetically and stepped back as if to leave, but she stopped him with a wave of her own.

"Yoo-hoo? Nate? You still there?"

"Huh?" Nate jerked. "Oh, right. Sorry. Listen, someone's here, can I call you back?" She tried to smile at Colin, but had no idea if she succeeded.

"Oh, sure," Frannie replied. "That was all I needed. See you at lunch tomorrow?"

"Lunch. Yeah."

"And don't forget that—"

Nate cut her off. "Paperwork. Yep. Got it. Thanks."

She thought she detected a snort of amusement as Frannie hung up, but immediately forgot all about her friend when Colin stepped over the threshold.

"Hello, there," he greeted her shyly. "Rose isn't at her desk, but your door was open. I'm sorry if I interrupted."

She dimly wondered where Rose had gotten herself to so quickly, but no matter. Colin was *here*. She wasn't sure if she should feel relief or not, but he was such a sight for her sore eyes, she didn't care.

"You're not interrupting at all." Nate waved dismissively at the phone. "Just my friend from accounting about a nitpicky paperwork thing regarding my mar—" *Oh, shit.* "My, um, marital status," she finished weakly.

Way to go. He's finally here, and that's the first thing out of your mouth?

His typically tweed-clad chest rose and fell forcefully as he sucked in a breath. "Ri—"

He cut off in a violent, choking cough.

She jumped up and ran to him, ready to pound on his back.

"Jesus, are you okay?"

He held up a staying hand, his face positively purple. "I'm fine," he wheezed. "Something just went down the wrong pipe, is all." He tapped a fist against his chest and let out one more croak.

She watched him carefully, but he seemed to be calming. His skin settled on a less-alarming shade of red.

"Sorry, if I had any water in here, I'd offer you some. I do have some pretty decent booze in my desk drawer though?"

He cocked a surprised eyebrow at that. "I'll do, but thanks anyway."

"Okay."

After one more steadying breath, he raised sheepish eyes to hers. "Pardon me. I ran into Max on my way over here, and he offered me…some delicious pastry I don't know the name of. But I suppose a crumb or two lingered, and…" He trailed off with an embarrassed smile.

She smiled back. "Hey, it happens. As long as you're all right."

He nodded. Now that the immediate danger had passed, an uncomfortable silence descended between them, as memories of the previous day flooded back with a vengeance.

Nate closed her eyes for a brief moment and exhaled sharply around the ache below her breastbone. "So. What brings you by?"

From the look on his face, it was highly doubtful he had changed his mind about that kiss, but a girl could hope.

"Right," he said again. "You, um, left this in my office yesterday." He held up her portfolio case.

"Oh. Thanks for bringing it back. I…I've been swamped all day. I didn't know when I'd get a chance to pick it up." She didn't trust herself to take it from him yet, lest their hands touch. So she simply stared at it instead.

"Sorry." He focused his attention on the carpet. "I'm probably the last person you want to see right now."

"No!" *Shit, that was too forceful.* "No," she offered more quietly. "You're always welcome."

His throat worked around a swallow, as he clearly weighed his words before answering. Suddenly desperate not to hear whatever it was, she took a chance and slipped her portfolio from his grasp. She returned it to her desk, keeping her back to him.

"Thanks again for bringing this back."

"Nate, please allow me to apologize." His quiet voice resonated behind her, much closer than she expected. She gripped the edge of her desk to steady herself.

He continued, "I am so tremendously sorry for what happened after…what happened yesterday. The last thing I would ever want to do is hurt you, and yet I did just that."

"I'm sorry, too," she breathed.

"I…I would very much like to still be your friend." He cleared his throat, and her eyes squeezed shut at the sound. "That is, if you can forgive me, of course."

There was nothing for *her* to forgive. She'd been the one to make a fool of herself, and yet here he was, ever the gentleman.

She wanted to throw her arms around him all over again. But they both knew where that would get them.

Could she still be his friend, when she wanted so much more? Doubtful. But the thought of not spending time with him at all? That prospect filled her with dread. She squared her shoulders and turned to face him.

"Of course I can." She plastered a smile on her face. "Can you?"

Relief flooded his face, along with something faintly resembling resignation. "You know I can." The edges of his smile trembled slightly before he firmed his lips. "Still friends, then?"

"Friends." *Even if it fucking kills me.*

Colin heaved a breath. "And I would also like to say, Nate, if you ever need… I mean, I know it's none of my business, so please feel free to tell me to buzz right off, but…if things regarding…your marital status…are too much and you'd like to talk… I'm here. I only want your happiness."

Nate gaped at him. His offer landed like a punch to the gut. What on earth was she supposed to say to that? It was a nice gesture, to be sure, and certainly something friends did. But did he really expect her to confide in him about *that*, after everything that happened?

His throat rumbled again. "Anyway. Something to think about."

"Um. Thanks." It came out as more of a question, but he didn't seem to mind.

Colin took a step back and cast a frantic glance around the room, and to Nate's relief, his eyes landed on her drafting table, and a telltale flash of red amid her sketches.

"Say, are those by any chance the lobster costume?" he asked.

She lunged for the table, pulling the sketch in question from the pile. "It is." She handed it to him. "What do you think?"

His handsome face bloomed into a charming smile, and she felt at ease again for the first time since he'd come in. "Oh, it looks just brilliant, Nate."

"Thanks. I have another one here somewhere." She crossed back to the table and rifled through the pages there. "Wait till you see. You're going to love it."

Out of the corner of her eye, she caught Colin moving to the window behind her desk.

"My goodness, you have the best view on the whole lot," he admired.

"Second best." She shot him a grin. "Lois has the best, naturally."

"Naturally."

They passed a few minutes in companionable silence as Nate continued to flip through the organized chaos of her work.

"Nate?"

"Yeah?" Something in his tone sent a vague, strange sensation prickling up her neck. She shook her head at her own silliness, how absurdly prone she was to melodrama lately. They would get back to their normal ease. She could do this.

Momentarily distracted by finally finding her quarry, she let out a triumphant "aha!" before Colin answered.

"Why does this ball smell like Nick's trousers?"

She barked out a laugh as she turned around. Of course he'd

choose this moment to bring up their prior inside joke, charming man. "I beg your pardon?"

Only he didn't look like he was joking.

The smile wavered on her face as she took in his alarmingly suspicious expression. Her blood crystalized into ice as her gaze fell to his hand, holding up the phony DiMaggio baseball.

Shit.

He gestured with the ball. "This baseball. That I presume your husband gave you. It smells like Nick's trousers."

At a loss for words, she feigned ignorance as a cover. "Nick's trousers?"

"Yes. Trousers. Or *pants*, as you call them. From the pirate costume. I remember him mentioning a waxy, flowery smell. The one you said came from your aging materials?" He cocked an eyebrow and stared pointedly at her.

Shit. Shit. Shit.

Nate forced a hollow laugh out of her throat. "Huh. That's funny. You know, maybe the teams use the same stuff to treat the leather of their gloves."

Not bad, Nate. That sounded completely reasonable.

"I suppose they might."

She released a small exhale. He sounded like he believed her. Didn't he?

Colin slowly rolled the baseball around in his grip. "You know, I've never played baseball."

"No?" *Damn it, why isn't he dropping this?*

"I believe cricket's our closest match, and I did play a bit of that when I was a lad." He looked admiringly at the ball. "The ball in your hands is rather remarkable, you know. The way it grips, the worn ridge of the seams. Almost as if...you can feel the history in it. The way it's been thrown. The impact of all those cracks of the bat." He paused. "It's funny."

Colin raised his eyes to hers, and she resoundingly identified with a deer caught in headlights.

"This ball doesn't have that feel."

All the coffee she'd consumed suddenly burned her from the inside out. She swallowed, desperate to keep it from making a return appearance. "Doesn't it? Maybe it had only been used in one game when DiMaggio signed it."

Colin assessed the baseball again, ignoring her speculation. "It certainly looks the part. And yet. There's something oddly familiar about it. Almost has the distinct air of…movie magic."

Someone screamed helplessly inside her own head. She fervently hoped she was the only one who could hear it. Judging by Colin's face, she was. But the world was violently tilting on its axis, so she couldn't be sure of anything.

And he hadn't stopped talking. *Why* did he have to keep talking?

"I haven't been at this studio very long, but one thing is eminently clear to me. You're an expert at movie magic, Nate." He held up the ball, an unreadable expression edging past his glasses. "This has your stamp all over it."

"I…I…" *Ah, fuck.* There was no sense in denying it now, was there? She exhaled forcefully as her entire body deflated. "You're right. I made it."

She closed her eyes, unable to meet his. Here it came. Exactly what she'd feared. She supposed twelve years had been a pretty good run. But it didn't feel good at the moment. She wondered if anything ever would again.

"Nate."

Oh, god.

She raised her head, bracing for the disappointment. The censure. The anger. She didn't know which would be preferable.

"Why?" Colin asked, a universe of emotion behind his tone. If only she could figure out *which* emotion.

"Why would you do this?" he continued.

She picked out a hint of frustration, and lashed out as a bit of her own rose up in response. "It's complicated."

Colin shook his head. "Of course it is. You wouldn't have gone to all this trouble if it wasn't. What I want to know is *why.*"

His frustration had morphed into anger. She gulped.

Before she could respond, he slammed the baseball on her desk and crossed his arms. "Are you all right? Really all right?"

"You don't have to be insulting about it," she snapped.

"Insulting? I'm not..." He waved that away as he took a few steps closer. "Nate, are you...? It's bad enough he doesn't seem to be around much, but... Is he holding something over you?" Colin's hand closed into a fist.

Wait. It's Walter *he's angry at?*

Well, that was unexpected.

"No. It's nothing like that. Far from it, I swear. I'm fine."

He relaxed a bit at her assurance, though not nearly as much as she would have liked. "If you're sure..."

"I am."

He hesitated, before the question nearly exploded out of him. "Then why the hell are you covering for him?" He didn't give her the chance to respond—not that she knew how to answer him anyway—and instead added energetic pacing to his questions. "Hell, why the devil are you even still married to him? You don't seem to love him, and he clearly doesn't either, given how little he's here."

As if the pacing wasn't enough to make her head spin, Colin began lobbing the baseball between his hands with alarming force, punctuating each exclamation. "And then you throw yourself at me!"

That one stung.

But no, he wasn't finished. "You've gone to tremendous effort to make everyone think he's the kind of fabulous guy who gives you impressive gifts. What is the point?"

Nate watched the ball zip back and forth like a nauseating metronome, trying valiantly to marshal her thoughts.

Okay, she could come up with *something* to tell him, right? *Zig.* The whole truth? No... Maybe? *Zag.* Panic skittered up her spine, clashing with the small fragment of logic still left in her.

He knew she'd lied about the baseball—there it whizzed again

—and yet most of his anger was still on her behalf rather than pointed directly at her. He *cared*.

You can do it. Just rip off the Band-Aid. No time like the present, right?

There wouldn't be, if she wasn't such a damn chicken. *Did that thing actually just make a zooming sound? No. Focus.* Colin's beef was with Walter; she should keep the narrative on what an absent dope he was.

She excelled at that, after all.

She frantically grasped for the right words. So focused on her churning thoughts—and that damn churning ball—she almost missed the fact that he was still speaking.

Almost.

"I mean, if I didn't know better, I'd think you weren't even really married to him." He concluded with a bitter chuckle, to accompany the baseball slapping against his palm.

So much for that fucking Band-Aid.

Time stopped along with the ball's motion. Nate swayed a little on her feet. Every last shred of warmth drained from her face. She forgot how to blink. Belatedly, vaguely, she noted that it would go a long way if she reacted with something other than guilty shock, covered her tracks in some way.

The resulting shriek of unhinged, maniacal laughter was most assuredly *not* her finest work.

Please let that not have sounded as bad as it did in my head.

The lingering bitterness on Colin's face seemed to solidify. The crinkles around his eyes dipped downward as they began to narrow. He was calm—*too calm*—for just a moment.

And then the crinkles disappeared completely as his eyes flew open, wide behind his glasses. His jaw slackened. A gasp, an actual gasp, sounded as he raised a pointed finger at her.

"Oh. My. God. You—"

Nate flew forward and clamped a hand over his mouth. "Will you shut up?"

With a chill, as she suddenly remembered her obscenely open

office door, she whirled around and ran over to close it. She snuck a frantic look around the vestibule before she did, thanking every deity imaginable for Rose's continued absence. She'd never in her professional life wanted so much to give someone a raise for *not* doing their job.

The door nestled firmly in its frame, she turned back to Colin at a glacial pace, her heart picking up where the baseball left off, erratically bouncing off her other internal parts. This time she knew it had nothing to do with all that coffee. She felt like those characters in the monster movies. The ones who know the creature is going to be exactly as awful as they remembered, but moronically face it with some misguided sense of cautious optimism anyway.

Colin remained silent, but stared at her with a wide-eyed mix of bewildered shock and…*was that wonder?*

Stupid, naive optimism. The other shoe's gonna drop any second now. And you won't need it because the monster will have just chewed off your foot.

"Nate. Your husband…" He looked around the empty room and dropped his voice to a whisper. "Are you…not actually married anymore?"

She attempted to swallow around the tightness in her throat. Her voice decidedly uncooperative, she shook her head.

And then her brain caught up to that "anymore." He hadn't pieced together the *whole* truth, then.

"Jesus. That's…" He shook his head incredulously. "So that mix-up with your paperwork…was not, in fact, a mix-up. And when you kissed me…" His eyes flew to hers, a spark of anger rising there. "Why the hell didn't you tell me? You let me think… And then I pushed you away…"

Oh, no. There it was. Frozen in place, she stared at him as he resumed his pacing. Fuck, if he started up with the baseball too, she might throw up right there on the carpet.

"I'm sorry," she whispered, unsure if the words actually made it past her lips.

"Nate, do you have any idea what it's been like inside my head these last few weeks, since I found out you weren't single? Stuffing down the urge to take you in my arms and tell you how extraordinary I think you are. To ask you on a proper date. Cursing my luck that some lousy arse-wit who doesn't appreciate you found you first. Nicknaming him 'Wanker' and desperately willing myself not to slip and call him that to your face. Hating his guts, yet unable to stop feeling sympathy for him because of what I want to do to him, to take from him."

Her pathetic heart thudded in hope. And then a thoroughly inappropriate snicker escaped her. "*Wanker?*"

He fixed her with a sardonic glance.

She flushed. "Right. Sorry. Go on."

"Why didn't you say something, Nate? I've been making such a fool of myself. And my god, that night at the barbecue! In front of everyone... You all must've had a right good laugh at how stupid the new bloke is."

"No, of course not. They..."

He cocked his head to one side at her unfinished sentence. "Wait a moment. Do they...not know?"

She managed a small shake of her head, fighting a new wave of dizziness.

"But..." Confusion clouded his features. "Max I could understand, and Nick I suppose." His eyes narrowed in examination. "But Lois...surely she must...?" He trailed off, and the concern rising in his eyes did her in.

A tide of panic clawed its way to the surface to overshadow everything else.

"Colin. You can't tell anyone." She rushed forward and clutched the lapels of his jacket in a death grip, a move that normally would've bruised her costumer's heart. "They don't know. No one does. Absolutely no one. Not even Lois. You can't say anything!"

His hands came to her shoulders. "Whoa. Don't worry. I would never."

Nate nodded jerkily. She wanted to believe him, but then, how long had she known him anyway? Based on the roaring thunder in her ears, her body didn't seem to be in any rush to catch up with his assurances.

"Just breathe," Colin intoned. "Where's that alcohol you mentioned earlier?"

She sniffed. "Desk. Bottom drawer."

"Right." He guided her to the couch. "Sit. And breathe."

She forced herself to heed his gentle command, as he left her to fish through the drawer. Returning to sit beside her, he uncapped the bottle and handed it to her.

"Here. You look like you shouldn't wait for a glass."

Her chuckle came out as a hiccup, and she took a long swig, welcoming the warm, slow burn. Thank god he'd thought of it. A second sip calmed her further, a bit more of herself returning in the process.

Which finally allowed the events of the last few minutes to sink in.

Colin knew she wasn't married.

But he *did* think she had been.

Should she tell him the whole truth, or just go with this new lie? If she opted for door number two, did that mean she could kiss him again?

She closed her eyes, biting back a groan. Her carefully built world still teetered on the verge of collapse. Her libido needed to back the fuck off until she figured out what Colin was thinking.

Keeping her head trained on the bottle in her hand, Nate slid her eyes sideways as surreptitiously as possible. He seemed... normal. Still watching her warily, but with nothing more than concern. That was a good sign, wasn't it?

"Better?" Colin asked quietly.

Finally meeting his eye, she nodded. "Thanks."

"Of course. You had me worried there for a minute."

"Yeah, sorry. Just took me by surprise a little."

"You and me both." His furrowed brow softened. "I'm sorry, Nate."

Huh?

"*You're* sorry?"

"Well, yes." He bit his lip. "Not only do I unwittingly uncover a secret you have—undoubtedly, I'm sure—good reasons for keeping, but then I pile on and make it all about myself. Please accept my apology."

"Really, Colin. There's nothing to apologize for. You're being far nicer than I have any right to expect." She sighed heavily. "I suppose I owe you a bit of an explanation, don't I?"

He smiled warmly, if tentatively. "You don't owe me anything." He hesitated. "I am willing to listen, though, if you want to tell me?"

"You *are* curious, aren't you?"

"No!" His face flushed with color. "Well, fine, yes. I do have questions. But as I said, you don't have to answer them."

"It's okay. I...I'd like to try." Not that she had a fucking clue what those answers would be. But she wasn't lying—about wanting to try, at least. She glanced at the office door, suddenly wondering if this was the place to get into any of it, whatever *it* ended up being.

Picking up on her train of thought, Colin asked, "Would it be easier if we went somewhere else, somewhere other than the lot?"

The corners of her mouth tipped up. "Yeah, I think it might."

His matching smile soothed her. "We could go for a walk. Or a drive. Or a drive to a walk, depending on our scenery preferences."

"That sounds perfect."

Colin stood and extended a hand to her. "Shall we?"

Chapter Eleven

_N_ate pulled her car into a spot on Ocean Avenue and turned off the engine. As she and Colin got out and made their way over to the railing that overlooked the California Incline and Pacific Coast Highway below, she smiled at the wonder on his face, grateful for the distraction from her still-churning thoughts. As many times as she'd reveled in this view, it never got old, but watching him take it in for the first time was even better.

It was especially beautiful at this time of day. The slowly descending sun glittered off the water beyond the moderate cliff where they stood, turning the sky into a stunning array of pinks and oranges. Off to their left, the lights of the Santa Monica Pier would come blazing to life any minute now.

As Colin so adorably suggested, they had indeed taken a drive to take a walk. Because sunset approached, and she wanted to draw strength from some natural beauty, Nate had proposed coming to this spot. The fact that Colin had never been sealed the deal, and here they were.

They'd stayed quiet on the ride over. Despite everything that had just transpired—and whatever the hell was about to—his presence next to her had been a welcome balm. She detected relief coming from his direction as well.

"My god, this view. I've never seen anything like it," he marveled, leaning his hands on the wooden rail.

"It's one of my favorite spots in Los Angeles."

"I can see why."

Nate leaned her arms on the railing. "You know, I've been trying for years to recreate these colors on fabric. I keep experimenting with different dye combinations, but nothing ever quite captures the real thing."

"I'm sure you'll crack the code someday. If anyone can do it, it's you."

Forget the fabric—she had a feeling her cheeks displayed a pretty accurate recreation of the sunset at the moment.

There he goes, making me blush again.

"What would you do with it, do you think? The fabric, I mean."

"Oh, I don't know. A gown maybe?" Nate laughed. "I've never actually gotten that far with the idea. I just wanted to capture the image, and fabric's my favorite medium, after all."

"Makes sense."

They stood for a few minutes, taking in the view. A slight breeze carried the salty scent of the ocean past them, along with a faint hint of hot dogs from the pier.

Finally ready to break the silence, she started speaking at precisely the moment Colin came to the same decision. Of course.

They laughed.

"I thought it might help if I started with a question?" he asked.

"Probably. Sure."

He paused, rubbing the back of his neck. "So, are you…divorced?"

She swallowed hard. "Divorced. Yeah."

And here I go. The famous Reynolds Foot-in-Mouth Disease strikes yet again.

But could I really tell him the truth?

Taking advantage of the fact that his gaze was trained on the distant waves heading toward the shoreline, she closed her eyes and leaned on the railing again. When had lying become so effortless?

"I see. That's good, I suppose. Only..." She felt him turn toward her. "Why go to such effort to keep that to yourself? Wouldn't it be easier if...?"

"If everyone knew? It would be, in some ways." She took a breath before looking up at him. The care etched on his features stabbed her with a fresh burst of guilt, but she continued anyway. "But you know how some people get over divorce. Especially toward the woman in the situation."

"But everyone already believes your husband to be so absent."

"They do. Now." She paused. Might as well try for at least a kernel of truth. "But when...it...first happened, I was just starting out my career. It seemed better to keep it to myself. I didn't want to be seen as a scandal."

"I can see that." He watched her cautiously. "And...Lois really doesn't know?"

The guilt knife twisted in her gut. "By the time I met her, I'd been...keeping up appearances for so long already... It was part of the package that is me. Once we became friends, real friends, I just...never knew how to tell her. And now she's my boss, too."

"Ah. And the last thing you want is to bring scandal to her new studio."

"I... No. I don't."

"I believe she'd understand, you know," he said softly. "If you told her."

Nate swallowed. "She might. If I hadn't been hiding it from her for quite so long."

They lapsed into another silence. His calm acceptance of her story would have been immensely comforting...if that story was the truth. If her fear over losing yet another person from her life didn't keep her, once again, telling lies.

Colin broke into her thoughts. "Does it not get lonely for you?"

The soft question broke her heart wide open. *So lonely, you have no idea.* Not ready to admit that, she deflected.

"It's not so bad. I've had my fair share of 'affairs' over the years."

She bit back a groan. *Why* was that what chose to come out of her mouth?

"Oh."

"Not that I'm saying I get around. Or that there's anything wrong with that either. A woman has needs, after all, and when they're not being met…"

"You do what you need to do," he supplied. Without judgment. *Huh. Okay, then.*

"Exactly."

She ventured a glance at his face, and the encouraging feeling faded. Despite his apparent lack of judgment, he seemed… resigned. Sad, even?

Oh, no. Did he think…

She blurted, "And I don't mean to say that you're just one in a long line of…" *Shit.* "Oh, I am just making this worse and worse, aren't I?"

"No, of course not."

She let her skeptical eyebrow do the talking for her this time, and he smiled.

"Really, you're not. I…think I understand." The smile faded back into introspection.

"I don't think you do." She couldn't stop from reaching out, touching his arm lightly. "Colin, this…" She gestured between them with her free hand. "This isn't anything like the others. *You're* not anything like the others."

The admission should have felt wrong, too much. She'd hardly acknowledged it to herself. But it had come even easier than her lies, and somehow that encouraged her.

A fierce hope blazed up behind his glasses, further warming her to the core. "Am I not?"

"No. You're…quite special, actually."

He raised his hand to cover hers, still on his arm. "As are you, Nate."

Her breath whooshed out of her.

A wild urge overtook her, to hurl all her remaining fucks over the railing and tell him the truth. All of it.

But what if it ruins all this instead?

She survived without her sister in her life. She knew that wouldn't be the case with Lois. And realization was dawning, much to her horror, that it also might not be the case with Colin.

It had been easy to classify him as a fling at first, but even his friendship filled her life tremendously after such a short time. She was nowhere near ready to push him completely away, which would surely happen if he knew. Wouldn't it?

Out of the corner of her eye, she saw Colin move to face her. It gave her a slight boost of courage.

The breeze ruffled his hair, and he met her eyes with tenderness. "I can't imagine the burden you're carrying. And the last thing I want is to add to it."

Oh, you dear, dear man.

He slid his hand along the railing until it reached her elbow, and his thumb came up to graze her arm in a featherlight touch. "Your secret is safe with me; you have my word."

"Thank you."

"And as much as I'd like to explore whatever is growing between us, I understand why that might not be the best idea right now."

"Oh." Her confusion, her disappointment must have shown on her face, because he offered her a tiny smile.

"You have so much on your plate. And as you said, you don't need to be courting scandal on top of it. Appearances being everything and all."

"Right." She squeezed her eyes shut.

His thumb continued its gentle caressing motion, while his other arm slid up around her shoulders. His lips came down on the crown of her head, and all the tension vacated her body, despite what he'd just said. She leaned into his side, feeling…safe. So extraordinarily safe.

"I understand you need me to be just your friend right now," he whispered into her hair. "But if that changes, when you're ready, I'll be here."

She nodded against him. A part of her wanted to push, to argue that she was ready now, damn it. But he was right. All her new realizations aside, a little patience was likely for the best, especially with the new lie she'd just told him looming over them.

And it felt glorious to simply be here with him, his solid weight supporting her, his arm fitted around her so snugly. His thumb still tracing her elbow. She inhaled deeply, and another scent surrounded her, this one not carried to her by the breeze. Warm, woolly—*ah, all that tweed*—and laced with the tang of ink and a hint of wintergreen. Every bit Colin. She'd never smelled anything as delightful.

And so she remained quiet, absorbing his strength. She had no idea what lay ahead of them, but for the moment, she decided to revel in the peace of being here, in one of her favorite places, with the man who was fast becoming one of her favorite people.

Chapter Twelve

*C*olin risked a glance at Nate for easily the millionth time, as he once again found himself a passenger in her car. Only a couple of days had passed since their evening at the Incline when Max followed through on his invitation. Now, they were headed to his bakery for the after-hours gathering he'd arranged. After Colin mentioned in passing that he had not yet been to the Burbank area, Nate offered to drive him over, so he wouldn't get lost. They'd both known it for the excuse it was— new as he might be to Los Angeles, his sense of direction was fairly decent—but in no way did he want to pass up the chance to spend extra time with her. And she'd looked thrilled when he accepted.

Max's timing could not have been more perfect. Earlier that morning, Colin received a telegram from an old buddy from his war intelligence days—now a private investigator—whose aid he'd enlisted in the search for his sister. Unfortunately, his most promising lead had turned up yet another dead end, and they were back to square one. At this rate, Colin despaired of ever finding her.

He shoved aside his disappointment and self-reproach, focusing instead on his mother's advice to create a soft spot around himself for his sister to eventually land. He'd spend the evening among his growing reasons to stay in California, the newfound friends he cherished more each day.

And Nate, of course.

Even as his search pulled his attention, Colin's mind hadn't stopped reeling from the revelation that she was not, in fact, married after all. Once the shock—and the misplaced anger he still wanted to kick himself over—had subsided, his prevailing desire was to scoop her up into his arms and kiss the hell out of her again.

But throughout the entire exposé in her office, and on the bluff, an uncharacteristic, panicked fragility hovered about her. It, quite frankly, scared him a bit. And made him want to protect her, make sure he didn't put that anxiety on her exquisite face again. He firmly believed it was right to apply the brakes, assure her that he wouldn't push for anything more than friendship until she was ready.

More kissing would simply have to wait. No matter how much it pained him.

He could at least take full advantage of her concentration on the road to sneak as many extra looks at her as possible.

She was so utterly dazzling.

Her maroon skirt fit her curves perfectly—though he valiantly held his eyes away from the spot where it had risen above her knee as she worked the car's pedals. It wouldn't do at all to ignite a cockstand while sitting a mere handful of feet from her, with nothing but his hands to cover his lap.

So instead he focused on her blouse, which had made him laugh as soon as she shed her jacket. On the surface, it appeared to be an ordinary cream blouse. But on the right pocket, where a monogram might typically sit, an embroidered single brown eye, complete with saucy curled eyelashes, stared at him. Nate in every way.

Realizing his attention now hovered in close proximity to her breasts, which would get him into equal amounts of trouble, he shifted his gaze north to her highly sophisticated, much safer tortoiseshell sunglasses. Just in time too—as they reached a quieter stretch of road, she smiled over at him, flirtatious and shy at the same time. His heart melted several additional degrees.

Colin bit back a groan as he stopped himself—in the nick of time—from reaching over to take her hand.

"Everything okay over there?" Nate asked.

"Of course. Why?" He hadn't actually groaned, had he?

"No particular reason. Just getting the sense you're thinking a lot, is all." He could hear the grin in her voice.

"You can smell the exhaust fumes, eh?"

"Got a little bit of steam coming out of your ears, too." She lifted her sunglasses and took her eyes off the road for a millisecond to give him a wink.

Colin clapped his hand to the side of his head with a dramatic flourish. "Damn. I thought I was keeping a lid on that lately."

"Don't worry, it was only a little."

They both laughed softly, settling back into a more comfortable quiet. She certainly had the power to make him feel calm, centered. When she wasn't making him daft with longing and desire, that was.

Standing there on that cliff, watching the beautiful sunset, something had shifted inside him. He supposed it had begun to shift during their first phone call, but he'd stuffed it down upon finding out about her husband's existence. After learning the truth, however, it clicked firmly back into place.

Colin had been unable to resist putting his arm around Nate, drawing her in to him. It broke his heart to see her in distress. He wanted to reassure her, wanted her to know she could trust him. She hadn't chosen to reveal her secret to him, but he'd do his damnedest to protect its precious weight, especially after yanking it into the open so unceremoniously.

Holding her close, feeling her warmth nestled against him, the subtle scent of her perfume teasing his nose—something citrusy, he'd thought. The way her head had fit under his chin in such perfect snugness. It had all felt so right. As if they were both precisely where they belonged.

He sighed quietly now as he looked over at her. She chose that moment to shift gears on the car, as they neared a stop sign. Her motion on the handle extending behind the wheel should have been innocent enough, but to his one-track mind, it reminded him of nothing short of a caress. He imagined those long, graceful fingers on his own gearshift and—

He squeezed his eyes shut. *You're doing a bang-up job keeping those thoughts out of your pants, aren't you?*

Friendship. She needs your friendship *right now.*

He turned his head back toward the window before he risked opening his eyes again. He was in deep, and he knew it.

He'd better turn his attention to safer subjects; otherwise, he'd end up launching himself at her. At this rate, they'd be lucky if he even asked her to pull the car over first.

"So, any idea what Max has planned for tonight?" Colin asked, hoping his voice didn't sound as strangled as it felt.

"Nick said he promised something new and exciting to lure us in," Nate replied with a grin, thankfully oblivious to his previous train of thought. "Knowing Max, that could be just about anything. But I've yet to taste any of his creations that were even remotely questionable, so it should be good, whatever it is."

Nate slowed the car as the bakery appeared on their right. *Bit of perfect timing, that.* She pulled into the small parking lot, empty save for one car, presumably belonging to Nick and Lois. Colin and Nate exited and rounded the corner to the front door.

"Why *Mom's* Bakery?" he asked.

"I honestly don't know. Never thought to ask. Maybe his mom taught him everything he knows?"

"Sounds reasonable."

They found the door locked, as the shop was closed for the day, but light spilled out the windows, illuminating their three friends, chatting inside. Nate leaned her face close to the glass of the door, making a silly face as she knocked. Colin's laugh bubbled up and out of his chest.

Max came to open the door, trying—rather unsuccessfully—not to laugh himself. "Sorry, we're closed. And we don't allow weirdos in, anyway."

"Are you sure that's the best way to run a business, turning away patrons like that?" Colin teased. "I thought the customer was always right?"

"Sometimes, you just have to draw the line," Max retorted as he stepped back to let them in.

"Thank you for coming to my defense, Colin." Nate swept in ahead of him, as her face lit up with a wicked grin. "But you got it wrong. It's the *costumer*, not the customer, who's always right."

"Well, I don't suppose I can argue with that, now can I?" Colin grinned right back at her.

He caught Max's raised eyebrow out of the corner of his eye, and distantly wondered if they should keep the flirting to a minimum in front of other people. But Max didn't press it, to Colin's relief, considering he was having far too much fun to stop anyway.

Lois and Nick met them with warm greetings, and the group gravitated to a couple of the little cafe tables Max had pushed together for them. As they settled into their chairs, Colin took note of the overwhelmingly delectable scents surrounding him. It was an interesting mix, to be sure. The mingling of sugar, cinnamon, and chocolate was hardly a surprise, typical of any bakery. But several more savory notes layered on top of the sweet ones—hints of onion and garlic, if he wasn't mistaken. Intriguing.

"Anyone else joining us tonight?" Nick's question was casual enough, but Colin detected a hint of ulterior motive lurking behind it.

"Nope. Just us." A muscle in Max's jaw twitched, and his lips compressed for the briefest of moments, but he recovered in the blink of an eye. "Anyone want coffee? Tea?" He popped up from his chair, barely waiting for their answers before moving behind the counter to fetch the drinks.

Nate raised her eyebrows at Lois, who shrugged. They both looked to Nick, but he carefully avoided their eyes, even when Lois narrowed hers with a smirk that indicated he'd be getting an interrogation later.

Colin smiled at the wordless conversation happening in front of him. He had a strong idea that all of it had something to do with the friend Nate and Lois mentioned from time to time. He vaguely remembered their saying she worked at the studio as well, but he had yet to meet her. There was clearly a story there regarding her and Max. But as friendly as Max had been with his advice the other day, Colin gleaned from that quick show of tension that it wouldn't be the wisest idea to ask him about his own romantic situation, at least not right away. Nate might tell him, if he could find a way to bring it up without sounding like too much of a gossip.

Max brought their mugs over on a tray. He set them down, all traces of disquiet gone. He set his hands on his hips. "Okay, as much as I enjoy spending time with you lot, I must confess I didn't bring you here for purely social reasons."

Nick rubbed his hands together. "I knew it. We're guinea pigs, aren't we?"

Lois shook her head with a smile. "My husband, the sugar fiend."

He nudged her playfully.

"Sugar, right..." Nate added, and Nick actually stuck his tongue out at her in response.

Max chuckled. "While you are correct about being guinea pigs, I'm afraid you might be a little disappointed tonight, Nick."

"Please. In thirty-odd years, have I ever been disappointed by your offerings of sugar?"

"You have not. But..." Max trailed off, leaving them in anticipation as he ran to the back. He returned a moment later with a large, towel-covered baking sheet. "I've been trying to come up with ways to branch out, and so I would like you all to be the first to try…a little something savory."

He whipped the towel off with a flourish, revealing an array of small baked concoctions. Some were shaped into golden balls of dough, others rolled into little wraps. And then there were a handful of oh-so-familiar crescent-shapes.

"You've made pasties!" Colin exclaimed.

Nate snorted. "Pasties?"

He gestured to the tray. "Yes, pasties. Those right there. I suppose you call them something more boring over here? They're meat pies. Right?" He looked to Max for confirmation.

Max grinned. "Exactly." He pointed to the crescents. "The meat pies have chicken." His finger moved on to the wraps. "Those are cheese rolls. And these"—indicating the balls—"are potato balls. Stuffed with beef, among other things."

Colin was relieved to have been right. "I thought I smelled onions."

"Good catch," Max replied.

Nick eyed the pastries skeptically. "So they're not sweet at all?"

"You don't have to sound *that* wounded."

"Well, I have come to expect certain things from you, brother." Nick turned to Colin. "These are pretty common in England, huh?"

Colin gave him a reassuring pat on the shoulder. "Indeed. Don't worry; they're quite good, I promise."

"Well, I, for one, am game to try them," Nate chimed in.

Lois echoed her enthusiasm. "Me too."

Colin felt a jolt of warmth sizzle up his leg. The act of leaning forward to inspect the pastries on offer had brought Nate in closer proximity to him. Her leg brushed against his, thigh to thigh, with light but glorious friction. He could tell the moment she realized, because she started to pull herself back. Not wanting to lose the warmth of her, he acted on impulse and moved with her, prolonging the touch.

She stiffened slightly, and he worried he'd made a mistake, before the tension dissolved and her leg relaxed against his.

"Excellent." Max clapped his hands once.

It certainly is… Oh, right. Food.

Max grabbed a stack of plates from the counter and passed them around. "I want your honest opinion." He shot a warning glance at Nick. "Obviously, none of this is going to replace the sweet stuff. But I'm hoping it might pull a little bit of a lunch crowd. I'm still tweaking the recipes some, experimenting with different meats. Any ideas are welcome. Dig in, everyone."

The baker watched them expectantly, protective of his food offspring, as they filled their plates and started the taste test. To no one's surprise, everything tasted utterly delicious.

"I have to say, Max, I haven't had anything like this since leaving London," Colin said. "And I will most assuredly be coming back for more."

Max exhaled. "Thanks, mate. That means a lot."

"They really are delicious," Lois remarked. "Every single one."

"I could easily make a meal out of an assortment of these," Nate added, before gesturing to the half-moon pasties. "And as delicious as the chicken is, I'd for sure want to try these with some kind of beef too."

"Ooh, or even pork," Lois suggested.

"That's exactly what I was thinking," Max replied. "This is good."

Nick finally weighed in, speaking around a mouth still full of food. "My sincere apologies for doubting you. Seriously, how do you do it, every single time? You made a deal with the devil when we were kids, didn't you?"

"I'll never tell," Max intoned.

Lois smiled warmly at him. "How is it that no woman has snapped you up yet?"

Max blushed at that, and a little of the earlier tension returned to his eyes, even as he joked. "I like to keep my options open."

They continued to eat and jest. Colin was genuinely starting to feel, as Max had suggested at the studio, like part of a team now. And a wonderful team at that. It was only the second meal he'd passed in their company, but it felt like he'd known them all for years. Eating food so reminiscent of home added to his delight.

And then there was Nate's leg, still pressed against his, under the table. A man could most definitely get used to this.

He hated to pull away from her, but the evening was starting to wind down and Nick had already gotten up to help Max clear the table. Colin didn't want to look like a tosser for not joining them.

As he rose, concentrating hard on trying to hold onto the essence of Nate against him, he completely miscalculated how close he still was to his chair, and therefore promptly lost his balance. His backside fell back into the seat with a thud. It was all he could do to maintain his grip on the mugs he had picked up.

So much for not looking like a tosser, you tosser.

Nate shot a startled smile at him, but thankfully said nothing.

Colin cleared his throat and stood, more slowly this time. "Let's try for take two, shall we?" He managed a weak laugh and cleared the table. Successfully this time.

Empty mugs—and plenty of shame—in hand, he followed Max and Nick to the bakery's kitchen.

"Need help washing up?" Nick asked.

"Nah, I've got it. All I needed from you tonight was your taste-buds." Max glanced toward the doorway before turning to Colin and continuing, his voice lowered slightly. "So I see Nate agreed to talk to you again."

Colin felt heat seeping into his cheeks. "She did. Thanks again for the advice."

Nick looked back and forth between them. "Advice? What did I miss?"

"Nothing much, really," Colin replied, eager to respond before Max could. "I ran into Max at the studio the other day, and after patiently listening to me unload on him, he offered me some excellent guidance."

"Ah, it was nothing. I'm glad it worked out." Max raised an eyebrow. "Nice to see you being *friends* again."

Colin scratched the back of his neck, prickling at Max's subtle emphasis. "Yes. We had a good talk. Cleared a few things up."

Max grinned. "Enough to have a date tonight."

His blush grew furious now. "Oh, no. This is *not* a date."

"Really? Because it looked to me like you arrived together."

"Well, yes. But we just rode here together. As friends. That's all." This conversation skirted the preposterous. He and Nate were not on a date.

Well, he supposed they rather were, when one got right down to it. But it wasn't supposed to *look* that way, damn it.

"You have been sitting awfully close to one another all night," Nick piped up.

Colin glared at him. "That doesn't… No. That is not what this is. You can't go on a date with someone who's married. And she is. Most definitely." *Oh, bollocks. Was that too obvious, too forceful?*

There was a reason his intelligence work had been limited to a desk and not field work. His acting skills were rubbish.

But Max and Nick didn't know about the divorce, and he had to keep it that way.

In an effort to dig himself out of this hole, he turned it back on Max. "And why are you so eager to call this a date? If it is—which I am absolutely *not* saying—that means you're the fifth wheel in this scenario."

Max opened his mouth to reply, then immediately shut it again. He crossed his arms and nodded. "You're right. It's not a date."

Nick smirked as he turned to Max. "That's right. Remind me again why we're an odd number this evening? Was there no one else you wanted to invite?"

"As a matter of fact, there was not. There were no other mouths I wanted tonight. I mean—" Max's glower was fierce as his lips clamped together.

"Uh-huh. Sure there weren't."

Colin leaned over to Nick, immensely glad to have the attention focused elsewhere. "I may be taking a wild guess, but does this have anything to do with that friend of Lois and Nate's who works at the studio?"

"Yup." Nick drew out the word with relish, popping the last letter as a grand finale.

"Nope," Max matched his tone and pitch as he retorted. "I can't stand her; she can't stand me. End of story." He leveled a finger at Nick. "Stop being a shit-stirrer. Besides, we are not talking about me. We're talking about Colin and his date."

Colin held up his hand. "Oh, that's quite all right. We don't need to." He exhaled with returning exasperation. "And for fuck's sake, please stop calling it a date."

Clearly miffed over his own turn in the hot seat, Max piled on Colin again. "You planning to kiss her again? Because if you are, that makes it a date."

"Whoa, wait just a minute," Nick interjected, eyes wide. "You kissed Nate?"

Colin threw a paranoid glance over his shoulder at the door. "Keep your voice down, would you?" He cleared his throat around the sudden obstruction lodged there. "And yes. Once. But I am a gentleman, and that is all I am going to say about it."

"Huh." Nick regarded him thoughtfully. "Does this mean she's finally going to kick that lousy husband of hers to the curb?"

"Oh...I...um..." Colin had no idea how to respond to that.

A funny smile teased the corners of Nick's mouth, raising Colin's hackles.

"What's up with that look?" Apparently, Max smelled something fishy as well.

Nick's eyes went wide for a moment. "Nothing. Nothing at all." He bit his lip, deliberating, and then his composure cracked. "Do you realize what this means?"

Bloody hell. Why in the world were they *still* talking about this? "I'm not sure I want to know."

"Nate and Lois are always scooping me." Nick's eyes took on

a positively maniacal gleam. "And now I finally have a piece of gossip first."

Colin's stomach churned, all those lovely pasties now turning against him.

"What makes you think Lois doesn't know all this already?" Max retorted.

Colin wanted to hug him.

"Yes. Exactly." He thrust a finger in Nick's face. "And if you're a gentleman, you won't say one damn word. To anyone." He swallowed, praying he was convincing enough. "Including your wife."

Nick gasped in mock horror, but thought better of making a joke when he saw Colin's face. *Thank fuck.*

"Fine. Of course." Nick raised his hands in surrender. "But can I at least say how great I think you two would be for each other, once Nate's free?"

"I suppose I can grant you that." *Anything to end this conversation.* "Thank you."

Nick grinned like a kid in a candy store.

Max rolled his eyes and leaned in conspiratorially. "His optimism really is obnoxious sometimes. I can't think of anything worse than a guy so disgustingly besotted in love that he won't rest until he's foisted the same lot on all of his friends. Can you?"

Colin snorted, and pretended to consider it. "You know, I really can't think of worse, either."

Nick narrowed his eyes. "Go ahead, scoff all you want, the both of you." He pointed a smug finger at them. "But just wait. Just you wait. You'll see."

With that, he pivoted to exit the kitchen, cheerful as hell.

COLIN AND NATE spent the drive home in relative, contented quiet. But this time the gravitational pull of Nate's tempting proximity butted up against Colin's thoughts of his conversation with the guys in the kitchen. He fervently hoped he'd heard the last of it from Nick. Only a couple of days after promising that her secret would be safe with him, and he'd nearly blown it.

He'd gotten the impression more lurked behind Nate's reasons for keeping Lois in the dark than she'd let on, and he'd never forgive himself if Lois found out before Nate was ready, because of him.

But Nick was a decent bloke, and he decided to trust him. Once he relaxed a little, Nick's other pronouncement about his and Nate's compatibility washed over him in a comforting balm.

It had been a lovely night, and despite his fumble with the chair, he could indeed still feel the memory of Nate's leg against his own. The only thing stopping him from closing the distance again now was the necessity of that leg in her operation of the vehicle.

Before he knew it, Nate pulled the car to a stop in front of his apartment building. *Oh. That was far too fast.*

"Here we are," she said.

"Here we are. Thank you for the lift."

"It was my pleasure." Her eyes sparkled warmly in the dim light from the streetlamp.

The tremendous urge to kiss Nate overwhelmed him. That pull never hovered far from the surface, and now that he knew just what her lips felt like, the way her tongue tasted, he craved more. But his assurance of friendship to her loomed; the next move needed to come from her. So he settled on a compromise of sorts.

Colin reached over and eased her hand from where it rested on the steering wheel. He brought it to his lips, taking his time, slowly grazing her knuckles. Lingering longer than was strictly necessary. He breathed in the faint whiff of their earlier feast, still clinging to her hand. He couldn't say he blamed the scent for wanting to hold on to such a lovely host.

Nate's breath hitched, and his mouth curved into a smile

against her skin. He slowly straightened away from her, letting his fingers slide against hers before releasing her.

"Good night, Nate."

She swallowed audibly. "Good night, Colin."

He opened the door and slid out. Unable to resist one last look, he bent to offer her a smile and a nod.

The expression on her face almost yanked him back into the car like a magnet. He managed to resist, and walked to his front door with a satisfied grin. One kiss on the hand, and it seemed he'd thrown her nearly as off-balance as she made him.

Maybe Nick was more right than he even realized.

Chapter Thirteen

*N*ate stood in her kitchen, waiting for her tea to finish steeping, an absent smile on her face. She didn't understand how a simple kiss on the hand could retain the power to hit her below the belt, even after several days. Except it had been anything but simple. Wherever he applied them, hand or mouth, Colin's lips were even more talented than his fingers on a typewriter.

I wonder how those fingers would do somewhere other than a typewriter…

A shiver coasted over her, and she shook her head. After a busy few days at the studio, she had promised herself a nice, quiet evening. This line of thinking was anything but. One of her favorite books needed re-reading. She had tea to enjoy. It was not the time to add to her growing ache down south. The more she allowed herself thoughts like that, the harder it would be to relieve that ache by herself.

So she turned back to her tea, removing the bag and taking the mug to the living room. She switched on the radio and settled into her favorite squashy spot on the couch. She picked up her broken-in copy of Gypsy Rose Lee's *G-String Murders* and examined the jacket as she waited for the radio to warm up. She'd been looking forward to her latest re-read, more than ready to immerse herself in other people's lethal problems for a while.

Nate tucked her legs under her and opened to the first page, as music began to drift into the room. She relaxed more fully into the couch.

And was immediately jolted out of her little paradise.

Actually, physically jolted.

The whole room lurched, and she heard the unique and, unfortunately, all-too-familiar shuddering crack that always accompanied one of the few things she disliked about living in California.

An earthquake.

Nate tossed the book aside and sat forward, hands braced on the edge of the couch. She froze, waiting. Would this one last very long? Continue to get bigger? Did she need to move to a safer spot?

A few moments passed. Nothing more.

Whew.

She released a long, slow exhale, willing her limbs to stop their own slight quaking. Not a very big one, then. That was good. Just your average, run-of-the-mill, pesky annoyance variety of earthquake. The signal from the radio hadn't even been disrupted. She could go back to her tea and her book, and her Colin-tingle avoidance. Evening plans still in place. Excellent.

The telephone let out an obnoxious ring.

Of course it sat on the table at the opposite end of the couch. Nate groaned. Who could be calling her right now? She doubted anyone would check on her. Certainly not Lois. They'd experienced far bigger tremors together—this one would hardly rate a mention tomorrow morning. Damage to the building was unlikely, and even if it was something of the sort, her landlord would surely come to her door instead of calling.

The second ring filled the room, and she was sorely tempted to ignore it and go back to her book. It couldn't be anything that important. She stared the phone down, but some unidentifiable instinct moved her to pick up on the third ring.

"Hello?"

"What the BLOODY FUCKING HELL was *that*?"

All the usual polite restraint missing, the voice's volume had increased exponentially, and it was pitched a couple of octaves higher than usual—but Nate could still recognize that beautiful baritone anywhere.

"Colin, hi. Are you okay?"

"Okay? Of course I'm not okay! How could anyone be *okay* right now? What... That... That noise... And... My entire flat just...SHIFTED!"

Nate tried desperately to keep the smile out of her voice. "Yes, that does generally tend to happen during an earthquake."

The breath audibly whooshed out of him. "Earthquake. So that *is* what it was. Jesus. I wondered."

"First one, huh?" she asked gently.

"Mm-hmm. I'd heard talk, but... Dammit, that was dreadful." He sucked in a breath, seeming to remember himself. "Are you all right, Nate? You're not hurt or anything?"

Warmth spread throughout her entire body, and it was all she could do not to verbalize an "*awww*" that no doubt would have embarrassed him. "I'm fine. That was a pretty small one, actually."

Colin snorted. "Small? Please, you don't have to pretend for my sake."

"No really, it wasn't that bad. As far as these things go, it was definitely a mild one."

"Mild?" His voice sounded small, laced with disbelief and a hint of...fear? "In comparison to what, exactly?"

Nate chuckled softly. "Other earthquakes, of course. I've felt far bigger ones. Longer too."

"Bigger? Longer? Oh, god."

She would have reveled in the double entendre if he didn't sound so genuinely spooked.

"Look at the bright side," she tried for reassurance. "The smaller ones like this don't usually come with aftershocks."

"*Aftershocks*? What, you mean there could be more?" His terror was evidently mounting.

Oh, you poor, sweet British transplant.

"Don't worry. It'll be fine. Really. Like I said, this wasn't a big deal at all." She infused as much cheer as she could into her voice.

"If you say so."

She wanted very badly to reach through the phone lines and hug him.

"Everything is all right, I promise. And you have something to brag about now, Colin. You survived your first earthquake. You're practically a native Californian now."

That drew a hint of a laugh out of him. "I suppose so." He sighed heavily. "I'm sorry. I've been terribly rude about all this, haven't I?"

Nate grinned. There was her polite gentleman. "Not at all. If I remember correctly, my first one was a bit of an ordeal too."

"Somehow I doubt that. But thank you." He paused. "Well, I should let you go. I've been enough of a bother. I'm sure you're busy."

Nate looked at her book, and her rapidly cooling tea. She no longer gave two shits about either. "Not at all. And you could never be a bother." Listening to him fidgeting on the other end, an idea seized hold of her. She spoke before she could chicken out. "Colin, would you like me to come over? Keep you company for a bit?"

"Oh, no, Nate. You don't have to do that…" He trailed off, and she sensed him weighing the options in his mind. He really was rattled by all this. He continued in a quiet voice that slid right to the core of her. "Are you sure you wouldn't mind?"

"I can be there in fifteen minutes."

***

PRECISELY FOURTEEN MINUTES LATER, Nate stepped up to the door of Colin's apartment. She glanced down and immediately snickered. Like many of his neighbors, he had a welcome mat. Unlike his neighbors, his was painted to resemble the British flag.

Her good humor faded, however, when the act of looking back up brought her own appearance into her periphery. When she had prepared to settle in for the evening, she'd changed into a simple peach and white striped shirtdress. In her haste to get to Colin, all she'd done was throw a sweater over it. True, it was her favorite shirtdress, but largely because she'd worn it so much the cotton had softened to an exquisite coziness. Since its coziness was the only thing remotely exquisite about it at this point, the dress rarely ventured out of her own apartment. She had a reputation to uphold, after all.

And yet here she was, about to let Colin, of all people, see her in it. *Damn this clobbered brain of mine.* She hadn't looked at herself in a mirror. Just how worn was it? Enough to be see-through? She heaved a sigh. She was fairly certain she'd left her slip on, hadn't she? A little shimmy confirmed the existence of an extra layer of fabric between her and the dress. She had that at least.

Nate shook her head at her own ridiculousness, and pushed the button for the doorbell. The door flew open with alarming speed, and there stood Colin.

Now, that's *cozy cotton.*

If she'd thought his disheveled work appearance delightful, Colin-at-home looked downright breathtaking. His short-sleeved, pale green shirt was unbuttoned just enough at the collar that a tempting hint of golden hair peeked out at her. Like her dress, the shirt looked soft and quite lived-in. He wore it untucked and... *Christ on a cracker.* Were those *linen* pants?

Nate forced a swallow past her suddenly parched mouth, and moved her gaze up to his face. He smiled sheepishly at her and ran his hand through his hair. The infinite number of directions in which it stood out was a clear testament to the fact that he'd performed the act often this evening. The poor guy looked like he'd been through an ordeal.

"Nate, hello." He opened the door wider and gestured. "Please, come in."

She stepped past him and into the apartment. "Nice doormat. Are you British, by any chance?"

He chuckled as he closed the door. "How did you guess? Yes, that was a gift from my mum. She wanted to make sure I didn't forget from whence I came."

Before Nate could respond, he sagged against the door with a groan.

"I am so sorry for my behavior on the phone. I can't imagine what I sounded like. I think the earthquake shook all the manners right out of me."

"Colin, it was completely understandable. I didn't think you were rude at all."

"You're too kind." He leaned his head back on the door. "Ugh, I wish I could explain why it got to me so much. I mean, I was stationed in London during the Blitz, for god's sake. *This* should bowl me over?"

Nate smiled and stepped closer to him. "It's hardly an apt comparison. There was a war on. You were on high alert, all the time, ready for attack. I believe there were even warning sirens, weren't there?"

"There were."

"So, you see? You could at least prepare for that disaster. We've all been at peace for a few years now. And the last thing you were expecting was for the earth to move, without warning. In a way you've never felt before."

Colin smiled down at her. "When you put it that way…"

"I *am* always right, you know."

"I'm learning that." He reached over and brushed his hand down her arm, gently and all too briefly. "Thanks, Nate."

Can I push him against the door and kiss him senseless? I really want to kiss him senseless.

But he'd insisted they remain friends, so she squelched her urge and focused her attention on the box she'd brought with her.

Thankfully, she held it with the hand attached to the arm he hadn't just touched, so it still possessed enough sensation for her to raise it.

"I had a box of Max's chocolate hazelnut doohickeys. I thought they might come in handy right about now."

Colin's eyes lit up. "They would indeed. How well do you think they pair with wine?"

She shrugged. "I've never tried them together myself, but now sounds like a perfect time to find out."

"Indeed it does. Come on."

He led her through the small living area to the kitchen. Nate set the box on the table as he retrieved two glasses from a cupboard and brought them over with the wine bottle.

"Thanks again for coming over. I hope I didn't interrupt any plans you had for tonight."

"I wouldn't be here if that was the case," she replied. "I'm exactly where I want to be right now."

He met her eyes. "Good. Because I'm very glad you're here."

They remained frozen for a moment, before he broke the spell and turned his attention back to the wine. Nate took a shaky breath and busied herself with opening the pastry box.

"Do you have a plate, or should we just eat right out of the box?"

"I think we're still civilized enough for a plate. There's a clean one on the counter as a matter of fact."

She grabbed it and transferred a handful of pastries over. Colin picked up their glasses and gestured back to the living room. "Shall we?"

Nate nodded and followed him. She couldn't help stealing a surreptitious glance at his backside—still intrigued by the hint of quality ass-age she'd spied that day in his office—but unfortunately the tail of his untucked shirt kept the potential hidden. Oh, well. She'd get to the bottom of it sooner or later.

Bottom. She giggled to herself, biting her lip to keep it on the inside. *Oh, I am such a child.*

Colin bent down to peer at her, startling her. "What is it?"

"Huh?"

"You're smiling. Care to share?"

Nate curved her smile into a smirk. "Trust me, it's probably better if I don't."

"All right, then."

She breathed a sigh of relief as they settled on the couch. Colin handed her a glass, and she held it up for a toast.

"To surviving your first earthquake."

Colin laughed. "To invaluable friends who make said survival possible."

They clinked glasses. He reached for a pastry and took a bite. The resulting groan sent Nate diving into her glass for another gulp of wine.

"These are perfect." He paused, considering. "And really not bad at all with wine."

She reached for her own and tested the theory. "Huh. You're right. We should share our findings with Max."

"He could add them to his advertisements."

Nate smiled. His British was showing again.

"What is it this time?"

"Nothing. Just…" *Eh, what the hell? It's far less embarrassing than ogling his ass.* "The way you say 'ad-*ver*-tiz-ments.' Very British."

He leaned in and whispered, "Don't tell anyone, but…I *am* British."

She threw her head back with a laugh. "So I've noticed." Nate twisted to better face him and leaned her elbow on the back of the couch. "Tell me, were you in London for most of the war?"

Colin turned to mirror her pose as he answered. "I was. Mostly in a bunker office. In front of my typewriter."

"So, not much has changed."

He chuckled. "Not much."

"That sounds like such a fascinating job, planting coded messages. You must have had to get awfully creative."

"I did. It got a bit more difficult, the longer the war went on.

Some things I could use over and over, but I had to keep coming up with new bits and pieces to avoid detection."

"Wow. Okay, I've been wondering something."

"Uh-oh." He squared his shoulders, dramatically bracing himself. "Go ahead, shoot."

Nate felt the urge to lower her voice, even though it was just the two of them. "Being in intelligence, did you have to use an alias?"

Colin lowered his own voice to match hers. "I did."

When he didn't elaborate, she waved her hand. "And...?"

"I can't. If I told you, then I'd have to get rid of you."

She swatted his arm, and he laughed.

"You really want to know?"

"Uh, yeah. Of course."

He took another sip of wine before speaking. "Archibald Cruikshank."

Nate let out a choked sputter of mirth. "You're kidding."

"I am not. You are looking at one of the BBC's most prolific wartime radio play writers, Sir Archibald Cruikshank."

"That's... I think that might be the most British name I've ever heard."

Colin grinned. "Thank you. I thought so too. Precisely what I was going for."

Nate grinned back, glad all the leftover earthquake tension seemed to have left him. And boy, did she enjoy spending time with him.

Her eyes drifted to his still-grinning lips, and caught sight of an errant smudge of chocolate. Or maybe hazelnut? Whatever it was, she wanted to lick it.

She sucked in a breath. Did she dare? No, she couldn't. Of course she couldn't. But maybe she could at least brush it off with her finger? It would be rude to just leave it there, after all.

Ah, hell. Just do it.

She reached over before she lost her nerve. Her thumb grazed his lip, and he froze.

"You had a little…" She held up her thumb, now smeared with pastry filling.

"Oh," he breathed.

She noticed a patch of goosebumps where her thumb had just been, her satisfaction almost overwhelming. On impulse, she brought her hand up to her own lips and licked it clean.

The air in the room changed on a dime.

Colin's eyes widened, and his Adam's apple bobbed convulsively around a swallow. Together, they held their breath for an eternity. Or maybe only an instant. Their eyes locked, and then Colin whisked the wine glass out of her hand and set it down along with his own. She wasn't sure who moved first, but in another flash they came together, lips crashing against each other.

They both moaned into each other's mouths, as if it had been years and not days since they'd last done this.

My god, I missed his mouth.

Her fingers immediately moved up into his hair, eliciting another glorious rumble from deep in his chest, as she'd hoped. His arms came around her and pulled her closer, as his tongue began to do frankly piratical things with hers. Their first kiss had been good, but this… There was an entirely new level of urgency this time, as if they couldn't climb each other fast enough.

Colin's hand skimmed down her leg in a possessive caress, and she slid it across his lap to grant him better access. As his hand passed skirt and encountered bare skin, she thanked herself for not bothering to put stockings back on in her haste to come over. His little hum of satisfaction indicated he agreed with her decision.

His lips slid over to her jaw, and then nipped a path upward, ending with a gentle tug on her earlobe. An inarticulate sound escaped her, and she felt his mouth curve in a little smile. He retreated along the same path and continued over to repeat the process on her other side. This time, he released a groan of his own, right against her ear, sending a surge of wet heat pulsing directly between her thighs.

"Oh, god, Nate." He brushed the words against the skin of her neck. "I am so bloody tired of pretending not to want you in my arms, every second of every minute we're together."

Her eyelids fluttered, and she barely found enough breath to respond, "So am I."

He moved his way down her neck with tiny, sublime bites and licks, pausing to take extra care with the hollow at the base of her throat.

"I want you, Nate. I want you so damn much."

She bent her head back as far as she could, offering more of herself up to him. "I want you even more."

She nearly came on the spot at his resulting growl.

His lips were still moving south, and he paused when he reached the *vee* where the two halves of her dress met above her cleavage. Her breasts ached, desperate for him to keep going. His eyes met hers over the rim of his glasses, a question breaking through the roaring conflagration. Nate raked her fingernails over his scalp, tugging at him to keep going, as she nodded.

His face simmered with a wicked grin as he lowered his head again. His fingers went to work on the buttons of her dress, his breath hot as he explored each newly revealed inch of her. Once he finished with the fastenings, he eased his hands inside to graze her ribcage through the silk of her slip, thumbs finding the underside of her breasts. A gasp escaped her at even that small contact, and she shrugged to ease the dress over her shoulders and off her arms.

She gasped again when one of Colin's hands came up to cup a breast. The sound turned into a whimper when his lips found the other.

She had been using herself as a test subject for some new slip creations with enough support built in to be worn without a bra, so there was currently only one layer of fabric between her skin and Colin's oh-so-talented mouth. Said fabric now provided a brain-melting amount of friction, as his tongue gently flicked at her nipple through the barrier.

"Colin…" she moaned. The ache between her legs throbbed impatiently, and she slid her hips closer, bringing her in direct contact with… *Well, hello, sir.* He issued a startled groan, and grew even harder against her.

Oh, I need to get my hands on that.

"You do have a bedroom somewhere, don't you?" She practically panted the words.

He raised his head drowsily, chest heaving. "I do."

Nate leaned in, craving another taste of his mouth. They kissed hungrily for a moment. In one fluid motion, Colin hitched her further into his lap and stood, sweeping her off the couch and out of the room with surprising agility. He walked them down the hall to his bedroom, her legs wrapped around his middle. She took the opportunity to return the favor of nibbling on his neck as she unbuttoned his shirt. She had only reached the second button when she realized…

Oh, holy shit.

He wasn't wearing an undershirt, so her fingers grazed warm, wonderful skin, topped with coarse fuzz designed to drive her crazy.

As soon as they cleared the threshold of the bedroom doorway, she unhooked her legs and slid to stand, shimmying her dress down over her hips. The second it hit the floor, Colin gripped her waist, pulled her in and seared her mouth with his.

They tried to continue their walk to the bed without stopping, which turned out to be a mistake when they both tripped over her discarded dress and nearly went flying.

Breaking the kiss with barks of shared laughter, they managed to kick the dress aside and support each other enough to remain standing.

"Are you all right, dove?" Colin asked, tucking a loose strand of hair behind her ear.

"Fine. And you?"

"I'm fine." He bent to brush his lips against hers. When he

straightened, he met her eyes with a new intensity. "And you're sure you want to…?"

Nate leaned up to kiss him again. "I'm sure. You?"

"I am." He punctuated his answer with yet another kiss, this one lingering. She let herself melt into it, trying to ignore the concern she'd seen in his eyes right before he asked. Always so solicitous of her well-being, of making sure she was ready.

And she was still lying to him.

Colin continued their languid kiss as he walked them toward the bed, his tongue working its magic and bringing her focus back to sensation rather than thought. Her legs hit the bed, and she sank down to sit. He sat next to her, pulling her in for more kisses, taking his time now.

Nate wished for their hurried, frantic lust to take over and propel them forward again. Because the more, slow savoring he did, the more chance it gave her brain to regain control. And her body was fast losing the battle.

That little flicker of doubt had opened the floodgates. It didn't matter how gleefully they mauled each other. When the haze of lust wore off, her lie would still be there, like a boulder between them.

She suddenly wanted both of them going into this with open eyes, no secrets.

She had to tell him.

But then he'd be furious. He'd leave. Losing him would hurt like hell. But after every wonderful way he'd been there for her over the last few weeks, she owed him honesty.

Maybe she could kiss him just a little bit longer. She didn't have to come clean right this second, did she? She ran her hands up the swath of his chest exposed by the open front of his shirt, desperately hoping the feel of him would anchor her back in her body. It almost worked.

Tell him. You have to tell him.

He chose that moment to run his hand up her arm, while

trailing his mouth down her neck to her shoulder. He eased the strap of her slip down, his tongue following in its wake.

I can tell him when we're done here.

But then she'd still be making love to him with a weight on her shoulders.

As his mouth continued its ministrations to her neck and shoulder, she willed her mind to cede control.

Don't say it. Not now.

Don't say it.

Don't say it.

Don't say it.

"I...I...I'm NOT ACTUALLY MARRIED!"

Chapter Fourteen

Colin's lips halted on the delightfully soft skin of Nate's shoulder. That was funny. It sounded like she'd said... But he already knew that. There'd been a whole bloody ordeal about it. She must've said something else? Most of the blood in his body resided in his cock at the moment, so his brain was clearly not up to the task of processing words correctly.

But Nate had gone more immobile than a statue. Odd.

He fuzzily lifted his head. Her eyes bore an alarming resemblance to Bambi's, and her hand covered her mouth. She had shocked even herself. Which made no sense...

"What?" The solitary syllable was all he could manage.

Her hand slid down her chin to her throat, and she bit her lip. "I...um..." Her eyes squeezed shut. "I'm not...married." She reopened one eye and squinted at him.

He blinked in confusion. "I...know?"

"No, you don't," she whispered. "Not really."

"I don't understand. Are you trying to tell me...?" A terrible thought struck him. "Bloody hell, you *are* divorced, aren't you?"

She shook her head.

He tried for speech, but failed. Only Donald Duck would have understood whatever emanated from his throat.

He really needed to cut back on the Disney cartoons.

Focus. Nate. Divorced. Not.

Even the syntax of his thoughts was broken.

The unresolved, still-excruciating situation in his trousers didn't help. Colin raked his hand through his hair. It didn't feel nearly as good as when Nate did it. But it did have the desired effect of sharpening his faculties, just enough.

"Oh my god, Nate. We *are* adulterers now?"

She came back to herself with a jolt and dug her fingernails into his arm. "No, that's not what I meant."

"Are you separated, then?"

"Not exactly."

A strangled groan—pitched higher than his voice had sounded since childhood—clawed its way up his throat. His hand made contact with his hair again, and he suddenly needed to move. He stood from the bed and took a few paces, his legs shifting uncomfortably around his protesting cock.

"I'm not separated, or divorced," Nate protested with a gulp. "Because I've never actually been married."

"I… Oh."

He turned back to face her, swatting through the million questions zinging in his head like a swarm of termites. He seized on one at random. "Was it one of those—what do you call it here—common-law things? Although you implied he left a long time ago, so were you even together long enough?"

Nate chewed on her lip in earnest, before finally answering. "No. It's not…that."

Colin waited for her to elaborate. When she didn't, a small huff of impatience escaped him. "What, then?"

She scrubbed her hands over her lap, then stood and started pacing in the opposite direction from him. Putting distance between them. That didn't bode well.

Her entire back expanded as she heaved a breath. Colin fought the urge to rush over and take her back in his arms. He wanted to ease her discomfort, but he sensed she might not explain if he did.

And despite his mounting anxiety, he was rather desperate to hear what she had to say.

Nate squared her shoulders and turned to face him. "I've never been married to Walter. Not because we didn't get married. But because…" She swallowed audibly. "You can't be married to someone who…doesn't exist."

His jaw dropped. That swarm of termites could have flown right in without his notice. "What do you mean, he *doesn't exist?*"

She ran her hand through her own hair, and the motion of her arm set her slip's strap to rights. The sight pierced him with a deep and rather unexpected ache of sadness.

"Just that. I…I made him up." She began to pace in a little square, as the floodgates opened and her voice came out in a tumble of words. "It was years ago—I was just starting out in the movies, and I lost out on a job I would have been perfect for, because they were afraid I'd quit and get married, and so when I got to my next interview, I panicked. Next thing I knew, I had the job but I had to pretend I was married, and then it just…stuck. And here we are."

As Colin absorbed her story, his eyes fell on her strap again. The taste of her skin lingered on his lips. They burned, itched to return to her.

He tried to focus on how difficult it must have been for her, to make her panic to such an extreme. But his mind kept skipping back to that day in her office, with the baseball. When she'd lied to him.

Logically, he knew it was her secret to tell, or not. And as secrets went, it packed a wallop. Of course she'd be picky about who she shared it with. Hell, she hadn't even told her best friend. Assuming that part of her story had been true.

Still, he desperately wished she'd chosen to trust him with it before this moment.

"Why are you telling me this *now*, Nate?" His voice was surprisingly calm, his tone quiet. He felt anything but.

"Because I…I thought you should know." He hated the smallness in her voice.

"But now? Of all times? When we're about to…" He gestured to the bed, and a sudden spurt of insecurity hit him. "Were you not enjoying yourself? If you thought I wasn't up to par, you could've just said something."

"Oh, please. Was all my moaning not enough? Of course I was enjoying it. Believe me, my desire to screw you senseless has never been the problem here."

The rising pique in her tone sparked a match against the ire building in him, and he snapped.

"So again, I ask you. *Why now?* You had the perfect opportunity the other day, and yet you lied right to my face!"

"I didn't lie; you assumed I was divorced!" Her eyes glittered with accusation, but flamed out at his exasperation. "Okay, fine. Yes. I lied. But can you really blame me?"

"Yes!" Colin immediately sucked in a breath, fully aware of how unfair he was being. He studied Nate, the lovely brown of her eyes muddied with a riot of unreadable emotion. His remorse continued to boil over. "I'm sorry. But please…can you explain? Give me something to help me understand."

He held his breath as she took a moment to gather herself.

"It's not something I tell people. Ever." She squeezed her eyes shut. "I tried, once. And it…didn't go very well. And I refused to go through that again."

A surge of frustration lit her features, and Nate threw up her hands. "Yes, I told a really stupid, really colossal lie, a long time ago. But it got me where I wanted to be, where I *needed* to be. I landed the job of my dreams, and I have worked my ass off to build it into what it is now. All while keeping this fucking exhausting secret on top of everything else. My professional reputation is beyond solid. I'm really good at what I do, and people know it. People respect me. How many times have you yourself complimented me about it? If anyone were to find out, I'd…I'd be a laughingstock."

Her chest deflated as soon as she stopped, the fight draining from her before his very eyes. He'd never seen her so shaken, so closed in on herself, all her earlier confidence depleted. It killed him.

"Am I laughing, Nate?" She met his eyes and gave him an infinitesimal shake of her head. "You could have told me," he whispered.

"I was afraid to."

Nate filled her chest with a slow inhale, and closed the distance between them. "I wanted to tell you. I should have. But I was terrified of how you'd react. I couldn't face it. But I am sorry, Colin. And I'm sorry for telling you like this, for stopping..." Her hand came up to settle on his chest. "I wanted...*want* you so much. But I just couldn't bear the thought keeping it from you any longer. I didn't want to go into this still lying. Then I went and ruined it all anyway..." She offered him a small, sad smile. "I'll go now."

He held his breath, but she didn't move right away.

Now that she had finished speaking, all of his attention zeroed in on the spot where her hand rested over his heart. With his shirt still open, they were skin-to-skin. As light as her touch was, the warmth of it pulled everything into focus, anchored him. To her.

All the confusion, the anger, the frustration faded away in an instant, leaving the bare, irrefutable truth of her confession. The only part of it that really mattered, when it came right down to it.

The realization hit at exactly the moment Nate began to slide her hand away.

No.

Colin covered her hand with his own, molding it to his chest. Her eyes narrowed, questioning.

"Nate."

"Yes?"

"You *are* still single."

"Yes. Yes, I am."

In what was starting to become a habit between the two of

them, the air in the room stilled and then sizzled with electricity, changing everything.

Colin brought his other hand up to brush her jaw, to cup her cheek. A smile curved his lips. "You told me the truth. And the truth is, you're still not married."

Surprise flitted across her features, replaced quickly by relief and then fierce desire.

He bent closer to her. "Don't go."

Her own lips quirked up, right before she pulled his head down to hers and kissed him.

And then there was no holding back, for either of them.

His arms locked around her, tugging her body against his, while his tongue set to work in claiming hers once again. Beautiful awareness washed over him that nothing stood in the way of that claiming. She pressed even closer—if such a thing was possible—and her hands found his hair, staking a claim of her own. *Shite.* He groaned into her mouth.

Nate responded in kind, and it sent them desperately stumbling sideways, back toward the bed. They couldn't get there fast enough. Without breaking their stride—or their kiss—he reached up to whip off his shirt. He hated to let go of her, but he needed her hands on more of his skin. And she delivered, skimming first his chest and then his back, hands everywhere at once and leaving a trail of fire in their wake.

His own hands came up to remove the clip holding most of her hair up. He ran his hands through the impossibly soft strands and cradled her head, as his fingers raked her scalp. *Let's see how you like it.* She let out what could only be called a growl, and he chuckled against her lips. Great minds thought alike, then.

Their legs bumped the edge of the bed, and Nate let go of him. He was about to protest the loss when she bent down to grasp the hem of her slip and yanked it up over her head, while simultaneously settling on the bed. The smooth motion left her clad in only a pair of pretty knickers, and Colin was momentarily incapable of doing anything but staring.

Momentarily. The burning quickly took back over, and he followed her down, pressing her back into the mattress. They fell into a ravenous kiss, while his hands came up to find her breasts.

"God, your tits are just lovely, Nate."

She let out a small giggle, which promptly melted into a moan as she arched up into his touch. "Thanks," she breathed.

His hips canted up and his impatient cock found its proper place in the cleft between her thighs. Even through a few layers of fabric, the friction was blissful and perfect—*so damn perfect.*

Nate emitted a long, low sigh and ground up against him. "I need you inside me. Now."

He bent to the curve where her neck met shoulder and gave her a gentle but insistent bite. "You read my mind," he growled.

Her hands greedily caressed his stomach on their way to the waistband of his trousers; his fingers slipped inside her drawers and pulled them over the luscious curve of her hips. He'd barely gotten them past her knees when he realized she'd gotten his complicated fly—which was topped by an annoying amount of extra buttons—open and was sliding her hands around to his rear.

A laugh escaped him. "I've never gotten these open that fast."

"My very first costume job was as a dresser for a theater." She smirked up at him, smug. It was quite possibly the sexiest thing he'd ever seen. "I was the queen of quick changes."

"I'll bet you were," he grunted, whipping her knickers the rest of the way down her legs and standing to shuck his shorts and trousers off together.

He heard her sharp inhale, took in the raw, lusty appreciation in her eyes. *Guess it's my turn to be smug now.*

His vision was becoming increasingly hazy as his lenses collected the steam gathering between them, almost as bad as it would be without his glasses. It was well past time for them to go. He snatched them off his face and tossed them to the floor, dimly hoping they landed on something soft, like their discarded clothing. Though he really didn't care all that much.

Turning back, he found her half-sitting up, staring. As if she was trying to…get a better look at his eyes now that they were unguarded. It launched an unexpected surge of heat rocketing through him.

He descended on her. He couldn't tell which one of them groaned louder when every inch of their blessedly naked fronts finally met.

He reached under her to grab the soft, smooth skin of her rear, pulling her closer. The feel of her breasts pressed against his chest was pure heaven. One of her hands wedged between them, moving again over his stomach and down toward…

The one, tiny shred of cognition he had remaining kicked in just in time. As much as it pained him, he wrenched his mouth from hers. "Bollocks! Hold on a minute."

She blinked up at him dazedly as he rolled away and leaned over to root through the drawer in his nightstand. He pressed his cock firmly into the bed to keep it from throbbing too much—and leading him right back around to her like a magnet before he'd accomplished his goal.

"What is it?" Her voice was a hoarse, throaty whisper. He bit his lip and pushed harder into the mattress.

"Aha!" He triumphantly brandished the small envelope he'd been seeking, and shot a grin over his shoulder at her.

Nate's answering smile was equal parts sheep and wolf. "Damn, I didn't even think of that. You do turn my brain to mush."

She lightly trailed a fingernail down his back and over his arse as he opened the packet, impossibly sending even more blood rushing to his groin. "Nate, please. If we're to have any chance of… I need a minute to get this on first."

She chuckled behind him before withdrawing her hand. Despite how shaky she made him, his fingers thankfully found enough agility to get the rubber on quickly, and he turned back to her.

Their eyes met, and he pounced on her once again, unable to

hold back a second longer. She clutched his shoulders fiercely as their mouths devoured each other.

"I can't wait," he growled against her lips.

"Don't. Please."

He hitched her leg around his hip and drove into her, hard. Colin had never felt anything so magnificent in his life. Nate cried out, and her hands gripped his arse firmly this time, fingernails digging in, urging him on. He was happy to oblige.

He had wanted to take his time, draw out their pleasure, especially hers. But now that he was inside her, sheathed in her wet warmth that seemed designed just for him, pure sensation—pure, unabated *lust*—took over. He needed release. Needed to claim her.

Mine.

"Oh, god, Colin…" She moaned into his neck. "There. More. Harder."

He did as she pleaded, reveling in every hungry noise she made.

Her legs circled him, clinging tightly. One hand remained anchored on his backside possessively, while her other came up to take her favorite—and his—hold on his hair. *Mine*, her body echoed silently. Claiming him right back.

Tension built and sizzled down his spine. He was close. But no way was he going over the cliff alone. He could tell she neared her peak as well, and he wanted their mutual claiming to be total, complete. Wanted to feel her explode and contract around him.

He brought his hand down between them, found the swollen, oh-so-sensitive spot right above his continued thrusts. His thumb barely grazed it, and a shriek burst out of her. He pressed harder, and her fingers tightened in his hair. He experimented with one fast circle, and that was all it took.

"Shit, Colin!" she cried as she shattered under him, her muscles clenching around his length.

He tried to still his movements, wait while she rode it out, but her quivering was too much, plunging him over his own edge. He shuddered as he exploded into her with one more push, roaring her name.

He rested his forehead against hers as he rolled just enough not to crush her while their souls returned to their bodies. They remained there for a blissful eternity, their only movement coming from the breath heaving in unison in their chests.

Colin finally pulled back to look at her, to brush a stray lock of hair off her face. Even slightly fuzzy due to the lack of his glasses, she was the most beautiful sight.

And she was *not* married.

Chapter Fifteen

It had only been a few minutes, but Nate's shock had yet to wear off. After blurting out her confession, she had fully expected Colin's anger and disappointment, been ready —despite how much it crushed her—to leave. She'd only reached for him because she craved one last touch, to carry with her. She certainly hadn't planned for what it unleashed in him. In both of them.

She rolled to her side and watched Colin return to the bed after cleaning himself up. Now that she finally knew exactly what had been lurking under his clothes, she could indeed confirm her earlier suspicion—the *David* had nothing on this guy. Despite his lanky frame, his legs—and that magnificent ass—were far more muscular than she had imagined. And what resided between them…*definitely* dwarfed poor little *David*.

Fully aware of her lascivious scrutiny, he took his time walking across the room. Apparently, he also stashed a healthy ego under all that tweed. Looking at him now, and recalling what they'd just done, what he'd made her feel, that confidence was well-earned.

Nate had felt so free, so desperately alive, when Colin was all around her, inside her. She'd enjoyed some pretty decent sex in her lifetime, but this…this was something else entirely. As quickly as they'd both plummeted over the edge, he left her more satisfied than she'd been in years. Maybe ever.

Colin slid back into bed and rested his hand on the curve of her hip. He started forward as if to pull her close, but stopped himself, maintaining a bit of distance between them.

Before she could even think to question it, he huffed a sigh. "This is a pickle. My body wants to be sandwiched up against you, but my eyes want to see you. I'm afraid I can't do both at once."

Nate laughed. "As much as I appreciate the unabridged view of your eyes, you could put your glasses back on, you know."

"I could. But then I'd have to get up again, and…I just don't want to." He gave her a lopsided grin.

Nate leaned over and kissed him. Having thoroughly sated themselves, they were in no rush now, and relished in savoring each other. She was quickly learning that while his romantic skills were many, he very definitely excelled in the kissing department.

They finally broke apart and leaned back against the pillows, facing each other. Colin again scooted his upper half back a touch, leaving their legs tangled together. He brought his hand up to hers and laced their fingers together in the space between them.

Now that they settled, Nate felt a little of their peace slipping away. They hadn't quite resolved their earlier discussion before taking a break to ravish each other, and she knew his questions remained. As relieved as she was to no longer fear his censure, she'd much rather continue to ravish than talk, despite how much they needed to.

One of his admissions from her practice-run of confessions the other day pierced through the swirl of her thoughts, and she clung to the little bit of mirth. A decent place to start as any, she guessed.

"I still can't believe you nicknamed him *Wanker*."

Colin snorted. "Not terribly original, I know, but…"

"But still pretty brilliant. I wish I'd thought of it."

"You did think of everything else." A million inquiries lingered behind his beautiful eyes, underneath his hesitation.

"Colin, I'm sure there are things you want to ask, and I will answer. But first, let me say again, I am truly sorry I didn't tell you sooner. I..."

He reached up to brush her cheek. "Nate. I was angry in the heat of the moment, but... As much as I wish you'd confided in me instead of fudging the truth first, I understand why you held back. At least, I'm beginning to."

She relaxed into his touch—and his words. "Letting someone in... It's pretty new for me." Before she could let that admission sink in too much, she pushed on. "I can see you have more questions. What do you want to know?"

He remained quiet for a moment, but thankfully followed her lead to keep to details about Walter.

"I guess the big one is, how much of what you said the other day dovetails with the truth you just told me?"

"Most of it, actually. Minus the divorce. I invented him years ago, it stuck, and no one knows."

"Years...how many exactly?"

"Twelve."

His eyes widened slightly. "Twelve? My word, that's..." His face softened. "That's a long time to carry such a big burden."

She smiled ruefully. "You have no idea."

"I know you don't want to court scandal, but surely you could have found a way to get out of it?"

"I could have. But I guess I just...got used to the whole thing." Nate grimaced. "I know it sounds ridiculous, but as awkward as it is to keep a secret like this, Walter has been kinda...useful in a lot of ways."

At his curious—but not judgmental—look, she explained. "As a woman in this business, you encounter a fair number of creeps. In my particular field, maybe not as much as the actresses do. You wouldn't believe the shit Lois went through when she started out." Her lip curled in disgust, thinking about how her brilliant friend's career had almost been thwarted. "Still. None of us are immune. But when guys think you're married, they do tend to be less…"

"Creeping?"

"Yeah."

"Nate, I hope I didn't—"

She rested her finger against his lips. "You didn't. You have been nothing but a gentleman. I'm the one who practically threw myself at you, remember?"

"I suppose so. But…"

"Colin. No buts." She smirked and reached around to grasp his ass. "Well, maybe just one butt…"

He laughed heartily, the sound warming her through and through.

As much as she wanted to go on groping him indefinitely, his astonishingly firm rear end was a subject for another day. She owed it to him to continue with this discussion first, so she gave him one last squeeze and let go.

"So anyway, Walter provided me with a bit of cover. From the lechers, and…" *Should I admit this one?* "…from getting my heart broken too."

The care in his eyes was almost too much for her, but she soldiered on. "I got pretty badly burned once, by a guy who didn't understand my career ambitions. It happened not too long before Walter came along." She rolled her eyes. "Before I *invented* him, I suppose I should say. But he's made things a little easier, given me something to hide behind. Any time I've needed to"— she cleared her throat—"scratch an itch, I get to keep it on my own terms, with an easy out. An end date, if they turn out disappointing, one of us starts to get too emotionally invested, or… things like that."

"I see." His voice quiet, Colin's hand slid from its place on her waist.

Shit.

Her hand flew up to cup his face. "Colin. That doesn't apply to you. What I said that day at the Incline, about this—us—feeling different? That was the truth. What we just did…it was…" She shivered at the memory, immediately followed by a bout of insecurity. "At least it was for me, anyway…"

Colin covered her hand with his own and placed a kiss on her palm. "It was for me, too."

Her smile returned. "Good. And really, if I wanted an escape route, why would I have unloaded all this on you?" She paused. "You could easily turn it back around on me."

He brushed his mouth over hers in a featherlight, yet searing, kiss. "I would never. The details may have changed, but you still have my word, Nate. This stays between us."

"Thanks."

As he settled back on his pillow, his eyebrows quirked up. "And Lois really doesn't know any of this?"

Nate shook her head. She bit her lip, suddenly feeling miserable.

He traced a finger across her cheek. "Does that have anything to do with the time it didn't go too well?"

"You're very perceptive, you know that?" He huffed a laugh, but remained quiet, waiting for her to go on. "My sister. She didn't understand. At all." The sting of tears invaded her eyes and nose, and she blinked against it. "Right after I landed that first job, I told her. We got into a huge fight. We were always butting heads growing up. She'd also never understood why I wanted a career. Thought I should settle down and get married like she did."

"So when you invented a marriage…"

"Exactly." Colin's finger trailed across her skin, and she leaned into the contact. "We got past the big blow-up, but then… Things were never the same between us. Eventually we both just stopped trying. It had already been an age since we'd last spoken to each other when I first met Lois."

She inhaled sharply against the flood of guilt. "She became like a sister. More of one. And there might have been a time when she'd have understood, but now…" She hiccupped a sob. "I've kept it from her for so long, I don't know how to tell her. And I can't lose her. I *can't*."

"Oh, Nate."

He didn't question her further, or condemn her for being a lousy friend. He simply gathered her into his arms and held her close. She only barely held in her threatening tears as she melted into him.

Safe. So safe.

He hadn't rejected her. She had an ally now in this beautiful man. Someone to share the burden of her secret. The relief was overwhelming.

After a few blissful minutes, Colin pulled back to place a kiss on her forehead. When he bent his head to look at her, a hint of mischief mingled with the tenderness in his eyes.

"So, 'scratch an itch,' eh? That seems...hardly adequate."

Heat flooded her neck and face. "Oh, well, you know..."

His voice lowered to a soft rumble, the timbre of it obliterating her. "Tell me, Nate, when was the last time you really, truly had that itch...properly taken care of?"

The pure, molten lava in his gaze left her unable to do anything but gulp out a small confession. "I...I...honestly don't know."

His mouth curved into the most beautifully wicked grin as he rolled over her. "Well, then. We're going to have to fix that, aren't we?"

"Okay," she breathed.

He took her mouth in a slow, possessive, perfect kiss.

She would have been disappointed when he removed his now-swollen lips from hers, if he hadn't immediately moved to devour her neck.

"You know, I owe you an apology," he whispered against her throat. "I had planned to take my time with you earlier, but you stole all my patience." He found the place where her neck curved into her shoulder, and his teeth closed over it in a languid, gentle bite. "I suppose I'll just have to make it up to you now, won't I?"

All she managed was a moan as he proceeded to lick his way down to the hollow between her breasts. She grasped his hair, hoping to propel him to…well, she wasn't entirely sure what she wanted first, his mouth on her breast or his lovely cock between her legs. Either one would do. Or both. Yes, that was it. Both.

But he resisted her tugging for a change.

"Oh, no. You are not allowed to rush me this time."

"I'm not?"

"You are not. That would lead to scratching an itch, you see. And I'm not going to scratch your itch."

"Why not?" Her voice came out in a desperate wheedle, but she forgot to care.

He smirked up at her. "Because, my darling Nate, you deserve a hell of a lot more than just scratching. Think of me as your own personal calamine lotion." He dipped his head to graze his tongue just barely over her nipple. She whimpered. Jesus, he had her actually whimpering now.

He chuckled against her chest, and she groaned. "When I'm through with you"—her other breast got the same almost-flick of his tongue—"scratching will never"—a soft bite this time—"ever" —back to the first breast—"be adequate for you again."

He and his magical tongue got to work, first on her tits. After they were sufficiently conquered, he moved lower. He took his sweet time before finally getting to the core of her… And hell, he left every single, solitary inch of her completely claimed. He made a thorough meal of her. Her clit had never received so much beautiful attention. His fingers, his lips, his tongue—*holy shit, his tongue* —worked masterfully together to find spots, inside and out, that even she had never met before.

By the time she collapsed in a heap on the bed, Colin had made very, very good on his promise.

Calamine lotion, indeed.

Chapter Sixteen

The next morning, Colin made his way from the studio's parking lot to his office, whistling a cheerful tune. Feeling lighter, happier than he'd felt in an age. He'd gotten perhaps an hour of sleep, and he couldn't keep the smile off his face. Or the memory of Nate's taste, her sounds of satisfaction, from his mind.

He had quite thoroughly ravished her. But then, he felt pretty ravished himself. He grinned, thinking of how well matched they were.

And then there was her confession. How in the world had she borne that weight by herself all these years? His relief at her trusting him with the truth paled in comparison to how glad he was to be able to shoulder some of that burden for her now.

Granted, a few things remained unspoken between them. Chief among them, where precisely they went next. They weren't exactly at liberty to carry on a romantic relationship in public.

Colin wanted, more than anything, to ask Nate on a proper date, declare his intentions—not only to her, but to the whole big, beautiful world. But to most of that big, beautiful world, she was still a married woman. So they needed to proceed with care.

And since they'd only spent the one night together so far, he wasn't sure he'd earned the right yet to ask her to kick Walter to the curb. Especially given her reasons for keeping the truth quiet.

But at the very least, behind closed doors, they could finally be more than friends. His lips curved upward again, unabashedly smug. He'd torpedoed her itch, all right.

"Colin, good morning!"

He looked up to find Lois a few feet in front of him. He hadn't noticed her approaching.

"Lois. Hello."

"Sorry, I hope I didn't startle you," she smiled. "You looked a bit…lost in thought."

"I did? Oh…yes…I suppose I was." He hoped he didn't appear as sheepish as he felt, given that those thoughts he'd been lost in were quite lascivious, and about her best friend. Colin gulped. Her best friend who hadn't yet told her the truth about her sham marriage. Which he now had to keep from her as well.

Lois assessed him quizzically, but didn't press him further. "I'm glad I ran into you. Those pages you sent…they're fantastic."

He brightened. "You really think so? I know I didn't give you much…"

She swatted the air. "It was plenty. From that first scene alone, then reading the rest of the treatment—and knowing your work, of course—I can tell. It's just what I'm looking for. I'm already getting ideas of how I'd want to shoot it."

"I'm so glad. I'll admit, I did struggle a bit with the plotting, wanting to get it just right. But I think I've got it figured out now."

"I have no doubt you do. We'll talk more when you've finished." She hesitated, still smiling. "I was a little worried about you after last night, you know."

Oh, shite.

Colin felt the color drain from his face. How did she know? Would Nate have confided *that* in Lois, called her first thing this morning to tell her? She couldn't have seen her yet—he'd only just arrived at the lot himself, and since she had to return to her own apartment after leaving his, she couldn't have beaten him here by that much, if at all.

Lois watched him expectantly, and he realized he'd yet to respond. What could he even say?

"I...I...I'm sorry, what?"

Eloquent, real eloquent.

"The earthquake. It wasn't particularly huge, but I'm assuming you felt it?" She smiled sympathetically. "I imagine it was your first?"

Earthquake. Of course.

"Oh, right! Yes, it was. Definitely not fun, that."

"I've lived in some part of California for most of my life, and they never do get any more fun, I'm sad to say. I hope it didn't rattle you too much."

"I confess, it did at first. But I had a...friend...who helped settle my nerves." At the mere thought of Nate, a furious blush overtook his cheeks. He pushed his glasses up in an effort to detract her attention.

The arch of her eyebrow indicated the move had not. "Really? Well, that's good." Her warm smile was a strange combination of all-knowing and...excited? "I am glad to hear it. I was afraid it might send you running back across the pond. And we'd hate to lose you around here."

Colin was unaware of precisely how much Lois knew, or if she knew a lot more than she let on—or than anyone suspected. Either way, he was certain they were no longer talking about the earthquake alone.

He squared his shoulders and met her eye directly. Wanting to prove himself. Eager for the chance. "I assure you, you won't be getting rid of me that easily. I'm here...in California, for the long haul."

Lois held his gaze and nodded. "Excellent." She surprised him by winking. "Well, I've kept you long enough, I'm sure you have places to be." She sighed. "I certainly do."

Colin smiled as he gestured to her head. "Heavy is the head, eh?"

Lois chuckled. "Yes… Well, no, actually. Busy, certainly. But… not heavy."

"It suits you."

"It does." They shared a grin. "Have a good day, Colin."

"You too, Lois."

As he left her and continued on to the writers' building, he couldn't help feeling like he'd passed some kind of test. It warmed him tremendously.

NATE BLINKED WILDLY, trying to keep her attention on the sketches in front of her. She took a big gulp of her coffee, but that didn't work either. She finally gave in to a full-body yawn, which descended into a contented sigh. Her body protested the effects of how little sleep she'd gotten, but her mind—and, well, some parts of her body too—simply didn't care.

Every sleepless second had been worth it.

She leaned her chin in her hand and let herself stare dreamily into space, reliving some choice moments. Like feeling Colin's hair between her fingers. Falling into the inferno of his eyes. The feeling of his mouth…*everywhere.* As much as his voice sent her to the moon, she had grossly underestimated how thoroughly it would wreck her when laced with desire. And when he'd spoken to her, lips against her joy hole…

She shivered. Joy didn't even begin to…

A soft knock startled her.

"You okay over there?" Lois smirked as she leaned against the doorframe.

"Yeah, I was just…" Nate cleared her throat. "In the zone, I guess."

"Clearly."

Nate speared her with a look as she got up. "Did you need something?"

Lois pushed off the wall and came into the office. "Nah, I was just in the neighborhood and thought I'd stop by."

"Well, I hope you didn't need to borrow any sugar. I'm fresh out."

"You sure about that?"

Nate narrowed her eyes. "And just what is that supposed to mean?"

Lois held up her hands and laughed. "Nothing. Nothing at all."

Nate suspected that wasn't nearly the end of it, but Lois let it go for the moment, wandering over to look at the sketches for the lead actress in the French Revolution picture on her drafting table.

"Hey, these look good. They'll be perfect on Renee," Lois commented, picking one up for closer inspection.

"Yeah, she really does have the face for costume dramas, doesn't she?"

"She does. Ooh, this green one is gorgeous!"

They chatted over the drawings for a few minutes, until Nate's eyes fell on a sketch of the lobster costume for Colin's piece. And there went her concentration again.

Lois's subject change pulled her back to the present.

"So that was some earthquake last night, huh?"

Nate heaved a sigh. "It sure was."

Okay, maybe her thoughts were only on the periphery of the present.

Hoping her cheeks hadn't turned the same shade as her lobster, or that Lois hadn't noticed either way, she looked up into her friend's face.

Judging by her sly smile and the fact that she'd raised not one but *both* of her eyebrows, Lois noticed.

Damn.

Nate turned away from the scrutiny. "It's…um…been a while since we had one."

"Yeah, it has." Lois put down the sketch she held and—for some unknown, blessed reason—changed the subject again. She pointed to the door. "By the way, where's Rose? She's really never at her desk, is she?"

Nate laughed. "She does make it a habit, but I'm afraid I'm the one responsible this time. I sent her over to the art department to pick up some color swatches for me."

Lois tilted her head. "Isn't that the kind of thing you can call and ask them to send over with a page?"

"It is." Nate smirked. "But Rose has a bit of a crush on Danny, so I thought I'd give her the chance to make an in-person visit."

Lois laughed. "Huh. And here I thought she had a crush on Colin."

"Oh, I think she does. She's very generous with her affection."

Can't blame her for that *one.*

"Speaking of crushes on Colin…"

Uh-oh.

"…I ran into him earlier. As small as it was, I was concerned the earthquake might have put some fear in him, being new to Los Angeles and all." Lois shrugged. "But he seemed just fine. Remarkably well-adjusted, as a matter of fact."

"Oh, that's good."

"He said he had a friend who'd helped him deal with it."

Nate swallowed. "I'm glad."

Lois's lips curved into the type of smile a black widow spider probably had when she caught something in her web. "You weren't by any chance that 'friend,' were you?"

"Why would you say that?"

"Oh, I don't know. Maybe because you're wearing the exact same dreamy, distracted…*satisfied* look he was?"

Nate sighed and rolled her eyes. "You really could go into fortune-telling if this studio maven thing doesn't work out."

"I knew it! So…how helpful did you get?"

She could deny it, but really, where was the fun in that? "Let's just say, Mother Nature wasn't the only one who made the earth move last night."

Lois let out a whoop of laughter. "Well, it's about damn time!"

"You know, your excitement is a little much. You could at least try to rein it in."

"Oh, please. Do you know how long I've been waiting for this day?"

Nate folded her arms across her chest. "Seeing as I haven't known Colin all that long, it can't be *that* much time. Certainly not enough to justify this level of glee."

Lois rolled her eyes. "Trust me, I was lying in wait well before Colin. You were ruthless with me about Nick, and I have been dying for you to throw off that husband of yours and get some action of your own, so I can return the favor."

"I hate to admit it, but I suppose I have earned that, haven't I?"

"Indeed you have." Lois's smile softened. "All kidding aside, though, it does look like a good time was had by all."

Nate leaned against her desk on an exhale. "That is an understatement." She remembered Lois's earlier words. "He gave off a satisfied expression, did he?"

Lois chuckled as she came to join Nate on the desk. "Most definitely. If I hadn't called out to him first, he probably would have run right into me. He was that lost in thought. What'd you do, club him over the head?"

Nate huffed. "Well…I guess I did."

She *had* dropped quite a bombshell on him before they'd pleasured each other senseless. Her bliss dulled a little when she looked over at her friend. She'd need to deliver that bomb to Lois before long. And without the faintest clue how to do it. Couldn't they just stay like this, comparing dirty notes? Hell, it actually felt great to be on the receiving end of her own teasing medicine. It would hurt so much to lose this.

"Hey. You okay? You lost a little of that sated haze."

"Oh, no, it's nothing. Don't mind me."

"You sure?" Lois leaned closer. "Was the earth-shaking not so mutual? I mean, you looked pretty dazed when I came in."

Nate was grateful for Lois's assumption, because it brought her focus back to the previous night's...entertainment. And here she could be completely honest. "Believe me, it was absolutely mutual." She relaxed into a slow smile. "If anything, I may have gotten the better end of the deal."

"Oh, really?" Lois grinned back at her. "That good, is he?"

Nate closed her eyes and pulled in a breath. "The man has...talent."

"It's always the quiet ones, isn't it?" Lois nudged her shoulder. "Should I give him a raise?"

Nate snorted. "And here I thought you wanted to run this place more ethically."

"Yeah, I guess you're right. I'll leave giving him a raise to you then," she finished with a wink.

It was Nate's turn to nudge Lois back, and they both laughed.

Lois appraised her warmly. "You two bring out something special in each other, that's plain to see."

Nate found herself blushing. *We do, don't we?*

"Have you talked at all about where you go from here?" Lois kept her voice casual, but Nate could hear the seriousness lurking beneath. "I mean, it's obvious you two aren't nearly finished making a meal of each other, but...have you given any thought to how temporary this fling will be?"

Nate had no idea how to even begin to answer her. While Lois was right about them not being finished with each other, the subject of the future—even a future as immediate as that after-noon—hadn't come up yet. There was so much still to say, and the public perception and logistics of any kind of relationship would indeed need to be tackled first. She didn't relish the thought of that conversation.

But this didn't need to be anywhere near temporary—nor did she want it to be.

As tempted as she was to cling to the warmth that filled her at the thought, her friend's presence at her side kept it at bay. Nate couldn't fully share all that was going through her mind about Colin, couldn't turn to her for any real advice.

Because of that one crucial piece of the puzzle Lois didn't know about.

Damn Walter's nonexistence.

"I'm back, Nate," Rose called from the reception area, saving Nate from having to deal with her ongoing, self-made drama.

Her secretary's flushed face appeared at the door. "Got the swatches. Oh! Sorry, I didn't realize you weren't alone. Good afternoon, Ms. Ashford."

Lois pushed off the desk. "No need to apologize, Rose. I should probably be going anyway."

Nate met Rose a few steps into the office to collect the swatches. "Are you sure?" she asked Lois. "You could stay."

Not that she knew what else to say. But her avoidance of any serious discussion didn't mean she wanted her friend to leave so abruptly.

"We can talk more later. After all, we both have work to do. Studio can't run itself, now can it?"

"No, it can't."

Rose had turned to go, but whirled around in the doorway. "Oh, I nearly forgot. I passed by the drafters' room on my way back in, and the team was wondering if you had those pattern notes ready?"

"I do. Finished them before I left last night. Hang on a sec, if you don't mind taking them back over?"

"Sure thing."

Nate moved to the shelf behind her desk and began to hunt through the new stacks she'd created that morning—which covered the ones from yesterday, of course.

Lois chuckled. "Far be it from me to tell you how to do your job, but how do you ever find anything?"

Nate threw a look of long-suffering exasperation over her shoulder. "As I have told you on many occasions, mine is an organized chaos. Regardless of how it looks, I have never lost a single thing." Locating the notes in question, she extracted them with a flourish. "See."

"Touché."

She walked them over to Rose, who immediately left on her errand. Nate turned back to find Lois holding…

Oh, for fuck's sake. Don't tell me I have to go through all this again.

She really needed to get rid of that damn baseball.

Before she could unfreeze herself and start panicking, Lois tossed the ball from one hand to the other with an annoyingly enigmatic smile.

"You know, Nate, if you ever do decide to…clear out some of the clutter…I'm more than happy to help."

She tossed the baseball to Nate—how Nate managed to catch it, she'd never know—and sauntered to the door.

"I'll see you later, friend." And with a wink, Lois was gone.

Nate had the strangest feeling, almost as if…but no, it couldn't be possible. If Lois was onto her, no way she'd keep it to herself. Or behave so calmly. No, she must have simply been throwing her support behind splitting up with Walter. It was hardly the first time she'd suggested it over the years.

Nate shut her eyes with a groan. *I really have dug myself deep in this hole, haven't I?*

HER CONVERSATION with Lois achieved one thing at least. It tempered Nate's lovely, lascivious memories of the previous night enough for her focus to return. She did find it a little odd that she hadn't seen or heard from Colin all day, given the state Lois had found him in. Whatever the reason, it was likely for the best. They both had work to do, and it wasn't as if they could spend a whole lot of time together—let alone touch each other—on the lot without arousing suspicion and gossip.

And she did not trust herself to keep her hands off him the next time she saw him.

Still grinning to herself at the thought, she heard Rose's breathy greeting drift through the open office door.

"Oh, hello, Mr. Canfield."

Nate's head snapped up, her entire body suddenly a live wire.

Speak of the man with the devilish tongue…

"Good afternoon, Rose," his voice drifted in. "And do please call me Colin."

Nate suppressed a snort at Rose's giggle, grateful for the slight distraction in helping her keep a lid on her own control. It was all she could do not to run out and jump his bones, but she made herself stand slowly. She smoothed her skirt down, then ran a quick hand over her hair. Had she remembered to put lipstick on after lunch? She hoped so. The idea of leaving it all over him, marking him with it, sent a thrill through her.

Outside the door, Colin continued speaking. "Is Nate in her office? I know I don't have an appointment, but I had some… costume questions…"

"Come on in, Colin," Nate called out.

Did that sound too desperate? Hell, do I even care?

Colin appeared in the doorway, looking particularly rigid, stiff. Contained. Disappointment flared, until she caught sight of his eyes, alight and ready to devour.

Ah. Not so much rigid then, as keeping tight rein over *his* control. Barely contained.

Right back at you, sir.

He opened his mouth to greet her as he approached…but the only sound he produced was a grunt, as he promptly slammed his shoulder into the doorframe.

Nate winced. "I felt that in my own arm. Are you okay?"

"Mm-hmm." Sheepish eyes met hers from a face rapidly flooding with color. "I think my pride took the bigger hit."

"Eh, pride's highly overrated." She rounded the desk. She reached up to rub his shoulder, but remembered her open door—

and Rose—in the nick of time. She had the door halfway closed when he spoke.

"I suppose I really must watch where I'm going..."

He let his eyes finish the sentence for him—an explicit *but I'd rather watch you*—and the door landed shut with more of a thud than she'd intended.

Nate yanked him by his tie, all thoughts of nurturing his shoulder evaporated. His arms circled her waist in a flash, their tongues beginning a raw tango. She felt a low rumble of satisfaction echo through her chest, but honestly wasn't sure which of them it originated from. Maybe both.

She slid her hands up and around his neck, but the second they reached the hair feathering over his nape, Colin grasped her wrists and broke off with a groan.

"No, not the hair. Please," he breathed.

"Oh. Okay." Weird. He'd seemed to love her hands in his hair last night, hadn't he? Had she read him wrong?

"Nate."

The doubt must have shown on her face, and she tried not to cringe under his scrutiny.

He brought her hands around and placed a kiss on each one. "I love having your hands in my hair. As a matter of fact, that's precisely the problem. I know as soon as your magic fingers get going, there will be absolutely no stopping me pulling you down onto that couch, letting you utterly debauch me."

Well, then.

She curved her lips up, feeling smug and seductive, and slipped her hands out from his and around his waist. "Remind me why that would be a problem?"

He bent to whisper next to her ear. "Considering the noises we both made last night...and your secretary on the other side of that door..." His lips closed over her earlobe and gave a tiny tug.

Nate groaned. "Crap. You're right. Stupid office."

He chuckled, straightening a bit to look at her. "Not only that, even if we could somehow manage to be quiet, you'd still do irreparable damage. My hair is rather like toothpaste."

She snickered. "Toothpaste? How do you figure?"

"Once released from its containment, it is rather impossible to put back in its original place. And given that it's miraculously stayed somewhat tamed this late in the day, Rose would definitely notice if I went back out there looking like…"

"I'd had my way with you?"

"Exactly."

"Fair enough."

Colin leaned in for another, less fevered, kiss. Nate carefully kept her hands below his shoulders this time.

When they broke apart, he rested his forehead against hers for a beat.

"I've just realized, I don't think we actually greeted each other when I arrived… Hello, Nate."

"Hello, Colin."

They shared a smile.

"So, what brings you by my office on this fine afternoon?"

He blinked at her and took a step back, a bit of his formality—and shyness—returning. She wanted to drag him back against her, but resisted.

"Right. I did have a purpose."

"Kissing is always an acceptable purpose, you know," she teased. Trying to mask the hint of trepidation creeping up her spine.

Colin's eyes blazed. "Believe me, that was most assuredly a part of my plan." He took a deep breath. "But there is more. I realize this is all quite new, and there's rather a bit we haven't talked about yet." He gestured to the door. "How we proceed, keeping it quiet, particularly at work and all…"

"Right." *Pesky fucking reality.*

"And I want you to know that last night was tremendous. All of it. Of course, the"—he lowered his voice—"debauching was, well, fucking extraordinary." He paused. "Extraordinary fucking? Fucking extraordinary fucking."

Her laugh started low in her belly and burst out. "That is… very accurate."

"I am a writer, after all." He flashed her a smile before continuing more seriously. "But it wasn't only the fucking I enjoyed. It was everything, all that came before. And after. And during." He shook his head. "Anyway."

Nate wasn't sure where he was headed. Her nerves warred with her fascination at his adorable effort to get the words out.

Colin straightened to his full height, striking her again with how tantalizingly tall he was. He offered her a lopsided but determined smile.

"What I am trying to say is that I would very much like to take you on a proper date, Nate Reynolds."

The breath left her lungs, immediately chased by a flood of warmth. "Oh."

"And I know we'll have to figure out the logistics of appearances, because of…" He gestured broadly at the air around them. "…everything. But I've spent the whole day…wanting to ask."

His cheeks flushed as he pushed up his glasses. He watched her expectantly, and she realized she hadn't yet given him a coherent answer.

"Yes!" *Oops, that was loud, wasn't it?* She cleared her throat. "I'd love to. Go on a date. With you."

His entire body lit up. "Wonderful." He strode forward and captured her hand to place a kiss on the back of it. "May I call you later, then, and we can make a plan?"

"Sure." She hesitated. "Or…I mean…I don't have anything going on tonight, if you wanted to…"

Nate bit her lip. *Crap. There I go, sounding desperate again.*

Colin squeezed her hand. "Even better." He turned at the sound of a telephone ringing in the distance. "Shall I come back in a little while?"

"Why don't I meet you in the parking lot? Then we can figure out the rest."

"Perfect."

He cupped her cheek before giving her a scorching kiss.

"I'll see you later, Nate."

"See ya."

She touched her lip, feeling unabashedly giddy, and stared at the door for a long time after he left.

Chapter Seventeen

A few hours later, Colin and Nate sat on a bench overlooking the ocean, in almost the same spot on the Incline where they'd watched the sunset a couple of weeks earlier. At Nate's suggestion, they stopped on the way to pick up dinner at a nearby deli that she swore made the best sandwiches in Los Angeles. As they tucked into them, side-by-side on the bench, Colin had to agree. The perfect ratio of meat and cheese, with a tangy-sweet sauce unlike anything they had in England. He wondered if they bottled it; he rather thought his mum would love it.

The only drawback was how messy the meal was, and he worried he'd end up wearing most of his without a table to lean over. He'd hate to embarrass himself on their first date, especially after clobbering himself in the doorway earlier.

He still couldn't believe he'd done it, but Nate hadn't seemed anything but concerned. And then the way she'd grabbed him… He didn't think he'd ever tire of kissing her.

She smiled over at him now, nodding at the remains of his sandwich. "What'd I tell you? Good, right?"

He swiped a napkin over his mouth before answering. "Delicious. I see why they call it 'special' sauce."

"As many times as I've had it, I can't figure out what they put in it. But it works."

"That it does."

She sobered slightly as she finished her food. "Are you sure you didn't mind coming here? I don't know how 'proper' a date it is, but..."

Colin ensured his hand was clean before reaching for hers. "Nate, it's perfect."

"Really?"

"Really. How could it not be? It's like a picnic. We have this beautiful view, fantastic food, and best of all? You're here. By my side. That's all that matters."

The blush on her cheeks delighted him.

"Well. That's good to know." She glanced up at him. "Sorry, it's just...been a while, I guess. I'm not used to real dates."

He brushed a windblown lock of hair off her face. "And that is simply not right." He leaned in to feather a kiss over her cheek. "I'm going to have to remedy that."

Her breath huffed against his neck. "I'm looking forward to it."

She shivered, and he pulled back to check on her. "Are you too cold out here?"

Nate grinned. "Oh, no. I'm quite warm, actually." This she punctuated with a drag of her lips across his jawline.

Colin shivered this time.

He felt Nate's smile curve against his skin. "You sure *you're* not cold?"

Colin rumbled a laugh. "I'm English, remember? We invented cold."

"Oh, I don't know. I think you're rather good at generating the heat."

He turned his head to meet her lips, reveling in the taste of her. After a few moments, Nate broke off with a sigh.

"This is a very nice date indeed," she whispered.

"I wholeheartedly agree."

She turned to dreamily look out at the sun painting its last marks across the water below, and Colin took the opportunity to watch her. She was radiant, hair swirling gently in the breeze, cheeks bright, her lips slightly swollen from their kiss.

Realizing she was being observed, Nate faced him again. "What is it?"

"Nothing. I just enjoy looking at you. You're quite pretty, you know."

"Thank you. You're not so bad yourself."

"Thanks." He reached up to run a finger along the lighter streak gracing the front of her hair. "I like this."

"I probably shouldn't admit it," she smirked, "but it's not natural."

He chuckled. "I figured as much."

She returned his laugh.

"What made you decide to do it?" he asked.

Her smile turned rueful. "A bit of preemptive vanity, I suppose. My mother started to go gray early on, and the first place it showed up was in a streak, right in front. Seeing as my job can be pretty stressful, I thought I'd get out ahead of it in case it's hereditary."

"Very practical."

"I thought so." She shrugged. "Besides, I think we costume designers should have signature looks, you know? Edith Head has her bangs and those glasses; I have my streak."

"And it suits you."

"I thank you, sir." Nate bit her lip before shifting on the bench to face him fully. "Okay," she began, "there's something I have been dying to ask you."

That made him a little nervous, but the distinct hint of mischief in her eyes inspired hope. Not that he had any deep, dark secrets or anything. And considering what she'd trusted him with the previous night, he couldn't refuse her.

Hell, there's no way I could refuse her anything, for any reason.

"I am an open book. Ask away."

"How exactly does a man who sits behind a desk all day get off having such a positively divine caboose?"

The laugh burst from his chest, and ended in a snort, much to his dismay. "That is…not what I was expecting you to ask. I'm not sure what I was expecting, but not that."

"What can I say? I enjoy keeping people on their toes." She raised an expectant eyebrow. "So…"

"Ah…"

It wasn't exactly deep or dark, but he did tend to keep it to himself. He had a reputation as a tweed-clad, somewhat square writer, and he never knew how people would react to the other, long-buried side of him.

"It's…a touch embarrassing."

Nate sniffed. "More embarrassing than, say…inventing a husband and keeping it a secret for a decade?"

"I suppose you've got me there." He cleared his throat before meeting her eyes. *Here goes…* "Dancing. I used to be a dancer. It's been a long time, but I do still dabble. Hence my…caboose, as you say."

Nate blinked a couple of times. "Wow. Talk about not expecting… Huh." She paused, opening and closing her mouth a few times. "I have…so many follow-up questions."

"I imagine you do."

She shook her head. "How long ago… What kind… Why stop…" Her eyes flew open wide, and she snapped her fingers before pointing at him. "I knew there was more to that dance sketch!"

"Guilty as charged, I'm afraid."

"So, you really were speaking from experience."

"I was. I suppose it would be easiest if I start at the beginning, wouldn't it?"

Nate propped her elbow on the back of the bench and rested her chin in her hand, all eager anticipation. Colin couldn't help but laugh.

"You don't have to look so voracious. It's not nearly as exciting as it sounds."

"Only one way for me to find out." She waggled her eyebrows.

"All right, all right." He drew in a breath. "Growing up, the family that lived next door had a daughter about my age, and her mother, Jane, ran a dance school."

"Like Fred Astaire and his family," Nate interjected.

"Precisely. Fiona, the daughter, was really good, entered all kinds of competitions, a lot of ballroom and partner stuff. When we were about fourteen, her partner's father got a new job and the family up and moved, scant weeks before a big competition. Fiona was pretty devastated, and so was her mum."

Nate's eyes lit. "They recruited you, didn't they?"

He chuckled. "Indeed they did. There were only a handful of boys at the school, all either too young or too short. I'd had a pretty sizable growth spurt at that point, and was about the only boy in the neighborhood with any height on Fiona."

"But how did they know you had any talent?" She held up her hand. "No offense, of course."

"None taken. I asked the very same thing, as a matter of fact. But the boy's part in the routine they had in mind wasn't overly complicated, and Jane maintained she could make a dancer out of anybody." He smiled at the memory. "And as it turned out, I wasn't just anybody."

"Had hidden natural aptitude lurking, did you?"

"I did. And what's more, I found I really liked it."

Nate narrowed her eyes. "Let me guess—you went on to win the competition, and the rest is history?"

"Well…yes, actually. It was originally supposed to be a one-time thing, but by then I was hooked. Fiona and I made a good team, so we kept going. We danced together for the next seven years."

"Wow. Did you do anything professionally?"

Colin sighed. "That was our plan. It got a bit tricky when we both started university, but we found the time, because we wanted it so much. Fiona and I argued that we didn't need to go to university at all, but our parents wouldn't hear of it. Jane knew how fickle show business could be, and wanted Fi to have a backup. My own mum always harbored tremendous excitement at the idea of a son who was a writer, and she insisted I nurture that side of me, too."

"So that passion came up alongside the dancing, huh?"

"Before it, as a matter of fact." He shot her a sheepish grin. "Wrote my first one-man play at the tender age of six."

"Please tell me there's photographic evidence of your performance."

"Do you want to hear the rest of my dance saga or not?"

Nate suppressed a grin. "Of course. Do go on."

"Thank you." He shot her a wink. "Anyway. Fiona and I were readying for a particularly momentous contest, the winners up for a spot in a prestigious West End vaudeville show. The kind that opened doors to Broadway, Hollywood, all of that. We were determined to be the next Fred and Ginger."

"What happened?"

"My left hamstring happened."

Understanding dawned on Nate's features. "The injury that kept you behind a desk during the war?"

"Mm-hmm. About a month out from the competition, at a rehearsal, I felt something…snap, I suppose would be the best word. I went to the doctor, who told me to keep off it for six weeks." He grimaced. "It was painful, but not excruciating, so I didn't take it seriously enough. I did rest for a month. Luckily we had our routine down, and we knew each other so well we could afford to take time off."

"But you didn't have six weeks."

"No, we didn't. And the competition was so damned important. For both of us. I couldn't let Fiona down. And because I was young and rather stupidly convinced of my own invincibility, I went ahead with it."

Nate reached over and rubbed his shoulder.

"I was feeling much better, and our rehearsal the night before went well." He huffed a rueful laugh. "Hell, most of the actual performance went beautifully. Thank god." Colin closed his eyes. "But then, not far from the end of our routine... It wasn't even a terribly rigorous move, but..." He exhaled. "I discovered what excruciating truly felt like."

"Oh, Colin."

"Fiona saw it in my eyes. We had such a shorthand at that point, and I could tell she wanted to stop for me, but I refused. Luckily, most of my part was over at that point. The end was a showcase for her. To this day, I still don't know how I did it, but I finished the routine, took a bow, and Fiona got me off stage."

He had collapsed onto a chair in the wings, and the second he did, the adrenaline wore off, the pain overwhelming. He shuddered now at the memory of it.

At some point, Colin had brought his hand up to cover Nate's, and now her thumb soothingly stroked the back of it.

He met her eyes—their beautiful, warm brown depth filled with sympathy—and offered her a chagrined smile. "You should have heard the dressing-down my doctor hurled at me. He was furious that I'd pushed myself too soon. Rightly so. And then he got to work trying to fix me."

Nate rested her free hand on his thigh. "Clearly he did pretty well, but not completely?"

"Not completely. I mean, for all intents and purposes, I'm healed. It took two surgeries and endless bouts of sitting still, but most of the time I'm not even aware of it anymore. Dr. Brown gave me a stern warning, though—which I have heeded—that I would never be able to dance professionally. It's fine for exercise, as a hobby, but the rigors of dancing as needed for a career... would have pushed me back over the edge. He said I'd never be able to come back from further injury."

"I'm sorry."

"Thanks." He shook his head. "As awful as it was, in a way it was my own fault. I knew it was too soon, and did it anyway. But

I was lucky, a lot luckier than most in my position. I had another passion to fall back on, one that I loved almost as much as the dancing."

"And one that involved nothing more than sitting on that fine ass of yours."

Colin chuckled. "Precisely." He shrugged. "And I don't regret the path I've taken since. I'm happy where I am now."

"I'm glad." She leaned over to place a soft kiss on his cheek.

And if I'd stayed a dancer, I might not be here with her right now. Where I am is good indeed.

He didn't voice that sentiment aloud, as much as he wanted to.

Before he could dwell too long on the implications of how much he was coming to treasure Nate's presence in his life, she pulled back with another question.

"What happened to Fiona?"

"Well, despite my catastrophe, we ended up taking first prize that night. Fiona accepted the trophy solo, as I was on my way to hospital. And thankfully, they offered her the contract anyway, even without me." Colin smiled. "She's gone on to have an utterly marvelous career. Took Broadway by storm, headlined in the Follies twice. Just last year, she moved offstage to become a choreographer for the Radio City Rockettes."

"That's fantastic."

"It really is. She deserves every bit of her success."

A flash of something that looked suspiciously like insecurity flitted across Nate's face.

"What is it?" he asked.

"Oh, nothing." She paused, considering. "It's silly."

"I'm sure it's not."

She shook her head. "I just wondered... I'm assuming, since you speak so highly of her, that Fiona's not...the one who two-timed you?"

"Oh." Should he tell her that part of it? No, of course he should. She'd been so honest with him. "As a matter of fact, she was."

"Wow. Sorry, I shouldn't have—"

He covered her hand with his. "Don't apologize. It's fine. Truly. We...weren't right for each other. It was easy at first, because we grew up together, shared the same dream. But if we'd stayed together, we'd have eventually made each other miserable. We loved each other, but were never really *in love.*"

"But she still hurt you." The anger in her gaze warmed him.

"She did. But at that point, it was my pride more than my heart. We'd already split up the act. Our future was shaky at best." He shrugged. "And we got past it. Became friends again. As we always should have stayed. It's ancient history."

Nate's eyes searched his. "I'm sorry...if my Walter crap brought any of the hurt back for you."

"There's no way you could have known. And it didn't, really. Not in any way that matters. It's far in the past. And for the best." Colin cupped her cheek. "And a moot point anyway. Since Wanker's fake and all..."

She snorted. "I really do love that you nicknamed him that."

"It was a fairly easy leap."

Nate smiled, and while he could have seized the opportunity Walter's mention presented to ask her about practical things like logistics and where they went from here, he leaned in for another kiss instead.

They took their time, savoring each other. Colin swept his tongue against hers, eliciting a rich, throaty groan that sent a spark directly to his groin. She closed her teeth over his lower lip, tugging gently. Her fingers performed a less gentle tug of their own in his hair. After his admission in her office, he recognized the signal for what it was.

He drew back and took in the seductive curve of her lips, his own mouth hitching up in response.

"You want to get out of here?" Nate whispered.

"Your place or mine?"

"Yours, if you don't mind," she answered. "Mine's not exactly fit for human consumption right now."

Colin widened his eyes in mock horror. "Is your husband home?"

She smacked his arm as she laughed. "Oh, shut up and take me to bed."

COLIN DID PRECISELY as she asked.

He collapsed onto the bed next to her with a contentedly exhausted huff. Still breathing heavily from their exertions herself, Nate curled into his side and kissed his shoulder. "A bit tired, are you?"

He raised his eyebrows. "Are you implying I haven't earned it?"

"Oh, no. You most certainly did. Twice." The contented sigh punctuating her assertion sent a thrill through him. "You're cockier in the bedroom, you know."

"Am I now?" He did feel it. Drawing pleasure out of Nate brought out a more confident side of him, one he liked. And he most definitely enjoyed what it brought out in her.

"You are. I like it."

His entire body warmed.

"So," she continued, "is that a holdover from your dancing days too?"

"It's a reaction to holding you." He bent his head to run a string of kisses and bites along her neck, making her shiver.

Nate moaned her approval. "Mmm…good answer."

Colin continued his ministrations, thoroughly enjoying the way his own scent mingled with her hint of citrus as it clung to her skin. Her satisfied hums urged him on.

"I'm trying to picture you on stage," she breathed. "Dancing. Did you wear a tux?"

"I did." He trailed his lips across her collarbone and turned his attention to the other side of her neck, not wanting it to feel left out, of course.

"You do realize you're going to have to show me your skills at some point, don't you?"

"Oh, I'm sure you can just use your imagination." He added a few licks to his repertoire to keep her distracted.

She snickered. "You should know me well enough by now to recognize there is no way I'm letting you off the hook that easily."

"I don't know. I'd like to think I have a few tricks up my sleeve to keep you otherwise occupied..." He gave her earlobe a demonstrative tug with his teeth.

Nate groaned. But then her inhale ruffled his hair, as if she wanted to say more. Her skin under his mouth warmed.

"What is it?"

"Oh, nothing." She tried to pull his head back down, but he resisted.

"I can see it's not."

"I..." Nate grumbled. "I do have one more question, but I'm not sure I should ask."

"Whyever not?"

She shot him a sheepish smile. "I don't want to embarrass you."

"Ah, I think I understand." He maintained a neutral expression. "The answer is yes."

"Yes?"

"Yes. I did wear a dance belt."

Nate collapsed onto her pillow with a cackle. "As much as that visual intrigues me, that was not, in fact, my question."

"Oh. My apologies for the assumption." He winked. "Seriously, though, what is it? You don't have to worry. A bit difficult to be embarrassed right now, with nothing between us." He moved his hips flush with hers.

She grunted her approval. "True." She snaked her arm around his neck and brought his mouth down to hers.

He could have kissed her all night, but he wanted her to know she could ask him anything.

"Stop distracting me and just ask."

Nate smirked. "For your information, I was not trying to distract you. You're the one distracting me, actually. All that talk of dance belts and your lewd rubbing against me…"

"I beg your pardon? *Lewd*?"

"I didn't say I had a problem with it." She paused, but the twinkle in her eye remained. "Okay, here goes. With all your talents on the dance floor—and in here—how is it that you're so…" She made a circular motion with her hand, searching for the word.

Understanding dawned—along with amusement.

"Utterly maladroit?"

Her eyes went wide. "No, I…" She bit her lip adorably. "Okay, yes. Sorry."

Colin grinned. "No need for apologies. It is, sadly, an accurate description. And interestingly enough, not unique to me. Rather the affliction of most dancers, I'm afraid."

"Really? But how?"

He shrugged. "I'm in the dark about the science behind it, but it's true, a running jest amongst us that we save all our grace for the stage. We can achieve all kinds of feats with the right music and lighting, but when it comes to an act as simple as walking, we're alarmingly likely to trip over our own feet. And it apparently sticks with you even when you've stopped performing, as evidenced by…me."

"That is interesting." Nate batted her eyelashes at him. "If you ever have a clumsy episode and feel the need to recover your confidence, I do hope you know that I'm happy to help."

"Thank you. That is a very generous offer, Nate." He momentarily projected mock innocence before letting his inner wolf creep into his smile. "Funny you should say that, because I think I might be feeling a certain lack of confidence right now…"

"Oh, you poor thing." She rolled against him, pressing her breasts into his chest with delectable friction. She nipped at his jaw. "Let me take care of that for you."

He was already half hard, and the throaty promise in her voice instantly brought him to full mast. She grinned and pushed him onto his back, straddling him.

"Look at that, it's working already. My, how you've grown."

She rubbed her folds against his still-progressing arousal, and chuckled at his growl. She leaned over to the tin of rubbers on his nightstand and made quick work of sheathing him.

Nate bent close to his ear. "Let's see how graceful you can be, shall we?" She sank down onto him in one swift motion, and his back arched off the bed.

She rode him hard and fast, his climax building practically before he could blink. By the time she'd finished with him, he'd forgotten every memory of ever being clumsy.

It wasn't until later, both of them drifting off to sleep, that he realized he still hadn't asked her anything about what came next for them.

Chapter Eighteen

*O*ver the next couple of weeks, Nate and Colin fell into a satisfying tempo—inside and outside the bedroom. Nate's mind frequently wandered during even the slightest work breaks, reviewing the magical scenes they made together. Unsurprising, then, that she smiled to herself while walking across the lot this particular afternoon, returning from an on-set costume check.

Colin was so attentive and so…talented. He brought out sensations in her she hadn't known herself capable of feeling. And she relished pushing him over the edge as well. For all his buttoned-up tweediness, he was quite the adventurer when the tweed came off.

And oh, that ass…

How utterly intriguing—and stinking adorable—that he had once been a dancer. Honestly, Fred Astaire could eat his heart out.

As fantastic as their bedroom shenanigans were, Nate also delighted in the rest of their time spent together. When they weren't screwing each other senseless, Colin made it his mission to take her on the kinds of dates she'd rarely let herself experience in the past. He came up with endlessly creative places for them to go while avoiding being spotted by anyone they might know. Being behind the cameras, neither of them would ever garner the attention Lois and Nick did, but plenty around town knew who she was—and her supposed marital status.

Nate recognized, deep down, the time was fast approaching to bite the bullet and "divorce" Walter once and for all. As comfortable as he'd become, her security blanket developed more holes every day. But however she went about it, she needed to make sure it didn't blow back on her career in any way. Their split would have to be equally as believable as the marriage itself.

Most importantly, though, there was Lois to consider. It would be wrong to end her marriage before she'd even told her best friend it was phony.

The courage to tell her was just so damn elusive.

It multiplied every day that Colin was beside her, but the ghost of her relationship with her sister loomed larger.

So her charade remained in place. For now, anyway.

Nate redirected her mind to a more pleasant train of thought—one that included a catalogue of Colin's finer attributes. Wonderful, sexy, thoughtful Colin.

Before long, she spotted Frannie approaching. As nice as it was to see her friend, she hoped she wouldn't bring up that stupid paperwork again.

"Nate," Frannie called, "fancy meeting you here! I was just on my way to your office."

Can't I just have five minutes of peaceful, lewd thoughts?

Nate smiled around the worry. "Perfect timing, then. What's up?"

Frannie handed her one of several folders she had tucked under her arm. "Latest budget numbers. All your requests approved."

"Wow," Nate replied, relieved on multiple counts, and took the folder. "All of them? I aimed high this time."

"I noticed," Frannie sniffed. "But you came in under with your last two films, so we had a little extra to spare."

"Okey-dokey, then. Thanks."

Frannie's smile turned sly. *Ugh.* "So…how are things?"

"Just swell. And you?"

"Fine." She narrowed her eyes. "I'm not letting you off with that non-answer. You look like the cat that swallowed the canary. You know me, I need details."

Nate widened her eyes dramatically. "About what?"

She received a swat on her arm in response. "You know exactly what. I'm guessing it has to do with your new man that Lois hinted about. She said he's British, didn't she? Has he finally stepped up? God knows that husband of yours never will. Spill."

As Nate considered how much detail she could get away with telling Frannie before the inevitable venture into dicey territory, Nick's voice interrupted her.

"Afternoon, ladies!" He strolled up with a smile.

"Nicholas! Your timing's as good as Nate's." Frannie dipped into her armload of paperwork again and extracted one for him. "Here."

"Why, Frannie, you shouldn't have," he replied. "It's not even my birthday."

She tapped a manicured finger against the folder. "Budget revisions for your upcoming comedy projects."

"Oh." Nick's mouth twisted into a grimacing smile. "Great. Thanks."

"Hey. You don't have to look so down-in-the-dumps. I gave you most of what you wanted, you know."

"Yeah," Nate chimed in. "She apparently worked wonders for me."

"Well, okay then." He smiled more genuinely this time. "Thank you, Frannie."

"Anytime."

"So," Nick interrogated brightly, "what are you two up to? Anything exciting?"

"I was about to convince Nate to finally kick Wanker to the

curb, and take up with her new English bloke on a more permanent basis instead."

Nate inhaled too much air and sputtered her way into a coughing fit. When she finally calmed down—after an oh-so-helpful thumping on the back from Frannie—she turned to her friend, debating whether to be alarmed or amused.

Amusement won out. "Wanker?" At Frannie's proud grin, she shook her head. "Funny, you're not the first to call him that."

"Oh, really," Frannie drawled. "Another point to the Brit, then? I've never met him, but I already like him immensely."

Nick snickered. "Wanker. That is good."

Frannie swept her hand in Nick's direction. "See. Nick agrees with me. Really, though, what are you waiting for? When are you going to chuck him?"

Nick crossed his arms and leveled her with wide-eyed expectation. "Yes, Nate, what *are* you waiting for?"

He was playing with fire, and judging by his grin, the little shit knew it. What she couldn't figure out was why.

Fuck me, does he know something?

But no. He couldn't possibly. Right?

She circled a finger at his face. "I don't like that look."

Nick huffed. "Why does everyone keep saying that? Is it really too much to ask that I get to unearth some gossip *first* for a change?"

Nate rolled her eyes, masking her relief. Simple angling for gossip, she could deal with.

So long as he didn't get too close to the truth.

Having reached the end of her patience, she made a show of looking at their surroundings and adopting her most arch tone. "As much as I hate to trample on your delicate sensibilities, I have no gossip to share today. And I am sure as hell not having this discussion with you two in the middle of the lot. Now, if you would excuse me, I have work to get back to."

Frannie flashed her a diabolically angelic smile. "Okay, but I'm only letting this go momentarily because I have work of my own to do… Don't think you're off the hook."

"I have no doubt." Nate held up the folder. "Thank you for this. I will see you later."

She started to leave.

"No goodbye for me?" Nick pouted.

"No." She aimed a finger at him. "Because you are evil."

His hearty laughter followed her as she walked away.

THE FOLLOWING WEEKEND, Nate tied a scarf over her hair and armed herself with a battalion of cleaning products, to ready her apartment for Colin's arrival that evening. Every time the question arose, she'd pushed for them to spend time at his place, since her busy work schedule—and complete lack of motivation—kept her from giving hers the tidying it desperately needed. Not only was the dust piling up, but she had a fair amount of men's clothes scattered around that she'd "borrowed" from the studio to pass off as Walter's in the event of any unexpected visitors.

But Colin she expected, and it felt rude to leave evidence of Walter—no matter how phony he knew it to be—where he could see it. Now that she'd finally invited him over, it was time to suck it up and clean.

She also needed to suck it up and come clean with Lois.

Her encounter with Nick and Frannie on the lot left her on edge. While she'd successfully put them off, it was only a matter of time before Nick's insatiable desire for gossip, along with his inclination to "helpfully" meddle, caught up with her. If Lois found out even a kernel of the truth from someone other than Nate… She shuddered to think of the consequences.

So, the time had come. As utterly nauseated as that made her.

Which was part of the reason she'd invited Colin over. A shot of his warmth and encouragement—along with a healthy dose of his quality horizontal recreation—would provide precisely the boost she needed. She hoped.

But first, cleaning.

She'd barely made two sweeps with her floor duster when the doorbell rang. Nate opened the door with a start.

"Lois."

Okay…maybe I'm doing this without a Colin boost.

"Please tell me there are no scandals looming on the horizon at Phoenix," Lois intoned, in lieu of a greeting.

"I… What?"

"Sorry." Lois offered her a rueful smile. "Can I come in?"

Nate shook off her surprised stupor and opened the door wider. "Of course."

Lois breezed past her, stopping to take in the state of Nate's apartment and the cleaning products adding to its dishevelment. She turned back around as Nate shut the door, spotting the sweeper still in Nate's hand.

"Oh. You're cleaning. It doesn't look remotely enjoyable, but if I'm interrupting…"

Nate propped the broom against the wall. "As necessary as it is, I don't mind procrastinating for a bit longer."

True, she'd much rather clean than have *this* conversation, but here she was.

Lois's earlier declaration suddenly hit her. "Wait. What's this about scandal? Did something happen?"

Please don't say it's about me. Not yet.

Lois pulled a scrunched newspaper page out of her purse. "Look at this."

Nate scanned the page, open to one of the gossip columns. Relief washed through her. Not about her, then.

"Oh, the Brookses' divorce finally went through." Nate continued reading. "And *she's* leaving Parkmoor Studios? How is that fair?"

Lois made an impatient gesture. "That's a tirade for another time. Keep reading."

Nate did, her attention sparked, and she glanced back up at Lois. "Is Ruth really signing with us? That's quite a coup."

"If I can make it happen, yes, it would be. But that's not the point." Barely contained irritation tinged her tone. "Did you read that last line?"

"What, the snide jab about a 'fallen woman' fitting right in with you? As crappy as it is, that's nothing new, right?"

"No, but shit like that had been tapering off." Lois paced away. "The studio's work was finally the main focus. But this is the third time in a month. It's like they're getting bored, and resorting to their old punching bag out of habit. Or spite." She waved her hand. "Whatever it is, I don't need this right now."

Damn it. Queasiness settled in Nate's stomach.

"I'm about to direct my first movie, Nate," Lois continued. "I need the focus to be on *that*. Not this same old shit. So. That brings us back to my question." She perched on the arm of the sofa. "You always know the gossip before anyone else. Have you gotten wind of anything I need to know about?"

Nate fought the urge run screaming out the door, opting for a quip instead. "You know I never dress and tell."

Lois snorted and flicked her fingers dismissively. "Of course I know that. I'm not asking you to be a snitch; I don't need details. All I want to know is whether there's any trouble brewing. Any shit venturing too close to the fan I might have to deal with should it come to light. *Please* tell me there's nothing coming." She raised hopeful eyes to Nate.

And Nate's heart sank. She knew of only one potential shit-raising scandal capable of coming back to bite Lois and the studio. Her own. And if she put that burden on Lois now…

She'd definitely lose her.

Lois would stop speaking to her. On her elegantly furious way out the door, she'd probably fire Nate to boot. She'd lose her beloved career and her even more beloved best friend in one fell swoop.

Fear roared to life with a vengeance. But Lois was waiting for an answer—for reassurance. And if that's what Lois needed, she could sure as hell give it to her. Nate forced calm into her face, her voice.

"No. I haven't heard about anything."

Lois studied her, and for a moment Nate worried she hadn't been convincing enough. But her friend nodded.

"Thanks." Lois exhaled. "I'm sorry to dump all this on you. I guess I'm nervous about my movie."

"I know. And you're always welcome to dump on me."

Lois laughed. "I will keep that in mind."

The sound of her chuckle echoed in Nate's hollowed-out heart, and she swallowed hard. This conversation put off the inevitable a little longer, but damn, it was going to hurt when she didn't have this anymore.

Shoving that aside, she suddenly remembered the concept of hospitality. "Hey, did you want something to drink? I think I've got some of Max's pastries too."

Lois rose from the couch. "As tempting as that sounds, I should get going. Nick and I are having dinner with a new investor tonight, and I have to go home to change." She gestured at Nate's forgotten sweeper. "And you have your exciting cleaning."

Nate huffed. "So exciting."

On her way to the door, Lois paused, eyes falling on one of "Walter's" sport coats. She pointed at it. "Walter's?"

Nate bit her lip. "Mm-hmm."

Lois cocked her head, studying the jacket. Nate had no idea what was so fascinating about it. Lois finally fixed her piercing gaze on her, and a chill made its way down Nate's spine.

"Nate, I…" She paused and shook her head. "Never mind." She smiled and gave Nate's arm what should have been a comforting squeeze. "Thanks for today."

"Anytime."

Lois slipped out the door, leaving a thundering silence in her wake.

Nate slumped against the wall. She wasn't sure who she'd been trying harder to protect, Lois or herself, but one thing was abundantly clear. Despite her earlier best intentions, she'd managed to dig herself even further into her miserable faux-husband hole.

Chapter Nineteen

After sinking onto the couch and staring into space for an hour, Nate finally remembered her date with Colin. She took in her living room. No way could she summon the energy to clean now. Which meant no way could she let Colin in. Not that she was up for seeing him in her current mood anyway.

No matter how much she wanted to tuck herself in his arms and not move for a week. Maybe longer.

She ventured a glance at the clock. He was due in two hours. She'd better get it over with and call him to cancel.

Heaving a sigh, she reached over to the end table and picked up the phone. Her eye fell on that damn sport coat and her lip curled into a sneer. At least it wasn't tweed; she'd hate to have that fabric ruined.

Colin answered on the second ring, his voice a warm balm to her soul.

Why am I canceling again?

She shook her head. Right, her apartment—and she herself—were in no condition.

"Listen, I'm going to have to take a rain check on tonight."

"Nate, what's wrong?" His tone flooded with concern.

"Nothing, really. I just… The day got away from me, and I think it's better if you don't come over."

"Oh. If you think so… But it doesn't sound like nothing. Are you sure you're all right?"

"I'm fine. Honest." She failed to keep a slight quaver from her voice.

Colin heard it. "Nate. You're not fine. I'm coming over right now."

"No, my apartment's a mess. I didn't do any of the cleaning I wanted…"

"I don't care about that. My place was hardly spotless the first time you were here, as I recall." He hesitated. "This is about a lot more than cleanliness, isn't it?"

Nate exhaled. "Yeah."

"Will you truly feel better if you're alone?"

"Probably not."

"Would you like me to come over? We don't even have to talk. I can simply hold you for a while."

She closed her eyes. That sounded…perfect. Absolutely perfect.

"Okay," she whispered. "Please come."

Colin arrived in record time. Nate stopped short on her way to answer the door when she remembered the old jumpsuit she wore and the scarf still in her hair.

Oh, well. Too late now.

She opened the door to his lopsided, slightly worried smile and promptly forgot all about what she looked like. She sighed as warmth flooded her chest.

"Hi."

"Hello," he answered.

"Come on in." She stepped back to wave him into the room. "Can I take your jacket?"

"Sure, thanks."

She closed the door, and he slid it off and handed it to her. She resisted the urge to sniff the lightweight fabric for his intoxicating scent as she hung it on the coatrack. Proud of her restraint, she turned to face him and noticed for the first time that he wore…

Oh, dear god.

A turtleneck sweater. He was wearing a fucking turtleneck sweater. A lovely, cozy, cream-colored creation that clung in all the right places. Perfect for snuggling into. Which she desperately needed to do.

A dam burst behind her eyeballs, leaving her powerless to stop the onslaught.

Colin's arms came around her in an instant. She sank into him, sobbing into his chest. Just as he'd promised, he held her tight, saying nothing but an occasional soothing word or two. One of his hands came up to cradle the back of her head.

Eventually her sobs tapered to small hiccups, and her breathing slowed to a more normal pace. Sensing her returning calm, Colin pulled back and grazed a kiss across her forehead. He brushed his thumb across her wet cheek, then took a handkerchief from his pocket to gently dab at the rest.

Nate sniffled as she took in the large puddle she'd left on his chest. "I'm sorry about your sweater."

He looked down absently and shrugged. "Eh, I needed to wash it anyway."

A startled, watery laugh escaped her, and he smiled down at her. She sniffled again, and took the hankie from him, gesturing to her nose. "Do you mind?"

"Of course not."

"I hope you're still saying that in a minute."

She blew her nose, rather loudly, but he was still smiling when she finished, which gave her a boost of encouragement. She took a deep breath and met his concerned gaze.

"Welcome to my humble abode."

Colin chuckled. "Thank you. It's lovely."

"You haven't even looked at it, have you?"

"No, not really. But it's yours, so therefore it's lovely."

Nate shook her head. "Flatterer." She gestured to the couch. "Would you like to sit?"

"Sure."

He followed her over and settled next to her.

"I feel like a terrible hostess. Can I get you anything?"

"No, I'm fine." He brushed a lock of hair that had escaped her scarf behind her ear. "I feel like I should be the one asking you that question. What can I do?"

"I'd ask you to grow me a spine, but I somehow doubt that's one of your many talents."

He moved his hand around to the base of her neck and traced the bones there. "I don't know… I'm pretty sure I felt one when you were in my arms over there."

"It's all for show." Nate let out a mirthless laugh. "I really messed up today. With Lois."

"Oh." His hand stilled. "Did you tell her, then?"

She couldn't bring herself to look at him as she answered. "I was planning to. I really was. As a matter of fact, I was going to run my plan by you tonight. But then she showed up out of the blue, and said she needed my help and I… I managed to make things worse. I think."

Colin grazed his thumb over the back of her neck. "Tell me?"

She bit her lip, then dove in, his presence at her side so comforting and solid. She clung to a desperate, albeit far-fetched, hope that maybe he'd reassure her it wasn't as bad as she thought.

His silence when she finished her grim tale didn't do much to kindle that hope.

She leaned forward and buried her head in her hands. "God, you think it's even worse than I imagined, don't you?"

His hand came up to rub tender circles on her back, his tone gentle. "I do not. I'm only taking a moment to think it all through."

Nate sniffed, voice barely above a whisper. "I am a terrible person."

"You are not a terrible person. You've only…made a few mistakes, that's all."

"Mistakes that are going to kill my relationship with my dearest friend in the world. And I pushed us even further off that cliff today, didn't I?"

"Nate."

She groaned into her hands in response.

"Nate. Look at me."

She took a deep breath and sat up, sliding her eyes to his.

"You're wallowing. Not that you haven't earned it, mind you. But I do not believe all hope is lost."

"You don't?"

"No, I don't. I won't lie, your situation isn't great, by any stretch of the imagination. But from everything I've gathered, the two of you have a long history, and you can get through this."

"But—"

He held up a hand, cutting her off. "You *can*. No, you didn't tell her today. But you at least got closer to it. And she did ask you *not* to tell her about any scandals, after all."

"Yeah, because she didn't think they'd be about me, of all people." She inhaled shakily. "Do you think… I mean, maybe she just needs to get through directing her movie? I hold on a little longer, and then…"

"And then you can tell her." Colin offered her a warm smile. "That sounds reasonable."

"You really think so?"

"I really do."

She bathed in his reassurance for a moment, before the never-ending doubts crept back in. "Even when I tell her the truth, I still won't know how to fix it afterward."

"Don't underestimate yourself." His face brightened. "Maybe you can fix it *during*."

"How do you figure?"

He hesitated. "I gather everything seems to go off the rails when you're in the middle of a situation, right? The panic takes over? So give yourself some armor, to help you say it right. Think ahead to what might help her understand. And then take a page out of my professional book and write yourself a script."

She considered his words. *Huh.* "You know, that's not a bad idea, actually."

He smiled at her. "See. I can tell you're feeling better already."

An idea took hold. "Hey! Maybe you could put your talents to use and write it for me…"

Colin chuckled. "As flattered as I am by the offer, I think it best if the words come from you." He gently took her chin in his hand. "But you are more than welcome to practice it on me when you're ready."

"Fair enough." She leaned in to kiss him. "Thank you," she whispered.

"You are quite welcome." He placed a kiss on her forehead. When he pulled back to look at her again, he had grown more serious.

"What is it?"

He shook his head. "Nothing."

"Colin. Tell me."

"I was…only wondering if you'd given any more thought to…"

"Phasing out Walter?"

He nodded. "I'm sorry. I know you're dealing with everything that happened today, and you need to tell Lois before you do anything."

"No, don't worry about it. I get it. And I have been thinking about it. I just have to go about it the right way, you know? Especially knowing Lois's concerns about scandal." Nate caressed his cheek. "Maybe that's something we could do together? Come up with a quality end-of-marriage story?"

His mood lightened considerably, gratifying her.

"An exit strategy for Walter. Sure, I'd like that."

"Good." She inhaled a sharp lungful of air and sank back into the couch, abruptly feeling every bit of the exhaustion setting in. "Oh, my head is going to kill me tomorrow."

Colin took her hand and brushed his lips across her knuckles. "My poor dove. I wish I could do something to help..."

His eyes scanned the room before lighting on something in the corner. He turned back to her and scrunched up his mouth, considering. He nodded once and sucked in a deep breath.

"Right then. I suppose it's time." He slapped his hands against his lap and rose from the couch.

Nate craned her neck up at him, not bothering to hide her confusion. "You've lost me."

He pointed to her record player. "Do you, by any chance, have some Gene Krupa over there?"

"I...I think I might. I'm not sure."

He strode across the room and started rifling through her stack of records. "Aha! Success." He pulled one out of its sleeve and began setting up the player.

"No offense to Mr. Krupa, but I'm not entirely sure how he can be of help right now."

Colin threw a twinkly glance over his shoulder at her. "Just wait."

Once he had the record set up, he paused and whipped around before starting it. Nate's eyebrows shot up as he bent and shoved her coffee table to the periphery of the room.

Now he's rearranging my furniture? What the hell?

Surveying the room and apparently finding it to his satisfaction, Colin put the needle down to start the music and returned to the center of the now spacious floor in front of her.

He shook his arms out and craned his neck side-to-side, finishing off with a few quick pumps of his legs. Another deep breath as the music began, and he cast his eyes up to the ceiling. She thought she heard him mutter, "I can't believe I'm doing this."

Before she questioned him again, he lowered his head and met her gaze full-on. And then...

Nate let out a delighted gasp.

Holy shit, he's dancing *for me.*

Colin marked out an energetic time step—shuffles, ball-changes, and a bunch of other steps she didn't know the names of —in perfect coordination with the rhythm of the drum-heavy music. And he was *good*. Damn good.

She could see why he'd won so many competitions. Astaire, Kelly, the Nicholas Brothers—they had nothing on Colin. It was a crime that his injury had forced him to stop. Although if it hadn't, he might not be here now.

He might not be *hers*.

The realization stunned Nate as it hit her, square in the chest. It terrified her, but she wanted him to go on being hers. She desperately hoped she could keep him, that she wouldn't find some way to inevitably screw it all up.

She didn't have time to dwell on the sudden maelstrom of her thoughts, however, because he caught her eye once again. His mouth quirked up saucily, then he winked as he turned his back to her. And began the time step again from the beginning.

This time with his glorious, firm, muscular ass on full display.

Crap snacks, that is the finest, hardest-working ass I've ever seen.

A laugh began deep in her chest and bubbled its way up and out of her. Here he was, doing the very thing the two of them had made fun of Nick for. Presenting his ass. To her.

Nate's cheeks hurt from grinning so widely. He'd done it, succeeded in pushing her heaping troubles far from her mind. She leaned forward, foot tapping in time to the music, and let herself thoroughly enjoy the view.

HOURS LATER, Nate lay spooned in Colin's warm, solid presence. She traced her fingers along the arm wrapped around her middle, fascinated by the way the moonlight through the window played against the hair there. His distraction had worked wonders, but now her mind drifted back to the incident with Lois. Somehow, it felt a lot less painful to examine it while safely ensconced in Colin's embrace.

Her guilt and fear weighed on her, but even if she had to wait a little longer, she at least had the beginnings of a plan to fix the situation. And a warm ally by her side to help her.

She sighed, and he tightened his arm around her, his lips coming to rest in her hair. *Ah.* He wasn't asleep either.

"What's your biggest regret?" Nate asked, suddenly curious. "I mean, you obviously know mine. But what about you?"

His chest expanded against her back, and he remained quiet for a moment. His hesitation didn't worry her—she trusted he'd answer. She knew him well enough by now to tell he was marshaling his thoughts.

"I've lost my sister."

She wasn't sure what she had expected—something about the end of his dance career, perhaps, or that partner who'd been stupid enough to walk away from him—but this admission caught her off-guard.

"I didn't know you had a sister." She turned in his arms.

"I do." He gave her a small smile. "She's my half-sister, technically, but…"

He looked so sad, she wished she could wrap her arms around him and leech out his pain by osmosis.

"What happened to her?" she asked.

He inhaled slowly. "I don't know." At her questioning look, he shrugged and continued. "When I said I lost her, I suppose I meant more precisely that I…lost track of her. I have no idea where she is now."

"Because of the war?"

Colin nodded. "The last I spoke to her was"—he rolled his eyes—"right after Pearl Harbor."

"Oh, wow."

The huff of his breath fanned over her cheeks. "Yeah. Frances came here for university, Boston, to be exact. Those early years of the war, it was a relief to know she was here, away from the fighting. With my radio work, we didn't have much contact, but I knew she'd met a young man whom she was pretty smitten with. But then the bombing in Hawaii brought your country into the thick of it all, and it changed everything. She wasn't in some neutral spot anymore. And despite my being behind a desk most of the time, my work was still exceedingly dangerous. Being in intelligence, the stories I heard…"

Nate cupped his jaw, stroking her thumb across his cheek. He shut his eyes and leaned into the caress.

"Maybe I was overly paranoid, but I was terrified of her being in danger because of her connection to me. That someone would trace her, hurt her because of the work I was doing. I thought it better if we didn't have any contact for a while." He opened his eyes, and one side of his mouth tilted up. "But I couldn't just walk away without saying goodbye, so I called her one last time to tell her, taking extra precautions of course."

"Of course." She slid her hand down to his chest.

"That was when she told me she and her young man were getting married. Apparently right away, since he was enlisting. I thought it was a bit soon, but I didn't tell her that."

"Smart man."

He chuckled at that. "She definitely would have bitten my head off if I'd tried. She's a stubborn one." Colin sobered. "I purposely didn't ask her what his surname was. I thought it was better if I didn't know. Paranoia, and all."

"Perfectly justified paranoia. The Nazis were a bunch of feckless shits."

"That they were." He shuddered. "But…that not knowing means that I haven't been able to find her. After all this time." His mouth twisted in a grimace. "I have no bloody idea where she is, if she's all right, if she's happy…" He squeezed his eyes closed.

"Colin." She leaned over and feathered a kiss across his lips. "You were trying to protect her."

"I know," he whispered. "But the war's long over. I should be there for her now. We may not have grown up under the same roof, but I'm her brother."

"I'm sure you've tried to find her, haven't you?"

"I have." He snorted. "Fat lot of good my intelligence connections did me. With her being here, marrying an American, there wasn't much anyone could find out for me."

"What about marriage records in Boston? I'm sure her maiden name would be on the license, right?"

He opened his eyes with a sigh. "I thought so too. My connections got me in there. You have no idea how many hours I spent combing through the records. I took the train up every weekend when I first got to New York. But I suspect she must have gotten married somewhere else."

"Which could be anywhere." She bit her lip. "And without knowing his name…"

"Precisely. I thought I had a lead, when my mum heard through the grapevine that her husband might have been stationed here on the West Coast somewhere. It's why I had no qualms about leaving Broadway behind and taking Lois up on her offer." He inhaled sharply. "But California is a damn huge state. Plus, so many marriages happened in those first few months after you entered the war. It's been overwhelming, and nothing but dead ends since I got here. It doesn't help that I've been so focused on my work at Phoenix. I haven't given her nearly the attention I should."

Colin let out a groan and rolled to his back, his arm sliding off her waist.

"And obviously she hasn't reached out to you, either?" Nate asked.

"No," he answered quietly. "I don't even want to think about why that might be."

An awful thought occurred to Nate. She propped herself on one elbow and placed her other hand over his heart. "There I was, going on about driving away my own sister, and you've been dealing with—"

"No." He cupped her cheek. "Do not beat yourself up over this. Do not. Our situations are completely different. But that doesn't make the pain any less, for either of us. A loss is a loss, no matter how it happens."

She turned her head to kiss his palm. "Okay, then."

His hand slipped down to cover hers, still resting on his chest, which rose with each deep breath. He'd gone inward again.

"You feel like you've failed her, don't you?"

His eyes widened briefly, and then his mouth eased into a wistful smile. "You're uncanny, you know that?"

She raised her shoulder in feigned casualness. "I know. In all seriousness, though, is there any chance you'll believe me when I say you haven't?"

"Probably not." He raised her hand to his lips. "But thanks, just the same."

"Anytime." She traced his lips with her thumb. "I hope you find her."

"Me too."

Nate snuggled closer to him. "So what's she like?"

His mouth finally relaxed into a wide grin. "Fish is loud, brash, boisterous. Loads of fun to be around. The first to call me on even the slightest hint of bullshite. But always ready to fight to the death to defend my honor."

She matched his grin. "Sounds like my kind of dame."

He laughed. "Oh, I have no doubt the two of you would get on famously." He glanced down at her. "At the risk of scaring you off, my mum would positively adore you, too."

Warmth spread through her chest. "I can't wait to meet them both." His initial words sank in, though, and she narrowed her eyes. "Wait a sec. Did you call her...*Fish*?"

A hint of color crept into his cheeks. "I did." When he didn't elaborate right away, Nate raised her eyebrows at him. He snorted. "When we were kids, we often went to visit our gran— our dad's mum—together on weekends. And Gran would always take us to a local pub, where we'd both end up having fish and chips, nearly every time." His lips curved in a soft smile. "Became a bit of a tradition. Before long, Gran started calling us—"

"Fish and Chips," Nate finished.

His eyes sparkled. "Fish and Chips. And it stuck."

She laughed. "But how in the world was it fair to her to get stuck with the *Fish* side of that pairing?"

"Well, I am older," Colin replied, suddenly—and adorably—full of elder brother self-importance. "And our names do begin with 'C' and 'F' respectively, after all."

She snickered. "And how did your sister feel about that?"

He attempted a half-hearted shrug. "She…" He caught her eye and let out a snicker of his own. "She positively *hated* it. Complained all the time. I'm not completely heartless, though. I did concede that if she had to be a fish, she could at least be a mermaid. I pull that nickname out on special occasions."

"I suppose that's pretty sweet."

He traced a finger down her cheek. "I do so wish you could meet her."

She caught his gaze and held it firmly. "Me too. And I am sure I will."

His eyes blazed. "I'll have to work harder than ever to make that happen, then."

Colin pulled her down and took her mouth. As she melted into him, thinking ahead to the growing list of things they'd started talking about doing *together*, a little more of her fear about her future chipped away.

Chapter Twenty

olin paused in the doorway of one of Nate's spacious fitting rooms. Absorbed in her work, she hadn't seen him yet, so he watched her for a few minutes, fascinated. Her arm laden with more ties than he could own in a lifetime, she held them up to a suit hanging in front of her, one at a time, deliberating their merits. It was a fairly simple task, but she looked utterly beautiful doing it.

He lifted his lips in a silly smile. He grew more smitten by the day.

It had killed him to see her so distraught over her encounter with Lois. He hoped, for her peace of mind, she'd be able to open up to her friend sooner rather than later. Sharing the dilemma over his sister with her had given him back a long-abandoned slice of his own peace of mind, and he wanted nothing more than to help her find hers.

God, the mischief those two could get up to together.

Colin still harbored a somewhat selfish—*all right, more than somewhat*—thrill at Nate's request for his help in disentangling herself from Walter. He was reluctant to push her, but the more time they spent together, the more he wanted to freely display his affection wherever they went. If she was willing to start coming up with a plan to be publicly single, then maybe it meant she felt as deep-down, long-term enamored with him as he did with her.

And so here he stood, having taken another of his newly habitual detours through the wardrobe building on his way back to his office. He supposed he should probably alert her to his presence, lest she startle upon spotting him unexpectedly. All those ties would make a rather large mess if they went flying.

Colin cleared his throat and knocked lightly on the doorframe.

Nate was frowning in concentration as she turned, but her face brightened into a grin when her eyes lit on him.

His heart stopped before resuming a much faster rhythm.

"Colin, hi."

"Just wanted to say hello." He gestured to her arm. "I hope I'm not interrupting."

"It's all right. My eyes could use a break from all this paisley." She set her armload down and those eyes raked over him in warm invitation.

Colin gave the door a bit of a careless shove and made his way over to her. Somewhere in the back of his mind, it registered that he probably should have ensured it shut all the way, but it had closed enough that they wouldn't be seen. His primary concern at the moment was having his lips on hers.

After enjoying a proper greeting, Nate drew back to smile at him. Her smile widened when she took in his lips.

"Oops. We're both wearing my lipstick now." She rubbed it off his mouth with her thumb, leaving sparks behind in her wake.

"Are you sure it's not a bad time? You were pretty deep in Tie World there."

Nate laughed. "I was. I have back-to-back actor fittings this morning. My first is coming by in about half an hour, so I should keep an eye on the time. But you're a welcome break, believe me."

"Good. I figured Rose wouldn't have sent me back here otherwise, but…"

"That is true." She kissed his cheek lightly. "But thank you for checking."

Mentioning Rose reminded Colin of the secretary's continually strange behavior. "By the way, is everything all right with Rose? She tends to act very…odd when she talks to me. Sometimes she actually giggles. I kept worrying something was amiss with my suit or my hair, but she even does it on the telephone."

Nate smirked. "I can't exactly blame her."

His face scrunched up. "Why? Am I that amusing?"

"That voice of yours is anything but amusing." At his continued confusion, she tilted her head. "Do you really have no idea what you sound like?"

Oh, bollocks. What do I sound like?

She smiled, shaking her head. "Remember when you told me that my tugging on your hair pushes you beyond your control?"

He nodded.

"Well, let's just say," she continued in a seductive purr, "your voice completely, thoroughly incinerates mine."

A slow grin broke over his face. "Does it now?"

"Yep. Ever since our very first phone conversation."

Pride beamed through his chest. "That's good to know." He bent to lean close to her ear. "So if I were to remain at this close range…"

He felt her shiver in his own bones. "Do that for much longer, and I'll take you right here on this pile of ties," Nate growled.

"Ooh, tempting," he whispered.

Unfortunately aware of their surroundings, they both let out heavy sighs before straightening away from each other.

"I'm gonna have to take a rain check on that," Nate lamented wearily.

"I'll hold you to it."

"You better," she retorted with a wink.

Feeling the need to return them—and his nether-regions—to safer territory, he brought the conversation back to Rose. "Wait a minute. Are you implying that Rose acts the way she does because she…"

"Has swoony feelings for you? I'm afraid so. But you don't

need to worry—you're not her first swoon. Or her last." She exaggeratedly narrowed her eyes. "I don't need to be jealous, do I?"

Colin dragged his eyes leisurely over Nate, head-to-toe. "You know you don't."

She visibly gulped and picked up a few ties again. "Good."

He chuckled and crossed his arms. "What about you?"

"What about me?"

"You must see all kinds of swoon-worthy people come through your doors. Anyone ever get to you?"

He didn't ask out of any jealous musings over her past, not really anyway. He was genuinely curious what type she usually gravitated toward. *Am I an exception?*

Nate adopted an air of importance. "I am a professional. I'll have you know, I never swoon over the people I dress."

"So there isn't even one who—"

"Cary Grant."

"Wow, you had that one ready fast."

She lifted a casual shoulder. "What can I say? He's my one weakness. Or rather, he would be, if I ever got the chance to costume him. Luckily for my professional reputation, that hasn't happened yet." Her eyes turned molten as she zeroed in on him. "But you know, I've always thought actors were highly overrated. Now, writers…they're a different story."

"Lucky for me."

"Indeed." She winked at him again, and they both laughed.

Nate returned to contemplating her neckwear, and Colin perched on the arm of the loveseat lining the wall.

"So I've been giving some thought to Walter." He wasn't entirely sure it was the best time to bring it up, but the mood was light, so he took the risk.

Nate turned her head to him. He caught a brief flash of hesitation before she stifled it. He tried not to let it sting, but a tiny sliver burrowed in anyway. But when she smiled again, her trepidation vanished, and he smothered his own.

"Have you? Come up with anything good?" she asked.

He purposely maintained an easy tone as he answered, "Well, of course, there's the obvious divorce solution. A touch salacious, but not all that unexpected, especially if we frame it with the right context."

"That's likely true."

"Unless of course… You're not Catholic, are you? I mean, can it really be considered a sin under these particular circumstances?"

Nate smirked. "Probably not. Although I'm pretty sure the lying would be." She waved her hand. "But it's moot anyway, since I'm not Catholic. Besides, the situation is complicated enough—let's not add theology to the mix on top of everything else."

"Fair point. So divorce is most definitely on the table."

"It is." She cocked her head to one side. "Did you have something else in mind?"

"Depending on what you're up for, we could also go a more… inventive route."

Nate's eyes sparked. "You know, over the years I have thought, on more than one occasion, of giving Walter some kind of rare, tropical disease."

Colin hummed his approval. "The possibilities there are endless. So many symptoms to choose from…"

"Huh. Maybe too many to narrow down?"

"Perhaps." He adjusted his glasses, then brought his finger to his chin, tapping. "There's always the odd workplace injury. A well-timed baseball to the back of the head…"

"At just the right angle…" Nate pursed her lips. "Might be believable."

He snapped his fingers. "Or, along those same lines—and with a nod to your Mr. Grant—a ballpark hotdog topped with some arsenic-laced relish."

"Ooh, not bad. Except Walter's really more of a mustard guy."

Colin snorted and raised his eyebrows. That was an awfully specific detail to know about someone who didn't exist.

Catching his unspoken meaning, Nate smiled sheepishly and shrugged.

He shook his head and continued. "We can make it mustard just as easily."

She considered for a moment. She started to say something more, but stopped and bit her lip. Their eyes met, and they both burst into laughter at the absurdity of the conversation.

Nate tossed the ties aside again and came to stand in front of him, slipping her arms around his neck. His hands found their place on her waist as he looked up at her from his perch on the couch.

"What does it say about us that we're having so much fun talking about this?" Nate asked.

"Not sure I want to analyze that one too much. It is pretty morbid, isn't it?"

She nodded before resting her forehead against his with a groan.

"Don't worry," he soothed. "We'll figure it all out."

"I know."

The two of them remained still for a few heartbeats, arms around each other and heads together. Despite their unusual circumstances, Colin once again marveled at how perfect it felt to be with her.

The ghost of a noise pulled him from his reverie. "What was that?"

"Hmm?" Nate looked up. Something behind his shoulder caught her attention. "Oh, it was the ties."

She stepped away from him and over to the other end of the couch, where some of the pile had slid to the floor.

"Let me help," he offered. As he rose to follow her, a strange feeling crept up his spine.

Was it really the ties I heard, or something else?

He aimed a look over his shoulder at the door, and of course saw nothing amiss. Colin rolled his eyes. All that talk of morbidity had muddled his thoughts. Of course it was the ties. He heard nothing but silence coming from the hallway.

After he assisted Nate in cleaning up, she turned to face him, resigned. "All macabre laughs aside, we're forgetting one crucial problem with offing Walter."

Afraid of the answer, he asked anyway. "What's that?"

She grimaced. "My having to play the role of grieving widow."

Colin's shoulders relaxed a fraction. "Worried that Lois has all the acting talent in your friendship?"

Nate huffed. "Hey, do I need to remind you I've been acting the part of put-upon *wife* for years now?" She sobered again. "But no, it's not that. It's only…"

Understanding hit him. "After the war…"

"Exactly. So many actually lost their husbands, a good friend of mine included. The thought of pretending to feel that pain…" She shook her head. "It just feels too crass. I couldn't do it."

He reached up to stroke her cheek. "I don't blame you." He smiled. "So. A quality divorce story it is, then?"

Nate smiled back. "I know it's not as creative…"

"Eh, I'm a writer. I can still make it shine."

"I have no doubt." She sighed and brushed a quick kiss across his cheek, her lips leaving a trail of fire behind despite their feather-light pressure. "As much as I hate to break up this party, I should get back to work. My actor'll be here pretty soon."

"And it would be easier for everyone if I'm not here when he arrives."

"Yeah."

He nodded and bent to kiss her. "I'll see you tonight?"

"We can have that rain check." She leaned in for one more kiss. "It's a date."

Chapter Twenty-One

A couple of hours after Colin's departure, Nate walked her second actor out after finishing their fitting, and returned to her reception area to find Rose.

"Hey, how'd the fittings go?" Rose asked.

"One was great," Nate replied truthfully. "But my first actor never showed. You didn't hear anything from Alex Madison, did you?"

"No, I didn't." Rose popped her gum as she thought. "That's weird. He's usually such an eager beaver. I've never met an actor so disgustingly early for everything."

"That's what I was thinking. I hope he's not sick or anything." Nate nodded to Rose's phone. "Can you call around, see if anyone's seen him?"

"You got it, boss."

Nate started toward her office door, but stopped when Rose held up a hand.

"Oh! I nearly forgot. Mr. Bradley called and asked you to stop by his office a-sap. Said it was urgent."

Huh. That was odd. The pirate movie was almost finished, and her next immediate project didn't involve Nick.

"Did he say what it was about?"

Rose shook her head. "No. But he did sound pretty serious." Her eyes lit up. "Ooh, maybe he needs help with a gift for Ms. Ashford or something!"

"Uh, yeah. Maybe. Whatever it is, I should go see what he wants." She headed back for the door. "If you do find Mr. Madison, can you try to reschedule him for tomorrow?"

"Absolutely."

Nate bit the inside of her cheek as she made her way to Nick's office. His summons puzzled her, especially if Rose, of all people, thought he sounded serious. A tiny, tickling worry nagged at her, but she dismissed it quickly. All that earlier talk with Colin lingered, making her paranoid. No need to make too much out of this. Rose liked to turn everything into a story. As a matter of fact, her secretary's theory was likely accurate—Nick's dramatic streak enhancing a simple request for help with a gift idea or something.

Nate stopped short when she reached the hallway outside Nick's office at the same time Colin did.

"Nate, hello." He gave her a warm grin. "I didn't expect to see you here."

She returned the smile, already feeling calmer. "Right back at you. Do you have an appointment with Nick? I don't want to intrude."

He paused to let her precede him into Nick's reception area. "Nothing officially scheduled, but Nick just called and asked to see me. He said it was—"

"Urgent? Yeah, me too."

Surprise registered on Colin's face. "Huh. Wonder what it's about…"

A strange current of electricity skittered down Nate's neck, but she tried to ignore it.

Nick's assistant, Jerry, smiled up at them, but before he uttered a word, the office door swung open.

"Oh, good, you're both here," Nick greeted them. He turned and handed Jerry a stack of manila envelopes. "Jerry, would you mind hand delivering these?"

"No problem." He got up to leave, waving on his way out. "See you guys later."

"Come on in." Nick beckoned to them as he turned back to his office.

He does sound somber. What gives?

Nate quirked an eyebrow in question as she and Colin followed him, but Colin shrugged, looking as confused as she felt.

That confusion only multiplied when they entered the office to find Lois waiting for them as well, leaning on the side of Nick's desk. She shot Nate a look of concern, accompanied by the tiniest lift of her shoulder, implying Nick hadn't clued her in either.

Nick gestured Colin and Nate to the two seats in front of his desk. "Please, have a seat." He shut the door with a firm click. "That errand should keep Jerry occupied for a while."

She decided to start out light. "Why, are you planning world domination, Nick?"

He didn't answer, but came to perch on his desk, directly in front of them, crossing one ankle over the other. It was a deceptively casual power move.

Highly unusual, coming from Nick.

"I just had Alex Madison in my office."

"So that's where he was," Nate replied. "He never showed up for his fitting, and now I have to reschedule him."

"Oh, he showed up to the fitting. Early, as a matter of fact." Nick crossed his arms over his chest and split a look between the two of them. A serious, un-Nick-like look. "Would you care to explain to me how it is that Mr. Madison came to be convinced the two of you are plotting to...*murder*...Nate's husband?"

Deafening silence filled the room.

Lois's head snapped in her husband's direction, before her gaze slid incredulously to Nate.

A shocked laugh burst from Nate's chest. "That's ridiculous. We weren't..." She froze.

Oh, shit.

They had been doing precisely that. Sort of.

"I knew I heard something!" Colin exclaimed. "It *was* more than just the ties."

"That's your big takeaway with this? And besides, the door was closed. How could you possibly have heard him—or vice versa?"

Colin visibly swallowed as guilt flickered across his face. "I…um…think I may not have latched it completely."

She stared at him in disbelief. "Are you kidding me?"

Out of the corner of her eye, Nate detected Lois crossing her arms. But she remained eerily silent.

Nick inhaled sharply and pinched the bridge of his nose, bringing her attention back to him. "Can we please focus? Madison was spooked enough as to be a bit fuzzy on the details, so it would be really nice if you could reassure me this is not nearly as bad as it sounds." He looked back at them, hopeful. "All he heard was you saying something about, say, 'getting rid of' Walter, right?"

She frantically searched her memory of their conversation. In her panic, she was probably remembering it as far grimmer and more graphic than it had been.

Rare diseases and poisoned condiments weren't really all that terrible, were they?

Colin let out a strangled noise as his shoulders slumped forward. *So, yep. That terrible.* Nick's sharp eyes flew to him.

"Colin?" Nick's voice held an amount of steel she'd never before heard when he wasn't in front of the cameras.

"Ah, well…the, um, word…'arsenic' may have been uttered at one point," Colin bit out.

Crap.

"Jesus Christ," Nick hissed, pushing up off the desk and past an unnervingly calm Lois. He paced away, then turned back to them, gesturing wide. "What the hell were you thinking, joking about something like that in the office?" He sucked in a breath. "You were fucking joking, weren't you?"

Nate's face flamed. "Of course we were. And we didn't exactly expect to be overheard, you know."

"Clearly," he shot back. "And yet here we are. In the last place we need to be right now." He shot a concerned glance at Lois.

Whose continued silence grew more and more ominous with every passing second.

Nate gulped. She'd assured Lois there was no looming scandal. Forget Walter. Lois was going to kill *her*.

Nick continued, "Look, I know I've probably been a little obnoxious, urging you to dump your husband so I can push you two together. But I didn't mean you should just throw caution to the wind. Plotting *murder* in your office? Really?"

Well, when you put it that way…

Temporarily distracted—again—from panic over what Lois was taking away from all this, she seized on the unfortunate rightness of Nick's point. For all her being a vault around Lois, she had been slipping up when it came to her phony husband. A lot. Too much, in fact. Her sense had fled completely out the window.

Because of Colin.

Who spoke now. "Wait just a minute. We were not 'plotting murder,' as you say. You can't exactly murder someone who doesn't—" He clamped his mouth shut so quickly, she thought she heard his teeth crunch together. Colin carefully avoided looking in her direction.

She carefully avoided kicking him in the shins.

Maybe the others hadn't noticed what he'd been about to say? She risked a look at Nick, startled by the wry mirth on his face.

"Someone who doesn't what? Exist?" Nick chuckled. "Of course he exists, we've—" He stopped abruptly. "We've…never met him. Not…once." He turned his head toward Nate at an agonizingly slow pace.

Still not enough time to school her features, though.

Nick's jaw dropped. "Holy. Fucking. Shit," he whispered.

Once again, silence descended on the office. The kind of silence where breath was audible.

If anyone in the room was actually breathing. Nate had certainly stopped.

She slid her eyes over to Lois, who watched her carefully, stone-faced.

Oh, god. Why didn't I just bite the bullet and tell her the other day?

One of Lois's eyebrows arched slowly northward, in direct opposition to the southern decent of Nate's stomach.

Keeping her eyes trained on Nate, Lois finally spoke. "*Is* that the way that sentence was supposed to finish, Colin? 'You can't murder someone who doesn't…*exist*'?"

Nick's head jerked in Lois's direction.

"I…um…" Colin stammered.

Nate squeezed her eyes shut. This was it. Exactly the moment she'd been dreading. Her friendship was about to go up in flames, along with her career. Lois could easily fire her for this. She *should*.

Drawing a huge breath, she opened her eyes, raised her chin, and met Lois's trademark stare, scarily potent, and trained on Nate for the first time since they'd known each other.

"Yes," Nate declared. "That's what he was going to say. That you can't murder someone who doesn't exist." Another inhale. "Because Walter doesn't."

They held each other's gazes for a long minute. Nate imploring. Lois…unreadable.

She wished Lois would say something, but instead she only nodded slightly, with a brief twist of her mouth.

"Geez, when I said I wanted the dirt, I never expected fake bodies buried in the fake basement," Nick muttered.

Lois turned her gaze on her husband, who shrugged with a mix of sheepishness and mild defiance. In the space of a few seconds, they seemed to have an entire silent conversation.

That over with, Lois straightened off the desk. "So. We're all on the same page. Now what?"

Shiiiit. That's it? That's all she's going to say?

Nick cleared his throat, regaining some control. "Right. Well, as we've established"—here, he flashed a simultaneously apologetic and sardonic glance at Nate—"it's not actually murder when the subject of the plot is fictional. *Jesus.* However, there are precisely four people in this town who know that Walter Guffman does not exist." Another glance. "There are only four, right?" At Nate's pathetic nod, he continued. "And they are currently sitting in this room. Which does not help us in the slightest."

"I suppose not," Colin responded, attempting to rally. "But even hearing what we said, would he really believe it to be true anyway? Do we strike anyone as cold-blooded killers?"

"Maybe not, but he's a young, impressionable actor. Apparently with a healthy imagination. And three of the five films he's made here have been noir." Nick lifted a shoulder. "It's not all that surprising that his mind would go there."

"Ugh. Actors," Colin muttered. He glanced back up at Nick and Lois. "No offense."

"None taken," Nick fired back.

Lois said nothing. Again.

Nate looked back and forth between the men. Lois—and Nick, for that matter—knew her secret now, causing her queasiness to increase exponentially. All the while, these two were holding a discourse on the gullibility of actors.

She bit her lip and craned her neck to look skyward. Wishing for a lightning bolt to put her out of her misery. Or maybe an anvil. Where was that beeping cartoon bird when a woman needed him?

A terrible thought broke through the chaos in her mind. "Nick, what did you say to Madison? Where is he now?"

"I did manage to calm him down. Somehow. I assured him that it must have been a gross misunderstanding, that knowing the two of you, there was no way he could have heard what he thought he did." He rolled his eyes. "God, you've turned me into Charles Boyer in *Gaslight* now."

She wanted to argue, in principle, but he wasn't exactly wrong. So she held her tongue.

Lois mysteriously continued to hold her own tongue, doing absolutely nothing to temper Nate's anxiety.

Nick shook his head and continued, "I also swore to get to the bottom of it immediately, and extracted a promise from him to keep his mouth shut."

"Do you think he will?" Colin asked.

"Yes, I do. For now, anyway."

That should have reassured her, but Nate felt miserable. Her lie—her *life*—was unraveling faster than a sweater at a moth buffet.

She dropped her head in her hands, not bothering to contain her groan. "When did my life become such a farce?"

"That's it!" Colin's voice held a disgusting amount of optimism.

"What?" Nick asked.

She looked up at Colin. "Yeah. What?"

"A farce. That's what we tell Mr. Madison. That I'm writing a farce."

"I...huh?" The whole situation must really be getting to her, because Nate's brain felt astonishingly sluggish. More so than it usually did in fraught circumstances.

"I'm a writer. A comedy writer. So we say that what he heard were lines...from a noir parody I'm working on."

"That's not bad," Nick ventured, sounding genuinely intrigued.

"No, it's not," Lois agreed, finally inserting herself into the proceedings.

"You're joking, right?" Nate asked. Peripherally she caught Lois's head snapping in her direction, but she remained too petrified to look at her directly. So she pressed on with Colin. "Why the hell would he believe *I* was reading dialogue with you?"

Colin shrugged. "It's no secret that I've been consulting with you on some of my upcoming pieces. And we writers read our stuff aloud all the time. It's really helpful, actually."

"Yeah," Nick chimed in, "and most actors think writers are a bit odd anyway, so this wouldn't be much of a stretch." He nodded to Colin. "No offense."

"None taken."

The echo of their earlier exchange had Nate feeling like she was in some sort of sick time warp. She couldn't stop blinking at them.

Nick nodded as he started pacing again. "This is good. I can use this." He pointed a finger at Colin. "And I can sweeten it by promising him a part in it."

She looked at him in horror. "A part? In a film that..."

"Doesn't exist?" Nick smirked. "Believe me, the irony is not at all lost."

She curled her lip and practically snarled at him. "Seriously, though, what are you going to do when the part never manifests?"

Lois's cool voice answered, "Projects get shelved all the time."

Nate's sneer promptly deflated.

"Right," Nick agreed. "And we can find something better for him in the meantime. He might be a pain in our ass right now, but he's a pretty decent actor."

"It sounds like you all have this under some semblance of control now, and I have a very busy afternoon, so..." Lois straightened the hem of her jacket with a sharp tug. "Keep me posted on any further developments." She placed a quick kiss on Nick's cheek—which could have lessened the impact of her pronouncement, but somehow didn't—before sweeping out of the room.

The click of the door behind her echoed like a cannon blast.

Nate swallowed around the lump in her throat. Over the years, she had witnessed all manner of incredibly impressive tantrums from Lois. The woman had reigned supreme as the biggest diva in Hollywood for nearly a decade, after all. But this. This icy, quiet...*stillness* from her.

It terrified Nate.

As if her world hadn't just imploded, Colin let out a small

cough. "I...um...I could actually write it, you know," he offered. "The script, that is. The genre's so popular right now, it's just asking for a satirical take."

Is he shitting me?

"I don't know." *Thank you, Nick.* "You've got a lot going on right now, Colin. I don't want to stretch you too thin."

Thanks a lot, Nick.

She rolled her eyes. Neither of them noticed.

This typically would have been the moment when she turned to Lois in search of agreement on the absurdity of men, but Lois had left the room. And likely their friendship.

Nate's heart sank even further.

Colin was still talking, though. "I'm sure I can fit it in."

"Hold off for now," Nick replied. "Although maybe it would be a good idea to at least put together a treatment. Even just a page would do. The more concrete things we can present to Madison, the better it'll sell the story."

"That much I can do right away. This afternoon, even."

"Good." Nick inhaled. "Yes, this is good. I think this will work."

Do they remember I'm still in the room?

Nate split her glare between the two of them, finding it much easier to dwell on her anger over this part of the conversation. "Great. Well, if you two have this all figured out, are we done here?"

Colin took her hand. "Nate. Don't worry. I think Nick's correct. We can make this right. All of it."

The earnest concern in his eyes nearly unhinged her. Her heartbreak over Lois's reaction simmered, ready to boil over, and the last thing she needed was for him to stoke the fire by being his usual comforting self. If she stopped directing her ire at him and Nick, she'd turn it on herself. And focusing on them was so much more satisfying.

Nick interjected, "Why don't you go start on that treatment, Colin? The sooner I can set things up with Madison, the better."

"Of course." He stood. "Can I walk you back to your office, Nate?"

She rose to follow him, but Nick stopped her with a hand on her arm. "Actually, Nate, can I have a word? If you don't mind."

Delightful. There's more.

"Yeah. Sure."

Colin looked uncertain about leaving her, but her half-hearted attempt at a smile evidently reassured him. He nodded, thanked Nick, and was gone.

She sucked in a breath to steady herself before turning back to Nick. She did at least owe him an apology. "I am sorry you had to deal with this today."

He nodded. The way he stood there, hands in his pockets, regarding her with sympathy, but still dead serious—did nothing to calm her already obliterated nerves.

Nick inhaled, eyes locked on hers. "Lois didn't know." It wasn't a question.

"No. She didn't."

"How in the hell...?" He shook his head. "Sorry. That part doesn't matter at the moment. I apologize for bringing Lois in without giving you any warning. I didn't mean to ambush you, but time was of the essence, and I didn't want her hearing about this from anyone other than us. And I assumed..." He trailed off.

"That she was in the loop."

"Yeah." He offered her a small, sheepish smile. "You've got to admit, it's more than weird that she wasn't."

"Believe me, I know." She had no idea why Nick was so calm, so supportive. She'd earned his anger nearly as much as Lois's, what with Madison having come to him with this.

"If it helps, I was planning to tell her soon. Ish." She tried for a steadying breath. "I really, truly am sorry."

He nodded. "I'm sure you had your reasons. God, this explains *so* much. You know I'm going to need all the details at some point." He smirked. "Don't tell anyone I said this, but you might be a better actor than I am."

She huffed a laugh, grateful for his attempt to lighten the mood.

All too soon, he sobered. "Even without knowing the details, I understand how complicated this is for you, especially when it comes to Lois. But that's just it. Now…it's not only complicated for you anymore. What happened today makes this complicated for a lot of people. Lois. Me. It affects the studio now."

Hearing it spelled out in such stark terms… Forget the floor. Her stomach was subterranean now. What part of the globe was opposite California? Wherever it was, that's where the organ fell, probably bursting through the ground and scaring everyone in its immediate vicinity. *Maybe Colin could turn his farce into a B-movie— "The Stomach that Ate…Europe?"*

She groaned inwardly. Nick was absolutely right. She'd had no business letting things get this far. Leading Lois into exactly what she'd feared with regard to Phoenix.

"We're damn lucky I'm the one Madison came to with this," Nick continued. "He could have easily gone to the police. Or worse, the gossip rags." He offered her a small smile, which she felt too sick to return. "He also could have taken it to Lois first."

"But he didn't."

"No. He didn't. But probably only because she terrifies him. And he played my kid brother in a film last year, so he trusts me."

Nate latched onto that, desperate to find a silver lining somewhere. "And you are confident about Colin's idea?"

Said idea still pissed her off, but if it made all this go away without everything crashing in on Lois and the studio, then she could get behind it.

"I am," Nick replied. "As rattled as he was, Alex really did seem like he hated believing the worst of you two. That, and wanting to keep his career on track, were probably what kept him from taking this outside the lot. I'm pretty confident I can fix this, keep it contained, but…there is always that slim chance I can't. We have to prepare for all of it." He took a breath. "And that's why I included Lois in this meeting. Why she needs to know every detail now."

His reasoning was absolutely sound; she knew that deep down. But it didn't ease the pressure in her chest.

Nick's comforting hand settled on her arm before he continued. "Nate. You know I have your back. And I'm going to do everything in my power to set this to rights." He hesitated, growing even more sober. "But you also know that Lois is my everything. And this studio is her dream. Protecting it, protecting *her*, is always going to be my number one priority."

"I know," she whispered.

"You've known her longer than I have. She's worked her ass off to get here. But there are still plenty of people in the wings, just waiting for her to fail, ready to pounce the minute there's even the slightest whiff of blood in the air. If it were to get out that she was harboring a real-life Stanwyck and MacMurray?"

Nate groaned. "Disaster wouldn't even begin to cover it."

How did I let this get so *out of control?*

"Hey." He bent down to meet her eye. "I don't think it's going to come to that. But if it does...it would've been that much worse if she didn't see it coming. She can't get out ahead of it if she's broadsided."

"I get it."

She just wished it hadn't cost her the whole of what existed between them. If Lois had at least gotten angry... But she hadn't, and that awful silence felt like a death knell.

The abject misery churning through her must have been evident on her face, because Nick pulled her into a bear hug. "Come here."

Her head met his chest with a thunk as she groaned again.

"She'll come around," Nick said, voice filled with a quiet certainty she didn't feel.

"You really believe that?"

"I do. Just be honest with her now. Tell her the whole story."

"Any chance I could just spill my guts to you, and then you can tell her for me?"

Nick chuckled. "As tempting as that offer is, I think it'll be better coming from you." His chin came to rest on the crown of her head. "But I can be there with you, if you want."

She smiled at that, and pulled back to look at him. "You really want that gossip, don't you?"

"You know it." He winked.

"Thanks, but I need to do this on my own."

"Makes sense."

Nate filled her lungs, wishing she could inhale courage like air. Even a smidgeon would do.

"I've really created a big fucking cock-up, haven't I?"

"Yeah."

She smacked his arm, eliciting a grin.

"But," he continued, "you can fix it. *We* can fix it."

"You think so?"

"I am absolutely certain of it."

"She was just so…cold," she breathed. She looked up at Nick again. "I don't see how she'll ever forgive me."

She didn't dare hope. But then Nick nodded.

"If you can stop underestimating yourself—and your friend-ship—I have no doubt in my mind that she will."

Tears sprung to her eyes at that.

She could do this. She could. She had to. Come completely clean with Lois and beg for a second chance, somewhere down the line when all the smoke cleared. It was time to rip off the Band-Aid. Dive into the deep end. Out of the frying pan. Bite the bullet. And all that rot.

When this was all over, she needed to get Colin to write her some new metaphors.

Chapter Twenty-Two

 ate's shoulders sagged, her mind endlessly reeling from the chaos. Twelve years without a misstep, and now everything had gone to complete and utter shit.

As much as she needed to get it over with and talk to Lois before she lost her nerve, she had to wait a few hours. It was the middle of a workday, after all, with deadlines that couldn't be put off. Plus, given her track record lately, the studio was hardly the place to have this conversation. The last thing she needed was to be overheard. Again.

Complete and utter shit—what an understatement.

Well, that wasn't entirely true. Despite how much he scrambled her brain, Colin did make her happy. Happier than she'd been in...she couldn't remember when. If only they could stay alone together in their little bubble. Far from eavesdropping actors and friendship-killing mistakes.

And her *farcical* life.

With all the awful things that occurred in Nick's office, she had a veritable buffet of crap to dwell on. But as she forced herself to push everything with Lois aside until she could properly deal with it, the farce idea rose up to tap persistently on her last nerve. She wished it didn't rankle so much. That it had come from Colin stung the most. Even the times when he'd questioned her decisions, he'd made it clear he was simply trying to gain a better understanding of her. He was always so solicitous of her feelings, rarely judgmental.

A knock at her door pulled her from her thoughts. Though not very far.

Colin stood in the doorway, a tentative smile on his face.

"Do you have a minute?" he asked.

Nate managed a wan smile. "Sure. Come on in."

He did, making a point of fully closing the door this time, despite the fact that she'd sent Rose home early. He walked over to stand in front of her desk, examining her face closely. She should have been touched by his concern, but the emotion eluded her.

"What's up?" Her voice came out even more flat than she intended.

"I wanted to make sure you're all right."

"I'm just swell. Thanks."

"Nate."

She opened her mouth to retort, but the words stalled when she truly took in his face for the first time. Filled with not only worry, but that fierce expression she was growing used to—the one that hinted he'd cut off a limb if he thought it would ease her discomfort. She started to melt.

Her mouth eased into a smile. "Okay, I'm not swell. But I'll get there."

Colin reached across her desk to trace his fingers down her cheek. "I am so sorry I didn't make sure that door was closed."

Nate shrugged. "I should have been more careful too. It was hardly the conversation to get into here at work."

"Well, I meant what I said earlier. We will make this right. I'm sure of it." He looked as if he wanted to say more, but stopped himself, instead reaching into the inside pocket of his jacket. He pulled out a sheet of paper. "That's the other reason I'm here, in fact. I wanted to show you this before I take it over to Nick."

She took the paper from him and glanced at it. *Oh.* "The treatment. Right."

And there was the sting again.

Confusion flitted across Colin's features. "Do you not think it's a good idea?"

"No, it's great. Should do the trick."

"What is it?"

"Nothing." She handed the page back to him. "You and Nick seem to have it well in hand. So much so that I am a bit surprised you'd even need to show this to me."

"Of course I would show it to you. It's your concern, more than any of us. It's your life."

Nate snapped. "Yes, Colin. Yes. It *is* my life." She pushed out of her chair and threw up her hands. "My *farce* of a life."

She watched as his surprise morphed into understanding.

"Nate...surely you don't think... You know I don't believe you're actually a farce."

"How, Colin?" She practically shouted now. "How am I supposed to know that? Your perfect little solution certainly implies otherwise."

"My..." He shook his head. "You were the one who called your life a farce in the first place."

"And you jumped on the idea awfully quick." She waved her hand impatiently. "Hell, you're ready to write the whole damn movie!"

"To get us out of being perceived as homicidal noir villains!"

Nate let out a growl of frustration and turned from him. Her anger continued to mount and contort, the early pricking of tears stinging behind her eyes. She ground her teeth together. She refused to cry in front of him. Not again.

When she moved to lean on the shelf under her window, of course her gaze landed right on the baseball. That *fucking* baseball.

It was all too much.

She picked up the ball and hurled it across the room. It hit the wall with a dull thud and rolled down behind the couch. She slumped forward, bracing her arms on the shelf, exhausted.

Nate felt Colin's warmth at her back. His hands gently came to rest on her shoulders. Of their own volition, they began to relax under his touch.

"Nate," he began, his lovely voice rough with emotion, "I do not think you are a joke. Far from it. I think you are… extraordinary." She squeezed her eyes shut against the tears that threatened in earnest now. "I never meant to hurt you, not in a million years." His thumbs rubbed slow circles on her neck. "I was only sparking off what you said. And it made sense to me, because I'm a comedy writer. It's where I'm comfortable. It's what people would believe. It's what *I* can do to fix this."

He brushed her hair aside and his lips came to rest on the back of her neck. Her entire body pulsed with warmth, her anger ebbing away.

"And I'm desperate to fix this, Nate." His voice vibrated against her skin. "For you. Because you've…come to mean the world to me."

She let out a long breath and turned to face him.

He ran a finger under her chin. "You do believe me, don't you? You are not a farce to me."

She nodded. "I do. And I'm sorry too."

"What do you have to apologize to me for?"

Nate huffed and gestured to…everything. "All of this. But also because…I suppose it's a hell of a lot easier being mad at you than at myself."

"Perhaps. But I should have realized the implications of what I was suggesting."

She slid her arms around his waist and leaned into his strong, tweedy chest. "What really kills me is that if it were happening to anyone else, I'd probably be the first to call out the comedic gold of it all."

His arms wrapped around her and held tight. "It's rather different when you're the one living it, though, isn't it?"

"Yup."

They both chuckled, remaining still for a few minutes. It wasn't long before their breathing matched up, and Nate began to feel that beautiful Colin safety again.

As much as she wanted to linger there for the rest of the day, they both had places they needed to be. She pulled back to look at him.

"You should get that treatment over to Nick."

"Are you sure you don't want to look at it?"

Nate shook her head. "No, it's okay. I'm sure it's fine."

"All right." He bent to kiss her, his lips warm and soft. "Dinner tonight?"

She smoothed his tie, more out of habit than actual necessity. "I'd love to, but I can't." She peered up at him. "I have to go talk to Lois."

Colin drew in a breath. "Right, of course. I was going to bring it up earlier, but I wasn't sure if you were ready to talk about it yet." He hesitated. "She did take the news rather…calmly."

Nate snorted. "That's for sure." She met his concerned eyes. "And that, quite frankly, terrifies me."

"Oh, Nate." He cradled her cheek in his palm.

"Nick seems to think she'll forgive me once I tell her the whole sordid truth."

Colin offered her a tiny smile. "I'd like to think he knows her pretty well at this point. He's probably right, no?"

Nate chewed on her bottom lip. "I don't know. I hope so, but…" She drew in a huge breath. "But there's only one way to find out. I can't put it off any longer. Not now. I owe her an explanation. Among other things."

He nodded. "I'd offer to accompany you, but I'm guessing you wouldn't want that."

She smiled. "I'd love the moral support, but no. It does need to be just us."

"Do you want me to at least drive you over? I could wait in the car, or come back for you when you're finished?"

"That's tempting, but I have no idea how long I'll be."

"I don't mind."

She gave him a lingering kiss. "That means a lot, but I'll be okay. Really. I think I'll lose my nerve if I don't drive myself. If that makes any sense." She shrugged.

"Hey, whatever you need to do." He glanced at the treatment on the desk behind him with a resigned sigh.

"Go. Get that to Nick so he can start the damage control." She nudged him toward the door.

"I really do think it'll work."

"I think I do, too."

Colin turned before opening the door, and took her hand. "Call me when you get home tonight? It doesn't matter how late. I want to be sure you're all right."

Warmth bloomed again, starting in her chest and working its way everywhere.

"Thanks. I will."

He nodded. "Trust Lois, but even more…trust yourself, Nate. You've got this." He bent down and pressed his lips to hers. "And I've got you."

She hoped he was right.

Chapter Twenty-Three

*T*he setting sun cast an orange glow as Nate trudged up the walk to Lois and Nick's front door. She felt like she should be humming Chopin's *Funeral March*. She paused with her hand hovering over the doorbell, desperately attempting to muster what little courage she had.

Positive thoughts, Reynolds. You are a confident, competent woman. You can make magic with a scrap of fabric. You can come clean and earn Lois's forgiveness. Eventually. Maybe.

Oh, what she wouldn't give for some courage in the form of Max's cake right now. Maybe she should make a run to Burbank first...

No. Get it together. Focus.

Lois. Walter. Whole truth.

She cast her eyes skyward in a last-ditch plea to every goddess who might be listening. And maybe a few saints. Was there a patron saint of film noir? Or farce? Or lying?

Come to think of it, could one even pray to a saint if she wasn't Catholic?

Quit. Stalling.

Right. Her finger made contact with the bell, and she heard it echo on the other side of the door. No turning back now.

Footsteps sounded right before the door swung open to reveal Lois, in wide-legged pants and what looked to be one of Nick's cardigans. She was clearly in for the evening and ready to relax, and Nate's resolve wavered. That resolve took a nose-dive when she glanced at Lois's face, dispassionate despite Nate's unexpected arrival at her home.

"Nate. Hi."

"I can come back another time…"

Lois's voice was careful when she spoke. "You're here now. Come on in."

Nate crossed the threshold and Lois closed the door behind her. It was no louder than most doors, but the sound of it latching reverberated like a boom in her ears.

Lois came to stand beside her. Waiting.

Nate gulped. Somehow she'd fix this. *Whatever it takes.*

"I…" she began, unable to meet Lois's eyes. "I wanted to… um…talk. To you."

Quality beginning there, smarty-pants.

Before she could continue—not that she knew how—Nick bounded down the stairs, all relaxed energy despite the chaos she'd plunged them all into.

"Lo, I was thinking—" He looked up as his foot hit the bottom step. "Oh. Nate. Hey."

"Hey."

"Nate dropped by for a little quality chatting time," Lois said drily, before giving him an affectionate smirk. "Think you can fend for yourself for a while?"

Nick looked between them, hope warring with trepidation. "Of course. As a matter of fact, I was just thinking about something Max was…dealing with…the other day, so maybe I'll pop over and pay him a visit instead of picking up the phone. See if he's…got it under control and…stuff." He flashed Lois a brilliant grin. "That way I'll be out of your hair."

"Perfect."

Nate fought the urge to roll her eyes. He didn't need to invent a pretense to leave. But Lois didn't seem perturbed—by him, anyway—so perhaps it was simple over-sensitivity on her part.

He strolled across the room and grabbed his jacket off the coatrack, along with a set of keys from the hall table.

"I'll be sure to take my time." Nick bent to give Lois a peck. "Love you."

"Love you, too. Say hi to Max."

When Lois turned her back, he gave Nate a small smile and a nod, punctuated by a gentle squeeze to her arm. It was surprisingly reassuring.

"See you later, Nate."

"Bye, Nick."

When he left, Nate followed Lois over to the couch. Lois's cat, Lady Macbeth, sent a mewing noise in their general direction from her position in front of the fireplace. Nate wasn't sure if the cat was offering her moral support or simple acknowledgment, but she'd take what she could get.

As soon as Nate settled into the cushions next to her friend, Lois wasted no time. "So."

Why the hell is she so calm? Couldn't she at least raise her voice? A smidge? That *I could work with.*

All this time, she'd braced for an explosion when Lois finally found out. But this reaction was positively *killing* Nate. Perhaps Lois knew that, and was simply twisting the knife as she waited for her to start.

Nate tried. Several times. But forcing the words past the boulder lodged in her throat proved damn near impossible.

Seeming to sense her incapacitation, or maybe out of her own impatience, Lois broke the awkward silence. "You know, when our little party in Nick's office began this afternoon, I half expected it to come out that Walter found out about Colin and challenged him to pistols at dawn on the lot."

Nate's strangled laugh finally dislodged that boulder.

"But the story was much more intriguing than that." Lois

continued to speak quietly, deliberately. "Walter does not, in fact, exist. Because you fucking made him up." She folded her arms across her chest and cocked her head, studying Nate.

Who tried to swallow. A little more successfully this time.

"I suppose I should start at the beginning, shouldn't I?"

She owed Lois a hell of a lot more than that, but she did have to start somewhere. The beginning was as good a place as any. She sucked in a huge breath. "I don't know if I ever mentioned it, but when I was starting out, I interviewed at RKO before I landed at Parkmoor…"

It was as if she'd pulled the plug on the bathtub drain, all the details crowding at the edge of her larynx, fighting to pour out. *Or maybe a stopped-up toilet is a better analogy?* She ran through that god-awful interview when her mouth had first shoved her down this yellow-bellied brick road, then proceeded to walk Lois through everything. The counterfeit DiMaggio, the years of cover-ups, the way it had started catching up to her the minute she'd met Colin.

At some point, she pushed up off the couch to pace around the room. She didn't dare look at Lois for fear of what she'd see on her face. Now that she'd at last started, she couldn't let anything stop her from getting this all out.

After the grand finale of the day's misadventures in murder-plotting, Nate collapsed back onto the couch and buried her head in her hands.

"So there you have it. My whole sordid little tale."

Lois inhaled next to her, and she braced for the impact.

"Well, it's about damn time."

What?

"What?" She lowered her hands, but was still afraid to look at Lois.

"Do you have any idea how long I've been waiting for you to fess up about Walter?"

That jerked her head up.

"Wha… I…" Nate shook her head in a futile attempt to clear it. "You *knew*? Before today? *How*?"

Lois speared her with a sardonic glare. "Do you really think so little of my intelligence and perception skills—of our *friendship*—that I wouldn't figure it out?" She crossed her arms. "I will admit, I didn't know for certain until today. But I have had my suspicions for quite some time now. Give me a little credit, won't you?"

Nate blinked.

Is it too much to ask that one *person react to this the way I expect them to?*

"I…um… But you were so awfully quiet this afternoon. Does this mean you're…not mad then?" Nate held her breath.

"Oh, I did not say that. I've just had some time to simmer."

And there it is.

"Plus, I will admit to a perverse desire to let you stew in it for a while," Lois conceded. "And look, while I know all the details now, you still have some serious explaining to do. The last thing I —and I'm guessing, you—expected was for this to come to light in such a spectacular festival of fuckery this afternoon. How in the hell could you not tell me before, Nate?"

Nate swallowed. "I…I don't know. I'm sorry. I've just been terrified of…this. The end of a beautiful friendship. But here we are anyway."

Lois jerked back, startled. "Whoa. Hold on a minute. Who said anything about our friendship being over? Do you really have that little faith in me? In us?"

Nate could only stare at her, stunned.

And then she dissolved. The sheer weight of it all hit her in a sudden, overwhelming wave. Hot tears ran down her cheeks before she even realized she was crying.

She sensed Lois's alarm, but was powerless to stop the waterworks. Needed them to come, even. Nate had expected anger, anguish, loss. She'd assumed the worst. Feared the worst. But she should have known, should have trusted Lois. Just as Colin, and Nick today, had told her to. She saw now how right they'd been.

But she'd let her fear—her stupid, stupid fear—overrule everything. And that was what killed her now. She realized, with perfect clarity, that what hurt Lois the most—what actually threatened their friendship—was how easily Nate had believed it couldn't survive this.

A loud sob escaped her. "God, Lois, I am so sorry."

Lois didn't say a word, simply scooted closer and wrapped her arms fiercely around Nate.

Which, of course, made Nate cry even harder.

But her dearest friend in the world held on tight, riding out the tsunami with her. Lending her strength.

She must have truly been a mess, because even Lady Macbeth jumped up on her other side to offer a nuzzle and a purr, in a rare display of comfort and solidarity.

Eventually their ministrations worked, her calm and control returning. Lois sensed it too, because she eased her grip and rested her chin on the top of Nate's head.

"You're a fool, you know that?"

Nate let out a strangled laugh. "I do know that, actually."

Lois joined her laughter for a moment before pulling back, all seriousness. "I need you to listen, and listen good. Yes, I am angry—and hurt—that you kept all this from me, and would have continued doing so if not for all that ridiculousness that transpired at work, of all places. And we are going to talk about *all* of it. You're not leaving this room until we do." She inhaled sharply. "But I am not going anywhere, Nate Reynolds. You are my family. Hell, you're more of a sister to me than my own sister."

That elicited a choked sob from Nate, but Lois continued. "You were there for me when absolutely no one else was. I'm not happy that you haven't let me return the favor, but now that I'm in the loop, you better believe I'm going to start now. There is no way you are getting rid of me that easily, do you understand me?"

She nodded. "I do."

Lois pulled her into another hug. "Good."

She released her and reached into her pocket to extract a hand-kerchief, which she handed to Nate. "Here. You need this."

"Thanks."

Lois patted her lap definitively and stood. "Now. You have a ton more explaining to do, and then we should probably do some serious strategizing in case Nick can't win Madison over. But if we have any hope of accomplishing either, we are going to need sustenance first. Nick opened a bottle of very good Scotch last night, and there's still most of it left. Or…I've also got a couple slices of Max's chocolate cheesecake. Which would you prefer?"

Nate looked up through her lashes at her. "Both?"

Lois's answering grin warmed her through and through. "That's my girl." She pointed a warning finger at her. "Don't move. I'll be right back."

Nate did as instructed, head swimming. She absently scratched Lady M's head, continuing to draw calm from the cat's warmth. While she didn't relish the conversation to come, she could barely contain her thrill that Lois was still in her corner. At the same time, she was furious with herself for letting it all get to this messy, awful point.

She really was too dramatic for her own good.

Lois returned with two glasses, the bottle of Scotch tucked under her arm, and a plate bearing a huge slab of cheesecake and two forks.

"I figured it was easier if we just shared," she explained as Nate took the plate from her.

"Fine by me."

Lois settled back on the couch and opened the bottle.

"Are you sure Nick won't mind if we drink that?" Nate asked.

"Nah. That sexy little fucker was far too excited at the prospect of gossip this afternoon. We're taking the whisky."

Nate snickered. "I won't argue with that." She paused. "Speaking of gossip… I'd been working up the courage to finally tell you. As a matter of fact, when you came over the other day—"

Lois handed her a glass with a raised eyebrow. "Now, hold on just a minute. You didn't know I was coming."

"No, I didn't. But I *was* already planning to talk to you when you surprised me. And I would have…"

Lois's mouth twisted. "If I hadn't led with a request to warn me about potential scandals?"

"Absurdly enough, yes. And it blew up in my face anyway." Nate shot her a small smile. "I really was agonizing over it, though. If it makes you feel any better."

"It does." Lois shook her head. "Twelve years. That is…quite the long con, my friend."

"You have no idea." She set down her glass and went in for a bite of the cheesecake perched on the cushion between them. "So how long have you known?"

"I suppose not that long, in the scheme of things. But my suspicions have been getting bigger for a while now. I mean, I've always thought your situation with Walter was weird, but you were so reluctant to talk about it, I didn't bother to examine it too closely. Not until everything you did for me last year."

"What did that have to do with Walter?"

"Nothing, really. But I was more appreciative than ever for the way you always are, so ready to march into battle on behalf of the people you care about. You don't take shit from anyone, Nate. Plus, you've always been the first to call me on my bullshit. I started to seriously wonder why you seemed to take it from a husband, of all people." Lois shrugged. "And then once I started paying more attention, little things jumped out. I mean, never meeting him was one thing, but then I realized I'd never even seen a photo of him. It didn't add up."

Nate chuckled ruefully. "I should've known I wouldn't be able to put one over on you forever."

"Damn right, you should have."

"I mean, Colin figured it out, and he's only known me a fraction of the time you have."

"I knew you weren't only interested in that velvet sin voice."

She smiled. "I'm actually surprised you didn't figure out that I had figured it out."

"How do you figure?"

Lois snorted. "Oh, come on. I haven't exactly been subtle lately, trying to draw you out." She waved her fork at Nate. "Why do you think I've been so eager to push you at Colin? Granted, I do think you two crazy kids are fantastic for each other. But I also really wanted to see you crack and fess up, thus proving my hunch."

"Of course you did."

A rare hint of chagrin sparked in Lois's eyes. "I have to admit, that was part of the reason I stopped by for my little fishing expedition last week. Yes, all the junk in the paper annoys the shit out of me. And I most certainly want Phoenix to stay as scandal-free as humanly possible." She offered Nate a small smirk. "But I also wanted to see if you'd avail yourself of the opening I was presenting on a silver platter."

Nate stared at her, open-mouthed, for a long moment.

Lois nudged her. "See, you should've just come right out with it." She huffed. "I really thought you would when I spotted that jacket."

Nate found her voice. "The jacket? Why the hell would that have done it?"

Lois inclined her head as if Nate was a small child. "Because Nick wore it in that screwball a few months back?"

"No, he… Oh, fuck me. He did." She buried her face in her hands with a groan.

Lois chuckled. "So you've been embezzling my husband's costumes from my studio to make it look like a man lives in your house, in case anyone drops by unannounced?"

"You say that like it's a problem."

Nate dropped her hands and met Lois's eye, and they both laughed. It was beautiful.

Lois smacked Nate's arm. "See, that is exactly the kind of fun charade we could have been pulling *together* all this time. I do have a few acting skills myself, you know." She sipped her whisky, sobering as she swallowed. "Why didn't you tell me, Nate?"

Here it was. Her real moment of truth. Nate knew her reasons were likely to sound ridiculous once finally spoken aloud, but there was no way she could avoid it any longer. Especially since Lois was being so wonderful, despite her more than justifiable hurt.

"It's stupid, but at first it was…embarrassment more than anything." Lois regarded her with serious attention, so she found the guts to continue. "When you came to Parkmoor, I'd already been living with my lie for a while. And you met me as exactly the person I liked presenting to the world. Excellent at my job—all the parts of it. Not just the obvious ones."

"The counseling aspect. The listening and advice."

"Yeah. What was I supposed to say? 'Here's how to solve your problem, and oh, by the way, I invented a husband and have been lying to everyone about it for years.' Hardly lends itself to credibility, that." She huffed. "And then when we got to know each other, really become friends, I still didn't know how to tell you. I guess I didn't want you to think less of me."

"That's absurd. I couldn't possibly think less of you." At the look Nate leveled her, Lois winked. "Really, though, I would have understood."

"My sister didn't."

Lois drew in breath. "Wait a minute. *That's* why you and Mallory haven't spoken in years? Over this?"

Nate nodded. "She let me know, in no uncertain terms, how much she disapproved of my life choices. Before I knew it, we'd drifted so far apart that she was just…gone from my life." Her voice cracked. "I couldn't let that happen with you."

"Jesus, Nate." Lois grabbed her hand. "I am *not* Mallory. I meant what I said earlier. We may not be related, but you're my chosen sister. And I'm yours."

Nate squeezed Lois's hand back, unable to find the words.

"Your sister's never known the ins and outs of a career in this business. But I have. I know better than anyone that we all do what we have to, to survive."

"But I guess that's part of it too, Lois. All the shit you had to endure to get where you are? You had so much to put up with, all the time. I didn't want to pile on by burdening you with my secret on top of it."

"The way I burdened you with my problems?"

Nate's eyes flew wide. "That's not what I meant..."

Lois held up a hand. "I know you didn't. But we're friends, Nate. That's part of the beauty of having friends—being able to share each other's burdens. And it sounds like you held back because you thought your load was less significant than mine?"

"That's exactly it." Relief washed over her at Lois's understanding.

Lois nodded slowly. "That's bullshit."

So much for that relief.

"I beg your pardon?"

"You heard me. It's bullshit."

Nate opened her mouth for rebuttal, but Lois cut her off.

"No. It's my turn now. You honestly think that you're not a survivor too? Yes, you told a lie. A big one. But why? Because some idiot man denied you a job you were more than qualified to do, for an asinine reason. So you did what you had to do to secure the next one. And then you went on to carve out the career you wanted. You've more than earned your reputation as one of the best designers in this business."

Lois laid her hand on Nate's again before continuing. "But, hon, just because the shit you had to put up with wasn't as extreme as mine, or your path wasn't as dramatic, does not mean you had it easy. Everything you've built, you built while carrying a huge secret. All by yourself. Your pain might be different, but that doesn't make it any less."

Nate nodded, letting Lois's words sink in. She felt that familiar prickling behind her eyes again, and leaned her head back on the couch, in the vain hope it would keep them in this time.

She grunted. "When the hell did I become such an unstoppable fountain?"

Lois laughed. "Hey, even the best of us need to let it out sometimes."

"But lately it's been happening at the drop of a hat. And the actual dropping of actual hats used to be the *only* thing that could make me cry."

"Well, hats or no hats, you are dealing with a lot. Living in fear of unburdening yourself to friends, mind-blowing sex with a dashing Brit on the regular, murder accusations... I can understand how you could be overwhelmed."

That brought a laugh to the surface, and Nate leaned into it gratefully before returning to reality again.

"Speaking of murder accusations, I am so sorry I let that happen. Nick does seem to think he can get Madison under control, though."

Lois waved it off. "I'm sure he will. My husband could sell turtlenecks to a burlesque stripper."

"I hope so. I don't want my mistake reflecting back on you, not after everything you've gone through to get here. I can't believe I let it get this far. I can't apologize enough."

"No, you can't. But I'll be fine." Lois rolled her eyes with a flourish. "Honestly, it's not that much worse than some of what they've tried to accuse me of over the years. And now that I know about it, I can have some fun with my response." She held up a placating hand. "Not that it's going to get to the point where I need to respond. But I will be prepared just in case."

"Thanks. I think."

Lois's smile quickly turned to a snort of laughter.

"What?"

"Sorry, I was just thinking of what Madison's face must've looked like when he overheard you. The poor guy's eyes must have bugged out like a cartoon."

Nate let herself laugh as well. "Yeah, I can only imagine. I do feel kinda bad that we have to pull the wool over his eyes."

"He'll get over it." Her hand came down on Nate's shoulder. "And so will we."

"I'm really lucky to have you, you know that?"

"I do. And you are."

Nate shook her head.

But Lois wasn't finished. "Now, what are you going to do about Colin?"

Nate looked over at her, confused. "Colin?"

"Yes. When the dust settles from today's little melodrama, you are going to throw your fictional man over for him, aren't you? Twelve years is a long, lonely time. I know better than anyone the need to protect our hearts from the losers in this business, but Colin's like Nick. One of the rare good ones. He makes you happier than I've ever seen you."

Heat crept into Nate's cheeks. "Yeah, I am…"

"Uh-oh. But?"

"No buts. I'm going to get rid of Walter. I want to, now more than ever. But that's just it. I hate that what happened today makes the situation stickier. You have to admit, if I announce to the world that I've split up with my husband, right after someone thought I wanted to kill the guy, it might look a little fishy."

Lois considered for a moment, then nodded. "You're right. It is best to make sure this blows over first, what with the studio being involved and all." She leveled a finger at Nate's face. "But I do not believe you have to wait too long. Colin's good for you, so do not muff it."

She certainly didn't want to. Unease flitted through her, sharp and sudden, at the prospect of keeping up appearances even a little longer. Now that the weight of coming clean to Lois was off her shoulders, she wanted the rest of Walter's invisible dead weight gone as well. But the charade remained necessary. She shook off her impatience and instead focused outward.

"You know, you and Nick have become quite the matchmakers. You'd better be careful—you're starting down the road to 'old married couple' territory."

"Oh, shut up and have some more cheesecake."

Lois took a big bite herself, and Nate followed suit. She let herself revel in the fact that she was here, eating cake with her best friend.

She still had a best friend, even in the face of her deception. She could survive anything now.

Chapter Twenty-Four

"*I* can't tell you enough how sorry I am for missing that fitting, and for..." Alex Madison swallowed. "For everything else."

Nate had been surprised to see the young man show up in her office doorway a few minutes earlier, for the second time in only a few days. He'd arrived for his rescheduled fitting the day after everything hit the fan and spent most of their time falling all over himself, apologizing profusely. She honestly couldn't tell if he thought she'd be more upset with him over his having called her a murderess, or missing the fitting.

Either way, it fostered her hope they might just get away with all of this. Thank god.

And now here he was, back again. Before Nate could formulate a response, Alex thrust an arm in her direction. At the end of it was...quite possibly the most hideous bouquet of flowers she'd ever seen.

"These are for you," he finished with a sheepish, hopeful smile.

"Oh." Pushing away her morbid fascination over whether some of the handful could, in fact, be considered flowers, Nate schooled her face into a reassuring expression. "You really didn't have to, Alex."

"But I did! I feel just terrible, Ms. Reynolds."

So do I, looking at these flowers.

Instead, she replied, "Well, I appreciate the sentiment. Please, consider the whole thing forgotten." *And please forget it yourself.*

"Oh, you are so nice," Alex replied, with genuine sincerity.

"Don't mention it. And do enjoy your new part." Feeling generous, Nate winked and flashed him her most brilliant smile.

He blushed. "You heard about that?"

"I did. Congratulations. I'm sure you're going to knock it out of the park." The baseball reference might be laying it on a little thick, but given the circumstances it couldn't hurt.

Alex's cheeks gained even more color as his smile brightened. "Thanks, awfully. I hope I'll do it justice." He met her eyes briefly before his gaze darted off to the side. "I truly can't believe you're being this kind to me, after everything. Thank you again."

She leaned in conspiratorially. "What, did you think I'd leave some pins in your costumes? Or worse, dress you in yellow?" Not that she hadn't been tempted…

His wide eyes flew to hers again. *Oh, god, he really thought I would.* Nate beamed another dazzling smile, and they both laughed as his face relaxed.

"Perish the thought, Alex. Even I wouldn't be that cruel."

"No, you wouldn't," he sighed. "You…you really are just wonderful, Ms. Reynolds." He lurched toward her, but then stopped short. "Oh, geez. I'm so sorry. What am I thinking? The last thing you want is a hug from me."

Nate suppressed a snort. She could be intimidating when she wanted, but she was starting to wonder how much of a number Nick and Colin must've done on the poor man as well. Feeling magnanimous—along with wanting to help her case—she raised her arms and waved him in.

"Come on, then."

Alex's countenance melted in relief as he launched himself at her, squeezing tight for a flash before letting go just as quickly.

"You're the best, Ms. Reynolds."

He turned on his heel and fled the office. Nate stared after him in bewilderment, feeling more hopeful than anyone in her situation had a right to.

NATE SAT at her desk a few hours later, unable to tear her attention from Alex's strange bouquet—truly, it looked as if he'd gone around the florist's shop and asked for one of everything, heedless of form or color—and contemplated the odd turn of events that unfolded over the last several days.

Most surprising in the swirling jumble of her thoughts was her growing desire to throw caution to the wind. Not so much because it was unusual for her to do so, but more that it was actually premeditated for a change. Now that her twelve-year-old, tightly controlled bubble had burst, she had no desire to go back inside it.

Talking with Lois had gone so much better than she imagined, they'd managed to stave off Alex Madison and his assumptions, and she had a tweedy, deep-voiced, marvel of a man she wanted to parade around, announcing to all the world, "He's *mine*."

Not that she wasn't scared. The specter of Walter had been her security blanket for an age. A little part of her worried she'd have no clue how to operate in the world—in a relationship—without her parachute, her safety net, her out. But that was part of falling, wasn't it? Opening up to someone, building trust. And she'd never met someone who made her feel as seen, as *safe*, as Colin did.

She realized that her newfound determination to whip off her "married" cloak might be leaving Colin with a bit of whiplash—hell, she was feeling it herself too—but her determination mounted. She wanted it for both of them. And now that she had a team behind her, with Lois and Nick in on it too, her confidence grew exponentially. They could find a way to do this. Together. And *soon*.

With impeccable timing, Colin knocked on her open office door, looking delectable as always in his tweed.

She couldn't contain her bright smile. "Hi."

"Hello," he twinkled back. "We probably shouldn't be seen together too much right now, but I wanted to pop in and let you know, I saw Alex Madison again yesterday, and he seemed sufficiently contrite."

"Ah, that explains it. I was going to ask, what exactly did you and Nick say to him? I've never seen someone so apologetic."

Colin shrugged. "Only that..." He trailed off, eyes lighting on the explosion of mismatched color on her desk. "Good god. *What* is that?"

She grinned. "Alex gave it to me this morning."

His eyebrows lifted. "Well, then." He studied it for a moment, then scrunched his nose adorably. "Those orange things look more like mushrooms than flowers. Are you sure it was meant as an apology?"

Nate laughed. "If it had arrived by itself, I'd question it, but you should've seen his face. And his matching boutonnière." She shuddered. "This is really working, Colin."

"I'm glad."

Yes, they could absolutely do this. She took a breath to say just that, at the precise moment Lois appeared in the doorway behind him.

"Oh, hello." Lois shot Colin a sardonic glance. "I wasn't expecting to find you here, Colin."

He inclined his head. "Don't worry, I was just leaving."

"Actually, if you have a minute, the reason I'm here involves both of you."

"Of course."

Nate's excitement to share her plans with both of them grew exponentially, so she barely registered Lois's serious demeanor.

"Absolutely. As a matter of fact, there's something I'd like to run by you both, too."

"Okay then."

Was that hesitation in Lois's voice? No, she must be imagining it.

Nate ushered them over to her sitting area, as Colin shut the door behind Lois. When they were settled, Nate rushed in. "Mind if I go first?"

"Not at all. I—" Lois's lip curled. "Nate, you know I think your taste is flawless, but... I think perhaps the stress of everything is getting to you." She gestured at Nate's desk.

Colin snorted. "Are you insulting Nate's apology bouquet from Alex Madison?"

Lois whipped her head back around. "Oh, really? Well, then, do forgive me. He bought you flowers?"

"He did," Nate replied. "The groveling has been quite impressive. Even if the flowers are...not."

"The thought that counts, and all that, right?"

"Exactly. Which is a perfect segue." Nate took a steadying breath and split a look between Lois and Colin.

"I realize we've been talking about patience and caution, but... I'm ready to ditch Walter." A pang of trepidation zinged through her chest at their blank looks, but she soldiered on. "I mean, it's funny. This whole situation with Madison could have been such a disaster. I really thought it was the end of the world—for so many reasons. But it might just be the best thing that could have happened. I feel a new zip of courage. If we play this right, I don't see why we have to wait much longer at all."

Colin gave her a wan smile, but didn't say anything in response. Odd.

Lois looked resigned. "Oh. Right. That's great."

"Try to contain your enthusiasm, would you?"

Lois chuckled at Nate's sarcasm. "Sorry, I really do think it's wonderful that you want to move forward. I'm just...caught up in part of the reason I dropped by."

That didn't sound good. "Oh. What's going on?"

Lois visibly swallowed. *Uh-oh.* "I'm sorry to say it, especially given my encouragement the other night, but I believe it's not the best idea to dump Walter publicly just yet."

"But why? Things are going so well." She looked to Colin for support, but his already unsteady smile continued to waver. "Don't tell me you agree?"

"I..." He hesitated. "I do, actually."

She blinked at him. "I don't get it. You've been the one pushing me to get rid of him all along."

"I know. But that was before. When it was still only the two of us involved." Colin leaned over to cover her hand with his. "It's a lot bigger than us now."

Lois jumped back in. "I've been giving some more thought to the Brooks divorce, plus the resurrection of all those barbs at me in the press of late."

Nate nodded.

Lois continued, "I figured it couldn't hurt to pay a visit to our legal department this morning. I used all of that as an excuse to ask if we were prepared for any significant scandal happening here. In purely hypothetical terms, of course."

Nate's stomach flipped. "We're not, are we?"

Lois sighed. "Yes and no. I have every confidence in our team, but...they were pretty clear. This studio's reputation is still far too untested. Especially given the columnists' continued attempts, no news is good news coming out of here. At least for the time being."

Nate shut her eyes tightly. Colin gave her hand a squeeze, as Lois took her other hand.

"Look," Lois said, "I'm not overly worried about what happened with Alex Madison. Nick's taking him for a 'casual' lunch day after tomorrow, to really lean into his excitement over putting him in the new farce."

"And he has been so fantastically apologetic, what with the flowers and all," Colin offered.

"Exactly." Nate found her voice again. "So why—"

"The last thing we need is for news of your split getting out there and making Alex question everything we've told him," Lois argued firmly. "And then using it to grab some attention for himself."

Nate sighed. "And with the studio unprepared to weather the storm…"

"Right." Lois cocked her head to the side. "If I'm being truthful, you're not prepared to weather it either, Nate."

Nate's head snapped up. "What exactly does that mean?"

"Exactly what I said. There are always at least two—sometimes more—people involved in high-profile splits." Lois inhaled sharply. "And you know who bears the brunt of almost every single derogatory thing printed?"

Nate's mouth twisted wryly. "The wife?"

Lois nodded. "The wife. The words *harlot* and *jezebel* tend to get hurled about with abandon."

"I still remember all that uproar over Mary Astor years ago," Colin added. "The news reached all the way to London. Even we got wind of how much the studio heads were pissing themselves over the scandalous mess surrounding her case."

Lois sneered. "Her reputation barely made it past that."

A feeble hope flared in Nate's chest again. "But she *did* get past it. Hell, she's gone on to be everything from a femme fatale to Judy Garland's mom. Once everyone found out how terrible her husband was, the tide turned in her favor."

"True," Lois conceded. "But that was largely because we could witness his asinine behavior firsthand."

Colin engulfed her hand in both of his. "Lois is right. You're hardly in the same boat, dove. All they'd have here is your word."

Nate deflated. Again. "I suppose you're right. You'd think I'd remember that people can't see Walter make an ass of himself with their own eyes and know that I married a jerk. It's not possible, and we all know why."

"We do." Lois's voice brimmed with sympathy. "But even if

that wasn't a factor, discretion would still have to be key right now. All it would take is *simple* divorce gossip getting out in the wrong way, and Phoenix Pictures won't be the only thing to suffer. You'll always have a job here, but outside these walls I doubt you'll walk away completely unscathed. And having been on the receiving end of garbage like that for a decade, I can tell you, I would only wish that on my worst enemy." Lois took her hand again. "There's no way in hell I want to see my best friend go through it."

"Neither would I," Colin breathed.

All the air rushed out of Nate. While she knew gossip over a salacious—fictional—divorce would be much easier to withstand than the actual truth getting out, especially with Lois's support behind her, the idea of it still gave her pause. Her fear for the studio's reputation loomed once again with a vengeance, outweighing her own concerns. She couldn't let Lois down.

Colin's hands around her own were a warm, solid weight. As much as she wanted him to agree with her original plan, she didn't want to let him down either. He might fare better than her, but he'd still be embroiled in infamy, at a time when his screenwriting star was on the rise.

"So I need to wait."

"I hate to ask it of you," Lois answered, "but yes. And perhaps the two of you should cool it on spending quite so much time together here on the lot as well. At least for a bit longer. It's better for everyone this way."

"I agree," Colin added quietly.

"I wish I didn't have to put you in this position."

"But you do have to." Nate sighed. "I know."

"It's only for a little while, until the next big scandal comes along." Lois straightened in her seat. "On that note, I did come here with a touch of good news. Ruby Church and Bobby Frasier's big party is coming up. And you know every one of their legendary soirees ends with at least two or three people making colossal fools of themselves."

Nate perked up at that. "That's right. Ronald Carter fell in their pool almost six months ago now, and the gossips still call him the Drowned Rat every chance they get."

Lois smirked. "Precisely. And I know you're already on the guest list, Nate, but I talked to Ruby and managed an invite for Colin as well."

"You did?" Colin asked.

"I did." Lois paused. "Although maybe that's not such welcome news after all. You'll need to be detachedly friendly with each other from opposite, neutral sides of the room. But you'll have front row seats when someone hopefully steals this month's spotlight. And then, in a couple of weeks, maybe you can revisit the idea? I'll help, and we'll do it right, I promise."

Nate nodded. "I can do that." She groaned. "I think."

Colin rubbed her back. "*We* can."

Lois studied them for a moment, a small smile playing at her lips. She extracted a fancy envelope from her pocket and handed it to Colin. "Here's your invitation."

He took it with a smile, clearly trying to lift the mood. "I've been looking forward to meeting Ruby one of these days. With everything you all have told me about her, she sounds like quite the character."

"Believe me, she is." Lois laughed.

Nate nodded, and took a moment to smile herself. Ruby had started her film career at the tender age of five, and had grown into quite the talented young woman. She was bright, vivacious, and irreverent as hell. Nate thought the world of her.

"You'll like her," she agreed. "And she and Bobby always throw fun parties."

"I do like parties." He gave her back another reassuring circle of his hand, and she leaned into his warmth.

Lois rose to her feet. "Well, I should be going." She smiled at Nate. "It'll all work out, Nate, I'm sure of it."

"Thanks."

Colin stood as well, leaving Nate cold in his wake. "I'd best go as well. Better if we leave the office together, right?"

Lois nodded. "Right."

They both looked back to Nate, and she narrowly resisted the urge to become one with the couch cushions at the sympathy wafting toward her. She waved a hand at them.

"Right. Gotta keep up those appearances."

Lois shot her an apologetic smile as she headed for the door. Colin bent to press a quick kiss to Nate's cheek.

"See you tonight?"

Nate nodded. "See you tonight."

After they left, Nate was sorely tempted to give in to her urge to wallow on the couch. But work called, as usual, and so she stuffed down her disappointment and threw herself into it.

$\mathscr{N}$ate and Colin's dinner plans that evening hadn't changed, and since Colin finished up his work before she did, they agreed that he would pick up some food for them on the way home, with her meeting him at his apartment as soon as she was through. Her attempts to muster at least the projection of a good mood were largely failing when she arrived on his doorstep.

Colin greeted her with a kiss. "I picked up Chinese food, that all right?"

That did brighten her spirits. "Ooh, that's perfect. Please tell me you got extra cream cheese wontons."

"Always. I may have overdone it, as a matter of fact. There's probably enough of everything in there to feed a small army."

"Plenty to choose from, then." She leaned in for another kiss, savoring the taste of him. He took her coat and led her to the kitchen, where he had laid out the food containers, ready and waiting for them to dive in.

"Wow. You weren't kidding. Impressive spread."

Colin's mouth turned up in a lopsided grin. She sighed at how truly adorable he was. And cringed over their current state of affairs. The effort to keep things publicly slow with him was so damn draining.

And because the thought alone apparently wasn't draining enough, Colin's invitation to the party sat on the table next to their food, its fancy calligraphy taunting her. *Colin Canfield and Guest.*

She traced that last word with her fingernail, her gloomy mood back with a vengeance. She looked up to find Colin watching her, concern all over his lovely face.

"I am sorry you can't be that guest."

She turned abruptly to fetch some plates from the counter.

"Nate."

She didn't turn back. She sensed him stepping closer, but she didn't dare turn around.

"It's not like you won't be there too. You will."

"We just won't be going together." She couldn't make her voice anything but dull. Lifeless. "Because we need to be cautious. It can't look like we're on a date."

His hands settled on her arms, and he turned her to face him.

She tried to force a smile. "It's fine. Really."

"It's quite clearly not." He grazed a finger under her chin. "If it makes you feel any better, I am sorry that I agreed with Lois this afternoon."

"But you *do* agree with her."

"I do. Unfortunately."

"And you have a point." She heaved a sigh and leaned her forehead against his chest with a thud. "Ugh."

His lips brushed the crown of her head, before he pulled back to cradle her face in his hands, his gentleness too much for her. She rested both hands on his chest. His heart hammered against her touch.

"I wish it was different," he whispered. "We just need to be patient."

She studied him, taking a small comfort from his sincerity. She brought her hands up to cover his. "You're right. And it'll be fine.

I'm fine." She pasted a strained smile on her face, willing herself to feel it. "Come on, let's eat before everything gets cold."

SOMEHOW, Nate pushed aside her lingering discomfort enough to share a pleasant meal. Her forced cheer eventually relaxed into the real thing, as she shoved aside her worries and focused on her food, and on Colin's handsome face, his lovely voice. Once they could eat no more, they packed up the leftovers—there were, indeed, plenty for at least two more meals—and miraculously found room for them in Colin's icebox.

They wandered to the living room, wine glasses in hand, and Colin switched on the radio before settling next to her on the couch.

He gave her a sheepish glance. "Would it be terribly rude of me to squeeze in a moment or two of work right now?"

The question surprised her, and she hoped he wasn't trying to avoid her. "No, of course not."

"I wouldn't normally ask, but there's a scene that's been eluding me all day, and now that I've let it sit for a while, I've just had a flash of enlightenment. I'm worried if I don't jot down a few quick notes, I'll lose it completely by tomorrow morning."

She smiled at his rushed, polite earnestness, feeling silly for thinking it was avoidance. Sympathy washed through her at his conundrum as well. "I know what that's like." She kissed his cheek. "Do what you need to do."

He beamed at her and reached for a notebook from the coffee table. "Thank you. I'll only be a minute, I promise."

"Take your time."

Nate spied a trade magazine on the table and picked it up, entertaining herself with trying to decode the "*Variety*-speak" on the pages.

At one point, she looked across the couch at Colin, lost in thought as his pencil scribbled across the page. He was oblivious to her notice, so intent on his writing. But something in his posture caught her attention. His body was angled ever-so-subtly, leaning toward her. The magazine slipped to her lap, and she took advantage of his single-mindedness to watch him.

This. This is it.

For years, she had let herself be solitary, content to hide behind the fiction that was Walter. She had invented an entire relationship, an entire life, for herself. And it wasn't even a good one. She could have chosen Prince Charming, but no. She'd settled for one lousy fake husband.

But here was Colin. More than a good one, he was the best of them. Plus, he actually *was*, period.

She felt his warmth emanating in her direction, even with his concentration elsewhere. Since the moment she'd met him, he'd been present in a way no one ever had. In a way she'd never let anyone be, even the product of her imagination.

And she'd be an absolute fool to let him go.

She knew he had been right earlier, that the best way forward for both of them in light of the chaos surrounding them—that was ultimately of *her* creation—was indeed caution. But that didn't stop her sudden, impatient surge of frustration. Followed immediately by a fierce desire to turn around and reassure him the way he had for her. To *claim* him. She didn't want to interrupt his hard-won concentration, but her desperate need to touch him, even in some small way, built. She reached out, thinking a quick brush of his arm would be sufficient. But when he looked up, surprised but present, so present—so *hers*—it wasn't nearly enough.

His work instantly forgotten, he asked, "Nate, are you all right?"

The look in his eyes nearly did her in. Even with everything that hovered unresolved between them, his affection shone through. Attuned to her well-being, as ever.

She launched herself at him, closing the distance and pressing her mouth to his. He froze for a millisecond, then his hand cupped her cheek and his tongue tangled with hers.

A tiny shred of sense came back to her, and she pulled away. "I'm sorry; you needed to work."

Colin shook his head before diving in to claim her mouth again. Between kisses, he breathed, "Work can wait." He tossed his notebook to the table without breaking contact.

She poured as much of herself—of her heart—into her kiss as she could, willing him to understand everything she felt for him. All the reasons her patience had run out.

God, I wish I'd never dreamt up Walter.

Hardly the first time she'd acknowledged it, but the thought hit her with particular force at this moment. On its heels came a powerful urge to banish her creation to oblivion for the rest of time. To erase all traces of the mess she'd made.

Possessed of an overwhelming desire for him to lay thorough claim to her, leave no trace of her invented husband or any of her past—or current—doubts, she ripped her lips from Colin's. His eyes, full of fire that matched the heat consuming her, sought hers. She ran her hands across his chest, fingers skimming the relief of his chest hair through the fine weave of his shirt.

Bold energy rocketed through her. "Take me." She held his gaze, refusing to hide the defiance surging in her veins, her nerve endings. "Take me. Here. Now. Make me forget I ever invented Walter."

His eyes widened slightly in surprise, followed immediately by a defiance of his own. His mouth crashed back onto hers as he pulled her against him. With unspoken agreement—and passionate impatience—they didn't bother to move to his bedroom.

Neither of them said a word as they undressed each other with lightning speed, oblivious as to where their clothes landed. When they crashed back onto the couch, skin-to-skin, the heat between them could have lit a forest fire.

Nate sensed a desperation in him as well, fueling hers even more. She pulled him close, ready to obliterate any time she had ever hesitated with him earlier in their relationship. She needed him to know that she was in this, in all ways. Starting right now. Her hands raked over his back, trying to will her attraction, her—*whoa*—love, into him.

She was in *love* with Colin.

Her breath hitched as the revelation hit her, and she tightened her hold on him, if such a thing was possible. His muscles stiffened under her touch, as if he sensed her deepening urgency. She expected him to push back, to match her claw for claw—eagerly anticipated it. Primed for him to claim her, vanquish the ghost of Walter, with that raw, primal energy that propelled so much of their lovemaking.

So it surprised her when he softened, his own arms wrapping more firmly around her, now tender and gentle in their strength. He slowed his movements, pressing her down into the couch cushions as he languished deep kisses on her neck, her jaw, and finally her mouth, his tongue taking its sweet time in exploring hers.

She moaned as she melted into him. She couldn't even complain about his new pace, because he was somehow everywhere around her, covering her with his warmth. Setting fire to every bit of skin he touched, all the while making her feel safe. Sheltered.

It was utterly intoxicating.

And its own kind of claiming, she realized as he made his way down her body. He took great care to mark every inch of her as his own, completely, thoroughly. In his Colin way.

And then he reached her core. He slid to his knees on the floor in front of her, dipping his head between her legs and sliding his tongue inside her. Her back arched off the sofa, and all thought departed her on the heels of her cry.

In no time at all, he drove her to the edge of her sanity, but withdrew abruptly just before she went over. She gasped, trying to pull him back down by his hair, but he resisted. A small shake of his head, as he speared her with admonition—astoundingly sexy admonition—mixed with raw, animalistic lust. Nate nearly expired on the spot.

With a staying hand on her stomach, he rose to his feet, bringing his rock-hard, straining cock right to her eye-level. She swallowed convulsively as her mouth watered.

Before she could reach out and take him for herself, he glided away from her, and she whimpered her frustration. An amused rumble emanated from Colin's chest as he grabbed his pants from where they'd landed on top of the radio and fished through a pocket to pull out a condom. He smirked wickedly at her as he tore the envelope open.

As he rolled it on, his eyes never left hers, pinning her in place with their fiery intensity. He whipped off his glasses and dropped them on the coffee table as he stalked toward her.

He sat on the couch and pulled her to straddle his lap. He positioned himself quickly at her entrance, digging his hands into her hips to steady her. It shouldn't have surprised her that Colin teased that as well, gripping her firmly while he eased her down on him at a maddeningly measured pace, one blasted inch at a time. By the time he finally had her seated to the hilt, every muscle in her quivering legs had turned to jelly, and she was gasping for breath. Only one thrust up into her, mercifully faster this time, and her fingers frantically grasped the back of the couch as she exploded around him with violent shudders that obliterated every remaining bone in her body. She tried to call his name, but suspected it came out as nothing more than an unintelligible shout.

All the while, Colin continued to tilt up, driving into her again and again, chasing his own pleasure. Nate found the strength to clamp her knees around his hips, desperate for him to keep going, to draw out her orgasm as long as possible. He stiffened, and growled his release before collapsing back against the couch with her slumped against his chest.

He eased her off his lap, giving her one more all-consuming kiss before retreating from the room to rid himself of the rubber.

She tried in vain to collect her senses from where they'd scattered, strewn all over the room along with their clothes. When Colin came back, they remained silent as he stretched out and somehow wedged both of them comfortably on the couch, chest still heaving as much as hers. He pulled an afghan from the back of it and draped it over them before gathering her in. As she nestled into his side, he tightened his arms fiercely with a sharp intake of breath, and continued to cling to her as their bodies quieted and began their descent into sleep.

Nate drifted off to the comforting rhythm of his slowing heartbeat, as two thoughts echoed over and over.

She was very much in love with Colin Canfield.

And as soon as she got through Ruby's party, it was time to say good-bye to Walter Guffman once and for all, consequences be damned.

Chapter Twenty-Six

The day of Ruby's party dawned, and Colin found himself unable to concentrate on work at all, his thoughts an absolute mess. The way Nate had pulled him in, asked him to take her, had seared itself on his brain—and his cock. He'd been more than willing to oblige her. Something different, almost primal, had possessed her that night, and it took no time at all for him to join her.

As desperate as she'd been for him to make her forget Walter, he was even more desperate to ease the obvious ache within her. She tried to pretend otherwise, but there was no mistaking how much it bothered her that they couldn't go to this party together. She'd maintained the myth of Walter longer than most people would've been capable of, but the near-fiasco with Alex Madison seemed to break some kind of dam within her. And it absolutely killed Colin that now he was the one asking her to put the brakes on everything.

At this rate, he'd be an absolute wreck by the time he arrived at the party, which would never do. So he put his head down and forced himself to work.

By the time afternoon rolled around, he'd banged out what he hoped was a fairly decent scene. As soon as he stacked the pages into a neat pile, though, his mind zipped back to Nate.

He wished he could offer her some comfort tonight. With any luck, Ruby's party would be precisely the distracting spectacle they all needed, and they could revisit the possibility of phasing Walter out of their lives for good.

He suddenly remembered that Nick was supposed to have had lunch with Alex Madison the previous day. Colin assumed it went well, since he hadn't heard anything to the contrary. And if it had proceeded according to plan, perhaps that was one small kernel of hope he could deliver to Nate this evening.

Grateful to be alone in his office, Colin picked up the telephone and called Nick…only to find that he'd already left the studio for the day. *Right, party tonight.* He tried Nick and Lois's home, with better results.

"Colin!" Nick's cheerful greeting boded well. "What can I do for you?"

"Sorry to bother you at home," Colin apologized, "but I tried your office first and they said you'd already gone."

"Yeah, with the party I didn't want to get stuck. Wait, are you still on the lot? You are coming tonight, right?"

"I am. Leaving soon," Colin reassured him. "Besides, how long could it possibly take *me* to get ready?"

"Fair enough. So, is everything okay?"

"Yes. I wanted to check in; how did it go yesterday with Alex Madison?"

Nick hummed his approval. "Of course. Sorry I haven't had a chance to update you. It went great, actually."

Colin let out the breath he'd been consciously holding. "That's a relief. He really is buying this whole farce cover, then?"

"Yep." Nick chuckled. "You wouldn't believe how excited he is for this role. I think we're really going to have to follow through on it."

"Honestly, that's fine by me. I feel badly we're pulling the wool over his eyes, but as long as he doesn't suspect a thing, he deserves a giant reward."

"That's for sure." Nick lowered his voice. "And listen, Lois told me how bad she feels about making Nate wait on the divorce announcement. Hopefully you two won't have to put it off much longer."

"I hope so." Colin's sigh turned into a snort. "You know, sometimes I wish we could go back to the original arsenic plan."

Nick laughed. "Eh, you can at least throw it into your script."

"That would be grand, wouldn't it?" He exhaled. "Thanks, Nick."

"I truly am glad I could help. See you tonight?"

"See you there."

Colin tidied his desk and gathered up his jacket and briefcase, his mood much improved. They were making this right for Nate.

He'd just stepped out his office door when he felt something crunch softly under his foot. He glanced down, expecting to see a discarded scrap of paper, but instead...

He cocked his head, peering at the floor. Was that...?

Attached to a lapel pin, an orange, mushroom-like flower.

Colin's eyes widened, horror descending on him.

Bloody fucking hell. Not again.

He whipped his head up and broke into a run. He charged into the bright afternoon sunlight, eerily similar to the color of that damn flower, frantically searching the area.

Nothing.

But he couldn't have gotten far. Colin would find him.

He had to.

WITH EVERYTHING GOING on in their lives, it had been forever since Nate and Lois prepped themselves for a Hollywood soiree together. When Lois called to invite Nate over for an afternoon of primping and accessorizing for Ruby's party, Nate jumped at the chance to spend some quality time with her friend. She was her own chauffeur for the evening, and Lois had a much bigger bathroom than she did, so why not take advantage?

Plus, it gave them extra time to spend chatting. Because they were still friends, thank god.

And she had some important plans she wanted to set in motion that she needed to run by Lois. A small announcement in the papers about a certain costume designer's split from her husband to be met with her approval—and the legal department's. At this point, Nate didn't even care what it said, as long as she didn't have to wait too long for it to see the light of day. She wanted everyone ready to sneak it into the news on the heels of whatever stupidity—*fingers crossed*—occurred at this party. Thankfully, Lois had been cautiously optimistic about the whole thing.

Arriving at Ruby's right behind Lois and Nick, feeling more positive than she had in days, she scanned the jolly, gregarious—and already substantial—crowd for Colin, but didn't spot him yet.

Nate knew they weren't supposed to linger together here, but that didn't curb her eagerness to see him.

She'd thought of little else but him since the night before last, when he'd pounded away so much of her uneasiness. When she'd vowed anew to waste as little time as humanly possible in fixing her future once and for all.

When she'd realized just how over-the-moon in love with him she was.

And now she wanted nothing more than to take in his smiling face, hear his sexy velvet voice, and, after a sufficient taste of a Ruby Church party, fill him in on her talk with Lois and take him home to have her way with him. Again and again.

Before making it too far into the gathering, Nick turned to her and Lois. "I spy a gentleman making Bobby's signature martinis. May I get you lovely ladies a drink?"

"You may, thanks," Nate replied.

"Thank you, darling." Lois gave him a peck on the cheek.

As soon as Nick disappeared into the throng, a giant ball of energy appeared in front of them in the person of Ruby Church.

"Nate! Lois! I'm so thrilled you're here!" Her grin could easily power an entire sound stage. Ruby greeted them both with oh-so-continental kisses on each cheek, before grabbing Lois's arm.

"There's someone I'm simply dying to introduce to you two. She's new to Hollywood, but has just oodles of talent, and I'm trying to connect her with as many killer-diller dames as I can in this town. We have to stick together, after all." With barely a pause to breathe, her gaze flitted over the crowd, before she turned her bright eyes back to them. "I can't imagine where she's gotten herself to now. I'll have to introduce you to her later. Don't go too far," she added with a wink.

Nate smiled. "Of course not."

"Oh, you're a doll!" She squeezed both of their hands before scampering off.

Before long, Nick reappeared with their drinks. They attempted to move further into the room, but the teeming mass of shiny people impeded their progress. Nate didn't mind, not wanting to miss Colin's arrival.

She took another sip of her drink—Bobby's martinis were among the best—as something near the door behind her caught Nick's attention. He narrowed his eyes, but before she could turn around a vaguely familiar voice rose above the din.

"There she is! That's her, right over there!"

Nick's eyes widened. Lois's jaw dropped. The crowd fell into a hush.

A sick, sinking pressure pushed against the edges of Nate's happy Colin bubble. In spite of every instinct telling her not to, she slowly turned around.

Alex Madison stood near the door, a furious expression marring his blandly handsome face. An accusatory finger pointing directly at her.

Fuck.

Behind him...no, it couldn't be. Two police officers.

Fuck fuck fuck fuck fuuuuuuuuuuck

Pure horror and disbelief froze Nate in place. Colorful spots danced on the edges of her vision. Maybe it was the resulting spray from her bubble of happiness bursting into stupefaction.

She dimly registered Lois hissing to Nick behind her, "You said he was fine at your lunch yesterday."

"He was, I swear," Nick fired back.

Nate was incapable of words, her voice content to sit back and enjoy the oncoming wreckage, despite the panic building in her chest.

Alex started toward her, officers in tow, and the crowd parted for them like a *vee* of Busby Berkeley chorus girls.

So much for letting some other fool be tonight's scandal du jour.

Her heart threatened to pound right out of her ribcage, her breathing growing shallower, probably due to the fact that her stomach had lurched into her throat. What the hell could possibly have happened to change Alex's tune? Had this dopey actor not actually believed them, and been snowing them all this time?

But he'd seemed so sincere in her office the other day. Those flowers…

After what could have been a few seconds or a few years, Alex reached her, his finger now hovering in uncomfortable proximity to her face. She resisted the urge to throw her drink in his.

"This is her, officer. The one I told you about." Alex glanced around the room, and seeing he had everyone's attention, puffed out his chest. *Little asshole.* "She's plotting to *kill* her husband!"

Nate let out a strangled, high-pitched sound she'd never before made in her life.

What in the name of Edith Head's glasses is happening right now?

Every goddamn eye in the place was trained on her. Which meant she couldn't bolt for the door.

Nick, bless him, stepped up next to her. "Now, wait just a minute."

The policemen had been watching Nate warily, but one of them perked up at the sight of Nick.

"Why, Mr. Bradley! Good to see you." He stepped forward to shake Nick's hand heartily.

"Officer Harris, hello." Nick offered him a weak smile.

"You look a damn sight better than the last time I saw you." Harris leaned toward Nate conspiratorially. "High as a kite, this one was." Without giving her a chance to respond, he clapped Nick on the shoulder. "Glad to see you walking the straight and narrow again, sir."

"Of all the gin joints…" Nate muttered.

Shit on a shingle, my life really is a farce, isn't it?

Nick cleared his throat. "Right. Thanks. But enough about me." He adopted an authoritative air. "I'm sorry to say, you've wasted your time here, Officer Harris. These allegations against Ms. Reynolds are completely false."

Nate wanted to kiss every director who'd ever cast Nick as a lawyer.

Lois drew herself to her full height, her most glacial mask firmly in place, and joined the fray. "Of course they're false."

"They are not," Alex sputtered. "I heard the whole thing. You know I did!"

Lois raked a haughty sneer from his head to his toes—how the man didn't piss his pants right then and there, Nate'd never know. "How *dare* you disrupt this lovely soiree with such a trivial, ridiculous fairy tale."

"Fairy tale? *Fairy tale?*" Alex's vocabulary clearly hadn't caught up to his face, which was turning an alarming shade of red.

"Now, everybody just remain calm." Harris held up a steadying hand. "Let me get to the bottom of this."

"There's nothing to get to the bottom of," Alex whined. "I told you. This merry murderess and her lover are going to off her husband! Probably for the insurance money."

"I said, remain calm, son," Harris warned Alex.

The stunned silence of the partygoers had begun to give way

to whispers as soon as Nick stepped forward to defend Nate, and now the murmur escalated to a dull roar.

The pulse pounding in her ears harmonized with the crowd's buzzing, but Nate needed to wrest some control from this madness before it completely got away from her.

"Excuse me, Officer Harris?"

The chatter in the room ceased abruptly at the sound of Nate's voice.

Fuck me.

Harris turned to her. "Yes, little lady?"

Masterfully controlling her lip's impulse to curl at his patronizing tone, Nate heaved a breath and pasted a smile on her face.

I can do this.

"I assure you…sir. This is all a big misunderstanding. There's a perfectly simple explanation"—a snide snicker sounded inside her head—"for everything. It's quite funny, really."

An even snider cackle erupted from Alex. "Oh, please. I suppose you're about to trot out that stupid farce bit. Don't fall for it, Officer. *That's* the fairy tale."

Nate, Lois, and Nick turned to glare at the actor en masse.

Seriously, what the hell crawled into his underpants and died since yesterday?

Out of nowhere, Ruby popped up at Nate's elbow. "I believe this nice officer told you to pipe down, you pipsqueak. This is my party, and I can toss you out of here like that." She snapped her fingers, startling the shit Nate didn't know she still had left out of her.

Ignoring Alex's now-purple glower, Ruby put a reassuring hand on Nate's back and continued. "You go ahead, hon."

"Right. I…" Nate trailed off for a moment. As grateful as she was for Ruby's support, her presence cast an even brighter spotlight on the sordid scene. A trickle of sweat slid down Nate's back, as panic skittered past it on its way up.

This is a nightmare. She glanced around the room. *And I'm on full display.*

Her eyes returned to Officer Harris, waiting with a patient but stern expression. It hit her with sudden, powerful clarity. The only thing that would get her out of this unholy mess was the absolute truth.

All of it.

She swallowed around the lump in her throat, wishing it was Colin's hand on her back instead of Ruby's. Where the hell was he, anyway?

The mere thought of him unearthed a crumb of sense, and Nate addressed Harris. "As I said, Officer, I can explain every-thing." She lowered her voice. "But perhaps it would be better if we did that…somewhere a little quieter?"

Sympathy fluttered across the policeman's features, igniting a spark of hope. If she could get away from all the revelers stuffed-to-the-gills in this room, maybe—just maybe—she could still salvage a shred of her reputation.

"Of course, Ms. Reynolds. That's probably a good idea."

Alex let out the beginnings of a protest, but Lois whipped her head in his direction—*did she actually growl?*—and he snapped his lips shut, shrinking in on himself.

"You can use our library," Ruby offered politely.

Chagrin took over Harris's face, and Nate's stomach sank. "Well, actually, miss, if we're going to relocate, it's best I take you down to the station."

"The station? Swell…" Though if it meant she didn't have to confess her deepest, darkest secret in front of…*all* of her peers, she supposed it would have to do.

Lois gripped her elbow. "Nate—"

She held up a hand. "It's okay, Lois. Really. The officer needs my story. If the station is the best place for it, then that's that."

She split a glance between Lois and Nick, willing them to catch her meaning. Thankfully, she knew how to pick smart friends. Nick blew out a breath, and Lois nodded briefly.

"STOP! It's not what you think!"

Despite its panicked shout, that rich, beautiful voice coasted over her battered soul like warm honey.

The entire room whipped around to look at the disheveled Englishman who'd just burst through the door. Nate's heart leapt at the sight of her Colin—tweed rumpled, tie askew, hair sticking up in every imaginable direction—even as his sudden appearance sent a foreboding shiver down her spine.

A few voices in the crowd questioned who the hell this newcomer was.

"Who the hell are you?" Harris echoed.

Alex flung an impatient arm in Colin's direction. "He's her lover. And her accomplice! Arrest him too!"

"There's no reason to arrest anyone," Colin seethed. "And if you'd find something better to do with your time than eavesdropping outside every office on the bloody lot, you'd know that."

Ah, so that explained it. *Jesus, what did Colin say this time? And to whom?*

Lois took a cautious step toward Colin. "Okay, let's just take a breath, shall we? Everything's under control."

Nate watched the rapid rise and fall of Colin's chest. She'd never seen him so upset. And it was in defense of her. Her heart melted—along with her undergarments.

Not *the time, lady. Get yourself out of this fiasco first.*

She adopted Lois's calm tone, as much to soothe him as to steer this runaway bus back in the direction of saving her own skin. "Yes. I was just about to go with Officer Harris." She sent him the same pointed look she'd aimed at Lois and Nick. "To clear up everything."

"That's right," Harris agreed.

"I'm sorry, but you are not taking the woman I love anywhere, when she hasn't done anything wrong."

Love? Hot damn.

Too late, Nate caught a gleam of metal out of the corner of her eye—right before Harris slipped the first half of a pair of handcuffs on her wrist. She jerked, as a collective gasp rippled through the room.

"Oh, come on," Nick intoned. "That's hardly necessary."

Nate willed her breath to remain steady. But when she looked to Colin for aid in the process, her lungs abandoned all hope of ease.

He was positively feral now.

Oh, no.

"No! You can't arrest her!" He barged toward them.

"Colin..." Nate warned.

"You need to remove those handcuffs right now."

"And you need to step back and let me do my job, sir," Harris shot back.

Nate stuffed the dread back down her throat. "Colin, it's fine. Let me handle this. Please."

He ignored her. "I'm telling you, no crime has been committed."

"Yet," Alex muttered.

Colin whirled on him. "Ever."

"Colin..." This time she said it in unison with both Lois and Nick.

But he was too far gone.

"You can't murder someone—or even plot to—who doesn't bloody EXIST!"

Nate's heart plummeted to the floor.

Along with her career.

Chapter Twenty-Seven

"Well, the police are gone." Nick shut the library door behind him with a click. "And Bobby's herding the last of the party stragglers through the front, while the staff clears you a path out the back. A car should be waiting in a few minutes."

Nate massaged her wrist, numbly managing a nod of thanks from amid the creeping fog of her exhaustion.

Pure chaos had descended upon Colin's confession. Nick and Lois had taken charge, shepherding the key players down the hall to the library, while Ruby and her husband Bobby calmed the storm with the rabble in the great room.

While Harris and his companion took Nate's full statement, Lois and Nick flanked her, Alex sat by like some wide-mouthed guppy…and Colin hovered in the corner, looking shell-shocked, but finally silent.

At the end of her grisly little tale, the police officers had—thank all the gods and goddesses—believed her and concluded no actual crimes had been committed. Nick ushered them out, but not before Harris delivered a stern admonition to Nate about the dangers of lying.

He also leveled a few parting shots at Alex for wasting their time and jumping to conclusions, so that was something, at least.

"Where's Alex Madison?" Nick asked.

"Ruby came and snagged him," Lois answered. "Wanted to make sure he wouldn't cause any more trouble before everyone's gone." She snickered. "She might have actually locked him in the wine cellar."

Nick shook his head. "Poor guy."

Lois huffed. "After that stunt tonight?"

"Well, we did lie to him. A lot."

Nate's pulse pounded in her temples, and she slumped forward, resting her forehead on the huge desk in front of her. She pushed her voice out in a hoarse whisper. "Do you think he'll slink away quietly?"

"I hope so," Nick replied.

"I can't decide if I want to punch him in the nose or fire him," Lois muttered. "Or give him a damn raise to keep him from shooting his mouth off again."

Nick's mouth quirked up. "Well, between you and Ruby, at the very least we owe him a new pair of pants. I'll go talk to him now." He glanced at Nate. "Anything specific you want me to say to him?"

Nate raised her head to shake it. "I trust you."

With a nod, he was off, leaving Lois and Nate. And Colin, still quiet.

She supposed they needed to talk about...everything. But she had no clue where to begin. And she was so damn tired.

Lois, being Lois, took charge. "I'll go check on your car. Give you two a minute."

She raised her eyebrow in silent question, and Nate nodded. Might as well get this over with.

The minute Lois left, Colin stepped closer.

"Nate," he rasped. "I am so sorry."

She'd held it together pretty well, if she did say so herself. But the sight of his lovely face, crumpled in anguished concern, finally set off the prickling tease of impending tears behind her eyes.

"What the hell happened, Colin?"

His Adam's apple bobbed. "He overheard me. Again. I was on the telephone with Nick, and…I truly didn't think anyone was around." He closed his eyes for a long moment. "By the time I realized…I tried to find him, desperately. But…"

"You were too late."

"Mm-hmm."

"So then you came here and…" She swallowed around a sudden, hot burst of anger. "And you announced to all of Hollywood that I'm a big, huge liar. I thought you respected my career."

"You know I do. I…" His brow furrowed. "Wait, that's what you're most upset about?"

"Of course it is."

"But…the police. They were going to arrest you, Nate."

"I had it handled." Heat crept up her neck. "Which you would have known, in the moment—when I told you—if you'd taken your head out of your ass long enough to listen to me."

"My head…*my* arse? I was trying to help you."

"But I didn't need saving! All I had to do was go with them, and I could have cleared up the whole mess *privately*."

He stared at her, incredulity written all over his face. "Are you saying you'd rather have been carted away in handcuffs than—"

"Than be outed as a fraud in front of all of my peers?" She shot to her feet. "Yes, Colin. Yes!"

"But that's absurd!"

"More absurd than not knowing how to close a fucking door when you're having a sensitive conversation?"

"That's not fair. And none of us would be having these 'sensitive' conversations if you hadn't invented a bloody husband in the first place!"

She reared back as if slapped.

Colin's face crumpled in remorse. "Nate. I'm sorry. I didn't mean it like that."

Nate held up her palm and turned from him, the walls closing in on her. She wasn't sure whose shoulders to lay the blame on for this fucking mess, his or hers. Either option felt lousy.

Colin came up behind her to rest his hands on said shoulders. But it was too much, and she shrugged him off.

She inhaled a shuddering breath and faced him again. "Look, I'm really beat. And I don't want to fight with you on top of everything else. Maybe you should just go."

"Nate..."

"My car will be here in a minute, and I think..." She closed her eyes against the pain radiating from behind his glasses. "I need to be alone right now."

His exhale drifted across her cheeks. "Right. Of course. If that's what you want."

"It is." She risked another look at him. "Please."

He nodded, and backed out of the room, unable to tear his eyes from her. She wished he would.

The snick of the door closing behind him was louder than any gunshot.

The weight of all that had just happened slammed against her chest, and she sank back against the edge of the desk behind her. The breath left her in a wracking sob, even as her eyes remained dry.

She didn't know how long she remained there, frozen and completely empty, staring unfocused at the busy pattern of the carpet a few feet in front of her. A soft knock sounded, and she found enough energy to lift her head and see Lois peering around the door.

"Your car's here."

Nate nodded.

Lois stopped in front of her, and didn't hesitate a moment before pulling Nate into a tight, wordless embrace. The contact should have broken Nate open, but instead she simply clung to her friend, the deep fog of numbness surrounding her.

Chapter Twenty-Eight

"Well, tits." Frannie huffed as she sank back in her chair.

"Tits, indeed." Lois agreed.

"Yeah," Nate replied.

The three of them were gathered in the living room of Frannie's apartment, two days after the events of Ruby's party had laid waste to Nate's career—and heart. The *Titanic* had fared better against that iceberg.

They'd managed to avoid peers and press alike as Lois spirited Nate out of Ruby's house, but figured it likely someone could track her down at some point, to her own apartment, or even Lois and Nick's house. Luckily, no one would think to look for her at a studio accountant's abode, and Frannie had unquestioningly welcomed her with open arms.

It was a bit cramped, what with both Frannie's daughter and mother also sharing the tiny apartment. As much as Nate hated to impose on them—and her back protested Frannie's sofa—it was largely a blessed escape. If she was at home, she'd have to contend with the memories Colin had stamped on the place—like his dancing for her in the living room. And *everything* they'd done in her bedroom.

She'd spent most of the previous day unable to do much more than wallow. And consume a dinner that consisted of a glass of wine and one of Max's cheesecakes almost in its entirety.

Between her pity fete and Lois and Frannie's busy schedules at work, the three of them were only now getting around to catching Frannie up with the details of what transpired at Ruby's—and all that led up to it. Frannie had politely avoided the papers, wanting to hear her friend's side of the story first. Nate spilled everything, with a few assists from Lois.

After keeping it bottled up for so many years, it was astonishing how much more easily her story flowed from her lips these days.

"I don't even know where to begin," Frannie said. She glanced at Nate and reached out to grab her hand. "That certainly explains your pathetic state these last couple of days."

"Gee, thanks." Nate groaned. "Aw, hell, who am I kidding? I am pathetic."

"I didn't say *you* are pathetic, only your current state of affairs." Frannie tittered. "Really, though, all this time! You let me go on badgering you about what a turd your husband was, and he wasn't even real?" She gave Nate a playful swat on the shoulder. "You should've told me."

Lois snorted.

Nate shot her an exasperated look, before giving in to a rueful chuckle. "Okay, yes, I know. But in my defense, inventing a husband is a pretty embarrassing thing to admit, even among friends."

"Yes, but where better to admit it than with us?" Lois responded. "I mean, who among us isn't harboring some shit that's embarrassing? I used to have rules for throwing temper tantrums at work on the regular."

Frannie nodded with a grimace. "And my phenomenal kissing talents once had a bloke booting up his lunch, right at my feet."

Lois winced. "That really is terrible." She leveled a finger at

Frannie. "Though I am sure it didn't have anything to do with your skill."

Frannie sent her eyes skyward. "I have my doubtful moments. But thanks."

Nate laughed. "This hardly feels the same, but thank you both."

They smiled back, and she felt a genuine, if slight, easing of the pressure in her chest for the first time in days.

"So what now?" Frannie asked. "Gossip always hits the accounting building dead last, so I have no idea what everyone's been saying."

Nate shrugged. "There's not much to do, is there? Maybe if I hide out for a few more days, no one will notice when I slink out of Hollywood with my tail between my legs." She glanced at Lois. "Got any Broadway connections who're looking to hire a disgraced designer?"

Lois rolled her eyes. "Even if I did, I am not calling them and you know it. You have a job with me until you die, remember?"

Nate rolled her eyes right back. "And what good will that do either of us, when everyone else at the studio refuses to work with me?"

Lois smirked. "First of all, I'm the boss. They'll do what I tell them to." Her smile softened. "And second, I'm going to throw a piece of advice you once gave me right back at you. You shouldn't underestimate yourself and all the goodwill you've built up over the years."

Nate scoffed. "You mean the goodwill I just exploded into oblivion?"

Lois issued an enigmatic hum. "Not quite, my friend. I came over tonight not only to check on you, but to deliver some potentially good news. The strangest thing has been happening."

"Don't tell me the press has been cheering Nate on?" Frannie asked.

Lois snorted. "No, they're behaving exactly like the vermin they are."

"Wonderful," Nate muttered. "So, what is it then?"

Lois grinned. "I've had no fewer than a dozen women from other studios phoning my office in the last two days, mostly wondering what they can do to help you. But a few of them also hinted they'd be open to jumping ship and coming over to Phoenix if I have any openings. From all departments too—actors, but also editors, colorists, even some costume people."

Nate's head swam. "Really? But why? I rained scandal down on the studio."

Lois shrugged. "Seems we're building a bit of a reputation as a haven for rebel women. Who knew scandal could be such a draw?"

"As it should be." Frannie smiled slyly. "You know, I'd be willing to bet at least part of it is down to everyone thinking the world of you, Nate."

She bit her lip against the sting of tears.

Lois took her hand. "See, this is why you should have come to me ages ago, hon."

Nate sputtered a startled laugh.

Lois continued, quiet but firm. "As wonderful as you are at helping people solve their problems, you can be…pretty lousy at letting others in to help you with yours."

"I…" The objection froze on Nate's lips.

Shit. She's right, isn't she?

"I love you, Nate. You know that. And yet, you managed to keep all this from me, until a near-catastrophe forced the confession out of you." She brought her other hand up to further enfold Nate's. "You have a tendency to envision the worst imaginable outcome, and then allow your fear to build it up so much, you believe it's the only possible scenario."

Frannie grasped Nate's free hand. "And forgive me if I'm wrong, but most of the times the worst *has* come to pass, it hasn't turned out nearly as bad as you dreamed it would." She cleared her throat. "Apart from the whole handcuff stramash."

Nate rolled her eyes with a snort. Which promptly turned into a sob.

Lois squeezed her hand. "Nate, you and I are fine. And Frannie's fine." She glanced at her with a quirked eyebrow. "Right?"

Frannie waved her off. "Absolutely."

Lois continued, "I know I was afraid of what a scandal of this magnitude would do to the studio, and I'm sorry if that added to your burden. But it's not the first time we've turned shit into gold, and it won't be the last. Because *we* are in this together."

"Damn right," Frannie agreed.

Nate shut her eyes as she leaned her head back against the chair. "You two really are the best, you know that?"

"We do." Even with her eyes closed, Nate could hear the smirk in Lois's voice. "I'll admit, I was looking forward to unleashing the bitch—it has been far too long since she came to play, and for you, I will bring her out, every time. But I'm glad I probably won't need to now."

Nate laughed. "Thanks."

"So. Now that we've dispensed with your career issues…"

Nate cracked one eye open at Lois's tone. "Uh-oh. What?"

"Are we going to talk about Colin telling you he loved you at the party?"

That opened Nate's other eye.

"What?" Frannie shrieked. "How could you leave out a detail like that?"

"It's not like I had a chance to process it before Officer Harris whipped out the handcuffs."

"Right, but that's all over now."

Nate swallowed around the lump in her throat. "I think we might be, too." A mix of guilt and hurt speared her midsection.

"I doubt that. Have you talked to him?" Lois asked quietly.

"No. And he hasn't exactly reached out, either," she added mulishly.

"Well, he was right in the thick of it with you," Frannie offered. "He's probably feeling the need to lay low himself."

"I know," Nate grudgingly agreed. She looked to Lois. "Have you seen him?"

"I haven't. I'm surprised he hasn't sought you out. After his behavior at the party..."

Nate shot her friends a sheepish glance. "Yeah...we didn't part ways too well. I kinda yelled at him for making everything worse when I had it handled. And then sent him away."

"So *that's* what happened," Lois breathed. "Nate."

"Wow. You both had your heads up your arses, didn't you?" Frannie mused.

That got a laugh out of Nate. "We did."

"Will you believe me when I say that, when the dust settles, I think you can both still fix this?" Lois asked.

"Probably not." She slanted her eyes toward Lois. "You really think so?"

"You love him too, right?"

Nate heaved a sigh. Her heart, her *soul*, ached for him. "Yeah. I do."

"Then yes."

"I concur," Frannie agreed with a wink.

Completely wrung-out—again—Nate slumped against the back of the couch. "I am so fucking exhausted. Can we please talk about something else?"

They both squeezed her hands before letting go, and Frannie took Nate's request to heart. "Speaking of new additions to Phoenix... Lois, did I hear Anna right? You actually got a meeting with the Nicholas Brothers?"

"I did. Granted, it's only a meeting, about one picture. I still have to convince them to do said picture. But it's a start, at least."

"That would be fantastic," Nate said, latching onto the subject change. "Do you think you can get them on board? I didn't scare them away, did I?"

"You did not. And I'm keeping my fingers crossed." Lois turned to Frannie with a grin. "You want to meet them? We can arrange for you to happen by with some numbers at a convenient moment."

Frannie held up her hands. "Oh no. That would not be a good idea."

"Why not?" Lois asked. "I thought you loved their films."

"I do. That's exactly why I shouldn't be there. The last thing you need is your finance whiz turning into a giggling bobby-soxer and frightening them off. No, better to wait till *after* the cameras start rolling."

They all laughed.

"I had no idea you were such a fan of theirs," Nate said.

"Oh, sure. I enjoy Astaire and Kelly as well, but they're my favorites. The way they move is practically superhuman. Lucy's mad about them, too." Her smile took on a faraway cast. "I suppose my brother's to blame for my love of all things dance."

Lois leaned forward, resting her arms on her knees. "That's right, I forgot you have a brother. You hardly mention him."

"He's my half-brother, really. We had the same dad, but different mums. And you're right, I guess I don't talk about him much." Frannie twisted her fingers together. "Because I, um… don't know where he is. We dropped contact during the war, and I…I haven't been able to find him."

Nate touched the back of her neck, the ghost of a shiver raising the hair there.

"Fran, I'm sorry," Lois replied. "Is there any way we can help? Some avenue you haven't tried yet?"

"There are quite a few avenues I haven't tried." Frannie swallowed. "Honestly, I…haven't looked all that hard for him." She looked up at them sheepishly. "I lost an awful lot during the war. Lucy's father. My own. The thought that I might have lost Colin too…" She smiled at Nate. "Sorry for the reminder. My brother's a Colin as well. You know, I can't believe I hadn't noticed that before."

The ghost shiver was more potent this time.

Frannie shook her head and continued, "Anyway, I suppose

the not knowing is…easier somehow. I can still have hope, think of him out there somewhere, looking up at the same stars every night." She exhaled. "Sorry. What I was going to say, before I took the scenic route through melancholy, was that he's the reason I started taking Lucy to dance pictures in the first place, and got us both hooked."

"He loved them too?" Lois asked.

"Even better," Frannie answered with a wide smile. "He was a dancer himself."

Nate's breath stopped.

"You should have seen him." Frannie's grin brightened. "My mum took me to see a lot of his competitions. He was really going places, he and his partner, till he injured himself pretty bad and had to quit." She shrugged. "But all those dancers on screen, they're a reminder. And I figure if I can't introduce Lucy to Chips, I can at least expose her to something he loved."

Chips.

Nate's heart pounded out a rhythm Gene Krupa would envy.

"Frannie." She swallowed. "Or should I say, *Fish?*"

Frannie blinked at her in surprise. "How did you know I'm…?"

"The Fish to his Chips?"

"The Fish to his Chips," Frannie repeated, going still. She stared at Nate for a moment, and her hand flew to her mouth. "My god."

Nate huffed out a laugh. Regardless of the mess between them, it seemed she had one hell of a gift to give Colin.

Chapter Twenty-Nine

Colin stared dejectedly out the sole window in his office, alone. Again.

The life of a writer tended to be relatively solitary, but this week had been particularly quiet. He was still uncertain if that was a good thing or not.

His job here at the studio often involved a fair amount of meetings with producers, directors, and the like, but every once in a while he had a stretch where the meetings slowed. This was one of those stretches—made even more sedate by the fact that people appeared to be avoiding him, unsure what to make of him after his performance at the party.

He should be taking full advantage of such a perfect gift of uninterrupted writing time.

Except that he couldn't manage a single word.

His muse—his beautiful, vibrant, extraordinary muse—was gone. And he had no one to blame but himself.

Colin slumped against the window frame, ruminating on how thoroughly he'd fucked things up with Nate. For days, he'd done nothing but replay the events of that horrible night, wishing he'd done...*everything* differently. She'd been right. What was wrong with him, that he couldn't manage to close a single bloody door?

And then he'd been in such a frenzy to help her, to protect her, that he blundered his way into making the entire debacle a million times worse.

The silver shine of those handcuffs encircling her wrist was seared into his mind, and ran him through with fresh pain every time he closed his eyes. Hell, it haunted him whenever they were open as well. Could she really blame him for rushing in to save her from that fate?

She did. And she *should*.

Of course she had it handled. She was Nate. She'd invented an entire fictional husband and maintained the charade for years. It wasn't until *he* came along that it became difficult for her.

His breath fogged the window in front of him as he sighed. He'd even managed to botch the first time he professed his love. What kind of dolt blurted something like that out in the middle of a crowded room, at the worst possible moment?

Why didn't I tell her long before that?

He'd never loved anyone the way he loved Nate, and now it was highly likely the only time he'd ever see her would be in pathetic glimpses across the lot. He'd jeopardized her brilliant, beloved career, and she'd probably fix it with Lois so that the two of them never worked on a picture together again.

At least he hadn't killed her career altogether. He refused to pick up a newspaper, lest the drivel they were assuredly printing about her drive him feral on her behalf again. But Nick had told him that the blowback to the studio and—most importantly—to Nate was surprisingly minimal. Lots of her peers were rallying behind her.

Because she was magnificent, of course.

He groaned aloud. Not that there was anyone to hear him. He wished someone, anyone would stop by and distract him from the numbing, awful cavern where his heart used to be.

Fully aware that his current dramatic wallow wasn't doing him any good, Colin pushed up off the wall, determined to take action. If only he had a bloody clue what to do next. He wanted desperately to find Nate, pull her into his arms, and make things right.

But he doubted very much that she'd want to see his face at the moment, so he sagged back against the wall, leaning his forehead on the glass of the window.

He supposed he could attempt to use his natural gift, and write his way out of this catastrophe, but the chances were strong that Nate would simply toss anything he sent her in the rubbish bin, or perhaps set fire to it. She had endless destructive possibilities at her disposal.

Colin fervently wished the concept of a time machine was plausible, so that he could pay a visit to his last-week self and shout, "For fuck's sake, mate, close that door! And that one! All the doors!"

He heard a set of high-heeled footsteps approaching from down the hall. Two of them, actually. He straightened abruptly. One of the sets sounded like Nate's. Was it possible?

Colin turned in time to see the wise-cracking dame of his dreams appear in his doorway. She looked exhausted, and wary, but so very beautiful.

"Nate," he breathed.

"Hi, Colin." She bit her lip, hesitant.

"I'm so—"

"Your sister," she blurted. "I assumed she was English, like you, but she's not, is she?"

Colin blinked stupidly. Of all the things she could have said… "Um. No. She's not, as a matter of fact. She grew up in…"

"Scotland," Nate finished.

"Yes. But how…?"

A small gasp sounded behind Nate. An oddly, hauntingly familiar gasp.

He'd been so focused on his love that he'd hardly noticed the bearer of that other set of footsteps, who now emerged…

His miserable, sleep-deprived mind must be playing tricks on him. It couldn't be. *Could it?* It certainly looked like it could. But the way his life had been going, she could easily be a figment of his imagination. He lifted his glasses to rub his eyes, but she was still there.

Standing beside Nate, both hands covering her mouth, eyes beginning to tear up, was a woman who looked an awful lot like his sister.

He blinked a few more times, expecting her to disappear any moment. And then she spoke.

"Christ's teeth, she was right. It *is* you."

That light Scottish burr reached down into his icy, numb core and warmed him back to life. He didn't know which of them moved first, but before he knew it, they'd thrown their arms around each other and were clinging tight, in the middle of the office that had been so lonely just a minute prior.

"Mermaid! How?" He pulled back enough to look down at her face, starting to blur a bit due to the mist of his own tears. It felt glorious. "What are you doing here?"

She laughed. "I've *been* here. I work at the studio, in finance."

"Finance, of course." His eyes widened. "Bloody hell, *you're* the friend everyone's always talking about. You've been right under my nose this entire time."

"I have. And you've been under mine." She glowered at him. "Your name has *actually* been under my nose. Do you know how often you've probably come across my desk, and I had no idea it was you?" She smacked his arm. "What gives, using a different last name on me?"

Despite his wince, he couldn't contain his joy at her censure. "I felt like I needed a fresh start after the war. And my mum's the one who always wanted me to be a writer, so I thought it was fitting to take on her surname." He put his hands on his hips. "Besides, I thought you might be somewhere on the West Coast, but how was I supposed to know you were in Los Angeles, let alone at the same bloody studio! And it's not as if I knew your married name, either."

Which, technically, was his own fault, even though he'd made that choice for her own protection.

"And whose fault is that?"

He laughed. "I never could get anything past you, could I? My god, I've missed you."

Frannie hugged him again. "I've missed you, too." She stepped back with a small smile. "And it's Haynes, by the way. My married name."

Colin grinned back at her. "Frannie Haynes. Good to know. So how is…" *Crap, I really should know his name.* "Mark, was it?"

"Martin. Marty."

He grimaced. "Right. Sorry."

"He, um…" A wistful look spread across her features. No, a sad look. Colin studied his sister. *Oh no.*

"Fran…is he…?"

She met his eyes, resigned. Strong as always. "January of '43. The Pacific. That's how I ended up in California. He was initially stationed here before shipping out."

"Oh, love, I'm so sorry." He pulled her in for another hug. "I should have been here for you."

"It's not like there's anything you could have done."

He squeezed her more tightly. "I could have at least done this."

Her arms returned the squeeze. "You're here now." She looked up at him, smile brighter. "But there is a silver lining. The silver-est of linings, as a matter of fact. Marty didn't leave me completely alone. I have a daughter, Lucy. Your niece."

A new, warm sense of wonder spread through Colin. "A niece. My word." He huffed a laugh as he pulled back and rubbed Frannie's arms. "That's extraordinary. So, what's she like? Tell me all about her."

Frannie laughed. "She's six years old, and already such a handful. Curious about absolutely everything. Full of energy and feisty as hell."

"Hmm, so apple…" He gestured to Frannie. "…tree."

She swatted his arm, then nodded. "Damn right."

They laughed together. It felt positively wonderful.

"And she's your whole heart, isn't she?"

Frannie sighed. "She really is. I can't wait for you to meet her."

"Neither can I. My niece." Colin shook his head. "I cannot believe you're really here. How in the world did you find me, figure out we were both at Phoenix?" He snapped back to the present. "Nate, did you— Fuck, where did she go?"

And how the bloody hell hadn't he noticed her slipping out?

Frannie turned. "Oh. I suppose she wanted to give us a moment."

He rushed to the doorway to peer into the hall, but Nate was nowhere to be seen. His joyful mood plummeted once again.

When he returned to his sister, an odd mix of sentiments flitted over her face, her smile cautious.

"It was her, you know," she said quietly. "I probably could have gone on obliviously for ages, but after I mentioned you in passing, one thing led to another and…your Nate put it all together."

He swallowed around the sudden obstruction in his throat. "She's not *my* Nate. Not anymore."

She gave him a look that was equal parts sympathy and reproach, and then the Scot came out in full force. "Oh, your bum's oot the windae."

Colin barked a surprised laugh. "That is…astoundingly accurate." His shoulders slumped in resignation. "That's exactly what I did, didn't I? Hang my bum out?"

"I'm going to have to reeducate you in all things Scot, aren't I? That's not what I meant. Although, I suppose it could apply that way too…" Frannie shook her head. "But that's neither here nor there. The point is, don't be so quick to say it's over."

"Why not? You don't know how terribly I botched things, Fran."

"Oh, I know, believe me. From what I heard, you put on quite a show at that shindig."

Well, that's just great.

"But Nate contributed her fair share to the chaos too," she continued. "You two make some pair. You both need to fix this. But…I think you *can* still fix it."

"You really think so?"

"I do. She's crazy about you." She rested her hand on his shoulder. "And don't you dare argue with me. Just because she didn't make a dramatic declaration in front of all Hollywood, doesn't mean she doesn't feel it." She grinned wickedly.

Colin groaned. "Of course you heard about that, too."

"Aw, don't beat yourself up. It's sweet." She laughed at his eye roll. "Really, though. You're enough under her skin, on her mind, that she pieced our puzzle together from a few random facts I shared." His sister's face took on a rueful expression. "More than I was able to do. I've been so blind, willing you to be safe in London where I left you. All the times anyone's mentioned you… and it never once occurred to me that you were *you*." Her expression pierced his heart. "I could have tried so much harder to find you… I *should* have."

He folded her into his arms once more. "Hey. Don't. I didn't find you, either."

"All that time wasted…"

"You said it yourself, we're here now. That's all that matters. And I'm not going anywhere."

"Neither am I." She nodded against his shoulder. "You're right. And since we have loads of time ahead of us for catching up…" Frannie straightened up and her gaze turned steady, pointed. "We have a much more pressing matter to focus on first." One side of her mouth quirked up. "We're going to win your Nate back."

Colin sighed. "Frannie, I don't know if she—"

She waved her hand dismissively. "Yeah, yeah. And I told you, you're full of shite." She put her hands on her hips. "You love her."

He didn't hesitate for even a second. "With all my heart."

"Knowing just how big your heart is, brother, that's quite a lot of love." She'd been back in his life barely ten minutes, and already his sister was turning him into a pile of mush. Before he could start to dissolve, though, she poked him in the chest, hard. "Don't you dare give up without a fight."

"Ow." He made a show of rubbing the injured spot, mostly to cover his doubts. But he knew she wasn't going to let him off that easy. "I do want to fight for her. Hell, I'd do anything to fix this. I just...don't know where to start."

"Well, given the magnitude of your stupidity..." She glanced at the empty doorway. "And hers, sheesh. You two definitely need to start by bloody talking to each other."

"If I could get her to stay in a room with me long enough..."

She regarded him with sympathy before lowering the boom. "Have you actually *asked* her to talk to you, arse-wit?"

Colin chuckled. "Touché."

She tapped her finger against her lips. "And maybe sending a gigantic present with the invite might not go amiss either..."

"A gigantic present..." He adjusted his glasses and cocked his head to the side, considering. "Huh."

"Ooh, you've got something, haven't you?"

"I'm not sure. I've perhaps got...the beginnings of something, but..." He shook his head and perched on the edge of his desk. "I have no idea how I'd make it happen anyway."

Frannie stepped in front of him, forcing him to meet her direct gaze before she spoke. "Don't forget, dear brother, you now have one very important thing at your disposal that you didn't have last week."

He fought a smile, knowing what she was getting at, but unable to resist teasing her. "What's that?"

Her face broke into a delightfully cocky grin. "Your brilliant sister to guide you and keep you from putting your foot too far in it."

Colin's grin matched hers. "And that is a gift, indeed."

Despite the mess they'd gotten themselves into, he had Nate to thank for bringing this ray of sunshine back into his life. She'd slipped out before he could properly thank her for this miracle, but he'd be damned if he let it go.

And, if in the process, he could somehow manage to earn Nate's forgiveness, and her heart once again, then that would be the biggest miracle of all.

Chapter Thirty

"Hey, there. Got a few minutes?"

Nate looked up from her test photos to see Lois hovering in her office doorway. "Sure, come on in."

Lois walked over to her desk. "How'd things go with Colin and Frannie?"

Nate's face melted into a smile, remembering the sight of the pair of them, arms thrown around each other. "Great. They were so thrilled to see each other."

"That's fantastic. I can't believe they were in each other's backyards this entire time."

"I know." Nate glanced up, preemptively sheepish. "I, um, slipped out while they were catching up. After all the time they've spent apart, they needed their reunion time." She lifted her shoulder. "And I didn't know what to say."

"Hey, I'm not judging."

"Yes, you are." She smiled. "But thanks."

Lois laughed. "I hid out all the way in New York before I figured out how to solve my problems. Believe me, I get it."

"True. So what's up?" Nate asked.

"For starters, that list of people wanting to come work here is still growing. The press is starting to get wind of it too, and…"

Lois inclined her head. "Even the more obnoxious pieces are sending folks our way. It's quite the unexpected publicity angle."

"How is that possible?"

"Like I told you, we are capable of magical things when we work together, my friend." Lois grinned.

"I suppose we are." Nate let her shoulders relax.

"Never realized just how tired you were from carrying all that, did you?"

Nate chuckled. "Indeed, I did not."

She'd never in a million years wanted—or expected—her lies to hit the fan the way they had. But holy shit, the magnitude of relief she felt now that she no longer had to maintain them…

Lois crossed the room to Nate's window and picked up her DiMaggio forgery. "You know, the props department would probably love to have this."

"I'll teach them how to make their own." Nate took it from her. "There's something else I'd like to do with this one."

"Burn it?"

"Something like that." She inhaled sharply. "So if all that was the starter, what else can I do for you today?"

"Right." Lois held up a notebook. "I've started to make some preliminary notes about my film, and wanted to see what you think." She hesitated. "Assuming, of course, you still want to work on it?"

Nate jerked back. "Are you serious? Why on earth wouldn't I?"

"Well…given where things currently stand with the screenwriter, I wouldn't exactly blame you."

Oh. Right.

Lois continued, "And by asking, I do not in any way mean that I want you to withdraw. Quite the opposite. You're not only my best friend, you're also the best designer in the business, and the thought of doing this without you gives me hives." She smiled. "But if it's going to be awkward or painful for you, we can assign one of Phoenix's other designers to this one. I'll understand completely, and suck it up."

Nate huffed. "I appreciate that. But this is your directorial debut, and there is no way in hell I'm going to miss it. Especially not because of some…boy trouble. Besides, we have almost a month before we really start in earnest, and that's plenty of time for me to…"

Lois raised a gleeful eyebrow. "Throw yourself at him?"

Nate glared at her. "Don't push me, woman. Now, show me your damn notes."

Lois laughed. "All right, then." She came to the side of Nate's desk. "How familiar are you with the script?"

"I haven't seen the finished version yet." A memory stabbed at her heart, of a stick-figure storyboard. And fogged-up glasses. She swallowed. "But I did see a few early notes."

Lois studied her for a moment, but thankfully let it pass. "Right. So you at least know the characters, then."

They had only been bent over Lois's notebook for a few minutes when a knock at the door interrupted them. Rose stood in the doorway, more dazed than Nate had ever seen her. Which was saying something, really.

"I'm sorry to interrupt," Rose whispered breathlessly.

Nate and Lois shared a quizzical glance.

"That's okay," Nate answered. "What's going on, Rose?"

"You, um…" She half-swallowed, half-sighed. "You have a visitor." Her eyes darted to Lois before she rushed on. "And I know you're busy, but trust me, you *really* want to see this one."

Rose's behavior often verged on the unusual, but this was a bit much, even for her. A tiny ember of hope flared in Nate that perhaps it was Colin. But she'd seen Rose moon over him plenty of times, and never quite like this. This was a whole new level of Rose-ness.

Nate gave in to her curiosity. "All right, send them in." She shot one last look at Lois, who simply shrugged, as confused as she was.

Rose waved into the vestibule, and pressed herself into the doorway as the visitor breezed past her and into the office. Nate's jaw hit the floor.

An impeccably tailored suit. A glossy wave to his dark hair, slicked into perfection above his forehead. That familiar, all-knowing twinkle in his dark eyes. A suave grin sitting above the mother of all chin dimples.

Cary Grant.

Cary *Fucking* Grant.

Stood in *her* office.

"Good afternoon, ladies." How was it possible that his voice sounded even more posh in person?

Lois still had one hand resting on the back of Nate's chair, and she brought it down to poke Nate surreptitiously in the ribs. Nate's senses lurched back to life, and she jolted out of her chair.

"Mr. Grant, hello."

He strode forward, hand extended. "You must be Ms. Reynolds. It's a pleasure to meet you."

She managed a warbling laugh as she shook his hand—*I'm shaking Cary Grant's hand, Jesus*—and her voice came out in a croak. "Thank you. The, um, pleasure is all mine."

"It's a shame we haven't had the chance to work together yet, as I've always heard such wonderful things about you. And now that you're getting all this extra attention, we simply must remedy that. I do so enjoy working with interesting people." He winked devilishly. *Winked.* At her.

"Right. Of course." *Holy shit.*

He turned to Lois. "And Ms. Ashford, lovely to see you as well."

Lois shook his hand, cool and professional as always. "Like-wise. And please call me Lois."

"Well, all right, but only if you both call me Cary."

Nate looked back and forth between them in disbelief.

"Congratulations on what you're doing here, by the way, Lois," *Cary* continued. "I've heard good things, of course, but then

I saw Nick yesterday and he filled me in on all you've got going on. We should see about teaming up on something together in the near future."

"That sounds delightful. I hope we can make it work."

Nate watched Lois's calm composure with envy. She'd always joked that she'd lose her shit if this man ever walked into her office, but maybe she shouldn't have. Now that he was here, all her professional instincts had vanished into thin air, and the last thing she needed at this point was to make an utter fool of herself in front of this beautiful man. Not when her wild scandal apparently *impressed* him.

At least said beautiful man was still conversing with Lois. "You and Nick should join me and Betsy for dinner. We can talk shop over cocktails."

"Splendid."

He turned back to Nate and clapped his hands together. "But enough about work. You're no doubt wondering why I'm here."

"Uh, well, yes," Nate stammered.

Oh, come on, I really do have a bigger vocabulary, don't I?

"This might sound rather unusual, but I've been enlisted as a messenger boy today."

Huh?

Cary reached into his pocket and extracted a sheet of paper, which he proceeded to unfold.

Her favorite actor in the world cleared his throat dramatically. "'Mr. Colin Canfield requests the honor of Ms. Natalie Reynolds's presence this evening at sunset at *our spot*.'" He raised his twinkling eyes to her. "I trust you can interpret that one?"

Cary's handsome face swam out of focus in front of her. Nate nodded, blinking against her sudden tears.

"Fantastic. There's a postscript too: 'Do please forgive my not delivering this in person, but I thought perhaps the ever-dashing Mr. Grant...'" The actor paused mischievously. "Difficult to argue with him there." He resumed reading. "'...the ever-dashing Mr.

Grant might be of some assistance in convincing you to accept my invitation. Yours, Colin.'"

Cary carefully folded the page and handed it to her. "This is yours, my dear."

Nate gingerly took it. "Thank you."

"You know," he continued, "I only met him briefly, but he seems like a decent chap. I do hope you consider seeing him."

Nate managed a watery smile—both at his charm and the surreal situation. All she could say was "thank you" again.

"Don't mention it." He smiled. "I'm sure you're plenty busy, so I'll be on my way now."

Lois came around the desk to escort him to the door. "Thank you, Cary. It was very nice to finally meet you."

He paused at the door. "Likewise, Lois. Be sure to get in touch about that dinner. It was truly a pleasure to meet the charming pair of you." He gave them a courtly salute and was gone.

Nate stared dazedly after him, as Lois closed the door and sank against it. She waited a moment before speaking.

"He sent you an invitation via Cary Grant."

"Uh-huh."

"Cary. Grant."

"I know."

Nate opened the invitation in her hand and traced her finger over Colin's neat script, then glanced up into Lois's dazzling smile.

"Go get him, doll."

Chapter Thirty-One

Nate drove toward the ocean, likely paying less attention to the road than she should. She didn't care. The feeling of safety that reached her even through the few words of his invitation was nearly overwhelming as it wrapped around her.

It made a hell of a lot better security blanket than the lonely one she'd crafted for herself and clung to all these years.

And to have sent it in the person of Cary Grant? She shook her head as she drove, still in disbelief.

When she pulled the car to a stop along Ocean Avenue, she spotted the back of a familiar figure leaning against the railing, silhouetted against the breathtaking view. *He's pretty breathtaking too,* she thought, relief washing over her. She grabbed her handbag and left the car, slowly making her way over to him.

"Fancy meeting you here."

Colin whipped around at the sound of her voice. Despite his glasses, and the fact that he was mostly backlit, the intensity of his golden gaze reached her, burning brighter than the oncoming sunset behind him.

Mine. He's still mine.

"Nate," he breathed.

"I got your invitation. Clearly." Nate crossed her arms over her chest. "You know, I think you may have ruined Cary Grant for me."

His face fell. "Oh. I see. I'm sorry."

"No, I don't think you do see." She smiled as she stepped closer to him. "For as long as I can remember, Cary has been my gold standard. The perfect man, the ideal. The man I measured all others against. And I've always said that if I should someday find myself lucky enough to have him in my office, standing right in front of me, there'd be no holding me back.

"Then it finally happened. There he was. And do you know what was running through my head the entire time?"

"No, what?"

"Yes, he's handsome, suave, debonair." She shrugged. "But he's no Colin Canfield." His eyes widened, and she held his gaze, steady.

"Really?" His voice was barely above a whisper.

"Really." She shook her head. "When I wasn't looking, you tap-danced up and knocked my perfect man right off his pedestal."

Colin let out a shaky laugh. "If it makes you feel any better, I didn't set out to topple him."

"I know. Can I let you in on a little secret?" He raised his eyebrows in question. "I'm rather glad you did."

He froze, his breaths shallow. "You are?"

She nodded. "I seem to have fallen pretty headlong in love with you, Colin. I...I realized it before Ruby's party. I should have told you..."

"*I'm* the one who should have told you how I felt sooner. I hate that it came out the way it did, when it did..." He reached up, as if to touch her, but stopped short with a rueful huff. "I want so badly to take you in my arms, Nate, but I'm not sure I've earned that right back yet."

She wanted the same thing, but before she could say so, he

raised his eyes to her, and the fiery anguish she saw there stole her breath.

"I'm sorry," they said at the same moment.

Their laughter mingled with the crash of the waves below them.

"May I begin?" Colin asked.

She nodded.

"I am so sorry, Nate." His voice, always so smooth, was all gravel now. "I wish I could take it all back—blurting what I did to your peers, ignoring your request to handle things...*all* the times I let Alex Madison eavesdrop." He took her hand tentatively. "The last thing in the world I'd ever want to do is hurt you, yet I did just that. Has it been terrible, being back at work?"

"Astoundingly...no." She huffed. "Don't get me wrong, the looks I've been getting are something else. But the support is so surprising. And wonderful." She offered him a wry smile. "Lois has been fielding all kinds of requests to work with me. One actress told her I must be one hell of a trustworthy designer, that if I could keep mum about a doozy that epic, for that long, every-one's secrets must be safe in my vault."

Colin's gaze was warmer than the setting sun behind him. "I don't find that surprising at all. You are rather extraordinary, Nate."

"Thanks." She inhaled deeply. "All that aside, I wasn't exactly blameless the other night. You were right. None of this would have happened if I hadn't made up Walter."

He looked about to protest, and she held up a hand to cut him off. "We both could have handled that party, and what came after, better. But..." She closed her eyes. "I think, in a way, it needed to happen in a big, spectacular scene." Meeting his penetrating gaze again, she continued, "I feared the worst for so long. But it took all that shit hitting the fan for me to realize how much support, how much *love*, I have around me. To push me to let that love in."

"Nate..."

She shook her head, and closed the distance between them

further, taking his other hand. "I let my sister walk out of my life without a fight, and in my fear of it happening again, I almost pushed Lois away too. On top of all that, I spent such a long time avoiding romantic relationships that my longest one was not only terrible, it was fucking imaginary. So when I was finally in one—a *real* one—I almost didn't know what to do with you. With myself."

Nate cupped his cheek. The way he leaned into her touch sent a flood of warmth coursing from her head to her toes.

"I got so caught up in falling, and then it started to scare me how deep I was in. And in case you haven't noticed, I do *really* stupid things when I get scared."

Colin laughed. "Something we have in common."

"One of many things." She smiled up at him. "Can you forgive me for pushing you away after the party?"

He let out an incredulous groan. "Are you kidding me?"

Colin finally wrapped his arms around her, crushing her to him. She sank into the warmth of his body, inhaling his familiar scent.

Home again.

"Can you forgive *me*?"

"Of course," she replied.

"I love you, Nate," he whispered against her hair.

"I love you too, Colin. So much."

He tightened his arms around her before pulling back. "You've given me the first true sense of peace, of satisfaction, of *home* I've had in a very long time. You gave me…back to myself, in a way, by accepting all the many parts of me." He cradled her face in his palms. "You hold my entire heart in your hands, my dear love, and you always will. It won't ever belong with anyone else."

As she took in his blazingly hopeful expression, a tiny seed of trepidation bloomed in her. While wading through the massive fallout of everything that had happened over the last days, one revelation stood out, something she'd always known on some level. But it was clearer than ever now.

She didn't know how Colin would react, but she had to be honest. Had to share this part of herself and allow him to decide what he wanted to do about it.

Nate took a deep breath and waded in.

"Colin. I, um…"

"What is it?" The concern in his eyes gave her a boost of courage.

"With everything that's happened, I am finally, truly free. Of Walter. Of marriage. And I…I think I might want to stay that way. For a while. Maybe even…ever."

"Oh."

He looked positively crushed, and she rushed forward to explain. "I don't mean that I want to be free of *you*. Just that… Oh, how do I say this? I've spent a dozen years, my entire professional life, as a 'married' woman. I did what I thought I had to do to start the career of my dreams, and then I made it happen. I carved out almost exactly the life I wanted. The identity I wanted. But part of that identity, part of who I had to present to the world, was the long-suffering wife. And yes, I know how that sounds, given that I could have shucked that cloak off at any time. But I guess spending all those years pretending to be in a less-than-ideal marriage…"

"Soured you on the idea altogether?"

Nate nodded. "Yeah. I think it did. I didn't even realize how much until I let myself feel everything, *examine* everything, these last few days." She raised her eyes to his, hoping desperately that he understood. "I don't know if I'll ever want to get married. I might someday, but I might not. But I do know for sure that right now, I need to spend some time…not being a missus."

"That makes sense."

"Does it? Can you…are you okay with that?" She grasped both his hands in hers, bringing them up between them. "Because I meant what I said. I love you, Colin, and I do want to be with you." She squeezed tighter. "I love having you as a partner. And I want to try to be a better partner to you."

He squeezed her hands back. "As do I."

She swallowed around the lump of hope crowding her throat. "I may not be able to offer you a fancy ceremony, or a piece of paper with our names on it. But I can offer you my heart, Colin Canfield. Because it is yours. It's always going to be yours."

As Nate watched his face break into the biggest, most beautiful smile she'd ever seen, a tear escaped and made its way down her cheek. Colin let go of her hands and framed her face, arresting the tear's progress.

"I don't need the ceremony, or the paper. Your magnificent heart is all I will ever need, Natalie Reynolds. And I promise to spend my life keeping it safe."

They were both crying in earnest when he brought his lips down to hers. Their kiss started soft, but quickly ignited as they melted into each other. Several minutes ticked by as they devoured each other, finally home. Finally free.

They broke apart with identical sighs, foreheads leaning against each other. She shook her head against his.

"Cary Grant. How in the world did you pull that one off?"

One side of Colin's mouth quirked up. "I did have a little help. I enlisted Nick to reach out to Mr. Grant, who was just lovely about the whole thing. When Frannie suggested including a large present with my invitation, I thought he might be just the ticket." His grin widened. "Thank you for *her*, by the way. I can't get over how astoundingly wonderful it is to have her back in my life."

"You are quite welcome. I couldn't believe it when she started talking about her brother, the former dancer. It hardly seemed possible, but I'm so glad it turned out to be you."

"Me too." He shook his head. "The fact that we've been mere yards from each other this entire time…"

"I know. If it wasn't for Frannie's mysterious aversion to Max, you two probably would have crossed paths even sooner."

Colin chuckled. "*What* is that about, by the way? I've been dying to ask Fran, but I've only had her back for a few days. I'd hate to send her running for the hills again."

"Yeah, maybe it's best to tread lightly there. Lois and I still haven't been able to get it out of her." She tightened her hold on him. "Perhaps you'll have luck where we didn't."

"We can work on her together." He bent in for a quick kiss. "And you see, I was right."

"About what?"

"I knew you two would get along swimmingly. I just didn't realize you already did."

Nate laughed, unbelievably elated to be back in his arms, sharing their lives again.

"Oh! I almost forgot. I have something for you." She fished in her purse and pulled out the infamous baseball. "I'm long overdue in getting rid of this stupid thing. Want to help me figure out how?"

Colin tried—rather unsuccessfully—to adopt a serious look as he considered the ball. After a moment, he glanced to his left and inclined his head toward the ocean.

"Ooh, not bad." She held out the ball.

"Oh, no. My aim's not great. And you really should do the honors, dove."

"You're right." She hated to let go of him, but needed the room. "Here's hoping my aim's not shit." Colin's deep laugh warmed her to her core. "Okay, here goes."

Nate shook out her shoulders, wound her arm, and hurled her creation into the sea.

"Goodbye, Walter Guffman."

Colin leaned over the railing. "I'm pretty sure you've cleared land." He threw a mischievous grin over his shoulder. "We just dodged an attempted murder rap; I'd hate to see you get hauled in for beaning some random beachgoer over the head."

"God, I love you."

"I love you, too." He moved to pull her close again, but she stopped him, remembering something else.

"Wait, that's not all I have for you." She bent down to her bag, where she had dropped it, and brought out the bottle she'd picked up on her way over.

Colin barked a hearty laugh as he took it from her. "Calamine lotion."

"For our mutual itch-scratching." She grinned. "I'll have you know, I went to great trouble to procure that. Had to go to three stores before I found it. Apparently, it's very hard to come by when it's not summertime."

"Huh. Interesting. I will treasure this bottle then." He smiled down at her. "As I treasure you."

She blushed, and he drew her close for another kiss. They took it slow this time, exploring and savoring as if they had all the time in the world. Which they did. When at last they came up for air, she rested her head against his chest, and they held each other in comfortable silence as they watched the water below.

Nate rubbed her cheek against his jacket. She'd always thought of tweed as rough and scratchy, but his felt nothing but soft. Comforting. Perfect. She snickered as a thought occurred to her.

His smile curved against her temple. "What?"

"Just thinking. You know, tweed makes for a much better security blanket than thin air."

Epilogue

Six months later

$\mathcal{N}$ate descended the stairs at Lois and Nick's home, to find Colin staring reverently up at her. She was quite enthralled herself—he looked positively dashing in his tuxedo. Though his hair was a bit too tamed for her taste, she fought the urge to muss it, as the evening was still young, and she knew how much effort it must have taken him.

He took her hand as she reached the bottom step. "Nate, you look beautiful." He glanced down at her dress. "You finally did it. You captured your sunset."

"*Our* sunset." She swirled the diaphanous fabric of her gown's full skirt. "And yes, I cracked the code at last."

"I always knew you would."

"You'll never guess what I added to finally get the shade of pink I wanted."

"Well, don't leave me in suspense."

She gave him a sly grin. "Calamine lotion."

His surprised guffaw delighted her almost as much as the

molten heat emanating from behind his glasses. He leaned closer to her to whisper, "Will it damage your makeup too much if I kiss you right now?"

"It might." She pulled his head down to hers. Just before sliding her lips against his, she added, "But don't let that stop you."

"Ugh, would you two please take it somewhere private?"

They broke apart to find Nick smirking at them.

She narrowed her eyes at him. "You're never going to stop paying me back for all the grief I gave you when you and Lois were first married, are you?"

"Nope."

They had all gathered for a celebratory cocktail before heading to the premiere of Lois's directorial debut. Even Colin's mother had made the journey to Los Angeles, though Nate suspected it was as much about finally meeting her as supporting Colin. And Marjorie was exactly as delightful—and brash—as Colin had promised. They did indeed hit it off with flying colors.

As for the film… While Lois still planned to make Colin's original script at some point, she had pivoted to another of his creations for her first film. A certain farce about a potentially murderous affair, starring one Alex Madison.

Yes, they'd decided to lean into the momentum of their strange swirl of publicity. And somehow managed to patch things with Alex, who, despite his penchant for public spectacle, was not a bad actor at all.

Nate had lost count of how many times Lois checked in for her approval. But despite her initial, well-founded trepidation, Nate had to admit that Colin delivered a flawless script. And if she trusted anyone to present a story even loosely inspired by her life, it was Lois.

It wasn't entirely her story, of course. Colin had flipped the roles, with a wife inventing a lover rather than a husband, in order to make him jealous, and a happy reunion at the end. On-screen infidelity still pissed off those pesky censors, after all, and Lois needed them on her side for this one.

Nate had seen an early cut of the film, and as surreal as it felt, her hesitation had long vanished by the time the end title card flashed. She might be a touch biased, but she thought the movie was utterly brilliant, and could not be prouder of her friend's vision. And her love's words.

Though she and Colin were now living together, she knew how nervous Lois felt about the evening, so she'd agreed to their quasi-tradition of getting ready together. What she hadn't shared with Lois was her other, more selfish, reason for doing so. Since she'd finished her gown, Nate had been looking forward to surprising Colin in it, in a scene precisely like the one that had just played out.

Frannie's daughter, Lucy, bounded up to them in her adorably fancy dress. "Mom said I could stay up and come to the party later! Will you save me a dance, Uncle Colin?"

Colin scooped his niece up to eye level. "Are you kidding? For you, I'll save two." He glanced at Nate. "That is, if your Auntie Nate doesn't mind..."

Lucy turned comically pleading eyes on her.

Nate chuckled. "Lucy, darling, you are the only other woman I would spare him to." She winked.

Lucy leaned over to kiss Nate's cheek. "You're the best, Auntie Nate!"

Colin beamed at them both. She loved seeing how much joy it brought him to have both Lucy and Frannie in his life. He went out of his way to ignore his sister's repeated—albeit half-hearted—admonitions of his efforts to spoil Lucy rotten. The child's favorite present had been the pair of tap shoes he'd bestowed upon her, largely because the gift was accompanied by their standing date of dance lessons.

It was Nate's favorite too, as she often crashed the end of the lessons to watch. There wasn't an ocean big enough to contain the puddle of goo she melted into every time she saw him sharing his favorite hobby with his six-year-old niece.

Lois swept down the stairs in an elegant rush. "Please tell me Max is here. I cannot be late tonight."

The man in question bounded out of the kitchen, a bit breathless. "Don't worry, I'm right on time." He gestured back through the doorway. "And with quite possibly the biggest chocolate cheesecake I've ever made, in honor of the lady of the hour."

Frannie scowled as she followed him into the room. "You know, it really wouldn't have killed you to take into account the actual size of their refrigerator before you made that monstrosity."

"Hey, we made it fit, didn't we?"

She rolled her eyes at him.

Nate shared an eyebrow-raise with Colin. Months later, they still hadn't been able to get to the bottom of that one, and not for lack of trying.

She turned back to Lois, to find that Nick had taken advantage of the distraction to pull her close. Whatever he was whispering in her ear was clearly working, as her body relaxed into his and a smile overtook her nerves.

Colin started passing around the champagne flutes. "Let's toast, shall we?"

Nick raised his glass, the natural emcee. "To Lois, and a dream made real."

Lois beamed at him. "To love." She winked at her husband and Nate in turn. "To fake husbands of all kinds." She then raised her glass to the rest of the group. "And to friendship."

"To friendship," they all echoed.

Nate looked around the room at their little found family, Colin's hand warm on the small of her back. Not all that long ago, she'd thought she needed to maintain a certain distance around her heart in order to survive. And maybe that was true. But thanks to this bunch, she'd discovered that surviving wasn't enough.

She'd finally learned how to *thrive*.

Nate leaned against Colin's side. "I love you, you know that?"

He bent to feather a kiss across her lips. "Right back at you, darling."

She grinned mischievously at him. "Careful, you're starting to sound downright American."

He gasped in mock affront. "Perish the thought."

"All right, everyone, we don't want to keep the drivers waiting. Shall we?" Lois called.

As the group made their boisterous exit, Nate couldn't contain her smile. It remained all through the evening, in the crush of press outside the theater, and during the screening itself. As hard as it still was to believe, she'd spun her mess into a success.

Her fizzy warmth only grew at the party afterward—as Lois and Nick celebrated, Max and Frannie avoided each other, and Colin kept his promise to Lucy before turning his skills on Nate.

As he glided her smoothly across the room, she dared a graze across that magnificent ass of his.

The velvet that had captivated her from the first rumbled next to her ear. "Keep that up, and I'll have to find some dark corner to whisk you away to."

She flashed him a wicked grin and made another pass with her hand, punctuating this one with a pinch. He growled as he took her roving hand and led her off the dance floor.

Nate Reynolds might be single, but she certainly wasn't alone.

Acknowledgments

I know I am not the first to say this, but doing just about anything during the upheaval of the last couple of years has been a pretty difficult task. Writing a romance—and particularly a *screwball comedy* romance—felt herculean at times. But I fell very much in love with Nate and Colin while writing their story, and getting them to their HEA was immensely gratifying. I hope their adventures brought you some joy as well.

Speaking of screwball comedies, my love for them knows no bounds, as you might be able to tell by now. I couldn't resist giving the suave, undisputed king of screwballs, Mr. Cary Grant, a cameo in this book. I'd like to hope he'd be flattered. (If his ghost would like to stop by for a chat, I wouldn't exactly complain...)

It is, in no way, an exaggeration to say that this book would not be what it is without my Sploosh Sisters, my fantastic and immensely talented critique group. Genevieve Kersten, Amanda Pereira, Jillian Graves, and Daria Vernon—I cannot thank you enough for your friendship and all our regular check-ins, writing and otherwise. You kept me writing during everything, and your feedback and love of these characters helped me get through revisions (and revisions...and yet more revisions....) Thanks for all the laughs, comments, brainstorming sessions, and much-needed pushes to get this book where it needed to be.

To my editor, Michele Chiappetta, thank you so much for once again helping take my work over the finish line. Your insightful comments and encouragement are much appreciated, and I always enjoy working with you.

Daybed Books created another stunner of a cover for me, and I am ever so grateful. There is no one I trusted more to capture both the screwball and noir elements of Nate and Colin's wild ride, and you really knocked it out of the park. (Seriously, that baseball? It gives me so much joy!)

Angela James, Dan Stephensen, and all the members of the From Written to Recommended and Book Boss groups—thank you for creating such a warm, encouraging space for writers. Your cheerleading and advice has been tremendous.

A big shout-out to romance book bloggers and reviewers, who work so hard without nearly enough credit—and keep my own TBR pile the beautifully unconquerable mountain that it is! Special thanks to Silvana Reyes for generously hosting *Single Indemnity*'s cover reveal with such excitement, and Nick of The Infinite Limits of Love for including Nate & Colin alongside some of my recent favorite romance characters in your Valentine's celebration.

My heart overflows at the response I've received from all the friends, family, and work colleagues who have been so supportive of my writing journey. Thank you for your excitement about *Difficult* and now this book as well. It means the world to me.

As always, my Dad is the very best cheering section I could imagine. Thank you for absolutely everything. I love you so much. And Mom, I wish you were here to share my stories with, but I know you're watching from the stars. This one is, once again, for you.

And finally, a very huge thank you to all of you readers for joining me on this trip back to Classic Hollywood. My characters and I are thrilled to have you here at the party.

About the Author

Brianne Gillen is a romance author, costume designer, theatre educator, and life-long storyteller, based in the Los Angeles area. She loves classic films, especially the screwball comedies of the '30s and '40s, and will never turn down the opportunity to browse the treasure troves otherwise known as vintage clothing stores. She is also a voracious reader and firm believer in happily-ever-afters. She has done a bit of playwriting, and in recent years, has contributed her opinions to a few online publications centering on the art and craft of costume design. Her Phoenix Pictures Series centers around fierce dames and cinnamon-roll gents finding love in late-1940s Hollywood.

www.briannegillen.com